They were Roman soldiers—and they were still alive because there were no better killers in the galaxy.

The Galactics need fighters who could win battles without the aid of technology. That's why, when Rome's legions suffered disaster at Carrhae, secretive alien traders were waiting to buy them on the Persian slave market.

Now, virtually immortal, the Romans fight strange enemies on stranger worlds; and though they win every battle, the spoils of victory never include freedom. If the legionaries are ever to return to Earth, it must be through the beam weapons and force screens of their ruthless alien owners. But no matter the odds, two thousand years is a long time; the Romans are coming home.

DAVID DRAKE

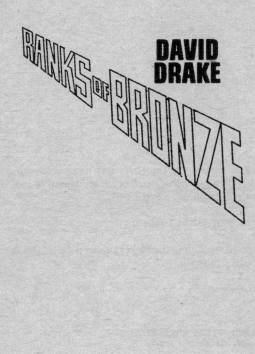

RANKS OF BRONZE

science fiction

Distributed in Canada by PaperJacks Ltd., a Licensee
of the trademarks of Simon & Schuster, Inc.

RANKS OF BRONZE

A Baen Books Original

In Canada distributed by PaperJacks Ltd.,
330 Steelcase Road, Markham, Ontario

First printing, May 1986

ISBN: 0-671-65568-X

Cover art by Alan Gutierrez

Printed in Canada

Distributed by
SIMON & SCHUSTER
TRADE PUBLISHING GROUP
1230 Avenue of the Americas
New York, N.Y. 10020

DEDICATION
For Jerry Pournelle

For numerous kindnesses over the years—including one off-hand comment that was worth any number of writing courses.

ACKNOWLEDGMENTS

To Jim, who bought the story ten years ago; to Janet, who reminded me of the BATRACHOMYOMACHIA; and to Jo, who liked the completed result.

PROLOGUE

On a farm in the Sabine hills of a planet call Earth, a poet takes a stylus from the fingers of a nude slave girl and writes, very quickly, *And Crassus' wretched soldier takes a barbarian wife from his captors and grows old waging war for them.*

The poet looked at the line with a pleased expression. "It needs polish, of course," he muttered. Then, more directly to the slave, he says, "You know, Leuconoe, there's more than inspiration to poetry, a thousand times more; but this came to me out of the air."

Horace gestures with his stylus toward the glittering night sky. The girl smiles back at him.

BOOK
ONE

THE FIRST CAMPAIGN

Gaius Vibulenus wore a white horsehair crest to mark him as a tribune. Fear turned the dew dribbling from that insignia into drops of acid on the back of his neck. Dawn was beginning to raise a bitter-flavored mist from the valley before them, and the occasional serpentine trees seemed to writhe as they bathed in the thick air.

The enemy was deploying from its camp in the shelter of great basalt pyramids that the sun revealed as a natural rock formation, not the godlike city which the young tribune had thought he saw against the night sky.

"Mother Vesta," Vibulenus whispered as his fingers tightened on the bone hilt of the sword sheathed at his left side, "let me live to see my hearth again. Father Hercules, give me strength to endure this time of testing."

A signal began to boom from the enemy camp. It sounded like thunder, a crash which built into a rumble and did not slacken though the whole valley began to echo with it.

"Mother Vesta," the tribune repeated, "let me live to see my hearth."

". . . ten feet tall," a legionary was muttering to his fellow as the Tenth Cohort lurched towards its posi-

tion on the left flank. "And they eat their enemies
raw."

"No talking in ranks!" snarled a non-commissioned
officer—Gnaeus Clodius Afer, the file-closer who ranked
second of the eighty-odd men in the cohort's Third
Century. In barracks, Clodius would have carried a
swagger stick, but here in the field he bore two javelins
and a shield like any other line soldier. He rang the
butt of the lighter javelin on the bronze helmet of the
man who had spoken.

The legionary yelped and stumbled. Dim light and
the helmet's broad cheek pieces concealed the man's
face, but the tribune recognized the voice as that of
Publius Pompilius Rufus—one of the few legionaries he
actually knew. Rufus and his first cousin, Publius
Pompilius Niger, came from farms adjoining that of
Vibulenus' own family, and the three boys had attended
school together in Suessula.

"Here, fellow," Vibulenus said in a squeak that was
meant to be a growl of warning to the non-com. He put
his arm around Rufus' shoulders and glared back at
Clodius. "No need for brutality."

"Sir, that's all *right*," the legionary whispered hastily,
jumping sideways and hunching as if the tribune's arm
were afire. Rufus collided with the trooper to whom he
had been speaking—his cousin Niger, of course—in a
clash of equipment much louder than that of the non-
com's blow a moment before.

"No need for little pricks too young to shave, neither," Clodius muttered, enough under his breath that
Vibulenus could pretend the words were lost in the
artificial thunder from across the valley.

Vibulenus stepped back, rubbing the lip of his Greek-
style helmet, more of an ornate bronze cap than func-
tional protection like those of the line soldiers. With his
hand raised that way, his forearm concealed the face
which he was sure glowed with his embarrassment.

Anyway, it wasn't true. He *had* shaved, and that first beard had been dedicated in a golden casket in the temple of Juno of Suessula which his father had refurbished for the occasion.

And would that the gods had struck him down in that moment. Then his family could mourn the ashes of Gaius Vibulenus Caper, and he himself would be spared all this.

Whatever *this* was.

How could General Crassus have bungled so badly at the end of a brilliant career?

Because of the noise around him, and even more because of the turgid echoes of his thoughts, Vibulenus did not hear the sound of the horse approaching until a legionary's curse was answered with, "Watch yourself, dog!" in the nasal bray of the rider, Rectinus Falco—another of the legion's six tribunes.

Falco was the last person Gaius Vibulenus wanted to see right now, but even that had its advantages: Vibulenus' shoulders straightened, his face became a mask of cool disinterest; instead of roiling with fear and embarrassment, his mind focused on the fact that he did not have a horse and that bastard Falco did because of the way he had made up to the Commander.

"Our commander sends me to check on the progress of the left wing," Falco said. His accent implied that he was born and bred in a townhouse in the wealthiest section of Rome. In fact, he was country gentry from Campania, just like Vibulenus himself; and the Vibuleni could have bought Falco's family three times over.

Not that questions of birth affected where the two tribunes stood, right now and for the foreseeable future.

"Not the level of progress one might have expected," the horseman went on, raising himself a trifle in the saddle by pressing his hands against the double front pommels.

"Tell the Commander that he needn't concern himself with this flank," Vibulenus replied in a tone of vibrant haughtiness that surprised him and would have surprised his declamation instructor in Capua even more. He had never shown signs of oratorical power. This was a hell of a place for it to turn out that he had talents in that direction after all. "Though I would have expected more cavalry to support us."

In all truth, this was a Hell of a place.

"Vibulenus, you'll go further if you learn to tend to your *own* affairs," Falco snapped angrily. He raised his torso higher with his hands and clamped his knees near the top of the saddle to peer at the cohort from a slightly better perspective. No doubt about it, the man was a natural horseman. "Which," he went on in his nasal sneer, "you seem to be doing a very bad job of, as ragged as these lines look."

"Then if you'll get yourself and your animal out of the deployment area," Vibulenus responded with ringing clarity, "we'll proceed with our business."

Falco might have continued the wrangle—which was not about war but rather status, and therefore of much greater importance to him. One of the line soldiers— was it Clodius Afer again, watching the ranks quick-step past—muttered, "Wonder how he'll ride with a spear up his bum?"

The horseman dropped back into a full seat with an alacrity that proved he considered the threat from the ranks more than rhetorical. The sun had risen high enough to clearly limn the anger on Falco's face as he tugged at the bridle and spurred his mount's right flank to twist it into a tight pivot. He continued to kick the horse as he rode back toward the command group at a twitchy canter.

Vibulenus drew a deep breath, obscurely thankful to Falco. Nothing like anger to drive out . . . weaker emotions. And he'd been worse places, they all had— trapped without water and without shade, facing Parthian

arrows that could punch through shield and breastplate
alike if a man's luck were out. Abandoned by their
allies, abandoned by Rome, and utterly abandoned by
hope.

Though it was doubtful that any of the three elements were closer to them now than they had been that
terrible day in Mesopotamia.

The tribune had a better view of the enemy across
the valley than he did of his own men; but the enemy
was not his job, not yet, and he determinedly concen-
trated on the deployment of the legion's left flank.

The legion had only a hundred and fifty attached
cavalry at the moment, and horses were in even shorter
supply than trained riders. There was a tiny squadron
of blue-plumed helmets bobbing in the sunlight ahead
of the deploying infantry. Weeks before, or what seemed
like only weeks, Gaius Vibulenus would have been too
ignorant to be bothered by the lack of cavalry. Nobody
who had survived the disastrous advance from Carrhae
could ever again be complacent about unsupported infantry. The tribune froze as his mind flashed a memory
of Parthians riding out of the dust, the sun glinting like
lightning on the steel heads of their arrows. . . .

A trumpet blew three short blasts, answered almost
immediately by three thinner, piercing notes from a
curved horn. The sound recalled Vibulenus to a present
which, bad as it might be, was better than that past in
Mesopotamia. The right-hand pair of the cohort's six
centuries had reached their proper spacing, and their
centurions had signalled a halt.

Like a bullwhip, the tip continued to move for some
moments after portions further back had stopped.
Vibulenus heard the centurion of the Fourth Century
give an order to his trumpeter, followed at once by a
two-note call and shortly later by the whine from the
Third Century's horn. The legionaries closest to the

tribune, three ranks ahead of him and as many behind, clanked and rattled to a halt.

Without a horse, the young tribune couldn't see a thing, not a *damned* thing, of the legion except the mail-armored torsos of the nearest soldiers. He strode between files, the alignment perpendicular to the legion's front, pausing as each man of the century dressed ranks by rotating one of his javelins sideways and horizontal. "Hey!" snarled a trooper whom Vibulenus jostled with his round shield in brushing past, but the man recognized him as an officer and blurted an apology even as the tribune stepped beyond the ranks and became, for a moment, the Roman closest to the enemy.

"Sir?" said someone in a concerned voice.

Vibulenus turned and saw, to his surprise, that Clodius Afer had spoken. They were all nervous. Perhaps the file-closer was as embarrassed at clubbing a man with his spear as the tribune was at butting into cohort discipline for purely personal reasons.

"It's all right," Vibulenus explained, "I'm—" To his amazement, he then said what he suddenly realized: "I'm less afraid out here. I think it's because—the arrows you know? We were all packed together, and the arrows kept falling. So in ranks I, I expect the arrows."

Clodius blinked in total non-comprehension. Several of the front-rank legionaries looked at one another with expressions which were too clear to permit doubt as to what they were thinking.

"Carry on," the tribune said sharply, flushed again with anger at everything but himself and the tongue that kept blurting things it should not. "I'm attending to the dress of this flank."

Well, that was the conscious reason he'd had for stepping out of ranks.

The legion was in fully-extended order, all sixty centuries in line with nothing held back for support or reserve. That gave them a frontage of almost a mile, a considerable advantage in keeping the enemy from swarming around both flanks—but it provided no margin for error, either on the flanks or in case an attack penetrated the thin six ranks into which the troops were stretched.

Perhaps the new commander knew what he was doing. Marcus Crassus had not. That was a certainty to the gods and to everyone who had served under that hapless general in Mesopotamia.

For all that, the ranks of bronze and iron and leather-faced wood had a look of terrible power. They made Vibulenus shiver with joy that he was on this side of the valley and not the other where the enemy fell to with the disorder of grubs spilled from rotting wood.

The ranks twisted like serpents crawling, for the slope across which the legion deployed was too irregular to accept the straight lines of the parade ground. These even curves had the sinuous power of a living thing, however, and within them the five-foot spacing between individual troopers looked flawless to Vibulenus despite the searing curses of non-coms who felt it could be improved. The First and Second Centuries locked into alignment with a final shudder, trumpet calling to horn. The sun behind threw the legion's long, spiky shadow across the grass toward the enemy.

A legionary—it should have been a mounted man—jogged across the front. He was coming from the pilus prior, the cohort's senior centurion. "Ready as ordered, sir," the man muttered as he passed Vibulenus, but he was on his way to the Commander waiting among his terrible body-guards behind the center of the legion.

The tribune nodded and tugged at one end of his sash, a token of rank like his trailing horsehair crest. Empty rank. *He* didn't command anything. It required a minimum of ten years' bloody service to become senior centurion of a cohort, and at least that—plus

family and connections—to become the legate in charge
of a legion.

When his newly-formed legion had marched away
from Capua with its standards sparkling, the horns and
trumpets calling triumphantly, Vibulenus had believed
that he was part of Rome's splendid conquest of barbarians. Mesopotamia and the gilded armor of the Parthian
cataphract horsemen had cured him of that mental pos-
turing; and disaster had left nothing behind but his
youth, and the empty "oversight" of the left flank which
his breeding gained him.

He could probably manage to die heroically, but it
was clear that the new commander would care even less
about such a death than Crassus would have.

Three cavalrymen trotted from the left flank, their
shields slung and their reins spread wide in both hands
against the chance of horses slipping and throwing them
down between the lines. Vibulenus stamped his right
boot to test the footing himself. The hobnails grated a
little, but the grass rooted the surface into sod and
there was no evidence of shingle to make a horse or
armored soldier skid.

But the riders were scouts, not fighters, and they
were understandably skittish about the potential problems which they were sent to search out. In battle
mode, these men would gallop across the same terrain
with shrieking abandon, each of them trying to be the
first to come to grips with the enemy. They and their
fellows had done just that under the leadership of Crassus'
son, disappearing in pursuit of Parthian horsemen who
fled until the Roman squadrons were out of touch and
support of the infantry.

It was so *easy* to blame others for the fact that Gaius
Vibulenus Caper was here. And it did so little good.

There was a series of horn and trumpet signals from
the right flank, distorted by distance and possibly multiplied by echoes. The thunder from the hostile en-

campment continued, but it was supplemented by deep-throated shouting.

A pair of vehicles drove from the mass of the enemy. With two axles apiece and a flat bed laden with warriors, the vehicles looked like wagons, but their drivers lashed them on like racing chariots. They were drawn by teams of six beasts which looked more like rangy oxen than like anything else in Vibulenus' experience, two pair pulling in yokes, and a beast attached only by hames to either side of the yoked leaders. They made for the scouting horsemen with the singleminded determination of gadflies seeking blood.

Mingled horns and trumpets from the command group called the advance. The signallers of the individual centuries picked up the concentus, until the massed call had spread past Vibulenus to the horn of the cohort's First Century.

"Cohort—" called the senior centurion, his voice audible because he had raised it more than an octave to pierce the bleating signals.

"Century—" the other centurions echoed with greater or lesser audibility, depending on their experience with getting real power behind a shout that was above their normal range.

"*Advance!*"

Raggedly, because some men did not hear the command and responded to their comrades' motion, the legion began to stride forward. Most of the men gave a shout, and a few clashed the javelin in their right hand against their shield boss.

The three horsemen were cantering back to their fellows, the task of scouting the intermediate ground accomplished by the enemy. The war carts bounded over irregularities, hurling the half-dozen warriors in the back of each into contortions as they clung to ropes looped around frame members. The vehicles lurched awkwardly where the opposing slopes met at the valley bottom, but there was no gully there and not enough of a bog or watercourse to affect the advance of the legion.

A warrior in the back of either cart was banging a mallet against a sheet of bronze slung from a pole. The rumble of changing harmonics explained the greater thunder emanating from the enemy camp.

"Ware!" called Clodius, and the tribune skipped aside as the legion rejoined him at the rate of two paces per second.

There was a slight gap in the frontage between the Third and Fourth Centuries—inevitable because the units dressed ranks within themselves, and useful because it provided a narrow aisle in which the non-coms could scurry between the six ranks for which they were responsible. Vibulenus fell into step between the Third Century file-closer and the centurion of the Fourth, a dull-faced veteran named Vacula whom the tribune had never heard speak a word which was not an order or the response to an order.

"How many do you think there are?" Clodius asked. "Sir?"

Vibulenus was trying to position his round shield. It was lighter and easier to carry than the big oval scutum of the line troops, but a similar piece of equipment had seemed horribly inadequate against the sleet of Parthian arrows. Startled by the question, but openly delighted that someone was treating him as if he had some purpose, he squinted across the valley at the army toward which they strode.

It was like trying to guess how many roses bloomed in the fields beneath Vesuvius, and an honest guess would have been in horrifying contrast to the five thousand, more or less, legionaries bearing down on those opponents.

So instead of blurting, "Thirty thousand, maybe as many as fifty"—the figures that clicked through his

mind—the tribune said, "They look like they're all naked, and only the ones in the chariots have shields."

They also looked like they were ten feet tall, just like
Rufus had said. Well, maybe eight feet tall.

"Yeah, well. . . ." said the file-closer. "At any rate,
they aren't shootin' arrows over their backs as they ride
away, this lot."

With no more organization than water bursting a
dam, and with the suggestion of equally overwhelming
force, hundreds of additional war cars charged from the
enemy line without appreciably diminishing the mass
that remained. The rumble of flexible bronze as they
approached had an omnipresence that horns or even
proper drums could not have equalled. It was as if the
legion were approaching a swarm of bees, each the size
of an ox.

The warriors were shouting as their vehicles galloped
onward, but their cries were surprisingly high-pitched
for all the breadth of their torsos. Plumes of single
feathers or perhaps blue-dyed plant fibers trembled
stiffly from the sides of each warrior's helmet.

The naked mass of infantry which remained on the
hillslope seemed, when Vibulenus squinted, to be armed
with clubs or maces. The warriors in the cars, however,
each carried a long spear tipped with the black glint of
iron. Some of those who clung to their vehicle with
their spear hand brandished huge shields, allowing
glimpses of breast-plates and swords or daggers in belt
sheaths.

"The chariots that came first," Vibulenus shouted.
He was in effect a rank of his own, a stride behind the
leading legionaries and a stride ahead of the second
rank, but he was marching in time with the centuries to
either side. The strap of his shield was already beginning to chafe the skin of his left forearm, and the
unfamiliar effort of holding the piece of equipment ad-

vanced was causing his biceps muscles to cramp. "What happened to them?"

Clodius Afer twisted his head enough to look past the cheek-pieces of his helmet at the tribune. He grimaced, a facial shrug because those were the only muscles not bound by armor or clutching equipment. "Not our problem," he shouted back; and he, like Vibulenus, hoped that was true.

The trees grew more thickly on the lower slopes of the valley. One of them forced the tribune to dodge aside to pass it between him and Clodius. Close up, the tree had even more of a snaky unreality than it and its fellows displayed at a distance in the mist that had already burned away. The bark was segmented into pentagonal scales, and the trunk, nowhere thicker than a man's thigh, terminated without branches in a single fleshy nodule thirty feet above the ground.

Vibulenus brushed the trunk with his left shoulder and wished he had not. His shield rim and the fabric of his tunic sleeve glistened with a thick fluid scraped from the bark. It felt slimy where it soaked through to his skin.

"Ready!" called the file closer, facing the men to his left.

Simultaneously, the centurion of the Fourth Century roared toward the mass of his own unit, "Century—"

The nearest war cars had rolled across the center of the shallow valley and were now climbing toward the legion. The draft animals looked distinctly unlike oxen now that the tribune had a closer view. They had four gnarly horns apiece, one pair in the usual place atop the head and the other on the nose. Vibulenus had not heard of anything like them, even among monstrous births catalogued with omens.

There were so many of the cars that they were jostling for position as they neared the legion. The unyoked draft animals fouled their opposite numbers in

neighboring teams, and one vehicle upset because its
driver did not have enough room to maneuver around a
tree.

"Charge!" shouted Clodius Afer, a fraction of a second before Vacula shrieked the same command in a
carrying falsetto. Both non-coms and their fellows from
the opposite flanks of each century in the line began to
run toward the chariots only two hundred feet away.

For a moment, the centurions and file-closers were
alone, a ragged scattering ahead of the legion like froth
whipped from the tops of waves. Then the whole legion
broke into a run as the right arms of the two leading
ranks cocked back, preparing to hurl the lighter of the
pair of javelins each legionary carried.

Gaius Vibulenus began to run also and tried to draw
his sword for want of a javelin to throw. He had to catch
up with the centurions because he was an officer and if
he could do nothing else, he could set an example . . .
but it wasn't that simple, except in the part of his mind
which refused to think and which was in control now.

Because he was young and fit, for all his relative
inexperience with the weight of his armor, Vibulenus
was beside Clodius Afer again when the file-closer's
arm shot forward and sent his javelin off in a high arc
toward the enemy. Clodius' heavy shield swung back
around the pivot of his firmly-planted left foot, balancing the heave of the missile.

The advancing line stuttered as each man lost a step
when he launched his javelin. The tribune, who had
finally gripped his flopping sword sheath with his left
hand so that he could draw the weapon with his right,
found himself once again in front of the remainder of
the legion.

The war cars were drawing up, apparently according
to plan rather than in reaction to the legion's advance.
Drivers swung their teams to one side or the other in a
scene of utter confusion, but with fewer real collisions

than the dense array had suggested would result. The
enemy were, after all, practiced at their method of
warfare even if they made no attempt at discipline in
the Roman sense. The warriors were springing from the
vehicles even as drivers sawed back on their reins as if
to lift the teams' forehooves off the ground.

Some fifteen hundred javelins rained down onto them
in a space of less than two seconds.

"Rome!" cried Gaius Vibulenus, while the legionaries
behind him were shouting that and a thousand other
things as they ran toward the foe.

The warriors' shields were big, even by comparison
with the bodies they had to cover, and they were solid
enough that even hard-flung javelins penetrated only to
the barbs of their heads. The teams had been in confusion before the missiles gouged many animals into rear-
ing agony. Now they were in chaos. Several teams
raced off in whatever direction they were pointing,
spilling their drivers and occasionally dragging an overturned car like a device for field-levelling.

Most of the warriors were unharmed, though a few
had been caught as they jumped from their vehicles
and now sprawled or staggered. Their chest armor,
even when studded with metal, did not turn or stop the
missiles the way the heavy shields had done. The weight
of the javelins stuck in the shield facings, half a dozen
in some cases, was an awkward additional burden. Many
of the warriors were trying to tug the javelins clear
when the second flight, from the third and fourth ranks
of the legion, hit them.

Vibulenus was running downhill, though the slope
was no more than an inch in twelve. When a Roman
javelin sailed over his shoulder, missing the back of his
neck by no more than the blade's width, his bloodthirsty joy and feeling of invulnerability washed away in
a douche of fear. The young tribune tried to stop. His
hobnails skidded out from under him, and the long

spear the warrior thrust at him gouged a fleck of bronze from Vibulenus' helmet instead of plunging in through his mouth and out the base of his skull.

The spearpoint's ragged edge was the result of forging at too low a temperature rather than deliberate serration, but the difference to Vibulenus would have been less than academic had the blade sawn a hand's-breadth slot through his face. As it was, the tribune's shin hurt more where his shield banged it than his head did from what would have been a deadly thrust.

The warrior who was trying to kill him had two feathery plumes that were part of his head rather than clothing as Vibulenus had assumed from a distance. He was lifting his spear again to finish the job with a second overarm thrust.

In panic that froze the events around him down to gelid detail but did not make them more soluble, Vibulenus swatted at the spear as he would have tried to bat away a spider which was leaping toward his eyes. The sword he held forgotten in his right hand clashed against the warrior's weapon. The iron spearhead shattered, victim of the best blade of Bilbao steel which Vibulenus' father could find for his boy to carry to war.

Something drained from the tribune at the shock—fear or weakness or concern for anything save doing the best job that could be done with the business Fate had handed him. He started to get to his feet.

Clodius Afer thrust his remaining javelin into the center of the warrior's chest until a foot of the point and metal shaft stood out through the back of the fellow's ribs.

"Eat *that*, pig-fucker!" screamed the file-closer as he released the javelin shaft and tried to draw the sword sheathed on his right side. Vibulenus jumped forward, his shield in front of his body as much by chance as skill, and blocked away the spear with which another warrior was stabbing for Clodius' life.

Close up, the warriors were half again as tall as the five-foot-eight-inch tribune, and their blue feather plumes waved a foot or so still higher. They gave off a smell like something chitinous and dead.

Vibulenus cut at the warrior whose spear he had just brushed aside. It was his first conscious attempt to use his sword, and he was clumsily ineffective: the blade chopped into the framing which supported the multiple layers of hide, scarcely making the heavy shield quiver. As the warrior tried to recover his spear, Clodius ducked under the shaft and hacked at the fellow's leading ankle with the skill of a butcher jointing a rabbit.

The warriors had howled as they came on, but when they were wounded they did not scream with pain. This one twisted silently, trying to brace himself with his spear and the shield whose lower rim he had slammed against the ground an instant too late to protect himself.

You're either lucky or you're not. You know that you *are* lucky from the fact that it's the other guy sneezing blood and bits of lung tissue onto the spear in his chest.

"He's got it!" Vibulenus shouted, as if he were a spectator at the arena instead of a participant in a full-scale battle. He was premature as well, because the warrior did manage to hold himself upright. The tribune tried a finishing blow at the feathered skull and only notched the shield rim again. Then Clodius put nine inches of steel in under the warrior's right arm and jumped back in time to keep from being struck by the toppling shield.

There were no warriors still standing within a spear-length of the Roman line. A pair of the enemy tried to scramble into action past an overturned war car. A dozen thrown javelins cut them down like wheat before the scythe.

"Come on, boys, we got 'em!" the file-closer cried as he jumped onto the vehicle himself.

"Come on!" Vibulenus echoed as he followed the

non-com. He was not really aware of the rest of the
legion, much less trying to encourage the men behind
him. His conscious mind was shouting to the instinct
that was ruling his actions, unnecessary except that it
was the only thing his intellectual portion could do at
the moment.

The overturned vehicle was floored with rope matting stretched on a dovetailed wooden frame. While the
mat supported and even cushioned the broad, bare feet
of the warriors, it was woven too loosely to provide safe
support for a booted Roman. Clodius Afer's left foot
plunged through an interstice which snared his knee
like that of a hapless rabbit.

The file-closer cursed and stabbed at the matting,
handicapped by his own shield. His point, bright already with warriors' blood, glanced from the tough
fibers of the mat and gouged his calf. He raised his
sword again.

Vibulenus hopped to an angle of the frame so that his
feet were splayed outward but had firm support. The
quality of the woodwork would not have disgraced a
senator's bed. "Wait!" shouted the young tribune without realizing that he had just given the veteran non-
com an order on the battlefield and that he instinctively
expected to be obeyed. Clodius looked up in surprise—
and he did not for the moment strike again at the ropes
trapping him.

Hundreds of additional war cars had drawn up short
of the wreckage of the first wave, delivering more warriors to the battlefield. The giant spearman came on in
clots, four or five together as they jumped from their
vehicles. They made no attempt to form a shield wall,
nor did the mass of naked infantry advance from the
position it had taken at dawn just below their encamp-
ment.

Individually, the warriors were as skilled and strong
as they were deadly. A quartet of them, leaping from a

car whose driver immediately lashed it toward the rear
again, saw Vibulenus and the trapped file-closer. Raising their shields and their fifteen-foot spears, the warriors advanced at a lumbering trot.

The tribune shrugged his left arm from the straps and
let his shield drop to the matting. The muscles of his
belly drew up as his body tried to twist itself out of the
way of the spears he imagined already criss-crossing his
flesh. He gripped Clodius under the right armpit and
dropped his sword also in order to lock the fingers of
both hands.

"Pull!" Vibulenus shouted, though what the file-closer
really needed to do was to push down with his shield
and right foot while the young tribune himself pulled.

Vacula and two of the legionaries from his Fourth
Century ran to meet the oncoming warriors. The centurion flung his heavy javelin so fiercely that the nearest
of the enemy staggered back, his shoulder pinned to
the shield through whose triple thickness of hide the
javelin had penetrated.

One of Vacula's men interposed his shield between a
spear and the centurion momentarily, but another warrior took the legionary out of the fight with a thrust
through the mail shirt and belly. The non-com was still
off balance from his throw and more intent on drawing
his sword than on swinging his shield into a posture of
defense. One long spear tore through the apron of
bronze-studded leather meant to protect the centurion's thighs. While Vacula thrashed like an eel on a
fisherman's trident, another warrior thrust through the
bridge of his nose.

The surviving legionary slipped aside, his javelin poised
as a threat to keep the warriors away from him now that
they had finished with his fellows.

Clodius Afer's leg came free. Almost as part of the
same motion, he vaulted down from the vehicle to
stand between Vibulenus and the warriors advancing

with bloody spears. "Watch it, sir!" called the file-closer. "Watch it!"

The tribune picked up his shield by the center strap, acting in too much haste to thread his forearm properly through the loop and then grip the real handhold at the rim.

One of the warriors stabbed at Clodius, but the veteran responded by shifting a handsbreadth to block the point with the thick, keel-like boss of his shield.

Vibulenus' sword stood pommel-up and ready to his hand, caught by the same matting which had held Clodius' foot. He drew it as he jumped down and almost lost the weapon again. The rope fibers snagged the notch left in the blade when it met the spearhead. A warrior thrust at him, and only Clodius' quick sideways chop with his sword stopped the spear from taking Vibulenus through the chest.

"Watch it, puppy!" the non-com screamed, barely able to block a thrust from his own left side.

The Pompilius cousins, Rufus and Niger, launched their heavy javelins as they scrambled over the wrack of vehicles and dead or dying animals. Neither missile was artfully aimed, but one wobbled into the throat of a warrior concentrating on another attempt at Clodius.

The wounded spearman bleated and staggered into one of his fellows. The third warrior, disconcerted, backed a step to take stock of the situation. Gaius Vibulenus, to whom everything since the attack had begun was a white blur, saw an opportunity with the clarity of the moon in a starry sky. He ducked low and swung the bronze-bound edge of his shield onto the bare instep of the warrior who was backing away. The way the small bones crunched made hair raise on the tribune's own neck.

"Come on, boys!" the file-closer shouted with his feet planted and his shield raised. The Pompilii and three of their comrades swept down from one side, and the

survivor of the legionaries who had accompanied Vacula
circled the hostile spearmen from the other.

The warrior whom Vibulenus had disabled bludgeoned
the tribune with his spear shaft. Vibulenus' helmet had
been knocked off at the start of the action, but he had
not noticed it was missing. The spear was too awkward
to be a good club, but the warrior made up with strength
and the shaft's weight for any lack of quickness.

Vibulenus sprawled on his back with his eyes and
mouth wide open. The sky was a pale orange, a complement to the color it had been a moment before, and
against it the young Roman had a double vision of the
spearhead which the warrior had poised to finish the
job he had started with the shaft. The weapon disappeared in a blur of armored skirts and the blocky,
powerful thighs of Clodius Afer, lunging between
Vibulenus and death.

The tribune thought he was getting to his feet again
only seconds later, but all the warriors he had been
facing were dead on the ground and no Roman he
recognized was anywhere around. The sixth rank of
legionaries had already marched by, disordered somewhat by the debris on the field but not by fighting.
Each of the men held one javelin in the right hand and
the other, heavier, missile gripped against the shield
back.

Beyond them, already starting up the slope toward
the enemy camp, were the leaders of the Roman advance. Among them Vibulenus could see the standard
of the Third Century and the stocky form of Clodius
Afer who was looking back over his shoulder to shout
encouragement.

The tribune's vision was clear again. If it had not
been. . . .

All of Vibulenus' muscles seemed to work, but when
he moved he had the feeling that his body had become
a water-filled bladder and that there were no bones

within his skin. The only war cars he could see were disabled ones and the few racing, empty but for their drivers, toward the shelter of the massed infantry.

Annihilation of the armored spearmen had scarcely changed the balance of numbers. Tens of thousands of the enemy remained; and Vacula, with pink brains leaking out of the hole which included both eyesockets, was only one reminder that the legion had suffered casualties as well.

The tribune picked up the sword he had dropped. The effort of bending and rising made the left side of his head throb as if he had just been clubbed there again. He retched, but there was nothing left for his stomach to heave up. When he wiped his mouth with the back of his hand, he remembered that he had vomited when he first tried to get to his feet. He had forgotten that. . . .

Horns and trumpets called from Vibulenus' right, and the young tribune turned toward the source of the sound. Well behind the last rank, the command group was picking its way through the wreckage—once living and otherwise—of battle.

There were two men on horseback, Falco and another of the tribunes. The rest of the command group was mounted on beasts which bore far less resemblance to horses than the four-horned draft animals of the enemy did to oxen. They were carnivorous, beyond doubt: giant lions, perhaps, or even huger dogs. They wore coats of iron scales, like the horses of the richest Parthian cataphracts. The score of inhuman riders mounted on them, the Commander's bodyguard, were armored in jointed suits which must have weighed hundreds of pounds apiece.

Gaius Vibulenus had not known where his place was. He still was not sure, but he knew he did not belong here, behind the legion, with Falco and those who had bought the Roman prisoners from their Parthian captors.

The young tribune began to jog down the remainder of the slope, clutching his sword but leaving his shield behind with the bodies. Every time his foot hit the ground, it pumped his skull airily lighter so that the pain resonating inside it became diluted to heat and a mild pressure.

When he opened his mouth to cry, "Rome!" he found that his constricted throat would not pass even a croak. He tried to shout anyway as he staggered like a drunk or a madman, reaching the sixth rank as its legionaries dodged the more numerous trees at the low point of the valley.

There were sounds of further fighting ahead, but the upward slope blocked vision. The slight decline from the opposite side of the valley had given the rear ranks an almost theatrical view of the start of the battle.

Gaius Vibulenus was an inch or two taller than most of the line soldiers, because his family could afford to feed him well as a child. That was not enough of a height advantage to permit him to see over the helmets and crests, short black brushes for the legionaries and red transverse combs to mark the centurions. He struggled through the ranks, bumping and once pushing aside the troops who were doing their best to keep their order: the only task they were called on to perform at this moment.

Ahead were the shouts of men and the clattering of weapons, brilliants of sound embroidered on the thunderous background still shuddering from the enemy camp. The young tribune thought of hogs stumbling through chutes toward the slaughterer's knife, fearful and unable to see anything but the gap toward which they plunged between high board walls.

But even if the victims knew their fate, they might run to it for the sake of certainty in a universe of spin and chaos; and for Vibulenus, there was nothing certain except that he wanted the identity of a man who was in the forefront of this battle rather than one who hung back when he had the opportunity to hang back.

As he dodged a legionary who was unconsciously swinging his sword back and forth in an arc which threatened everyone on his right side, Vibulenus slammed into another of the serpentine trees. Its top nodule waved, showering the tribune with gooey, sweet-smelling fluid. Vibulenus swung himself around the bole, unconcerned by the glue-like smear the bark left on his arm and breastplate and unaware that his hair was now gummy with effluvium from the tree as well as with his own blood.

The third and fourth ranks had closed up so that the legionaries stood almost shield to shield as they mopped up spearmen still living in the wake of the front ranks. There had been an attempt to open out again as the advance continued unimpeded, but there were still clots and gaps like the pattern made by frog eggs on a still pond.

The portion of Vibulenus' brain which was in control functioned like a racer's, not like that of a man in the midst of battle. It sent the young tribune through one of the gaps. Ahead of him he could see the standards and the leading elements of the legion already coming to grips with the hostile infantry.

There was a shower of stubby javelins from the enemy lines. One of the missiles, weighted near the head with a lump of stone, hit Vibulenus in the middle of the chest. The bone point shattered against the molded bronze of his breastplate, but the shock threw him back a step and brought him to his senses. Then he took the remaining two paces forward to join Clodius Afer as the file-closer hacked through the ribs of an enemy.

The tribune has lost both his helmet and his shield, but the hostile infantry were just as naked as they looked from a distance. They were taller than the Romans, but they were by no means the size of the spearmen who had ridden to battle on the war cars. Some wore peaked leather caps and bandoliers which held half a dozen javelins like that which Vibulenus' breastplate had stopped; but none of those whom the tribune saw carried shields or wore any armor that would slow an edge of Spanish steel.

One of the enemy swung his stone-weighted javelin at Clodius like a mace. It glanced off the file-closer's neck guard, making the man stagger and his helmet ring. Vibulenus stabbed upward through the enemy's belly and watched its feathers flutter as the creature toppled backward and died.

Gaius Vibulenus Caper had just killed someone—not a man, he supposed; but it might have been. And all that mattered to him at the moment was that his sword caught in something and he had to jerk very hard on the hilt to clear the weapon.

"Bastard," snarled Clodius, slashing at the dead foe who had struck him. His voice was hoarse, and he gasped out the epithet between huge breaths through his mouth and nose together. "Bastard!" and he waded forward over bodies still quivering and oozing fluids from their wounds.

"Rome," wheezed the tribune in what was meant to be a shout. He hacked down the enemy who had just stabbed his left arm.

Hostile infantry higher on the slope volleyed bone and flint-tipped javelins, but those in contact with the Roman lines attempted to use theirs as hand weapons. The points could deliver a nasty or even fatal gash, and their stone weights might have been heavy enough to crush an unprotected skull. Against Romans with shields and full armor, they were singularly ineffective.

For a minute or two, Vibulenus and the leading elements of the legion cut at opponents as thickly packed as wheat in a field—and as defenseless. Then the rear-most ranks of legionaries launched the javelins most of them still carried, arching them well beyond the line of hand to hand combat. The enemy reacted like a glass tumbler struck by a paving stone.

Roman javelins had been reasonably effective against the warriors in the first stage of the battle, creating confusion even when blocked by shields or body armor. In the naked infantry, anyone hit was a victim, and the enemy was packed so densely that most of the missiles punched through two or even three of them. More of the hostile infantry had probably died on Roman swords already, but the suddenness of this disaster in the heart of the mass blew the troops who saw it into panicked flight.

When the pressure of their fellows behind them ceased, the front line of the enemy gave up even the pretence of resisting the legion. Vibulenus fell to his knees when his sword slashed only air. The victim he had tried to decapitate fled backward before the stroke in a great rubbery bound, his feather plumes fluttering like miniature wings as he flung away his bandolier of missiles.

None of the enemy within fifty feet of the tribune were still standing when he got his own feet under him again. The ground writhed with bodies trying to stuff bright-colored intestines back into sword-cuts or withdraw javelin heads which extended as far behind as the shaft did in front of the wound. Survivors of the hostile infantry were loping away in all directions, faster than even the handful of Roman cavalry on the wings could pursue after the slogging effort of battle.

Within and ahead of the fleeing infantry were the war cars, empty now save for the drivers who were as furiously bent on escape as any of their fellows in the infantry. The vehicles (those which the legion had not overrun at first contact) had been drawn up behind the infantry, awaiting the signal to retrieve the warriors whom they had carried to battle. Now, like birds from a blazing forest, they bolted away with nothing behind them save raging disaster.

The thunder from the enemy camp ceased. Legionaries from the right flank were climbing over the low earthen wall, unresisted by those within.

Vibulenus tried to stagger forward in pursuit of the enemy. Someone grabbed him by the left shoulder. When the tribune attempted to brush off the contact in single-minded concentration on his task, he found that he had a nasty wound in the left biceps which he could not remember receiving.

All the strength and determination drained out of the young tribune. He slipped into a sitting posture on the ground. The lower edge of his breastplate gouged him as he slumped, but at the moment he did not have the intellect to care or the energy to do anything about the discomfort.

"That's right, boy," said Clodius Afer, releasing Vibulenus' shoulder and sprawling down onto the ground himself now that he had stopped the younger man. "We've done our job—leave the rest to those as are fresh."

The filer closer took off his helmet and gestured with it at the rear ranks of the legion streaming on in distant pursuit of the enemy. The legionaries would not catch many of their naked foes, but their pressure would keep the enemy from regrouping and launching an attack on men exhausted by victory. "You get so tired," Clodius went on musingly, "you run right up on a spear and you don't know you've done it. Got to know when to stop, boy." He began to massage the back of his neck. Vibulenus could see the skin there had been scraped when the hostile mace drove down the helmet edge.

The tribune looked at Clodius. The younger man's vision had, since he sat down, been an apathetic blur for want of brain capacity to process what he was seeing.

Now the non-com's face sprang into sharp focus. The skin was flushed, and ghostly red and white outlines remained from the pressure of the helmet rim and cheek pieces during the battle.

Clodius' eyes were open. They held no expression, but the crow's feet at their corners belied the youthfulness suggested by the man's thick black hair.

The file-closer was breathing through his mouth, though the breaths were controlled and not the gasping spasms which thrust Vibulenus' ribs against the inside of his body armor. The non-com had the look of an ox in the traces, tired but stolid and immensely powerful.

The tribune remembered the way Clodius had struck Rufus as the legion deployed. He realized now that the veteran had known too well what the next hours would be like, and his knowledge had made him savagely intolerant of lapses in discipline.

Vibulenus glanced at his sword. Fresh, the blood on it had looked normal enough; but as the fluid dried, it took on a purplish sheen. His face stilled to hide his awareness that his right arm to the elbow was covered with the same inhuman fluid, Vibulenus began to wipe the flats of his weapon on the grass and gritty soil. His left arm was too stiff to use, and when he tried to move it, the scab and exposed muscle crackled painfully.

"What's *that?*" demanded Clodius Afer in amazement, his fingers hesitating in the midst of releasing the laces that held the shoulder straps to the front of his mail shirt.

The tribune shifted his whole body to follow Clodius' gesture, finding as he did so that it was much more comfortable to be facing back down the slope anyway. Coming toward them was a device that resembled a piece of siege equipment. It was circular and turtle-humped, twenty feet in diameter and as high at the center as a man standing. The tortoise-like object was a saturated blue in color, and—though this might have been a trick of the angle—it appeared to move by drifting a foot or more above the ground.

"I don't know," Vibulenus admitted. He did not have enough emotion left to be concerned. "Maybe it's something like what they loaded us onto." And had later marched them out of, though neither he nor any member of the legion to whom he had talked could remember anything about the intervening period. "A boat."

He reached up to unfasten the studs of his cast-bronze body armor. Pain in his left arm brought the motion to a wincing halt.

The file-closer grimaced at the tortoise drifting over the bodies on the slope. Then, turning his attention to something within his experience and therefore not frightening to him, he said, "Here, let me bandage that," and took a folded strip of two-inch linen from the wallet he carried on the back of his equipment belt.

"Hold *still*," Clodius added sharply as Vibulenus turned his head with a bland expression and an unstated desire not to look at the damage to his body. The older man X-ed the fabric below the wound and began crossing the ends upward toward the shoulder as if he were wrapping leggings.

The front-rank legionaries who had not simply flopped on the ground were wandering in a daze of exhaustion, some of them dragging their shields and many with their armor unlaced. A line of shouting, laughing men climbed back over the wall of the enemy camp, carrying above their heads a single sheet of bronze three feet wide and at least ten times that length.

"Their drum," said Clodius, glancing in the same direction. His fingers, dark with blood and grime, tied off the bandage in a neat square knot. "Their signaller."

"Hey, Gnaeus," said one of the soldiers nearby, brought to awareness by the file-closer's voice. "Where do we get water? We're—oh. Hi, sir."

The last to Vibulenus, recognized also, and the legionary who spoke was Pompililius Rufus with his cousin Niger beside him. Both men carried their helmets in their right hands. Rufus' was missing its crest: the whole socket had been sheared from the peak of the otherwise undamaged headgear.

"They didn't bring the servants on the ship with us," said Gnaeus Clodius Afer, lifting his head and peering back in the direction from which they had deployed. The huge metal vessel onto which they had marched under Parthian guard and which they had exited again in a very different place was out of sight in a canyon lying parallel to this much gentler valley. "I lost three good slaves. Would've brought me a nice bit of coin back to Rome. . . . if we'd gotten back to Rome. . . ."

"I'll," said Vibulenus, alert enough again to be an officer responsible for the well-being of his men, "go demand—"

He tried to get up. Everything went blank for an instant, until the shock of his buttocks crashing onto the ground returned him to buzzing consciousness. His skin felt as if it were expanding because someone was stuffing it with hot sand.

"Steady there, sir," said one of the legionaries. Clodius had caught the tribune's left wrist as he fell, so that the wound did not bang against the breastplate.

"Hercules, I felt fine," Vibulenus muttered. He *still* felt fine, no pain except for an embarrassment that was worse than the transient burning sensation.

"Sir," asked Niger, "where did you get these?"

The young legionary's hand brushed Vibulenus' hair and then proudly displayed his capture, a glossy brown insect whose wingtips were now pinched together between thumb and forefinger. It was trying to arch its tail back against the prisoning fingertips, though the tribune did not see a sting.

"Well, that's a wasp, Niger," Rufus said with a tinge of "of course" in his voice.

Vibulenus reached up to squeeze the right side of his scalp, which had a crawling sensation in contrast to the severe throb on the left side where he remembered the spearshaft clubbing him. Maybe that was why he felt dizzy. . . .

"Who this side of Hades—" the file-closer began.

Rufus interrupted, "Watch that, Gaius!" and grabbed Vibulenus' wrist, treating him in an emergency as a boyhood friend rather than superior officer. "There's three on you and maybe they bite."

"I'm not sure it's wasps," Niger said, transferring the first-plucked example to his left hand and reaching for another. Something buzzed away from the tribune's scalp, brushing his ear as it did so. "They've got just the two wings, see—" He held out a second squirming captive.

His cousin reached for the tribune's head with thumb and forefinger extended, saying, "Well, these men we're fighting. *They* don't look like—"

What Vibulenus hoped was the last of the insects escaped ahead of Rufus' fingers, its wings beating what seemed to be an angry note. Perhaps he was projecting his own irritation onto the wasp.

"That's what I *mean*, don't you see?" explained Niger, gesturing with both trapped insects like a priest conducting some sort of bizarre rite. "Things don't look like what we're used to in this part of Parthia—"

Vibulenus glanced sharply at Clodius, but the file-closer appeared to have heard nothing to which he would take exception.

"—so maybe these're *bees*, not wasps, and I can make mead, honey-wine, if I can find their hive," the legionary finished triumphantly.

His cousin grimaced, then said apologetically to the tribune, "Niger's been fancying his chances to make mead ever since we boarded ship at Brundisium."

"Well, what *are* the damned things doing on his

excellency?" demanded the file-closer. The respect in his words was mostly formal, because as he spoke he unceremoniously squeezed at the edges of the pressure cut on Vibulenus' scalp to determine its severity. Clodius' touch syncopated the measured beat of the pain in the tribune's head, but it did not make it worse.

"Well, we always helped Daddy make it," Niger said defensively, "and I just thought as it'd make things, you know, more like home."

"There's something sweet . . . ," Rufus said, touching the right side of Vibulenus' scalp gently and bringing his fingertip back to sniff, then tongue. "Don't think it's honey."

He, his cousin, and even Clodius Afer reached out simultaneously to continue the examination. Vibulenus, feeling like a common serving dish at a banquet, lurched upright and this time gained his feet with only a momentary spell of dizziness.

"Pollux!" he muttered as he swayed, the others rising also with expressions of concern both for his condition and the way that they, also detached from routine by the events of the morning, had been treating an officer.

"I'm going to go over there," Vibulenus said with careful distinctness, pointing toward the command group which had at last reached the enemy camp, "and demand to know why there are no water bearers."

"All right. . . ," said the file-closer. He bent to pick up his helmet and shield. The vermilioned leather face of the latter had been gouged in a score of places, and a flint point had been driven deep enough into the plywood to cling there even after the shaft was broken off. "You two," he ordered the Pompilii. "Pick up your gear and come along. We're going to escort his excellency."

"There's water, sir," said Niger, pointing in a gesture distorted by the fact that he still held an insect.

At first the tribune thought Niger meant the gigantic turtle which floated down the line of first contact, moving toward the left flank. The device was particularly evident at the moment Vibulenus glanced back because it was lifting five or six feet in the air to clear the wreckage of two war cars, one run up on the other when javelins killed the drivers of both.

But besides the larger device, there were a dozen or more smaller scurrying constructs, coursing up the slope toward the victorious legion. A fountain on the back of each bubbled high enough to dazzle in the sun. The vehicles were each the size of an ox, small only by contrast with the metallic turtle. They moved at a respectable pace, faster than a man marching, but their jets of water were angled so that they fell back onto the vehicles instead of being wasted on the ground.

"I'm still going to see the Commander," said Vibulenus abruptly. He was not sure whether the decision was the result of reason or because he was dazed and as dangerously monomaniacal as he had been when he returned to the front of the battle without his shield or helmet.

What the young tribune *did* know was that he had been driven by fear ever since he met the Parthians as a member of Crassus' army, and the rain of arrows from those horsemen had continued for an afternoon that seemed eternity. The battle this morning had shown him that there was something in the world to strive for besides freedom from fear: there was success, in terms however limited; and there was the respect of men who were now his fellows, because he had been their fellow when the chips were down.

If it was not strictly the duty of Gaius Vibulenus Caper to find a place in the front rank of the legion, then it was surely the business of an officer to look after the welfare of his men. It was time to ask the questions that he had been afraid to ask when they were marched aboard the giant vessel or later when they were mustered again in its hold and deployed here—wherever *here* was.

"Well, come on, dammit!" Clodius Afer snapped to the legionaries. "Get your *gear* together."

Niger sighed. He freed his hands by tossing the maybe-bees off in ballistic arcs from which they did not recover until, ten feet away from their captor, they were beyond accurate sight range. They hovered for a moment to get their bearings, then sailed off as copper glints in the air. "I sure wish . . . ," the legionary murmured as his eyes tracked them. Donning his helmet and lifting his shield by one handle, he followed the others.

Vibulenus checked the blade of the sword he was carrying. He was pleased that he was so alert. Pleased, in fact, that he had not simply forgotten the weapon on the ground where he sprawled. His left arm was beginning to throb in the intervals in which his head did not, but there was no return of the nausea he had felt just after being clubbed down.

The sword was not clean, but what Vibulenus had not wiped off on the grass was at least dry. He sheathed the weapon, swaying a little because his balance did not seem to be everything it should have been.

"They're picking up bodies," said Rufus, squinting toward the floating turtle on the opposite side of the valley.

"No it's not," insisted his cousin. "Look, you can see there's bodies still lying there behind it." He paused before adding, "Maybe it's the *wounded* it's picking up."

The glance Vibulenus risked to the side told him only what he had expected: that he would fall down if he tried to walk without keeping his eyes straight ahead. He continued forward with thirty-inch marching steps. That stride, ingrained during training, was easier for him to maintain than shorter paces. Every time his left heel struck the ground, jagged lightning flashed in his arm. When his right boot came down, dull thunder echoed from his skull. The muscles of his face bunched tautly about the prominent bones.

"No, it's taking bodies," said the file-closer, "*some* bodies. I saw Crescens of the Fourth Century skewered the same time Vacula bought it."

And I *nearly bought it,* interjected the tribune's mind but not his mouth.

"Vacula's still lying there," Clodius continued, "and all the big wogs we chopped are there, but I don't see Crescens at all."

"Maybe—" offered Niger.

"And maybe he *didn't* crawl off with three foot of spear through his middle," the file-closer snapped to crush the suggestion even before it had been articulated.

A mobile fountain had halted nearby when a legionary stepped close to it. Now the vehicle was surrounded by thirsty men, baked in their armor by their exertions and the climbing sun. The vehicle was broader than Vibulenus had realized, so that thirty or forty men at a time were able to slurp, dip, or even duck their heads into the water. The fountain continued to dance playfully above them.

"Keep moving," Clodius Afer gruffly ordered the accompanying legionaries, but he himself angled toward the fountain. He jogged the first steps but quickly fell back to a walk.

Vibulenus noticed that the file-closer was favoring his left leg and felt pleased by the fact in a guilty way. It proved that he hadn't been the only one who took a battering this morning. Then the tribune remembered Vacula flopping backward with a ragged hole in the middle of his face. He touched two fingers to the bruise on his forehead left when his helmet was hammered off, and his skin flushed with embarrassment that he had felt his own injuries were exceptional.

Clodius doffed his helmet. Vibulenus thought he might plan to use it for a club to get through the soldiers already struggling for water, but the file-closer instead used the edge of his shield to slice his way expertly to the front. There, he dipped the helmet full without ceremony and wrenched his way out of the confusion again to rejoin his companions.

"Now, hold up a minute and *drink*," Clodius said, blocking the tribune's path and extending the brimming helmet from which he had not drunk himself as yet. "Sir."

Vibulenus swayed as he halted, but he squeezed his eyes shut and felt his body steady while his retinas pulsed alternately red and violet. He took the helmet, shocked by its weight, and managed to inhale part of the mouthful he awkwardly gulped. Coughing, he handed the makeshift container back to Clodius while trying to nod his thanks because he could not speak.

It was good water, cold at least. Though flavored by the file-closer's sweat as well as the dust and phlegm coating Vibulenus' own throat, the water left no mineral aftertaste.

The tribune looked at the fountain and thought about the larger equivalent of that floating construct, the vessel which had brought them here. He understood nothing about either, except that they *were* here, and that the water was water. . . . The arcs and circular dead ends in which the young officer's brain spun were so perfectly empty that they acted as an anodyne to the pain of his body, even after all four of them drank a second time and he prepared to march on toward the Commander.

"Everybody all right?" Clodius Afer asked in a cautionary tone, the helmet poised between his palms and the hinged cheek pieces flopping over the backs of his hands.

"Yessir," chorused the legionaries, while Vibulenus lifted his beardless chin in assent and said, "Yes, thank you, I feel much better."

That was true, though the tribune did not know whether it resulted from the water, the pause, or simply that the pain was beginning to overcome his capacity to feel it.

"That's fine," said the file-closer with a wicked grin. He put his helmet back on. The water that still nearly filled it poured over his head and down the links of his mail shirt like a stream cascading through rapids. *"Damn* but I needed that," the non-com remarked, continuing to grin.

Vibulenus found that the incident made his youthful honor prickle. Had the veteran made a fool of him, getting the officer to surrender the water that could have bathed him instead?

"You earned it," the tribune said, saved by his instincts. He clapped the older man on the shoulder as they strode off together toward the camp.

Legionaries who had scaled the enemy's sloping wall were now staggering back with all manner of loot, most of it as odd as the huge bronze sheet that early-comers had carried off. Vibulenus noticed a trio of soldiers returning through the gate, passing a skin of what he supposed was wine. They supposed it was wine also; but, like a scene from a farce, they spewed up the entire contents of their stomachs and collapsed on a count of three.

Another legionary tried to drag the skin out from under the third victim before all its contents dribbled out. A wiser companion tugged him away.

During the battle, the gate of the enemy camp had been closed by a framework around which were woven briars, a sort of vegetation Vibulenus had not encountered in the valley. Some of the panicked native troops had pulled the barrier aside to flee in one direction or the other. The opening made little difference, because the sloping wall was only a slight impediment without troops willing to defend it.

The Commander and his mounted entourage, who had entered by the gate, were making a dignified exit through the same opening when Vibulenus reached it. The bodyguards stalked out in pairs until six of them were aligned in front of the entrance, armored ankle to armored ankle, to block any Romans who might wish to accost the Commander.

As Gaius Vibulenus did.

The young tribune stepped ahead of his companions, to within six feet of the mounted guards and well within reach of their long-shafted maces. Two of the beasts growled, and a third hunched down on his forequarters, baring his teeth. A gap had been cut in the beast's upper molars to insert a bit.

The guard made no attempt to draw up on his reins. Gravel scattered beneath the creature's non-retractile claws, one of which was bloodied, as the paws extended toward Vibulenus.

"I wish to speak to the Commander," the tribune said in the piercing, inescapable voice which his throat provided at need. "I am Gaius Vibulenus Caper; citizen, military tribune, and member of the equestrian order." In fact, his family was wealthy enough that his father could have bought a Senate seat if he had wanted the trouble . . . and not that it made the least difference any more, except in Vibulenus' mind and the minds of those captured with him.

There were slotted disks a foot in diameter and four inches thick on the chests of all the lion-like mounts. Vibulenus had assumed the disks were part of the beasts' protection but now, as close as he was, he could see this was not the case: the actual armor was formed by blankets of heavy iron scales wired to a leather backing, cut away at the breast so as not to foul the disks—which moaned constantly. From the motion of dust particles, the tribune saw that air was being drawn in fiercely through the slots.

A guard raised the perforated visor of his helmet. The face beneath the iron was broad and brown and looked more like that of a toad than anything else in the tribune's previous experience. He could hear a gasp behind him—from Clodius, he thought. None of them had seen the guards' faces before.

"Get out of the Commander's way," the guard boomed, Latin in a voice so low-pitched that the words, though distinct, were barely intelligible.

Upright, the mount was as high at the shoulder as Vibulenus was tall. Even with its forelegs outstretched, the beast's eyes glared from behind filigreed protectors on a level with the tribune's. The eyes were set frontally, like those of a man or a lion, giving the good depth perception a predator needs but not the nearly 360° field of view that makes a horse sure-footed.

"I must speak to the Commander!" Vibulenus shouted. He set his shoulders, but he could not bear to front the line of guards squarely. Rather, his left side was slightly advanced, and he was glad that he had lost his shield because otherwise he could not have kept from cringing behind it.

The beast carried its rider a clawed step closer, breaking the alignment and bathing the tribune in an exhaled breath compounded of dead meat and less familiar odors.

Vibulenus heard the sound of metal behind him, the ringing of a sword edge as it cleared the lip of its sheath. He did not dare turn his back, but he opened his mouth to shout a warning to his companions—to his fellows, to his friends—not to escalate matters into disaster.

Before the tribune could speak, a voice from behind the guard advancing on him croaked an order made obvious by its timbre although it was not in anything Vibulenus recognized as a language. He thought another guard had spoken, but when those of the front rank reined their mounts aside, the Roman recognized his error.

There were three riders behind the front line of guards, two of them Roman tribunes on horses. The third mounted personage rode a beast like those of his bodyguard, though its only armored trappings were studs on the reins and the saddle between the beast's high, humped shoulders. Because it was not covered in iron, the mount had even more of a shaggy, carnivorous look than did those of the guards, but it was under perfect control as it advanced with measured strides into the gap the guards had provided.

"What is it you want to say, Gaius Vibulenus Caper?" asked the Commander, leaning forward as he spoke, past the bristly mane of his mount.

He looked tiny on his present perch, though he had seemed a man within normal limits earlier, when he presided over the mustering and reequipping of the legion in the hold of the vessel. Vibulenus had assumed the Commander was human, as he had assumed the warriors the legion met and slaughtered in this valley were human for all their height and the feathers which grew from the sides of their skulls.

But the toadlike bodyguards were not men, even if the tales were true of Nubia, where the Blemmyes were said to wear their heads in their bellies and other men sported tails. If the guards were not human, then there was no certainty of anyone except the legionaries themselves . . .

Falco smirked down from horseback. Vibulenus felt a rush of loathing greater than anything the face of the guard had drawn from him.

"I demand to know why we are here," he cried, speaking loudly because the intake whine of the disks on the guard beasts added to something like a howl. The disk on the breast of the Commander's own mount was connected to the beast's throat by a short metal hose, and similar rigging seemed to lurk beneath the armor of the other mounts. "We are Roman citizens!"

"You are here to fight, Roman citizen," said the Commander. There was a high squeal, the sound of an axle with an unlubricated bearing, but it came from the Commander's slight body as his bellowed order to the guards must have done. "To fight for my trading guild on worlds where the Federation does not permit weapons of higher than the local technology.

"And you fought splendidly, Roman. Superbly."

The Commander wore body-covering tights whose fabric was the same shade of blue as the mobile fountains. His face was the only part of him which the suit did not cover, and the flesh there returned sunlight in a direct reflection like that of metal or glass when the angle was right. The hands that gripped the reins, and the feet that rested on the pegs which the Romans were learning to call stirrups, each seemed to have six digits beneath the soft blue cloth.

"I don't—" the tribune said. "Understand," Vibulenus would have continued, but that would be pointless. "Where *are* we?" he asked instead, the timbre of his voice rising with desperate emotion instead of rhetorical effect.

"That doesn't matter," the Commander replied simply. Probably that answer would have done as well for the other statement, the one Vibulenus had swallowed. "You won't be asked to do anything unfamiliar to you. Anything—" his six-fingered hand gestured broadly toward the wrack of bodies lying on the far slope, giant warriors strewn like driftwood storm-tossed on a beach "—anything but what you do so well. And—" the Commander withdrew his hand and straightened in the saddle "—you will become immortal."

The sun glittered off a variety of new facets as the Commander's face drew up in what might be a grimace.

"That is," he added, "your bodies will not age. Not ever again."

His lips did not move when he spoke. The flawless Latin of his statements came from a black embroidery on the fabric covering his throat.

There was another sound in the air, like the suction wheeze of the beasts' equipment, but louder and from above. Over it, Vibulenus shouted, "Will you send us home? We can pay you. *Rome* will pay you a rich ransom."

As she had not ransomed the soldiers of Regulus, captured in similar ignominy, but even a slave could hope, could pray. . . .

"Release you?" the Commander paraphrased. He squealed again, in apparent humor. "Oh, no, Roman. You're far too valuable for *that*. And now, I must report to my superiors. You'll be given further details when you've mustered aboard the vessel for your next assignment."

The roar from above was expanding into echoing thunder beside which the warriors' vibrating bronze sheet faded to pale mockery and even a true storm would have been inaudible. Vibulenus looked up as men all over the valley were looking, shading their eyes with a hand or simply gaping in open-mouthed wonder.

The young tribune had guessed that they had come to this place in a ship, a vessel that sailed upon land as those with which he was familiar sailed on water. The thing that roared a hole in the sky as it slowly descended was a ship like that which the legion had marched aboard in Parthia, but it did not slide over the land.

"What—" the tribune began and paused when he realized that, even if he shouted, his words could not possibly be understood. Some legionaries were throwing off their helmets so that they could clamp both palms over their ears.

As if he were speaking within the tribune's skull, the Commander's voice answered the incompleted question: "Now that we have defeated the king who refused us trading rights, the trading mission can go ahead. But move aside, tribune, or you'll require a full physical rebuild yourself."

Vibulenus caught the hint of a croaked order like that which had opened a path through the bodyguard so that the Commander could speak with the young Roman. He stumbled out of the guards' way as they, having heard the new command as clearly as the tribune had heard the last words directed to him, spurred their huge mounts back across the valley.

The pair of Romans accompanying them yipped and kicked their horses, getting off to a less abrupt start than the carnivores of the guard but falling into a fluid canter that looked more comfortable than the others' loping gait. The remainder of the twenty-strong bodyguard followed, surrounding the blue spark of the Commander. Most of them had raised their visors now that the fighting was over, displaying their bulbous eyes and their broad, expressionless mouths.

The descending ship dropped below the ridge, toward the canyon in which the legion's vessel already waited. For a moment, the thunder was redirected upward and the ground quivered in trying to absorb the noise. Then it muted to a growl and ceased entirely. The silence that followed was so complete that Vibulenus could again hear insects buzzing in his hair, where the tree with which he had collided had sprayed him.

"What's it *mean*, sir?" begged Clodius Afer. The prospect of battle had made the file-closer tense and irritable, but he was a veteran of other wars. What he had just seen was an object the size of the Circus Maximus, descending slowly through the air as if it were a feather and not something that could hold a hundred and fifty thousand human beings. "What's going to *happen?*"

"I don't know, Gnaeus," the tribune said, using the file-closer's first name because he knew in his guts that there was no rank or class at a time like this. "But if we wait long enough, maybe we'll find out."

And if what the Commander had said about agelessness were true, they would be able to wait a very long time.

"All right, next lot," said the man whose blue body suit identified him as one of the vessel's crew. In fact, he would have passed in Vibulenus' eyes for the Commander, save that his garment did not cover his skull and there was no shiny surface between his face and the outside world. This crewman called himself the Medic, a diminutive of the word for doctor—medicus. The word was understandable though not a linguistic formation familiar to the legionaries before flashing, headsized floating machines summoned them back aboard.

There was a gassy wheeze; four doors opened in the wall of the room. Romans who had entered the cubicles nervously a moment before stood, bemused and wrapped in dissipating steam. Some of them were working limbs or kneading parts of their bodies.

"Come on, come *on,*" the Medic snapped from behind the piece of furniture—it looked like a writing desk—at which he stood. "Keep it moving or I'll be here all fucking *night*. And so," he added in an afterthought, "will your buddies."

The four nude men stepped out into the hall proper, still more focused on their own bodies than they were on what the Medic or anyone else might say.

"Hercules!" muttered Clodius to the tribune at his side, "Look at Caprasius. You saw how they near lifted him and his leg into the booth in two loads."

Caprasius Felix, a front ranker of Clodius' century,

had run into a cutting weapon of some sort during the
battle, wielded with enough strength to sever the bone
of his right thigh. Somebody had slapped a tourniquet
on the wound, but neither that field expedient nor the
amputation which was all surgery could offer such a
case was likely to help the victim long.

Two of his fellows had carried him, unconscious from
shock and as pale as the belly of a dead fish, into the
booth as the Medic directed. Now . . .

"Well, he's limping," said Vibulenus.

"What in *Hades*," Caprasius was muttering as he
walked toward the marked exit, past the quartet of
toad-faced bodyguards who kept order as the returning
legionaries processed through the medical check on
reentering the vessel. The injured man was clutching
his right thigh with both hands. Suddenly, he took the
hands away and tried to kick that leg high in the air.

There was a three-inch band of paint or discoloration,
bright Pompeian red, around the thigh, but there was
no sign of the wound which had gaped to splintered
yellow bone. Caprasius stumbled and fell sideways when
muscles caught in a way he had not expected, but he
was rolling again to his feet before his friends could
help him.

"*Hades*," he repeated, grinning like a man reaching
the head of a prostitute's queue. "It *works*, by Hercules,
it fuckin' *works*."

Others of the soldiers leaving the booths also bore
patches of red. They looked like wounds, but in fact the
stained areas *had* borne fresh wounds—and did so no
longer. A Sextus Julius—one of several in the legion, a
First Cohort non-com, Vibulenus believed—was massaging his scalp as he walked along. Half of it was
hairless and colored deep red; but when he had entered
a cubicle, his skull was partly exposed and the flap of
skin he tried to hold in place included the ear on that
side.

"Will you *bleeding* come on?" the Medic pleaded. "Next lot, *move* it!"

"*Move*," boomed one of the armored toads acting as proctors, reaching out with his long-handled mace. The four Romans at the head of the line moved with more or less haste, away from the spiked knob rather than toward the cubicles.

Nothing to be afraid of, Gaius Vibulenus lied silently as he hopped forward. Then he said aloud, "Nothing to be afraid of, men," turning his head toward Clodius Afer who was walking stiffly beside him.

Oddly enough, that worked. The young tribune strode firmly within the cubicle nearest the seated Medic. Acting like an officer to others made it easier to act like a man within yourself—even though you knew you were a coward and you were so frightened that your eyes didn't focus as you stepped close to the back wall of the booth and the door began to shut.

"Just get bleeding *in*, will—" the Medic whined to someone else, the words amputated by the door sealing.

The legionaries had stripped under direction of the Commander's guards in the long hallway stretching from the vessel's entrance to this room and the Medic. No one seemed to care about the cohort or rank of the men being ordered into groups of four: those who straggled back to the vessel first had run through this process hours before, and there were still a thousand or more soldiers behind the tribune and his immediate companions.

A blood-warm mist of water with an astringent odor sprayed Vibulenus from all directions. He jumped, but the spray at once relaxed the throbbing veins of his head. As the temperature rose, his left arm began to lose some of its sharp stiffness as well.

Vibulenus' right hand unclenched. The booming guards had insisted that the Romans pile every scrap of clothing and equipment against the wall of the broad hall-

way, saying that every man's belongings would be
returned at the proper time.

That was unimaginable, but probably true: when they
mustered in the Main Gallery before marching out
against the feathered warriors, Vibulenus had been issued the sword his father bought for him—lost irre-
trievably to some Parthian, he would have guessed. That
sword, the only relic of his previous life, would have
felt good in his hand as he stepped into the cubicle.

The water felt better. The booth had a diffuse light
source, so he could see the grime and scabbed blood
wash away from his body. Something else was happening as well, or perhaps the heat was affecting him after
the wounds and—when he had eaten last?

The light was pulsing with his heartbeat. Instead of
becoming dizzy, he was weak—too weak to stand, but
the solid walls of the booth extended limbs to grip his
body in a dozen places. His stomach lurched momentarily, but though the spasm passed it was followed by
the surge of well-being that usually followed vomiting
during delirium.

Vibulenus would have screamed, but he didn't have
that much control of his muscles any more. He was no
longer conscious of the water spray, but his scalp and
left biceps felt so hot that there was no discomfort. He
was wax, melting into oblivion and glad of the fact.

The liquescing heat ceased, leaving behind only the
damp ambiance of the warm room of the baths. The
light was normal again, and the tribune's head began to
sag as the cushioning supports withdrew into the wall.
Something pricked the skin above Vibulenus' heart before the wall reabsorbed the chest support. He staggered forward, but instinct threw his hands out to save
him against the back of the booth.

The bandage was gone from his left arm, and so was
the pain that had gnawed him even when he held the
injured limb clamped firmly against his chest. His torn

skin had reknitted beneath a coating—a dye, apparently—
of brilliant red. There was only a tingling in the muscles
to suggest a shard of flint had been rammed deep
within them.

The door hissed open. The last of the steam dissipated; there was no drain, but the spray with the ban-
dages and other sludge from Vibulenus' body had been
borne off somewhere. Fingering the side of his scalp,
now hairless but no longer cut and swollen, the tribune
stepped out of the cubicle as the Medic tiredly repeated, "Come on, next lot."

Clodius Afer bolted from the adjacent booth with his
face set in the same mask of fear it had worn when he
entered.

"Down the hall," rumbled one of the guards. The
creatures were wearing their helmet visors down. Not,
the tribune suspected, for protection, but rather to
cushion the shock the Roman captives were receiving
already. There had been none of this the first time they
were marched aboard the vessel in Parthia; none of this
that any of them remembered, at least. But then, they
remembered nothing.

Vibulenus looked at the squat figures who had spoken, visualizing the features behind the iron mesh. The
bodyguards were taller than most men—most Romans,
at any rate—but it was the breadth and the neckless
solidity of their bodies that made them look remarkable
when covered with iron. Their strength was in keeping
with their appearance, for their armor weighed more
than a man could lift, much less wear, and they wielded
maces on ten-foot hafts with the ease of a centurion
brandishing his swagger stick.

The guards, and the various implications the young
tribune drew from them, did not affect Vibulenus' present buoyancy at being suddenly whole, no longer wracked
by staggering pain. He clasped his left arm around the
shoulders of Clodius Afer, keeping his grip despite the

non-com's attempt to shudder away when he saw the patch of red dye next to his own skin.

Clodius' legs and forearms were so tanned that pocks of new skin showed up pink in places that he had received minor cuts and abrasions during the battle. None of his injuries had been so severe that the process within the booth had left him with red stains like the tribune and Caprasius Felix.

"Gnaeus," Vibulenus said, "don't be—" He started to say "afraid" but realized as his tongue touched the word that the veteran would hit him, rank be damned. "Don't be angry because they've cured your pain."

"I don't under*stand*," the file-closer whispered, but his calloused right hand reached up to grip Vibulenus' arm to him.

"We'll understand later," Vibulenus said with the confidence of health, not reason. Together, they led the remaining pair of men from their group toward the doorway at the side of the hall. "For now, it's enough that we don't hurt any more."

He looked up, at the toad-faced monsters to either side of the door. "Soon we'll understand," he said, and this time he spoke more in prayer than belief.

"All personnel, report to the Main Gallery for an address by your commander," repeated a well-modulated voice. "The red pulses lead toward the Main Gallery."

"They ought to let us form in centuries," said Gaius Vibulenus as he looked around at as many of the legionaries as he could see milling in the Main Gallery. The room was huge, with a smoothly arched ceiling that showed no sign of the groins and coffers that should have been required to carry the stresses. "I'm going to bring that up at the next command group meeting. This is absurd."

"This tunic don't feel right," said Clodius, pinching out the breast of the garment which had dropped at his feet from a wall dispenser as he left the Sick Bay. The file-closer peered down his nose at the tent of fabric between his thumb and forefinger. "Isn't . . . I dunno. Don't *scratch* the way it ought to, you know?"

"All personnel, report to the Main Gallery for an address by your commander," said the voice.

It sounded as if the words were being spoken a few inches from both of the tribune's ears simultaneously. He no longer jumped and looked around, but the effect still shocked him. Some legionaries covered their ears—uselessly, Vibulenus suspected—and hunched lower in growing fear at every repetition. Clodius Afer seemed to ignore the words, or at least their strangeness.

"Maybe it's Egyptian," the tribune said, trying to speak over the last of the announcement. The vessel was huge, even though it did not compare in size with the ship that had thundered in after the close of the battle. As soon as the announcements began, scarlet beads appeared in the ceiling of all the rooms and hallways. They flowed to the Main Gallery—to here. "The linen, I mean."

If it was linen. If it were even cloth. The walls and ceilings of the vessel were metal, totalling more metal than Vibulenus had ever imagined could be in one place; but sometimes the surfaces took on other semblances, as when the sheer wall opened to deposit garments, or ceilings that had been smooth and unremarkable glowed with light to guide the legionaries toward the assembly.

The floor of the Main Gallery was large enough to have held the legion fully equipped before it marched to battle. With the men—with the survivors—stripped to tunics, there was no hint of crowding, so that legionaries could stand in groups of their closest fellows or wander nervously, looking for somewhere to alight.

One of the latter was Pompilius Rufus who, before Vibulenus could speak, called, "Sir! Sir? Have you seen Niger?"

Clodius and the tribune dipped their chins together in denial as the young soldier paced over to them.

"I was just saying they ought to muster us properly," Vibulenus offered. "Issue standards to the standard bearers so that everyone would know his place."

"He insisted going looking for a cursed beehive," Rufus muttered, oblivious to the disembodied summons as well as to the tribune's conversation. "I thought, well, if I go back, then he won't stay out long. . . . But I don't *see* him."

"You know," said the file-closer, looking down again at the fabric covering his own broad chest, "The tunic *feels* funny, but it fits me. Yours wouldn't." He nodded toward the much slimmer tribune and added in an afterthought, "Sir."

"*Niger!*" Rufus shouted, through the megaphone of his hands. The acoustics of the room absorbed the sound so completely that the shout was lost in the buzz of conversation only ten feet away. A few men turned, then turned back to their own concerns.

"Let's go to the front," Vibulenus said. He was feeling increasingly restive, and there was nowhere else to move that made a difference . . . except back out of the gallery. What result would defiance have?

"What d'ye suppose they do when people don't come back when the little lights tell 'em to, sir?" Rufus asked miserably.

Vibulenus put his arm around the shoulders of his childhood friend. "Strait rations," he said as the three of them maneuvered toward the front of the gallery where they would have a somewhat better view of the gathered soldiers. "Maybe a flogging. Don't worry—the Commander says we're valuable." He began to believe the words as soon as he had spoken them.

"What I mean is," the file-closer continued, completing his own point, "you muster by rank and file so's you know who's there and who isn't. But if you know that already, and I guess they do or they wouldn't be dropping clothes the right size outa the walls, then you don't need that kind of order."

"I don't—" Vibulenus started to say before he realized that he could think of no objections to the veteran's formulation. Who in the name of *Hercules* were the Commander and his entourage?

"I guess the Commander must be a god," said Clodius Afer, tilting his head to peer at the curving surface of the ceiling eighty feet above. "D'ye suppose we're all dead after all?"

"*Castor!*" Rufus blurted. "*He* is."

The three of them had reached the area closest to the front of the Main Gallery where ten of the Commander's bodyguards stood with their maces held crossways at waist level. There was no door in the bulkhead behind them, but a hexagonal outline the size of a man's chest stood out against the shifting pastels that colored the partition.

The very presence of the toadfaced guards was enough to clear an area of almost twenty feet between them and the nearest legionaries. Facing the wall, and as separate from his fellows as from the armored non-men, was the waxen-faced figure of Arrius Crescens—the legionary whom Vibulenus had seen stabbed through the belly so fiercely that the bloody spearpoint burst through the links of mail in back as well.

Crescens was so still and blank-faced that the tribune thought he might in fact be a simulacrum, a death mask worn by a dummy in some unfathomable alien rite. While Rufus and Clodius started away, the young officer began to walk cautiously toward the figure of the dead man.

It was a dummy. There was nothing to fear.

"Crescens?" Vibulenus said, extending his hand slowly toward the figure's shoulder.

"I suppose," said Crescens, turning to Vibulenus with

the deliberation of an ox dragging a cart. "Except I'm dead. They all say that."

"Yeah, you are," whispered Vibulenus, uncertain whether he had mouthed the words or only formed them in his mind. He continued to extend his arm until the fingers touched the slick fabric of the legionary's tunic and felt the bone and muscle shifting beneath.

"You think *I* don't know it!" Crescens shouted, slapping the tribune's hand away and glaring at him as if he was on the verge of further violence. "I felt it go in, didn't I? *Hercules*, mister, it was like fuckin' *ice* all the way up me! And ye know what . . .?"

The legionary leaned closer and reached out to grip Vibulenus' wrist, the hand he had just struck away. The pores of the dead man's face were large, and the unnatural pallor of his skin magnified their relative darkness into freckles.

"I couldn't *see* any more when that big fucker pulled the fucker out agin," Crescens said. He held Vibulenus' palm against his belly, against a large knot in the muscles that felt like cartilage beneath the fat. "I could hear the edge of it grind agin my rib bones, though."

"You needn't let that bother, my man," the tribune said in his clear, detached voice. He stepped back, inexpressibly thankful that Crescens released him. The red dye on the legionary's belly made a splotch noticeable beneath the fabric of his tunic. "We've all noted how amazing the Commander's surgeons must be. My own—"

Vibulenus fingered his dyed left biceps, but before he was finished, he was stuck by the absurdity of comparing his recent wound to the way Crescens had been transfixed. His lips twitched silently for a moment. Then, almost without input from his mind, his mouth said, "You weren't actually killed, you see. Just wounded and repaired."

The tribune turned sharply and strode back to his

companions, willing his ears not to hear anything the
dead man might call after him. When he risked a glance
from the corner of his eye, he saw that Crescens had
resumed his blank-eyed stance. His right hand continued to rumple the tunic over his wound in a slow
massage.

"They, ah . . .," Vibulenus said, as Rufus and the
file-closer carefully looked at the floor or the ceiling to
avoid staring at him. "Well, I guess the Medic . . .," he
tried but paused again.

"You will live forever," the Commander had said.
Gaius Vibulenus Caper, eighteen years old, wondered
how long forever really was.

"Hey, *there's* Niger," said Rufus, striding across the
open space. He was willing to ignore the presence of
the guards in order to reach the farther side of the hall,
where he had glimpsed his cousin, in the shortest possible time. *"Niger!"*

"Your commander is about to address you," said the
clear voice in everyone's ears. "Before he does so, the
floor will shift so that everyone has a clear view. Do not
be concerned."

Relatively few of the thousands of men in the Main
Gallery listened to what their ears could not fail to have
heard. Even those few, like Vibulenus, who didn't tune
out the words as just another repetition of the summons, were still trying to process the information when
the back of the gallery began to rise.

There would have been panic even if every one of
the soldiers understood the statement, of course.

Clodius and Vibulenus, at the front of the long room,
felt only a trembling through the soles of their bare
feet. The tribune looked back over his shoulder, frowning in concentration, because he *thought* the voice had
said that—

The floor of the Main Gallery was slanting upward,
carrying legionaries with it. As their footing shifted,

men bolted backward toward the door by which they had entered. The screams were so loud and universal as to overpower the deadening effect of the gallery's acoustics.

The ceiling was lifting in synchrony with the floor, so there was no reason to fear that the surfaces would grind the men between them like millstones. Fear is emotional, not a matter of reason, however, and fear is the most human reaction to having solid become fluid underfoot. The door at the back did not open.

The only thing that kept the panic from being as lethally crushing as an actual mating of floor and ceiling was that the movement of the gallery lessened to zero in the front. Pressure from the crowd behind would have crushed men to death against the wall, as Vibulenus had once seen happen when a chariot crash started a rush for the stadium exits. Here, the men in the middle of the gallery poised, uncertain whether to rush the door or toward the front; and those nearest the front were more bemused than frightened by what they saw happening to others.

Over all the commotion, the disembodied voice kept calling angrily, "Everyone stop crowding! There is no need for concern! Stop this at once or there will be severe disciplinary measures!"

There *had* been a certain amount of crowding forward by men who closed their eyes so that they would not have to see that they were pushing their fellows closer to the guards. Clodius Afer, with a grimace that reflected his own distaste for the situation, thrust himself back into the press. Snapping, "Loosen up your ranks!" the file-closer slapped men alongside the head to get their attention.

The tribune took a deep breath. He had been trying to brace himself against the men pushing him from behind. Now he turned sideways, slipping back a rank or two, and shouted, "Stop this at once, you men!"

He tried to slap a grizzled legionary whose name he did not know. The man responded with a short punch that numbed Vibulenus' whole left side and blinded him with the pain. He couldn't fall down because the crowd was too tight, and when it loosened a moment later he had enough control of his body to stay upright.

The panic had ended itself in exhaustion and pointlessness. Men who had fought a grueling battle and undergone enervating rehabilitation in the Sick Bay simply did not have enough energy to long sustain a rush to nowhere. Sheepishly, shaking loose their tunics, legionaries drifted back to the center of the long room, leaving the front and rear to those who had preferred those extremes to the neutral median in the first place.

After all, there was nothing frightening about standing in a hall whose solid floor sloped toward the front at about the angle of the aisles of a theatre.

"What in Hades happened to you, sir?" Clodius Afer demanded, dusting his palms as he strode back to the tribune. The legion's front had advanced several feet as a result of the commotion, but the toadfaced guards had relaxed again and were no longer bracing their maces out in front of them as a physical bar to the humans.

"Somebody . . .," Vibulenus wheezed. He forced himself to stand fully upright, though his right shoulder was still an inch high to put less tension on the ribs and muscles of his other side. "I was going to help you," the young tribune went on with careful steadiness, "but somebody hit me. I don't see him."

He glared at the nearest soldiers. Some blinked in surprise and a few turned their eyes away, but the man who threw the punch had disappeared into the crowd.

"Umm," said the file-closer, sucking in his lips. He laid his hand on Vibulenus' shoulder; in comradeship, but also to face the younger man to the front again. "Gotta be careful about, you know, things like that,

sir," the veteran said. "Saw a first centurion tossed
right through an oak door, the once, when he broke his
swagger stick on somebody and turned his back to fetch
another one. You got enough people together, you can
lead 'em when there's someplace to go . . . but you
need be *real* careful if you're gonna push."

There was a series of crisp flashes from within the
hexagon on the wall, light like the edge-glints of swords
drawn in the sun. The figure itself spun, momentarily
circular with its velocity. Around it opened a rectangular doorway tall enough to have passed one of the giant
spearmen.

The Commander looked even tinier in the doorway
than he had when mounted on the carnivore.

"Brave warriors," said the voice in Vibulenus' ears,
and the tribune was close enough to see that the sound
now synchronized with the Commander's lip movements.

The door closed behind the figure in blue, and another glitter of light from the hexagon haloed his head.
The door pivoted from one side, but it did not seem to
be attached in any way to the lintel or jambs. Like the
vehicles which roved the valley after the battle, the
panel of shimmering metal appeared to float in the air
until its edges merged again seamlessly with those of
the bulkhead.

"Here, on a world far from your own," the Commander continued, "you have undertaken your first
duties as assets of the finest trading guild in the Federation. Your success was beyond our expectation—and
your reward will be beyond your dreams."

The Commander's chest rose and fell without affecting the words Vibulenus heard, so the pause was a
rhetorical one before the voice continued, "You will
never grow older. Throughout eternity, you will remain
as strong and agile as your are now."

There was so general a buzz of sound from the assembled Romans that the Main Gallery hissed and popped

like a fire in wet leaves. The young tribune glanced sharply at Clodius, knowing—presuming, at least—that the file-closer had heard this before, when they had confronted the Commander at the gate of the sacked camp.

Clodius' muscles were still, his eyes wide open and expressionless. His face was not so much blank as masked, and the knuckles of his right hand were grinding against the calloused palm of his left in proof of physical existence.

"This gift of immortality—so to speak," said the Commander, hushing the room with anticipation of what might come next, "is a very expensive boon, one which I myself received only upon being promoted to my present post. You have earned it by the technical skill which you displayed today."

"Have you seen anybody besides him and the Medic?" Clodius Afer whispered into the tribune's ear.

"Well, the guards," Vibulenus whispered back with a quick flutter of his hand that was all the gesture he was willing to make toward the creatures in plate armor.

"You will have no duties, no responsibilities," said the Commander, "save the duty for which you have proven yourselves so splendidly fitted: war against the enemies of my guild, the enemies of galactic progress."

"*Them*," sneered the file-closer, and it was a moment before Vibulenus remembered that the guards were the pronoun's referent. "*They* don't run this place. They're dim as six feet up a hog's ass."

The word "war" had drawn a restive murmur from the legion and another pause from the Commander before he continued, "For reasons that do not concern you, the Federation has interdicted trading guilds, my own included, from the use of military technology higher than that of the natives who must be subdued. It is the ability that you have shown in using your pitiful technology which has enabled you to become assets of a trading guild envied by all its rivals."

"What's he mean?" a soldier behind Vibulenus whined to his fellow. "Them barbs, they wuz nekkid, the half of 'em and the rest warn't much."

And that was true . . . but the tribune realized that what the Commander had said was true also. The warriors dead on the slopes outside had metal weapons—even had iron, unlike the demigods of whom Homer had written. Nobody could fault the strength and individual skill with which they used their weapons either; Vibulenus brushed a hand across his temple in memory of the blow that had almost cracked his skull.

But the giant spearmen didn't know how to use their weapons as an *army*, as a Roman legion moving forward in ranks as implacable as the metal of their armor. They were barbarians, only barbarians, and therefore of course they died when they met Rome. . . .

"During the period that some of you are convalescing from your wounds," chimed the Commander's crystal voice in Vibulenus' ears, "the ship is limited to proceeding in normal space. Therefore time will seem to pass normally, and you will be permitted to occupy it with recreation as well as training."

"Women!" called someone midway in the hall, loud enough that the tribune could understand.

The Commander's head swivelled minutely, and Vibulenus thought that his ears twitched beneath the fabric of his tight hood. The tribune remembered his own vain attempt to spot the man who had punched him in the crush. Perhaps there were ways other than floating doors and rooms that healed wounds in which the Commander's world differed from that of Rome. . . .

"Yes, of course, women," said the blue figure with a smile that was as perfect as his Latin diction—and every bit as learnedly unnatural. "Not just now, I'm afraid; but they'll be provided for you in what will seem to be a very short time."

He threw the crowd another crisp, uncomfortable smile. "I wouldn't want you to think that my company doesn't prepare properly, but the fact is that we did not expect your success to be so complete you would *deserve* so high a level of expense, you warriors."

"*Warriors*," Clodius Afer echoed in a whisper. "We're soldiers. Warriors are meat on the table for soldiers with discipline."

Gaius Vibulenus thought of what they were being told and what it implied about the alternatives had the legion *not* demolished its opponents so hastily. Well, in Parthia the alternative had been working the quarries under a mind-blasting sun. . . .

"Because you will be conscious and alert during the first portion of this voyage and the voyages that follow," said the Commander, "it is necessary that you observe certain limitations. Your skills, brave warriors, are extensive within the bounds of your technology—but your technology is very low in comparison to what is available to every officer of my guild."

There was a commotion on the far side of the room. Vibulenus thought at first it was a reaction to the statement, then that the floor must be shifting again because there was movement in the crowd both forward and back, like a ship's wake dividing a small pond.

The tribune set his palm on Clodius' shoulder and lifted himself on tiptoes, craning his neck to make the most of his height advantage over the bulk of the legionaries.

"There's no need to be alarmed," the Commander was saying. "This is only a demonstration of things you'll have to understand to make your voyage comfortable."

"It's not the *floor* moving," said Vibulenus to the file-closer who had gripped him unasked beneath the arms and lifted the tribune vertically, feet off the floor. The pressure of Clodius' hands made it hard to speak but not impossible, and the support the veteran offered was only peripherally physical. "There's another door opened in that wall."

If his feet had been on the ground, Vibulenus would have turned to see whether the wall on their side of the Main Gallery was also marked for an opening. Instead he squinted, his view aided by the way legionaries were clearing from the affected area.

"Okay, let me down," he muttered. Clodius obeyed by lowering, not dropping, the young tribune back to the floor. Vibulenus avoided massaging his ribs for fear that would look ungrateful.

"It's the rest of the bodyguards coming in," he said, indicating the line of armored toad-things. When the file-closer's eyes followed the gesture the tribune was able to quickly rub his chest where it ached. "Only half of them were here before. These must be the ones, you know, keeping an eye on things with the Medic."

They had entered the gallery by a side door near the front rather than marching all the way through the assembly. Nothing surprising about that. The fact that the previously-hidden portal had opened without the sparkle of light which accompanied the Commander's entry was just another datum, another scrap of information that might someday help Vibulenus again understand the world as clearly as he had until—he entered the here and now in which he had just started to live.

"Hercules!" he gasped as he *saw* what his eyes had been receiving while his mind dealt with other things. "They've got Rufus and Niger!"

"By Death and Hades. . . ," muttered Clodius Afer in a voice without emotion.

Vibulenus did not notice the file-closer's arms move; in fact, he noticed nothing but his one-time school-mates, each of them gripped by the elbows in the articulated iron gloves of two bodyguards. When the tribune's legs thrust him forward, toward the creatures who held *his men*, Clodius Afer's hands anchored him as solidly as they had lifted Vibulenus for a look only moments before.

"Now just hold on," said the file-closer in a voice that was soothing despite its raspy tone because it was totally controlled. "Let's see what's happening *before* we decide we're what's happening ourselves."

"Do not be concerned," the Commander's voice said coolly. "You will believe the evidence of your fellows where you would not accept another sort of demonstration."

In the instant before his reasoning mind took over again, Vibulenus would have lashed out with his fists and elbows to free himself if Clodius Afer had not dealt too often with men driven by a single emotion—hate or fear or fury—to give the younger man that play: His bear hug enwrapped the tribune's forearms so that Vibulenus' thrashing had no physical effect. The tribune's blood pressure shot up momentarily, and the crystal matrix in which he saw the Pompilii cousins became a blood-red haze.

But that passed: Clodius was right as well as being incomparably stronger, and the Commander was—in charge.

When he relaxed, Vibulenus saw the Pompilii were not being severely treated by the guards who had stepped out of the wall behind the foremost legionaries, grabbing the cousins as the two closest Romans before the men realized what was happening. For a moment, Rufus lifted both his feet and was carried, without slowing or otherwise affecting what the toad-things were doing with him.

Vibulenus noticed also that no Roman but himself seemed to have tried to rescue the cousins. Maybe they all had cold common sense like Clodius; maybe nobody knew the boys; and maybe Gaius Vibulenus Caper was a bigger fool than he'd felt since blubbering in fear while Parthian arrows whistled down. At least he knew this time that he was proud of his instinct—and that the file-closer's judgment had kept that instinct from getting him killed.

"Now *what*, by the Mother's tits," said Clodius Afer, releasing the tribune but not so completely that his hands did not hover near enough to regain their previous grip, "are they doing with a shield?"

The ten bodyguards marched with stiff deliberation to join their fellows already standing in front of the bulkhead. They clumped along two by two, the leading pairs carrying Niger and Rufus; and one of the last pair carried a shield, just as the file-closer had said.

It seemed to be an ordinary legionary's scutum of leather-covered plywood, twice as high as it was wide and slightly convex on the side toward the enemy. The rim was bound with bronze strips, and there was a rectangular boss of the same metal bulging out sharply to give room for the hand of the man carrying it.

Neither the boss nor the shield-facing had any of the fancy work, heraldic engraving and appliqued geometric designs, which distinguished the equipment Crassus' army carried into Parthia. Structurally the shield appeared to be the same, and the way Niger's arms flexed when the guard handed it to him showed that the piece was of at least the usual weight.

The guards who held Niger released the young Roman's arms so that he could take the shield. One of them boomed something to him, probably in Latin, but Vibulenus heard it only as a rumble of sound. Niger's brow knitted as he tried vainly to make sense of the order.

Clodius Afer's hand was back on the tribune's shoulder in a gesture of comradeship rather than control. The two men were blank-faced because they had disso-

ciated their intellects as completely as possible from
their bodies and from the memory that would flesh out
the data their eyes were receiving.

Two of the armored guards stood close to Niger, near
the corner formed with the front wall. Legionaries on
that side of the room shifted so they were farther from
the comrade snatched from among them than they had
been from the original line of guards.

"There's five thousand of us, aren't there?" said
Vibulenus softly, rationally. "Well, less after this morning, maybe." But Arrius Crescens stood, open-eyed and
stolid, no longer a subject of fear in the midst of newer
uncertainties. . . .

"And there's twenty of them," the tribune went on.
"Twenty-one, yes. . . ."

The file-closer's hand tightened enough to remind
Vibulenus that they would wait and watch, the two of
them.

Rufus and the guards directing him marched toward
the Commander who stood slim and aloof with the
bulkhead behind him and the legion in front—the one
with no more volition than the other.

The blue figure glanced toward Niger and perhaps
spoke something into his ears alone. The young legionary raised the shield over his head, holding it by the
lower rim so that the soft highlights of the boss were
toward the Commander. The shield wavered a little;
Niger steadied it and himself by backing a step to the
sidewall and bracing his shoulder there.

"Our own weapons—those of my guild," said the
Commander as his shimmering eyes swept the legion
again, "are of greater destructiveness than even this
demonstration will prove. Nevertheless, watch the shield
which your fellow is holding."

While the Commander spoke, his hands swung forward a black cylinder slung behind him, visible but
unremarkable in this interval that held so many remark-

able things. The cylinder was about the length and diameter of the Commander's forearm. The irregularities on it, including the handles by which the Commander raised the device to his shoulder, gave it the look of plumbing which should have been decently hidden behind stone facings or molded bronze.

The guards holding the other Pompilius cousin halted near the Commander—behind him, actually, now that he was facing the side—but the blue figure ignored them. There was a glitter in the air above the cylinder, something that could have been static electricity but suggested an image of the shield toward which the cylinder was aimed.

A jet of light so cohesive that Vibulenus thought it was a fluid spurted from the cylinder to the shield. The boss exploded in a fountain of green sparks as the flash-heated metal burned in the air. Niger was one of a hundred men who screamed in surprise. He flung the shield away from him as drops of molten bronze spattered twenty feet in every direction.

The shield hit the floor, walking on its rim in a slow pirouette before clanging down on its convex face. The hole burned through the boss was large enough to pass a clenched fist. Strips of wood glued to form the shield's core sprang outward at the edge of the burned metal so that they looked like ravelled ends of rope.

Pompilius Niger bolted back into the mass of legionaries from which he had been taken. None of the guards tried to stop him—but Rufus found, when he made a similar attempt, that his arms were still held firmly.

"When I or any employee of my guild give you an order," said the Commander with his usual cool precision, turning toward his audience again, "you must obey instantly and utterly."

He released the cylinder. It snuggled itself to his back, out of the way but quickly available at need.

Charred wood and burning felt created a musty reek in the atmosphere as the shield continued to smolder.

"He wasn't carrying it outside this building, though," said the file-closer thoughtfully, while his fingers gently kneaded the muscles of Vibulenus' shoulder.

"The shield will remain here after this assembly," said the Commander. "I had intended to have your fellow carry it among you himself, but I underestimated the effect our weapons would have on warriors of your— cultural level."

"Little *bastard*," whispered Clodius Afer because the Commander's voice in his ears had hinted at amusement.

"Maybe they can't use anything but, but maces outside this ship," the tribune murmured to the veteran. "Maybe their gods would strike them down for violating that law."

Though *why* would there be such a law?

"Almost the whole of the ship is yours to roam as you please," continued the Commander, "except when you are summoned for training or assembly. This bulkhead—"

He stretched out one delicate, overfingered hand to tap the shifting pastels of the bulkhead behind him "—is my territory and that of my crew and guards. You are not to attempt to enter it, and you are not to approach within three feet of its surface. If you do— watch closely, now."

Vibulenus was watching the Commander's hands, expecting one of them to reach back for the cylinder. The blue figure did not move at all.

Two of the guards flung Pompilius Rufus toward the bulkhead.

The boy did not thump against the lighted metal because his body disintegrated in the air with a tearing crash.

The Commander winced an instant before the noise erupted behind him, and his shoulders hunched against the sauce of pulverized body spitting back into the room.

There was a barrier three feet from the visible wall. The momentum of Rufus' body carried him against it, and the young legionary splashed across the plane of contact as if he had fallen from a high cliff. Bone and muscle, as fluid and finely divided as the blood with which they merged, squirted sideways in a vertical tapestry behind the Commander, thinning and disappearing ten or a dozen feet from the center of impact.

Occasional globules overloaded what was an almost instantaneous process of digestion. Those caused the pops and sputters that threw droplets as high as the ceiling and as far as the middle rows of men watching the demonstration.

The tribune's forehead felt damp. He wiped it with his palm, then wiped his palm on his tunic, telling himself as he did so that it was sweat.

He felt no urge to attack the Commander. In fact, his guts were filling with ice water and his legs began shaking so violently that he was afraid he would fall down.

"This is not something I or my subordinates *do*, you understand," said the Commander in the chill tones of nightmare, his words heard clearly throughout the Main Gallery despite the gasps and cries of the men assembled there. "It is something that happens automatically to anyone who steps close to the wall. Only those whose nerve patterns have been keyed into the— mechanism of the ship—can survive."

There were smells in the air besides those of the burning shield. Partly the addition was the choking sharpness that near-striking thunderbolts left at the back of a man's throat—but there was charred flesh in the air as well. Something lay on the floor just outside the partition between death and life which Rufus had limned with his body. Vibulenus could not be sure, but he thought it was the heel of one of the boy's feet, sheared off because it did not have quite enough momentum to carry it across the barrier on its own.

"Now," the blue figure concluded, pausing for a perfect smile toward the assembly which stirred like a wheatfield in a fitful breeze. "Go and relax. We are already under way to a new engagement."

"What's he mean by that?" Clodius Afer demanded querelously. He gave Vibulenus a rough shake in an attempt to get his attention. "We can't be going anywhere. We'd *hear* it. Wouldn't we? Sir?"

The Commander turned and manipulated the hexagon on the wall. The invisible barrier did not affect him, except that one of his feet slipped a trifle in the slime Rufus had left at the demarcation line. Light twinkled within the hexagon and the door drifted open. His bodyguard, pair by pair, shuffled through the portal behind him.

Gaius Vibulenus could not understand the words the file-closer was throwing at him in a desperate attempt to deny what he had just seen. The tribune's mind danced with a montage of images, from the first moment he realized the guards were throwing his friend toward the wall, to the flash of richly-saturated earth-tones as the legionary disintegrated.

"Sir, *please* tell me we're not moving," begged Clodius Afer.

The younger man blinked down at the file-closer's hands. They gripped his shoulders but no longer tried to shake him into a response. He was a Roman citizen and an officer. He had his duties.

Taking one of Clodius' hands in each of his own and lowering them, Vibulenus said, "I think probably we are moving if he says we are, Gnaeus. I don't understand how that is either, but perhaps we'll learn. We have a lot of things to learn, I think."

He looked at the bulkhead and the door closing with

another flicker behind the last of the guards. His eyes were again able to see what was there, rather than what had been happening there in the recent past.

He had a duty to Pompilius Rufus, also. Some day he would fulfill it.

"Get up now," repeated the voice in Vibulenus' ears. "This room is about to be cleaned."

The tribune snorted and turned his head on the pillow, thinking in muzzy error that he could muffle the intrusion that way.

A jet of cold—very cold—water from the ceiling played the length of his spine.

Vibulenus leaped up, screaming and certain that he was being burned alive. The water from what looked like an ordinary rivethead splashed momentarily on his chest, but he did not connect the spray with the beam from the Commander's weapon which had devoured him as he slept.

There were half a dozen other men in the room. Those who had started to get up at the summons were staring in bemusement at Vibulenus and two others, prodded by separate spikes of water. None of the men were known by name to the tribune, though he recognized a couple of the faces. He did not know how he had gotten here, but the pounding of his head told him that he had been drunk at the time.

"Leave at once," ordered the calm voice. It would have passed for the Commander speaking, but Vibulenus did not imagine the Commander concerned himself with housecleaning. "Other rooms are open for your use."

The studs which had jetted cold water were now wreathed in steam, and the temperature of the room was already beginning to rise as the Romans stumbled out.

It had been an odd room, now that Vibulenus was

alert enough to notice it. The floor was spongy, but its covering and the cushioned banquettes seemed to be of one piece with the walls—which were metal.

The only opening was the door into a broad hallway. That should have made the room stuffy or close under the circumstances, but the wastes voided by sleeping drunks were merely a whiff, not a suffocating reek.

"Pollux, but I need a *bath*," Vibulenus muttered. Out in the hall he couldn't blame the odor he smelled on his fellows.

"Follow the blue dot in the ceiling to the baths which have been provided for your comfort," said the voice.

The tribune jumped and looked around uselessly. There *was* a pulsing blue dot on the ceiling, right enough. "You there," he snapped to a legionary who had exited the room with him. "Did you hear something about the baths?"

"Hah? Nossir," said the other, giving a glance at the russet border of Vibulenus' tunic, marking him as a member of the equestrian order—and making the young tribune flush by recalling his mind to the garment's stains. "Good idea, though; if you know where one is?"

Something spoke to the legionary's hopeful question, and the man's eyes flickered up toward the blue dot. "All *right*," he said cheerfully. Nodding to Vibulenus, he strode off down the hall.

The blue dot preceded him; and the tribune, grimacing, followed an identical dot that waited until he stepped toward it before it slid on. There were other men in the hallway, some of them wandering with puzzled expressions but most seeming to follow beads of varicolored light, just as Vibulenus was. He vaguely remembered that Clodius Afer had said something about wine as the Main Gallery lowered itself after the assembly, and then the two of them had gone off after a bead of orange light.

The ship contained huge areas of open space, making

it more like a city than it was a vessel. Most of the
rooms flanking this hallway were similar to the one in
which Vibulenus had awakened, twelve feet to a side
with an eight-foot ceiling and no furnishings except for
the cushions built against all four walls.

A few had doors shut flush with the passageway. One
of these slid upward as the tribune passed, puffing out a
wisp of steam and humid air. He paused—the dot of
light halted a half step farther on—and peered in. The
room was of the standard pattern, glistening now as
steam cleared in tendrils sucked rapidly toward the
solid walls. It was clean and ready for occupancy; as, no
doubt, was the room Vibulenus had occupied until being
turned out.

The bead of light made a right turn down a cross hall
long enough that the tribune could not see to either
end. The hangover was only a dull shadow of the way
battle injuries had left him feeling. Nonetheless, he saw
other figures only as blurs. Afterwards he thought he
remembered being hailed by name—but he could not
be sure.

He would have stumbled past the paths, had not the
voice in his ears said sharply, "This is your destination.
The dot will go no farther with you."

Alerted if not truly alert, Vibulenus stopped at the
open doorway beside him. It was twenty feet wide,
opening onto a circular bay that was larger than any
room he had seen aboard the vessel except for the Main
Gallery. Despite its size, it was thronged by soldiers,
many of them bearing the deep scarlet dye of healed
injuries.

"Discard your garments here," said the omnipresent
voice as Vibulenus took a puzzled step within the bay.
"New clothing will be issued as you leave."

There was a shallow bin beside the door, empty; but
as the tribune paused, a legionary with less compunc-
tion wadded up his own tunic and tossed it in. The

garment melted into the bottom of the bin, leaving it empty again.

Shivering with youthful embarrassment, Vibulenus pulled off his tunic and promised himself that he would never again drink more than he could handle. The men around him were not slaves and social equals—the former beneath notice; the latter in no better state because of partying. These were social and military subordinates to whom he must provide an image of irreproachable dignity.

"Choose a location along the wall," said the voice.

The tribune stalked straight ahead, pretending that he did not see any of the other Romans and that they, as a result, could not see him.

"Hey, d'ye see him?" came a fragment of conversation, overheard but unprocessed until minutes later. "Right up t' the front knocking shit outa them bastids, and him without even a helmet!"

The ceiling was the usual eight feet high, the only dimension in which the gigantic vessel seemed less than generous by human standards. Nude men, some of them talking to one another with animation, were passing back and forth through the center of the room. The wall to which Vibulenus had been directed was unusual only in that it was curved, but the soldiers already standing within arm's length of it were in separate capsules whose boundaries were displayed by the water which leaped and sprayed within.

The tribune walked to the first open space he saw, ignoring the men who jostled him on their own slanting courses. Embarrassment about his condition kept Vibulenus from fear of undergoing a process strange to him.

Some of the men in this bath were hanging back in concern, watching cylinders of air glint to enclose their fellows before sprays from the floor and ceiling converged on them. Many of the common legionaries were so unsophisticated, however, that they had not seen a

seagoing vessel before Crassus sailed his army from
Brundisium. This bathing arrangement was only one
more of the unique circumstances they had learned to
expect since they left their farms in the Campania.

Gaius Vibulenus knew enough to be afraid; but to his
boy's mind, dissolution like that of Pompilius Rufus was
less to be feared than his present loss of dignity.

Somebody stepped in front of him to the space he
had chosen, but the air around the soldier next to that
place lost its sheen. That legionary sauntered away from
the wall with a refreshed expression; his skin was flushed
and gleaming as if from an expert massage. Vibulenus
took his place without hesitation.

There was a *ping* that could have been *in* his ears
instead of being *heard* by them. Everything in the
room as a whole was now glimpsed through a surface
that was perfectly clear but did not pass light in quite
the same line as air did. Vibulenus remembered the
way the Commander's face gleamed and wondered if
that were from the same unknown cause.

"Standard?" asked the voice.

Vibulenus looked around, surprised out of his fuzzy
internal dialogue.

"Or do you want to give instructions for changes in
the standard cleansing program?" prompted the voice.
It had a peevish tinge at such moments, unless the
young tribune was imagining the tone from memories
of house slaves skirting insubordination under similar
circumstances.

"Fine, that's fine," Vibulenus snapped, flushing again.
"I'll have the same that the men have."

Before the tribune could wonder whether he had
correctly inferred from the question that he was being
offered something special because of his rank and class,
needles of warm water with a slight astringence began
to scrape grime from his body. It was like nothing he
had ever felt before, but it was effective; and the steam

that clouded the invisible cylinder around him sheltered Vibulenus from eyes more effectively than his mind could do.

As a way of cleaning the body, this "bath" was at least as effective as the system with which Vibulenus was familiar. The sprays varied in termperature and were firm enough to knead his muscles like the fingers of a masseur. There seemed to be an ingredient added to the water which took the place of the olive oil with which the tribune would ordinarily have rubbed himself, then scraped off in combination with the dirt and body grease from his skin.

So it wasn't the result of the bath that bothered the young Roman, only the process. He had expected a social event—sitting with half a dozen others around the water vat in the steam room; racing a friend across the pool in the cold room; and at the very least, being oiled down by a slave in the warm room—a task no individual could effectively perform for himself.

Instead, Gaius Vibulenus Caper was more alone than he had ever been in the eighteen years since he left his mother's womb . . . excepting only what had happened to him in the Medic's cubicle; and this bath was too similar to that event to be comfortable.

The sprays became bitingly cold, then shut off. Blasts of hot, dry air wrapped Vibulenus for a moment, and the voice said, "New clothing will be issued to you at the exit from the bath."

Probably the *ping* Vibulenus thought he had heard before did have something to do with the invisible shield, because when he heard the sound again he was back in the room with no distortion. The air was cooler than the flows which had dried him, and the atmosphere had a freedom of movement that would have gone unnoticed except that during the bath the tribune had felt that he was circumscribed.

The shimmer of a cubicle next to him ceased without

a sound the tribune could hear. It reminded him to step back into the room, to give space to anyone else who wanted it. What were the bath hours here? *Were* there bath hours? Was it daylight now?

The man stepping away from the wall next to him was Lucius Rectinus Falco. He was two inches shorter than Vibulenus and within days of being the same age, but he always gave the air of being infinitely more knowledgeable.

Vibulenus would have let his eyes slide away from the other tribune, except that Falco was already starting to grin with recognition. To refuse to face him would be cowardly as well as futile, so Vibulenus started to nod a vague greeting in hope that it would suffice.

Falco reached out and gripped his forearm. "Well, Gaius my boy, how did you like our little demonstration yesterday?"

And while Vibulenus' conscious mind told him that he must have misunderstood the words, Falco went on, "You know, I suggested to the Commander that you were the sort of troublemaker who'd be of more use as a demonstration than for anything else. But since you were an officer, so to speak, he thought he'd wait. So I suggested—"

Falco really didn't expect the bigger tribune to hit him.

Vibulenus landed his first clumsy punch squarely on the sneering lips. Vibulenus did not immediately follow that blow with another, because of the pain that shot up his own arm from the knuckle he had broken on Falco's teeth.

"Stop!" called Falco. *"Commander!"*

"Fighting is not allowed!" shouted the ship's voice as Vibulenus tried to hit Falco with his left hand and wished he had a shield in it. "Stop at once, or this area will be gassed and corrective measures taken!"

"Don't!" cried Falco, throwing up his hands. His lip

was bleeding enough to spit droplets of blood. "You heard the Commander! He'll—"

It was impossible to hurt somebody with your bare hands, thought Vibulenus as he slapped at Falco to avoid reinjuring the knuckle while Falco scrunched up his face and punched back.

Neither blow landed, because arms grabbed Vibulenus from behind and rotated him around the man who was holding him. The tribune's bare feet hit the ground six feet from where they had been lifted. The voice continued, "Personal contests can be held through the simulator in the Recreation Room. No direct combats are allowed!"

"Gnaeus?" said Vibulenus.

"Right in one," agreed the file-closer as he released the younger man and stepped hastily away so that his peacemaking would not look like an expansion of the brawl. His arms were splayed slightly so that he could react if the tribune tried to dodge past him to get at Falco again. "Let's stay calm, sir."

Vibulenus was both drained and embarrassed to have hurt himself so badly and Falco not at all. Well, Falco *somewhat:* the other tribune was dabbing his fingers to the cut on his lips. The rage which he glared at Vibulenus could not have been more real if Falco had just been impaled at his command.

"The red bead will lead you to the Recreation Room," said the voice in a tone of satisfaction. "Private quarrels must not be worked out directly."

"I won't do anything about this now, Vibulenus," Falco said, his hand hovering midway between a gesture and soothing his lips. No one had moved to interfere with him, so he strode in a wide arc around the taller man, trying to look brisk but not cowardly. "You'd better mind your ways, though, or I swear by the gods of my house that the Commander will hear about it personally!"

Falco stepped into the hallway with his legs scissoring so quickly that the tunic which fell out of a wall
dispenser lay behind him unnoticed, its russet stripe a
reproach.

"He's not afraid of me," Vibulenus muttered as the
file-closer stared after the other tribune, disappearing
in naked haste. Class pride had not vanished when they
all were reduced to captivity together, to slavery. Besides, it was true. "He's afraid of what they'll do to both
of us. The Commander."

"He'll do wonders," sneered Clodius Afer. At the
time Vibulenus thought he meant Falco. Then, snarling
at the soldiers still watching them in hope of further
excitement, the file-closer added. "Get on with it,
damn ye, or see if *I* don't find something for ye to be
doing."

The tribune began walking because his muscles were
shaking with hormones that he had to work off—toward
the doorway because that was the direction he was
facing at the time. "He was the one who had Rufus
killed. I *knew* Rufus from the time he was . . . we
were—"

"Hold it, sir," interrupted the file-closer, taking the
first of the tunics that dropped from the wall and hand-
ing the next, with its narrow border, to Vibulenus.

"He's got the Commander's ear," the tribune resumed, the first words muffled as he pulled the garment over his head, "and he's using it to—"

"How do you know?" Clodius asked bluntly.

"Where are we going?" Vibulenus said, looking up
the hall and back behind him. There was no particular
difference: featureless walls and soldiers, most of them
going to or from the baths.

"To the Recreation Room, whatever in Hades that
may be," said the non-com. "How do you *know* Rectinus
has any control over the Commander?"

"He—" Vibulenus began, and stopped before he gave

credence to what at any other time he would have deemed nonsense. "Oh. Sure. Falco could say the sun rises in the east, and I still ought to check it if it matters, right?"

"I thought something like that, yessir," Clodius Afer agreed. "And I guess—"

"This is your destination," interrupted the ship's voice, the Commander's voice. "The bead will go no farther with you."

Vibulenus had expected a sports ground like Rome's Campus Martius, but perhaps safe javelin and discus courses were too large for even the volume of this monstrous vessel. Was there swimming, at least, available? He regretted not having been able to swim a few laps in the baths, where he had hoped there would be a pool.

The Recreation Room was circular again, sloping down from the rim to the center like a double theatre—amphitheater—designed for gladiatorial events. Instead of narrow stone benches for seating, there were couches set radially to the circle. Vibulenus found inexpressibly alien the notion of a couch tilted so that you looked down over your feet instead of reclining on one arm and facing the side.

"This place. . . ." said Clodius Afer. "Look, it must be *over* the baths. Or under them. The hall wasn't long enough for two rooms this big to be side by side."

"I don't see what they're doing," Vibulenus said. "There's nothing *here*."

The room was at least as large in diameter as the baths—surely the hall hadn't curved either up or down? But Clodius was right about its distance. This room was high from the center to the ceiling because of the way the ranks of couches sloped downward. There were six or eight doorways around the circumference, which made the room's alignment in the vessel even more confusing. Some hundreds of the thousand or more couches were occupied by legionaries focusing intently on the center of the room—

Which was empty. The rows of couches continued downward until the lowest row filled all but a ten-foot circle, where there was not so much as a pylon standing.

"Maybe if we ask—" Vibulenus began, looking upward though he did not think the voice *really* came from the ceiling. He was afraid of asking the—the vessel itself—for information in front of the file-closer, though he could not have explained what reaction he feared or why.

In any case, Clodius Afer responded to the problem in his own direct fashion by stepping down to the nearest occupied couch and shaking the man in it to full attention. "Hey!" the file-closer demanded. "What in Hades—oh. Hi, Epidius. Sorry, sir, but what in fucking Hades goes on here?"

The First Cohort centurion that Clodius had aroused grimaced angrily at the junior non-com, but he blanked his face instantly when he saw the tribune, as well, hanging on his answer. "Ah," grunted Epidius. "Well, it's the Battle of the Frogs and the Mice. Just—well, if you lay down on a couch, you'll see. And you sir—" nodding to Vibulenus "—if you please."

The nearest pair of unoccupied couches were some way down the aisle. "That horse's ass," the file-closer muttered to his companion. "What's he think his rank *really* counts for any more?"

"It's all we have left," replied Vibulenus in a flash of awareness spoken before he fully comprehended it. "It's *got* to count."

The tribune sat on the center of the couch and began to lower himself carefully into a reclining position. Even before his head had touched the cushion, he was seeing a battlefield in place of the amphitheater he knew was really there. Vibulenus thought he heard the file-closer say something, but he continued to lean back into a medley of clashing weapons and raucous challenges shouted in Latin.

The combatants were not Romans and not humans. Epidius was quite right: the tribune was now watching— had nearly become a part of—a battle of frogs and mice. His viewpoint swooped down the line of frogs . . . or *almost* frogs. The beasts stood upright and their legs were straight instead of splaying outward at the knees the way those of true frogs did.

The scene was without scale. Certainly there was nothing to prove that the facing armies were made up of minute individuals rather than things the size of men. The ground was very marshy, and the broad webbed feet of the frogs were an obvious advantage to them.

Their equipment was crude, however, and it seemed to have been adapted from local vegetation rather than being created by art. Their shields were of pale, heavily-veined leaves whose edges were wrapped but not smoothed to a regular outline. They wore breastplates of darker material which also seemed to be individual leaves; their helmets looked like Phrygian caps but on closer examination—the viewpoint froze even as Vibulenus considered the question—were seashells bound on with grass ropes.

Unlike their feet, the hands of the frogs were not webbed—though they looked strange enough, having only three digits to grip their shields and the long stone-pointed spears with which each warrior threatened the enemy.

That enemy was as surely an army of mice—and not mice—as they were frogs. In contrast to the smooth, mottled-green hide of the latter, the mice toward whom Vibulenus' unvoiced question slid his viewpoint were covered in brown fur. Their bellies were the same color as their backs and limbs, but the multiple dugs of many of the warriors were so full that they must be females.

The panoply of the mice showed greater artifice, though not necessarily greater efficiency, than that of their opponents. Vibulenus could not tell for sure the material of the spears and shields the mice carried, but they seemed to be ceramic—glazed at the spearpoints and, in a variety of grotesque designs, on the facings of the shields.

The mouse breastplates were of painted leather, framed and cushioned by wickerwork and bound to them with leather thongs. At first glance, their helmets were of leather also, fur side out—but the close inspection which the tribune's wonder granted him showed that the helms were gigantic nut-shells with the shaggy husks still clinging to them.

Neither army carried edged weapons; and, unless Vibulenus were wrong about the spears of the mice, neither army had any metal even as items of adornment.

The tribune's point of view swooped up to a godlike perspective from which the armies, beginning to flow together, were blurred into two unities: the individual warriors shrank from man-size to mere colors, a green jelly and a brown jelly, sliding toward one another across a pan of neutral gray.

"Gaius Vibulenus Caper," said the voice, "you have received the challenge of Lucius Rectinus Falco. Do you accept?"

"What?" blurted the tribune. Below—directly below, not "down" in sense that one looked down from the bleachers onto a gladiatorial combat—the field rang with the cries of the combatants, individually audible when the voice was not speaking in his ears.

"You must accept or not accept," the voice said tartly. "Do you accept?"

"Yes, damn you, but what—"

And Vibulenus spiraled vertiginously down to the marshy battlefield.

He was no longer watching the battle as he lay on a couch which he felt even if he did not see. The shield on his left side was supported by a strap of woven grass over his right shoulder and across his back. It weighed more than even a full-sized legionary's shield, and the leaf from which it had been formed was cured to the density of half an inch of oxhide. More awkward still was the breastplate, a harder, thinner leaf whose serrations prodded the skin of his belly when he strode forward.

That skin was green, with a dozen subtle shades ranging from almost black to almost yellow. His toes splayed at each step, giving him better support than his mind expected when it confronted soil so marshy that water stood around the stems of the coarse, knee-high grass.

Vibulenus was suddenly certain that he was going to die. It wasn't fear, exactly. The feeling was more akin to knowing that you would hit the ground even as you slid over your horse's shoulder.

"Caper, you little coward!" cried one of the oncoming line of mice. "Come out and take your medicine."

Couples of warriors were fighting at intervals between the waiting lines, though when a frog fell or a mouse there would be a general surge from either side and a struggle over the body. One of the mice, striding on hind legs much longer and more powerful than those of the little crumb-nibbler his head and torso mimicked, was coming straight toward Vibulenus. The voice of his sneering challenge was that of Falco, though it came from a furry throat and past great chisel-edged gnawing teeth.

"I'm here, Falco," Vibulenus shouted back. He charged the spear-brandishing mouse, trying to adapt his mind to the unfamiliar—multi-jointed—leg motion his new body found congenial.

Vibulenus held his spear overhand, a little before the balance, so that the butt joggled against his shoulder as he ran. The weapon was much longer than the javelins with which he had trained. That made it unwieldy; but in mitigation of its size, the spear was surprisingly light—certainly no weightier than the heavy pattern of Roman javelin.

All the items of Vibulenus' panoply felt awkward to him, but the frog body he wore was more skillful with them than the tribune had been in battle with legionary equipment. He was not a warrior, but his present muscles and the instincts which came bundled with them were those of a veteran.

The mouse with the voice of Rectinus Falco sank ankle deep at every step, but his shield and spearpoint had a hard glitter that suddenly frightened Vibulenus. His spear was longer than the mouse's, so he thrust in a panicky attempt more to keep his opponent away rather than to do injury.

The frog spearhead was narrow and slightly twisted because it had been flaked from a seashell. The instant it clicked on the face of Falco's shield, Vibulenus feared the shell would shatter and disarm him. The point broke, all right, but it broke into another wedge-shaped profile which would certainly pierce flesh with an arm's full strength behind it.

The mouse rocked at the blow and stumbled, his narrow feet less suited to the marshy surface. Vibulenus cried out in relief which replaced his foreboding as suddenly as lightning tears the limbs from a tree.

He could not follow up on the thrust because his weapon was too long. As his frog hand tried to shorten its grip, he remembered the similar plight of the spearman who had faced him that morning—and Falco, striking desperately, drove the dense, sharp point of his ceramic spear through Vibulenus' shield and into his thigh.

The wounded tribune screamed. The reasoning part of his mind—which had nothing to do with the struggle—noted that the sound was an unfamiliar croak, though when he cried "Wait, Falco!" an instant later the words were in Latin.

"I told you you'd pay!" the mouse shouted as he jerked his weapon free with a slime of pale blood on its tip. He had been off-balance even before he struck, and the effort of clearing the heavy spear cost him his footing. Falco fell with a splash and the terrified cry, "Father!"—his own or perhaps Jove, father of gods and of men. He probably did not know that he had spoken.

Vibulenus' leg trembled with cold fire, but his enemy was under the point of his spear. He stabbed downward as Falco struggled to rise. The shell point chipped again on the edge of the ceramic shield, crazing the surface, then dug into the mouse's breastplate.

Falco tipped over on his back again. The spearpoint was through the leather, but the wickerwork beneath held it for a moment. Vibulenus strode forward, dropping the handle with which he had maneuvered his strap-slung shield and gripping the spear with both hands.

His wounded leg buckled so that he fell sideways.

For a moment, the mouse was still pinned by the spear caught in his breastplate. He slid on his back, twisting, and the point sprang free.

Vibulenus tried to push himself upright with his left hand, but his shield was in the way. His frog body strained upward with terrified bellows, and the strap across his back tugged him down again with identical force.

Falco squirmed into a kneeling position. He had lost his ceramic buckler and held his spear with both hands as he poised with foam dribbling out the corners of his mouth. Vibulenus batted sideways with his own spear, but the shaft was light and an inadequate weapon even if swung with greater force than his exhausted muscles could manage.

The mouse struck back too hastily to rise to his feet first. The blow was clumsy and the spearpoint less sharp than the shimmering glaze had made it seem but the combination sufficed to drive the weapon a hand-breadth into Vibulenus' chest.

It didn't hurt although he could feel the point grate through bones. Vibulenus realized this was all a game. Then his frog body toppled flat in sudden weakness and pain blazed through him with the brilliance of the sun coming from behind a cloud.

Vibulenus was still fully conscious, but the only muscles he could move were those which focused his eyes. The world was wrapped in a pulsing white glow through which the mouse warrior withdrew his weapon and struggled to his feet. Falco must be exhausted also. It was not effort, really, not work done that was so draining. Rather, it was the tension of battle, the emotional tautness that kept every muscle keyed against possible use like a top spinning in place.

Until you collapsed, or you died.

"You've bought it now, dog-spittle!" the mouse wheezed through slobbering jaws, and he drove his spear down at Vibulenus' right eye. The pain stopped, and the universe snuffed all its lights.

The Battle of Frogs and Mice had proceeded considerably since Vibulenus' previously birdseye view of the struggle. The Frogs had their backs to a steep-banked pond, not the barrier to them that it would have been to a human army; but under pressure from the Mice, the green line was disintegrating as its members hurled away their equipment and plunged into the water.

Gaius Vibulenus screamed and jumped to his feet. The mythic battle dissolved instantly, sound and view together. The tribune stumbled and fell crosswise over Clodius Afer on the couch next to his.

The file-closer lurched upright, giving a shout and a display of muscles toughened by daily training with equipment weighted to make the real thing seem light. He relaxed at once, calmed by the change of mental scenery even before he recognized Vibulenus.

Clodius swung to his feet, permitting both men to pretend that the grip with which he had started to crush the tribune's ribs like a breadloaf was simply help in recovering the younger man's balance. "You okay, sir?" he asked solicitously, stepping away with his arms firmly clasped to his sides.

"Gnaeus," said the tribune when he had recovered enough from the grip of panic and the file-closer to speak. "I was down there." He glanced toward the pit, but there was nothing to be seen but rings of couches—more of them filled than before, though some legionaries were beginning to leave the hall. "*Down* there!"

"Right," said the file-closer. "Me too. Till you, you know, shook me out of it."

Vibulenus started to speak but paused instead with his mouth open, wondering how he could explain to the veteran that he had been a participant in the fantasy struggle, not merely a disembodied viewpoint.

Before he could find the words, Clodius Afer had said, "I was a mouse, myself. Were you? I've always *hated* slimy frogs. And look, wasn't there a poem about this, the Frogs versus the Mice? I swear I heard some

old bastard bellowing it out in the public baths years
ago, 'cause he liked what the echo off the tiles did to his
voice."

"Let's. . . ," said the tribune before he lost his train
of thought while his eyes drifted across the figures
reclining in rapt attention on something which did
not really hang in the middle of the amphitheater.
What would he do if he spotted Falco? He already
had his knuckle and his memory to regret from the last
time.

"Let's get out of here," Vibulenus said gruffly. The
knuckle at least could be cured. It didn't hurt at all
while he was a frog . . . but the scars of *that* experience, though mental, would never leave him.

"Let's go find the Sick Bay and see if this—" he
pointed to his puffy right hand with the other one
"—can't be taken care of."

As they walked up the narrow aisle, the tribune in
the lead, he continued over his shoulder, "I don't know
why they don't want us to fight each other. It doesn't
seem to matter even if we—" he hadn't admitted this
even to himself before "—get, get killed."

"That isn't true," said the file-closer in a voice that
surprised Vibulenus more for its peculiar thoughtfulness than it did by its content.

"What?" the tribune prompted, pausing in the hallway outside the amphitheater for his companion to
come abreast.

Clodius would not meet the younger man's eyes,
however. "Well," he said, squinting down the corridor
as if to estimate its length, "they offered me the centurion's slot in the Fourth Century. Told 'em I'd think
about it. You know, up a rank but down a century, and
I'm . . . you know, the guys came through real good
today."

"But Vacula. . . ," said the tribune, seeing what the
non-com meant.

"Yeah," Clodius agreed. "Vacula's gone, dead as Crassus. Some others, too. They said—the voice said, you—" He shook his head angrily, trying to clear the nervous mannerism from his speech. "Anyway," he continued, "they told me it was because his *brain* got stabbed they couldn't do a thing for him so they just left him lay. Brains and spines, they say."

The file-closer shook his head again, this time in puzzlement. "Why d'ye suppose that should be? Brains and spines?"

"Why should any of this be?" Vibulenus answered as bleak awareness descended on him. "I don't know. But I think—" and the bluntly gleaming spearpoint swelled again as it descended on the eye of his memory "—that Rectinus Falco had heard about brains and spines too."

He shrugged. "No matter. Let's find the Medic, and then maybe some food."

"Right," said the file-closer. "It don't bother me so much now things're starting to get organized."

Vibulenus' mouth was open to ask directions from the voice of the ship. He paused and swallowed. For a moment, he tried to pretend he did not understand what the file-closer meant.

"Lead us to the Sick Bay," Clodius Afer said nonchalantly to the ceiling, where a yellow bead obediently sprang to life.

And the blithe acceptance of their situation which the tribune felt also within his own heart frightened him as much as the spear plunging toward his eye had done.

BOOK
TWO

THE FIFTH CAMPAIGN

"Get your fuck—"

KA-BANG! rang Vibulenus' helmet under the impact of the crossbow bolt.

"—*head* down!" completed the new commander of the Third Century of the Tenth Cohort, Gnaeus, Clodius Afer, hunching along the rampart.

"Oh," he added as the tribune rolled out of the sprawl into which the bolt had knocked him, helmetless and recognizable. "Sorry, sir, but one a' those bastards has the communications ramp like he'd taped it."

Local auxilliaries, slightly-built bipeds like those who held the fortress with skill and tenacity, began banging shots over the rampart in what was obviously a pointless exercise. The light bolts sparked against the stone walls of the fortress or flew wildly over the crenellations.

It was notable that none of the auxilliaries raised their heads above the earthen rampart which protected them. Their right hands jerked the cocking levers of their repeating crossbows, while their left hands clamped the fore-ends to the fortification to roughly steady the weapons. As the archers' muscles worked feverishly, the dark green of their skin showed beneath ruffles in the short, almost translucent, gray fur that covered them.

A bolt slightly longer and heavier than those the

auxilliaries were shooting—and much better aimed—grazed the timber parapet and thudded into the guard-walk so close to the tribune's boots that he jerked them closer to the wall. The auxilliaries ducked down again also. A film of greenish poison colored an inch or so of the shaft above the buried head.

"Sorry," muttered Vibulenus, snatching up his helmet which had been ringing softly on the guardwalk where it had fallen. Near the crestholder was a dent with a gouge and a smear of poison in the center of it. The bronze was already beginning to verdigris where the poison touched it. The tribune sucked in his lips and rubbed the metal clean against the turf. "I forgot how *damn* much that tower overlooks us since they burned us out last."

"This's the sharp end, right enough," the centurion agreed grimly. "We're supposed t' be issued some oxhides t' cover the guardwalk so at least they can't *see* us so easy from up there."

Vibulenus nodded upward in agreement, then donned his helmet again. The blow had not hurt him as much as it surprised him, but three inches to the side and the quarrel would have been through his forehead.

The tribune's sweat was as cold as the morning air. There were no small mistakes; only times you were luckier than you deserved to be.

There were times you *weren't* lucky as well, and in the air as a reminder hung hints of the charred ruin of the siege ramp which the present one replaced.

Twenty-seven legionaries had been caught in the con-flagration which wrapped the first ramp in flames so hot that corpses could not be recovered, much less reani-mated. Hundreds of the local auxilliaries—archers mostly, like these—had died at the same time . . . but that didn't matter, because they were bound to die some day, finally and irrevocably, unlike the members of the legion.

Unlike Gaius Vibulenus Caper, whose fingers traced the dent in his helmet as he thought and shuddered.

Clodius Afer was thinking along the same lines because the breeze carried a whiff of roast flesh on the cleaner odor of wood smoke. It was there if you knew to sniff for it . . . and that was as hard for a legionary here to avoid as it was to keep from picking a scab. "Looked so simple," said the centurion.

"This much timber around—" Afer continued as he nodded toward the hills sloping everywhere within his arc of vision, covered with the stumps that had provided material for the siege works "—wasn't even a risk, just hard work muscling the frames into place and backfilling with dirt."

A trio of ballistas fired from the battery a furlong behind the rampart on which Vibulenus now crouched. The artillery's arms slammed against the padded stops, lifting the rear mounts from the platform until gravity thudded them back.

Two of the missiles were head-sized stone balls which crashed into the battlements of the tower. One ball disintegrated while the other caromed off nearly whole, in a shower of fragments battered from the wall. It would be possible to breach the fortress with ballista stones, but it would take bloody forever. . . .

The third ballista sent a pot trailing smoke in a low arc over the wall of the fortress.

"Eat *that*, you bastards!" shouted a legionary farther down the guardwalk, but the sight did nothing to improve Vibulenus' state of mind.

The locals in this place, where the sun was too white and the days too long, brewed a liquid that burned like the air of the Jews' Gehennum. Pitch, sulphur, quicklime, bitumen, and saltpetre were dissolved in heated vats of naphtha, the foul-smelling fluid that pooled like water in many of the valleys hereabout. Shot over the walls in firepots like the one the ballista had just flung, it destroyed the defenders' housing, panicked their live-stock and—who knew?—perhaps killed somebody.

But the same fluid, poured by the hundreds of gallons from the top of the tower, had devoured in flames the original siege ramp across which the legion had expected to storm to victory.

It wasn't that a flame attack had been unexpected. Galleries had protected the soldiers as they built the ramp closer to the walls. They were covered with raw hides over a layer of green vegetation that acted as a firebreak, as well as a cushion against heavy stones. The framing of the siege ramp was timber and theoretically flammable, but no one had believed that freshly-cut logs, none of them less than eighteen inches in diameter, were at any real risk.

The defenders had waited until the face of the ramp had advanced within ten feet of the fortress and the log-corduroyed upper surface of the Roman construction was nearly on a level with the battlements of the wall proper. Then, despite arrows showered by the trading guild's local auxilliaries, they had thrust spouts through the crenellations of the tower defending the vulnerable angle on which the Roman attack was centered.

From the spouts, dispersed and carried outward by gravity, came the fluid which clung and blazed and could not be extinguished. Water only spread the flames and made them burn the harder by igniting the quick-lime. Even dirt and sand, shovelled desperately onto the fires by some of the quicker-thinking legionaries, rekindled only minutes later when the hell-brew soaked to the surface.

There was an hour of havoc and terror, men lost and equipment destroyed—tools, battering rams, and the galleries which were meant to protect them. But, as the defenders continued to spew fluid on the ramp from which every living thing had been driven, the framing timbers themselves caught fire. The flames continued to spread until the entire quarter-mile width of the siege ramp had become involved.

The flames rose higher than the granite tower which had spawned them, and the smoke lifted a thousand feet before spreading into a pall that hid the sun for three days and wrapped the corpse of the legion's expectations. Artillery on platforms a furlong back from the nearest flames was ignited by the radiant heat, and the ramp's filling of earth and rubble turned to coarse glass which crumbled and gouged when the legion finally began the task of rebuilding.

The defenders' artillery was light, catapults which shot arrows from ordinary bows instead of using the power of springs twisted from the neck sinews of oxen. As a result, they could not hurl firepots against their besiegers and spread their yellow flames along the teams of men and oxen dragging fresh material up the ramp. Few of the legionaries doubted, however, that this attempt would end in as complete a disaster as the first, once the siegeworks advanced to within ten or so feet of the tower's face.

"The trouble is," said Vibulenus, "these little furry wogs know what they're doing."

He was on a needless tour of the advanced works, to inspect them and report back to the Commander. The tribune could by now have figured within a foot how closely the ramp approached the fortress, calculating from the amount of material that had been carried forward since the most recent tour of inspection. Timber was the limiting factor since the nearer slopes had been denuded to form the initial works. The legionaries were stretching the available wood this time by using fascines of rolled wickerwork to bind each advance of the siege ramp; but even so, heavy logs were needed as

pilings to anchor the fascines against the weight of the
fill behind them.

The unsteady ruin of the former ramp was more
detriment than gain as a foundation, and Vibulenus was
not alone in dreading the way the wicker underpinning
would burn, despite the layers of sod intended this
time to cover the works on the final approach.

"Too right," Clodius agreed, giving the trembling
arrow a nod which showed that he mistook the tribune's
meaning. "I don't think much of their bows—they're
quick, sure, but they're no problem with armor the way
the Parthians, they shot us t' dogmeat. But some of 'em
could shoot out a crow's eye, looks like."

"I mean. . . .," Vibulenus said, focusing on a great
timber, an entire treetrunk over a hundred feet long,
being dragged up the approach. The teamsters, locals
driving the draft animals which looked very similar to
the way the tribune remembered oxen looking, would
halt out of arrow range until darkness.

"I mean," the younger man continued now that he
thought he could phrase his statement so as not to seem
to rebuke Clodius, "They're too good all over. Good
with their bows—" one of the auxilliaries chose that
moment to rise and pump three arrows smoothly toward
the tower, ducking back before an answering shot
"—good on their fortifications, good on everything. We've
been fighting dumb barbs too long."

"They can't meet us in the field," said the centurion,
more sharply than he would have spoken had not his
pride been touched.

"We'd eat 'em for breakfast," Vibulenus agreed easily. He was watching now and thinking about the timber, suitable for a ship's keel, as it inched up the ram
under the labor of forty yoke of oxen. "But we don't
have anything like that fire of theirs, either."

"We don't *need* it," insisted Clodius Afer, misunderstanding again. "They've built with stone, and they got

the height besides. We could pour the stuff down the
face a' that wall all day and it wouldn't bring down the
tower. Hercules, they nigh *did* that when they, you
know. . . . The other ramp."

The works were lightly manned since the previous
disaster. The Commander might not care about the
legionaries as individuals, but he must have been telling the truth about their value to his precious guild.
The irretrievable loss of twenty-seven men at a blow
had shocked him as grievously as it had the survivors of
the conflagration. He had agreed without hesitation
when the tribunes and senior centurions insisted at the
following staff meeting that it was better to risk a sally
by the defenders than to risk the legion as a whole in a
sudden firestorm.

From the Fourth Century, picketed to the immediate right of the section which Clodius' century held, a
non-com was scrambling along the guardwalk toward
Vibulenus. It might be Niger, promoted to watch clerk
when Clodius took the neighboring century. That would
be a pleasure, because there was very little fraterniza-
tion across the ranks when the legion was in the field—
and they had been in the field an unexpected three
months already, with victory more distant every day
that brought no beneficial change. . . .

"Maybe they'll run out of food," Vibulenus said glumly.
He drew his sword and held it so that on the polished
flat of the blade could be seen the reflected tower,
blurred and less substantial than the reality that was
worth a man's life to view from this close up. "Or
water."

Three crossbow bolts spat down, thumping the bul-
wark, the guardwalk near the sword's shadow, and the
communications ramp where the corduroy surface had
been adzed smooth. "Or arrows, though there doesn't
seem much risk of that."

Niger, who was proud of his new red-tufted crest but

had better sense than to mark himself here with insignias of rank, squatted to a halt beside Vibulenus. "Third Century reports normal progress, sir. We have enough fascines filled to advance another row, as soon as it's dark enough to set the anchor posts."

Niger took a quick look over his shoulder, then rose on his haunches to be sure that no one save native auxilliaries were close enough to overhear anything he said to his immediate companions. "Hi, Gaius," the young legionary resumed. "Gnaeus. Not much happening, is there?"

"How's your mead coming, boy?" asked Clodius Afer in a tone so dry that the tribune was not sure whether the veteran was being sarcastic or just making conversation on a subject about which he was willing to be friendly.

The older veteran. Everyone in the legion had seen and survived at least five campaigns now.

"Well, you don't find bees in a pine forest, you know," Niger said, rightly doubtful as to whether Clodius did know what was to him obvious. "They nest in trees, but they need flowers to eat, and there wasn't anything open around here before we came."

Niger's eyes scanned the slopes behind them deeply gouged by run-off from the brief storms which added to the legion's misery—and replenished the defenders' water supply. "You know, sir," he went on, professionally respectful now that he was considering a professional problem, "I been thinking. If we build the ramp much nearer the walls, they're gonna burn us out same as before."

"You've got company in that opinion," Vibulenus said in something between agreement and sarcasm himself.

A ballista, reloaded more quickly than its fellows, banged. The crashing disintegration of its missile was followed, for a wonder, by the vertical collapse of part of the tower's facing. It left a patch of rock of a darker color across as great a width as a man could span with both arms. Perhaps in a hundred years. . . .

"So you see, sir," Niger went on with the enthusiasm of invention, "what we need to do is stop the ramp right where it is so they can't pour fire on it—"

"And see if the cursed place weathers to dust any time soon?" Clodius Afer interjected.

"No sir," the watch officer said in a tone of injured simplicity. "We can reach the wall from here with a ram or a drill, if it's long enough. If we use that tree—" he pointed at the long bole Vibulenus had already noted "—for instance."

"It'll—" said the centurion.

"*And,*" Niger continued with uncharacteristic determination, "if we cover the outside with bronze sheeting so's they can't burn it up no matter whether they try all night."

"Hey," said Clodius Afer in surprise. "You know, sir, that just might . . . ?"

Vibulenus grimaced, wishing he could be more hopeful about what was, after all, a more imaginative notion than any the Commander had offered. "No," he said, "even if it doesn't sag too much over the distance—" Twenty unsupported feet; the tribune knew from the Greek architect superintending construction on his family's estate how much a beam would flex, and this one covered besides with a heavy layer of metal . . . "—then they'd snag it with ropes from the top of the wall, and we'd be too far away to save it."

"What we really need," said Clodius Afer with gloomy thoughtfulness, "is one a' them lasers the Commander's got. Suppose we could ask him just the once, to turn the trick?"

The short answer to that was *no, you cursed fool*—the Commander's guild wouldn't have bothered to *buy* them from the Parthians, buy Romans who knew how to lock shields and use a short sword, if there'd been a chance of using the guild's own weapons. But Vibulenus would not have said that to a friend; and anyway, the implications of the question showed that the non-com had an idea that was still unclear to the tribune.

"Do you think the lasers could tear a hole in those stones?" Vibulenus said doubtfully. "I didn't think it was that. . . ." His voice trailed off as he tried to remember what the shield looked like after the bolt had struck it. That hadn't been so very long ago, except that . . . everything got mixed up between, between battles. They fought, they regrouped on the ship after the guild traders landed in their even larger vessel. And then the legion drank and slept and played in the amphitheater with whatever fantasy struggle was going on there now. Injuries that the Medic had repaired aged to true healing, sometimes with traces of scar tissue: the tribune's left biceps still had a twinge from the stab wound he couldn't remember getting in his first melee.

And then, when the deep red dye had faded from the flesh of even those who had been most seriously wounded—those who had been killed, and whose eyes never lost that awareness—everybody woke up in the morning, and the Commander was briefing them for another battle, at another place where the air was wrong and the sun was wrong . . . and nobody was sure any longer what was right.

"Right" was not getting your skull smashed by a ton of rock, and not being engulfed in a fire so hot it burned your bones to a pinch of lime.

"Gee, d'ye think so, sir?" Clodius Afer said, breaking in on the tribune's memory of flames shooting higher than the screams of the men they encircled. The centurion's brow furrowed as he made his own attempt to visualize the laser demonstration. It kept getting mixed up in his mind with what had happened to a kid in his century, Publius Pompilius Rufus, scarcely even blooded. . . .

"No!" snapped Afer, crushing that train of thought with his vision of the present situation. "No," less forcefully but still firmly enough to surprise the men beside him; "what I mean is, they couldn't pour their fire on us if we had that laser. And peckin' through the wall, then—Pollux, *that's* no problem. The mortar they're set with at the base, that's been burned to Hades. The stone're big enough but that just means you've got a hole you kin crawl through first time you get one clear."

"Yeah," agreed Niger while Vibulenus was still grappling with the unstated part of the equation. "Hot as everybody is after the first time, I betcha four men with picks'd have a block out in a couple minutes easy. Then she's kitty bar the *door*."

"Mustn't forget there's gonna be another layer behind the facing blocks," Clodius cautioned the junior non-com, professionally analytical now that he had begged the initial question of the laser. "Maybe fill, too, but that'll be rubble, and anyway, we tear a hole big enough and the fuckin' tower falls in, makes us a better ramp right damn through their wall than anything we're gonna build from the outside. Baby! *Then* we gottem."

To Vibulenus, it was all a variant of the discussion that began. "If that camel-fucker Crassus had had sense enough to march us along the river instead of trying to cut across the fucking desert. . . ." Hindsight was a useless waste of breath, and preplanning that started off with an impossibility was worse. That wasted not only time, the one commodity besides frustration which the legion had in great plenty just now; it wasted thought which might otherwise have been put to useful purposes.

But he still didn't see. . . .

"Gnaeus," said the tribune, interrupting Clodius Afer's description to his admiring junior of the way the legionaries should deploy after they had breached the wall, "how would the lasers keep them from pouring down fire? When they stick their spouts through the embrasures, they're still under cover behind the stone. Lasers wouldn't do any more than the archers did. Unless maybe they curve, do you—"

"No, no," the centurion said, harsher than he would have chosen because his dream was being assaulted from false grounds. Clodius had already convinced himself, at least for this moment with friends, that a deputation from the legion would convince the Commander to break the rules—in a way that would mean his death and the immediate dissolution of his trading guild by investigators of the Federation. "Sir, you see, the stuff *burns*, right?"

Vibulenus started to lift his jaw in agreement with the rhetorical question, but the centurion was already hastening on to cover his lapse of respect by saying, "And they've got, who knows, hundreds of gallons of the stuff up there—" he cocked his eyebrows to the breastwork beside him and the lordly tower beyond "—maybe thousands.

"Now," his voice sank with the beauty of the thought it was about to express, "what if *all* that fire-piss was to light up on *top* the tower instead of when they pour it down on us? How'd you like to see *that*, Gaius, see all them bastards jumpin' every whichaway and burnin' like fuckin' night games at the Circus?"

"I'd like that a lot," said Vibulenus slowly. Indeed, he could imagine it even as he spoke: the bolt of sudden light ripping apart the spout, scattering blazing fluid among the defenders and the open vats which they prepared to pour down on the legion. The fire would go where arrows could not—nor the laser beam itself, directly. That was very good thinking.

"But," Vibulenus went on, "there's no way we'll get a laser. The Commander himself doesn't dare carry one when he's out of the ship. You know that."

"Maybe," said Niger, hopeful even though both his superiors had lapsed into glum silence, "we could get the artillery to do it? You know, shoot a firepot into the battlements?"

As if supporting the suggestion, a pair of ballistas slammed missiles leaving smoke trails toward the fortress. One pot sailed into the hidden courtyard. The other splashed its contents in a great oval of flame onto the wall it had failed to clear. The blaze was lambent anger against the black stone, streaking and then shrinking into a score of orange hotspots that continued to sizzle around unusually large globs of pitch.

"Naw, not accurate enough," explained the centurion, thumbing in the direction of the fortress as if he or his companions could see it. Their ears and past experience told them as surely as direct sight could have done what had been the result of the ballista shots. "Especially with firepots, since they're lighter 'n stone and they wobble when the fluid shifts."

His listeners lifted their eyebrows in agreement. The smoke trails from the weapons that had fired held their corkscrew shape even as they drifted downwind, dispersing.

Niger's lips pursed, however, as he followed his own line of thought even while ceding the truth of what Clodius Afer had just said. "Well," he offered hesitantly, "if they don't hit it the first time, sir—and I don't guess they would neither—what's to stop they keep trying until they do?"

For a moment, it looked as if the senior non-com were about to snarl an angry put-down instead of giving the suggestion a proper reply. Perhaps if Vibulenus had not been present, that would have happened, but the tribune's expression of something between agreement and expectancy calmed Clodius Afer.

With a smile instead of a bark of haughty dismissal, he said, "If *I* can see the chance, lad, you can bet your hopes of a woman that this lot we're gettin' wiped by'll see it if we draw a line to it, plinkin' away with firepots.

Mayhap they do already and they store the shit down a floor with a layer a' stone between the tubs and anything we could touch with the splash if we *did* hit."

"All right, I see," said Vibulenus who at last *did* understand what had been so obvious to the centurion that it took him this long to realize what he had to explain to his juniors.

The tribune was smarter than the older man—either of them would say—and was certainly better educated. But Clodius Afer had the habit of looking at military problems and military solutions, putting himself in the other man's boots. At one time or another he'd *been* on the other side of most problems during service in Lusitania and Gaul, besides the catastrophic last thrust into the Parthian domains.

For some problems, there is no satisfactory substitute for experience. Learning that had been a valuable piece of experience for Gaius Vibulenus.

"Now, I don't think they're worried about that yet," the centurion continued, glowing now from the approval of his social and military superior. "The way they poured the stuff down the first time, they weren't takin' time to haul it up any distance—and why would they bother? They're no more used to our artillery than we are to their cursed fire! But I guess they're smart enough to learn."

Niger spat angrily beyond the edge of the guardwalk. "Learn quicker 'n some folks does, I reckon. Or else we wouldn't be buildin' right up t' the wall for another bath any time they get good and ready t' offer it."

Bows snapped faintly from the top of the tower. The missiles, moving in several flights as the archers pumped their cocking levers, quivered in the sunlight as they arched upward. When they dropped at last, it was almost vertically. They had been aimed at the teams laboring forward, dragging the hundred-foot timber that had been brought so far with such effort—and would blaze with empty magnificence in a few days or weeks, along with the remaining material of the rebuilt siege-works.

Even with their height advantage, the defending arch-ers were unable to get much more than a furlong's range from their bows. The breeze scattered the light missiles terribly, so that only a few of the dozen or more launched even landed on the track smoothed onto the surface of the ramp for transport.

Though the wood was soft, one of the bolts flopped back after it struck point-first, lacking the slight mo-mentum that would have enabled it to stick. With poison, of course, it could have left a dangerous wound on bare flesh or—possibly—the tougher hide of one of the draft animals. There was little chance of that, since the drivers had already halted fifty feet back of the zone of danger.

"Sure *wisht* we could borrow that laser," said Clodius Afer with a sigh.

"We won't get that," said the tribune, his voice calm but his mind dancing with a sudden thought as blaz-ingly splendid as the flames which had destroyed the siege works and twenty-seven men.

"Not *that*," he repeated, "but by all the gods, we *will* get something as good."

And before either of the non-coms realized his in-tent, Gaius Vibulenus had ducked down the steps to the gallery which led to the rear—and to the means of putting his idea, *all* their idea, into effect.

The shimmering surface of the Commander's face flowed and distorted as he drank something that was not ration wine from his goblet. "I don't see how this could possibly work," he said with less than his usual detachment. "Is this something you've used on your own planet?"

Vibulenus was familiar with the word "planet" from

the astronomical poetry of Aratus, which had formed part of his education. It was nonsensical in this context, so he ignored it and said, conscious that not even the friendly eyes around the circle held belief, "Sir, this is not a familiar technique for us—" He glanced to his side and got shocked disavowal from Pacuvius Semo, the tribune nearest to him, in place of the smile of solidarity for which he had been fishing.

They were all in this together, thought Gaius Vibulenus with an icy memory of spears—fantasy and real melded together—swishing toward his brain. Whatever others wanted to tell themselves.

Loudly, coldly, certainly, the tribune who was no longer as young as he looked continued, "Nor is the problem a familiar one. However, anyone who has seen a smithy in operation will know that the apparatus will work. Common sense indicates that the result will be what we desire. What *you* desire, sir."

"Nonsense," said Rectinus Falco forcefully, and the chances were better than half that he was right. Hades, that he was right on either assumption, the mechanics or the result of their successful use. But nobody was going to guess that by looking at Vibulenus' boyish, supercilious expression.

There were fifteen Romans in the command group, the five surviving tribunes and the senior centurion from each cohort. The legion's first centurion, a balding, glowering veteran named Marcus Julius Rusticanus, had held his post throughout the period of service beneath the Commander. Several of the other cohort leaders were recent promotions, since their rank and the deference afforded them were owed to courage in battle—which came with a price, even when the Commander's vast, turtle-shaped recovery vehicle roamed the field after victory had been won.

The Commander was the same man or not-man who had mustered them when they awakened aboard the ship which became their home. The Medic since the third campaign had been a turnip-shaped creature, shorter than the smallest legionary, with broad hands and fingertips that spread like those of a tree frog.

But they saw the Medic only at the end of a campaign, unless they were so badly wounded that their fellows bundled them on wagons or stretchers to the vessel. Nothing, including the recovery vehicle, left the ship between the time the legion disembarked and the victory they were landed to secure.

The Commander shared the legion's exile from the ship during a campaign, but he could not be said to share any unnecessary danger. The Commander lived a full half-mile back from the fortification, in a dry-stone blockhouse which had been erected before work on the first siege ramp even began.

The command group met in the courtyard of the blockhouse, rank with the smell of the lionlike mounts which were stabled there every night. While the Romans squatted supporting their backs with the stone walls, the Commander sat primly upright on a stool. Two of his bodyguards stood to either side of him, and a further pair glowered beneath raised visors from behind the stool.

Falco began to rise to take the floor, half way around the circle, but Vibulenus did not relinquish his position. The meeting was one he had called—requested, at any rate. Begged, if you will, of the Commander who, like any reasonable slaveowner, made an effort to accommodate the wishes of his chattels when that did not require unreasonable effort.

"Sir," Vibulenus continued. His voice cut the air like a swordblade while his own imagination told him that the wind blowing across the wall's jagged top was robbing his words of all life, all power. "The technique will succeed. Whether or not it does, the cost of the attempt is negligible. There—"

"The beam that our colleague proposes using," cut in Rectinus Falco, holding himself erect with his chin and chest outthrust in a posture as much theatrical as rhetorical, "is one of the few decent timbers remaining to us. The bronze that he would have us use—"

"Is available," said Vibulenus, and no one in the courtyard, even the speaker, could doubt the power of his voice. "And timber will be in much shorter supply the third time we build the siege works, a certain result if we proceed in the current manner for the next week or even days. Therefore, if your worship will—"

"You are—" interrupted Falco, twisted by anger from the Commander to speak directly toward his rival instead.

"*If* your worship will give the order," Vibulenus continued in a snarl as piercing as the sound of the Commander's laser cycling, "I will carrry out the necessary arrangements so that the fortress can be stormed after the wall is breached."

"How droll," said the Commander, sipping again from a goblet that shone as if studded with a thousand jewels. The liquid within was visible, rolling sluggishly; its color changing from blue through amber, depending on how the light struck it. "This isn't really covered, but I don't see how the Federation could object to it."

Ballistas loosed against the distant stronghold. The sound of their discharge was barely a whisper on the breeze, but the sharper crack of balls demolishing themselves on stone was clearly audible.

"All right, Tribune Gaius Vibulenus Caper," the Commander said, stilling with his words the remark that Falco, still standing, was about to interject. "The estimates of success through starving out the garrison have been revised downward again, and at this particular stage in my career I cannot afford. . . ."

His voice paused. He might have gone on, but Falco, driven by anger to a courage equal to anything his rival had displayed on the battlefield, burst out, "Your worship, there is a cost which our colleague is—passing over. I will not say—" but with venom in his tone he said it "—choosing to obfuscate." He glanced from the Commander to Vibulenus.

"Go on," said both together, the blue-garbed Commander interested; the taller tribune puzzled. If there were a point Vibulenus had missed in the triumphant structuring of his motion, then he deserved whatever punishment he received for wasting the Commander's time on a—nearly—disrespectfully determined presentation.

"He is neglecting the assault on the walls," Falco continued smoothly. " 'Under cover of my new device,' says our friend, 'so new indeed that even you cannot imagine it, your worship—'" Falco smirked.

The goblet which the Commander had been swiveling gently, froze although the fluid continued it's slow motion within.

Falco was terrified. He of all the Romans was most conscious of the blue figure's power over them and most concerned that the Commander was truly inscrutable, his face and gestures not those of a man—though they *might* be. Falco was too experienced to intellectually believe his rival was cool and collected, but his gut accepted Vibulenus' appearance as his reality—tall, calm, a hero in battle while Falco could claim only the Commander's ear in a place of safety.

Well then, this was *his* field. "My colleague proposes," continued the shorter tribune as his mind cut away the rhetorical flowers which he suddenly feared would bring his end, "that a party attack the walls with picks, drawing the attention of the defenders on the tower who will then be dispatched by his wonderful device. It is patent to all of us who were near the walls during the previous attack—" Falco had been well back, as always, but the chaos forebade certainty; and in any case, stating a "fact" loudly was most of the way to being believed. "—that this attention, if drawn, means the immolation of the attacking force."

The speaker paused. All around the circle, Romans frowned and pursed their lips as they considered the words and agreed with them. Neither the officers nor centurions who had cut their way to command through heroism were willing to damn the plan at once for its danger, but. . . .

"You have already lost twenty-seven valuable men to no effect," continued Falco, whose sole audience was the figure in blue who was more powerful than all the consuls and legions of Rome. "You must not throw away more on my colleague's hare-brained scheme."

"Must," realized everybody in the courtyard as the gerundive construction rolled off Falco's tongue, had been the wrong thing to say.

Vibulenus held silent with his tongue poised, letting the Commander break the hush by saying, "Starvation is still certain enough, I suppose. Eventually. But go ahead, Gaius Vibulenus, put your plan in effect, only—"

"Yes, your worship?" said the lips of the tall tribune while his mind watched and listened to his body appreciatively from a distance. He wondered if he were going to faint.

"Only don't spend more than twenty men on the feint, will you?" the Commander continued before he took another sip. "Perhaps you can get the locals to do it instead of your own people. Certainly we pay that lot enough. Or at least their chiefs."

"I. . . ." said Falco as he tried to clear himself. The argument was lost, that was certain. "I—"

The Commander's head turned. Falco could not meet the eyes which would not, in any case, have told him anything. He collapsed to a sitting position, wishing the sun were not so bright . . . wishing everyone else in the courtyard were frozen and he could hack through their throats with impunity, including the Commander and most *especially* Gaius Vibulenus Caper. . . .

"The attack will be real, your worship," said Vibulenus as he alone remained standing. His viewpoint had drifted back within his body as soon as Falco sank away, but knew his heart was beating abominably fast and he was sure he was going to lose control of his tongue before he could make the necessary explanations.

Plowing on regardless like a runner who knows his legs will give way if he slackens in the least, Vibulenus said, "We need to breach the wall as quickly as possible so that the defenders can't come up with another means of thwarting us—"

"Yes, I understand, Gaius Vibulenus Caper," said the Commander, rising in dismissal. One of the armored toads behind him snapped the folding stool closed with enough force to threaten the frame. "Your preparations will take some time, I'm sure, so you'd best get on with them if you're to be any use at all."

He waved a slender, blue, deformed-looking hand. Non-coms began lurching to their feet while the tribunes tried to rise with greater delicacy.

"Sir," said Vibulenus in a voice of such penetrating clarity that everyone paused and even Falco looked at the still face of his rival. "I'll be leading the assault myself, sir. I think we can make the attack in safety."

The Commander made a corkscrew motion with his free hand. "Whatever you choose, Tribune," he said. "Just no more than twenty men. And—" he was walking daintily toward the gate of the living quarters within the blockhouse, but he paused for a moment "—see that there's a follow-up squad at a comfortable distance. In case you're wrong about the safety."

The blue figure disappeared indoors. In the milling confusion of the courtyard, filled with glances and whispers, Gaius Vibulenus wondered what he did choose.

And why.

* * *

"You shouldn't *be* here, sir," said Pompilius Niger, and the flight of arrows which punctuated the statement thudded into the roof of the mobile gallery above them like rain on thatch.

"I ought to be in Baiae," Vibulenus replied. Floating in a one-man skiff in the middle of the Bay of Naples. Surrounded by the prismatic beauty of thousands of dancing waves and covered by an open sky colored the rich blue of indigo-dyed leather.

"Watch it!" called a soldier beyond the gallery. No way of telling what he was warning about. A thud shook the footing of the men preparing to lift the heavy roof covering them, but it could have been an accident to the Roman preparations as easily as a missile flung some distance by the defenders.

The impact brought Vibulenus quivering back to the fear and near darkness within the mobile gallery, however. "You do *your* job, Niger," he added harshly, "and let me do mine!"

"Sir," said the senior centurion of the Tenth Cohort, his voice deadened and attenuated because he was speaking from outside the protective walls. "We're about to lower the walkway. Wait the signal so's we get it straight before you step off."

Vibulenus nodded agreement, then realized that the centurion couldn't see him through the layered mud and wicker that shielded the assault party—for a time. "Fine," he said, "fine. Get on with it."

Bows nearby popped, though the hissing thunk of quarrels striking showed that the auxilliary archers were only responding to the defenders. There was a crash, loud for all its distance. Seconds later, the gallery and its surroundings were pelted by shards of a ballista ball which had disintegrated against the tower close above them.

The cohort leader shouted an order. Wood squealed,

and a section of men grunted together as they shifted a heavy weight.

"What he means," said Gnaeus Clodius Afer, "is you understand that business best, so it's you needs to be out there running it. *We* can handle this shit."

The twenty men under the heavy gallery were all volunteers and all from the Third and Fourth Centuries—paired according to a practice more ancient than any history that was not myth. Presumably they all knew how risky it was, since they'd also seen the first ramp destroyed.

Vibulenus doubted that any of them save Clodius and Niger had a real grasp of the plan, although he'd tried to explain it to them. The volunteers didn't much care—a normal attitude for soldiers, and one which the tribune was better able to appreciate now that he had become a soldier himself.

Siege work was boring and, in this case, apparently pointless. The Commander believed the works should be continued to put pressure on the defenders, but the legionaries were running lotteries as to what time the enemy would destroy this "threat" with the same off-hand precision as before.

An assault on the walls was something different, and a chance to come to grips with opponents who were invisible—unless you wanted an arrow through the eye you were looking with. One of the tribunes said it'd work, that he had some screwy contrivance that'd keep the wogs in the tower from frying the attacking party alive . . . but nobody really expects to die, coldly assesses the likelihood of that. And the near-magic available through the Medic and the recovery vehicle didn't much affect the equation.

Gaius Vibulenus Caper knew very well that he could die. In fact, he had no difficulty in intellectually convincing himself that he *would* die . . . but his gut didn't believe it any more than did the guts of the troops around him. That was a blessing and no small one, since it permitted him to function in this tight enclosure, already hot with the warmth of sweating bodies.

Functioning meant speaking in a normal voice to the men who shared the danger, convincing them by calm example that they were part of a military endeavor rather than a method of suicide by fire. "No, centurion," Vibulenus said in what he hoped were tones of composure. "The work outside is a matter of timing and military judgment. The leading centurions in charge of it are much better suited to the task than I am."

That the tribune's gut didn't believe, not for an instant; but his intellect did, and he had no choice anyway. He had to be part of the assault he had planned. Vibulenus was young enough to know that he could not otherwise live with himself if the result turned out as badly as it might.

The first centurion, Julius Rusticanus, shouted, "Forward!" Then: "Put your *backs* in it, you pussies!"

Rusticanus had the scars that had promoted him through the lower ranks, but he had also the exempla that fitted him for his current position. He could handle returns of the legion's equipment and personnel, duties that frightened many men who were willing to charge spears stark naked. Beyond that, he had the carrying voice and absolutely precise enunciation which would have suited him for a life on stage—if he had not been built more like an ape than a Ganymede. He was as likely as any Roman present to be able to understand the complex operation outside the tower, and by far the most likely to have his orders obeyed.

While Rusticanus had overall charge of the operation in lieu of the Commander (whose bodyguard would not protect him from fire), the Tenth Cohort's senior centurion had been delegated tasks involving the assault proper. That meant building a gangway of solid timbers and organizing teams of men to slide it into position when required.

Which was now. Without the gangway, Vibulenus' party and their mobile gallery could not have climbed down the fascine-bulging front of their own siege works. As it was, the descent would be a steep one for men so awkwardly burdened.

The cohort leader gave another muffled command, and the guardwalk shook with the pace of over a hundred men. The gangway was of four-inch planks, planed smooth on their upper surface so that no one would stumble in the quickmarch down from the siegeworks. The stringers were halved logs; and the whole contrivance, carried upside down, weighed the better part of a ton.

The important responses by the defenders were hidden thus far behind the tower's crenellations, but a storm of crossbow bolts was as obvious as it was expected. The siegeworks themselves could not cover the teams moving the gangway; even the light breastwork which shielded the guardwalk had to be thrown down so that the gangway could pivot into position.

Instead, other legionaries attempted to cover their fellows with a tortoise of shields locked overhead and to the sides. Between that formation and the gangway itself which acted as a roof, the legionaries were as safe as reason expected in the heat of battle.

The defenders snapped their volleys down as quickly as they could work the levers of their bows. Each time an archer pulled his cocking handle, a claw drew back the bowstring and the wedge which retained bolts in the magazine slid out far enough to drop the lowest missile. A sear released the string automatically when the bow reached its full draw—and the archer pumped his lever to repeat the cycle.

Bolts that hit the gangway pattered. Those which struck shields thudded on plywood or rang peevishly if they glanced from a metal boss. A scream pierced the confusion of shouts and shuffling hobnails, but the advance did not pause for one casualty running to the rear with a bolt in his shoulder and the pain of poison blazing in his imagination.

"Down *front!*" ordered Rusticanus in a voice like a scythe. The log surface of the rampart quivered on its base of earth and wicker as soldiers butted the forward end of the gangway in the pits provided for that purpose.

"Now *push,* curse you!" the centurion shouted. There was a lull in the volleys of missiles from the top and arrow slits farther down the tower face: most of the defending archers had exhausted their magazines and were ripping open fresh bundles of quarrels to shake into the feed lips of their weapons. Through the snap and patter of the occasional shot came a mechanical screech and the collective wheeze of scores of men as they lifted the far end of the gangway against the fulcrum provided by its stringers bedded at the edge of the rampart.

As the gangway lifted, legionaries waiting with stout poles ran up to continue the momentum of the end which hands could no longer reach unaided. The arrow storm broke again with a viciousness that equaled its first intensity. The gangway lifted to its zenith like a wall, but it was too narrow to provide full protection. Bolts clicked against armor, and less fortunate soldiers cursed or bawled according to their temperament as points gouged their flesh.

But the gangway continued to swing upward until it paused trembling, just short of vertical. *"Push!"* roared Rusticanus. He reached over the back of a legionary to add the thrust of one hand while his other braced a shield studded with half a dozen quarrels already.

The unlubricated stringers rotating in adze-cut pits shrieked louder than the triumphant legionaries as the gangway crashed over the edge of the siege ramp.

Released from duty at the same instant as their major protection toppled away, soldiers ran to the rear in a diminishing shower of bolts as archers emptied their magazines again.

Rusticanus and some of the lesser non-coms stepped deliberately to cover behind their shields. As was usually the case, it was much safer to face danger steadfastly than to flee it; but the experience that allowed a soldier to stand when he could flee was hard-bought and a long time coming.

The mobile gallery had no front or rear wall, but the roof overhung by three feet on either end to block plunging missiles. There was little to be seen, even for Clodius Afer and the other three soldiers in the front rank. Vibulenus, in the row behind them, was lighted dimly by what sunlight seeped past the heads and armored shoulders of the leading rank; and the twelve men arrayed behind the tribune might as well have been in a sealed tunnel for any view they had of what was about to happen.

Vibulenus felt a sudden urge to scream, hurl the gallery away from him, and rush toward the wall which loomed unseen somewhere before him. He couldn't have budged the cover of mud and timber, couldn't rush anywhere while the rest of the assault force packed him tightly . . . and he probably couldn't even scream through a throat which had gone as dry as old bone. He was shaking all over, and he had a terrible need to urinate.

That could wait until they started moving and the act became less obvious. Vibulenus relaxed, feeling enormously pleased that he had just demonstrated intellectual control over one of the few factors within his capacity to change.

A single trumpet signalled them.

"On the count, boys," said Clodius Afer over his shoulder as his own muscles bunched on the crossbar.

There were five transverse poles, as thick and sturdy as a quinquireme's oars. They would make it hard to move forward and back in the gallery, to exchange workers—or flee—but they had to be solid to accept the strain of moving so heavy as structure. Most of the men in the assault force would be unable to help prise apart the tower wall. They were present simply to add their strength in shifting the gallery.

And to swell the butcher's bill in event of disaster, but that was a purpose only for the gods—should they will it. Let the thought not be an omen.

". . . two," said Clodius, *"three!"* and the gallery lifted with a slight sway to the left as if the structure were a turtle just sober enough to walk.

"Pace!" the centurion ordered. "Pace. Pace. Swing right, boys, just a cunt hair—pace, *that's* the way, pace—"

Vibulenus heaved at his bar with a sidewall to his left and a legionary he didn't know grunting to his right. He was lifting with all his strength, but that strength was nothing in comparison to the mass of the gallery. He could feel it shift above him, and his instinctive attempt to counterbalance that thrust was as vain as trying to bail Ocean dry.

Guided and controlled by Clodius Afer, who at least sounded as calm as the stone wall, the assault party staggered onward. Bolts spat into the wet mud with which the gallery was covered, audible but unfelt as the protective roof swayed step by step across the guardwalk.

"Watch it here, now," the centurion called, as the motion threatened to become uncontrolled. Where the gangway met the surface of the rampart, there was a lip and a gap of several inches. The leading rank tried to hop the irregularity, but the gallery was too massive for that to be possible. Divided among twenty men, the weight was acceptable, but no individual had the strength alone to make the structure so much as quiver.

As the assault party jerked their loads high again, a poisoned quarrel flicked past the roof gable and thumped the guardwalk between Vibulenus' boots.

"*Pace*, curse ye!" shouted the centurion.

The quarrel that Vibulenus snapped off beneath his hobnails as his foot shuffled forward must have kissed Clodius' thigh on the way past. Perhaps the poisoned head had not broken the skin; probably the centurion had not received a lethal dose—and very likely they were all dead in the next few minutes anyway.

The gallery tilted down as rank by rank the men supporting it found footing on the slanted gangway. Vibulenus was straining so hard at his burden that fear of stumbling drove out his fear of what would happen if they reached their goal.

Behind them and to one side, centurions shouted hoarsely as their squads began to raise and swing the hollowed timber on which rested all hopes of success. The trunk that had given Vibulenus the idea, a hundred and twenty feet long and straight as a die, had been chosen to execute the plan as well. Legionaries had sawed the trunk in half lengthwise and hollowed it with adzes so quickly that the tribune himself marveled.

On the estate of the Vibuleni, such labor would have been performed by slaves—less well, and taking three or four times as long to accomplish. They *were* slaves, every man in the legion, and at some level they all knew it; but they didn't think like slaves. There were citizens of Rome and the best soldiers in the world, despite the vagaries of a consul who should have stuck to politics and similar forms of extortion.

"*Pace*, boys, don't let the bitch slide," Clodius ordered, his voice showing the strain of physical effort if not of fear. The gangway was narrow. If they let gravity carry a corner of the gallery over the side, they were well and truly fucked. The crossbows that sank bolts vainly in the mud roof would turn the force into a score of shrieking pincushions before any of them could be untangled from the overturned gallery.

Behind them, present only in their prayers, the log weapon was being swung into position. Like the gangway, it pivoted in a socket dug into the ramp, but the teams which lifted it did so through hawsers attached to a pair of shear legs. The hundreds of men hauling back on each hawser were covered by equal numbers of legionaries with raised shields, adequate protection for targets near the extreme range of the defenders' bows.

Nobody knew it all, thought Vibulenus as the archers in the tower shifted their aim from the gallery to the teams of men swinging the hollow log. The army Crassus marched into Parthia thought it had all the answers to war, but the squadrons of horse archers supplied with camel-loads of arrows had battered the legions the way the waves defeated a cliff.

But the furred, quick-handed autochthones of this *place* did not have all the answers either, despite their ability to spew flame as a fountain spurts water. Their missile weapons depended on the tension of bent wood. Real artillery powered by torqued skeins of ox sinew would have slaughtered the lightly-protected lifting teams faster than they could be replaced.

As the shear legs straightened toward vertical, the forward end of the log angled upward to the height of the tower's battlements. A third crew, protected by the rampart, marched along the guardwalk hauling a chain that drew the end of the device sideways. The log now formed the hypoteneuse of a right triangle whose straight sides were the platform of the siege works and the face of the tower.

The defenders must have expected the log to be used as a ram. Even now, as it lifted to an unexpected angle which displayed the hollow interior lined with bronze sheet, it looked more like a ram than it did anything

else in their experience—or in the experience of the
Romans who had built and were about to use the device.

At the base of the pivoting log was a high screen of
wicker and leather. It covered a final crew of legionaries, leavened this time with a few local auxilliaries, and
the great bellows made from whole oxhides. One of the
auxilliaries gave a high-pitched order as the log steadied
into position. The men on the arms of the bellows
poised, but only when the centurion relayed the command in a parade-ground bark did a pair of legionaries
grip the handles of a pottery jar and lift it toward the
broad funnel mounted on the base of the log.

Liquid spouted from the top of the tower. It had
began to burn halfway along its course toward the mobile gallery.

Vibulenus and his fellows had staggered off the lower
end of the gangway, to the glassy remnants of the
original siege ramp. At the tribune's first step, his leg
crunched through what had seemed to be firm ground.
It was like walking through a crusted snowdrift, except
that the edges drew blood as they scraped Vibulenus'
calf.

The gallery dipped forward as other Romans broke
through as well. The fire had consumed everything
flammable in the siegeworks; but wherever there was
enough silica in the earth to vitrify, glass had kept the
fill from setting under its own weight and the heavy
rains. The sprawled remnants were not impassible, but
they provided a barrier of hidden pits covering half of
the last twenty feet between the new ramp and the
base of the tower.

And that saved the lives of the men in the gallery.

The defenders were expert in their use of flame, so
expert that the first gout of blazing fluid travelled from
the spout with the conflicting pulls of gravity and outward inertia in an arc calculated to splash it under the
roof of the gallery. The autochthones knew that by

flooding the area when the assault force was directly beneath, they could destroy the legionaries as completely as they had the first siege ramp—but there was no need to runnel flame over the refractory roof of the gallery if the clinging, erosive liquid could be splashed onto the legs of the men inside.

The gallery wobbled to a halt three feet short of where the defenders expected it when they started their flame on its long fall.

Vibulenus' calves *itched* in a way that was more intrusive than any pain could be. Sweat that raced down his thighs paused and burned when it reached the grit and abrasions on his lower legs. He could not take a hand from the bar he carried to scratch the affected area. His palms were hot and the skin of them, though calloused by swordhilt and shield strap, slipped over the muscle and bone beneath. The unusual stress of carrying the gallery was reducing his hands to puffy, bleeding blisters.

The tribune could see only dimly. The assault force was in an artificial valley between the siege ramp and the sheer wall of the tower. Most of what sunlight did scatter through was blocked by the sheltering roof, and even the remainder was blurred by the sweat and tears which Vibulenus could not wipe away. The tumbling flame, striking and splashing before the gallery, instantly returned light and color to a microcosm of gray pain.

"*Mother!*" screamed Clodius, loud enough for the tribune to hear him and be surprised. Everybody was shouting, though, and the flames roared as they splattered and eroded the earth. The fire was deep red, with flecks of quicklime as white as rage and a shroud of ragged smoke that was visible only at a distance from the bubbling flame.

The gallery grounded before anyone had the presence of mind to order it down. Hands dropped the bars in panic as the men of the assault force tried to jump back. They tangled themselves with the structure and the men behind them.

A legionary in the fifth row did manage to leap out the rear of the shelter. Sunlight and the imprisoning hugeness of the structures before and behind drove the man back under the roof of a moment later. He brushed off his helmet on the eaves. As it rolled on the blackened rubble, a dozen quarrels snapped toward and clangingly against it.

"All *right*," ordered Gaius Vibulenus. His voice was as cool as the core of him which shock had disconnected from the sweating, punished body he wore. Clodius Afer and the other men in the front rank were being burned by the pool of fire which closed their end of the gallery, and the tribune's own shins were scorching. "We're going to *side*-step left, now. Take your bars and *lift*!"

He should have worn his greaves . . . and he was so disoriented that he almost failed to obey the orders he had given the men who were suddenly under his actual control.

The gallery bucked convulsively and grounded again as the sideways shift tripped several legionaries over the outstretched legs of their fellows. All the horns and trumpets in the legion brayed simultaneously while the shelter lurched another step away from the flames.

The ground shook as a huge fireball ignited on the roof of the tower. It was so bright that it shadowed the receding pool of flame near the assault force.

Ever since the gallery began its tortoiselike advance, the tribune had been too caught up in his immediate surroundings to think about the larger aspects of his plan. The professionals of the legion, rank and file as well as the centurions, had done their job with the stolid excellence of a grist mill grinding away its allotted task.

When Rusticanus gave the signal, two soldiers poured their jug of enhanced naphtha into the breech of the log. The local officer who advised on the process had suggested igniting it with water to spark on the quicklime. The legionaries had chosen to risk an open flame instead, something they understood as they did not understand starting fires with water.

The centurion in charge stepped to the log when the legionaries jumped back. He thrust a torch into the funnel glistening with the residue of thickened fluid. Fire bloomed from the touchhole.

"Bellows!" ordered Rusticanus.

Horns and trumpets cried out in a cacaphony intended to terrify the enemy rather than communicate orders. As the sky echoed, the twenty strong men on each lever of the bellows began to stride forward, ramming the air in the oxhide chamber into the base of the hollow log and the fire already blazing there.

Flame spurted twenty feet in the air from the touchhole before a pair of soldiers clamped a bronze plug down on it. The air surging from the bellows mixed with the fluid and rammed it toward the open end of the tube over a hundred feet in the air. When oxygen bubbled into and through the burning liquid, the combination puffed explosively up the hollow trunk—and out, in an orange-red flash, across the defenders on the top of the tower.

The spurt was of superheated gas, not fluid that clung with the tackiness of pitch and molten sulphur, but it crinkled the bowstaves, armor, and faces of those archers it enfolded as they crouched at embrasures. The two defenders pouring liquid through a spout wailed and dropped their open vat as flame burst from it to meet the puff expanding from the hollow log.

There were several hundred additional gallons of fluid on the tower in closed containers which shattered when spreading fire wrapped them. When half the jars had ignited in a matter of seconds, the remainder exploded simultaneously. Part of the crenellations, fragments of equipment, and the bodies of defenders too fiercely ablaze to be recognized as living things rained in all directions from the top of the tower.

The flare mounted in a hemisphere, like the cap of a mushroom thrusting itself through the loam, until it broke free of the stone and wrapped in upon itself to climb still higher on the reflected heat of its own cumbustion. The platform from which it had lifted was bare of any form of life save the few defenders who still thrashed in the blazing sheet which had devoured their eyes and lungs already.

Vibulenus knew his weapon had been successful when an object slammed the sloping roof of the gallery and bounced, then fell again to the ground before the assault force. It could have been a burning missile, heavy enough that its shock grounded the shelter again. What sprawled in a smokey wrapper of flames was not a timber, however, but a corpse that had been a crossbowman before his flesh melted and heat cracked the phial in which he dipped his quarrels. The resinous poison burned blue.

"All right!" ordered Clodius Afer in a voice burned skeletal by emtion and flame-dried air. "Left on the count, boys, and put your backs—"

"Out the front with your tools, men," said Vibulenus, speaking from a mind where everything had a place, like the markers of a board game awaiting the next shake of the dice cup.

It did not occur to him that he was countermanding the centurion. He was placing his game pieces in the illuminated security of his imagination. The dark and bloody reality—of which *his* body was a part—did not impinge on what was right from a standpoint of command.

"We're safe close by the wall if we move fast," the tribune shouted. When his words had no effect for a

further long moment save to turn heads toward him, he
added, *"Move!"* and prodded the ribs of Clodius and
Niger.

"Come *on*, soldiers!" roared the centurion, ducking
under the crossbar with the jerky certainty of a boulder
rolling downhill—after the tribune pushed it. "Let's
take this fucker down!'

No one else in the mobile gallery could get out the
front until the leading row clambered free. Those men
wouldn't have been in the front rank unless they were
willing to leave cover. They scrambled from under the
shelter, and Vibulenus followed them in the irrational
certainty that the remainder of the assault force was
coming also. He was playing a complex game of Ban-
dits, and they were the carved-stone counters on the
board moving as he willed.

For that matter, they did follow him—every man of
the assault force, because they were Romans . . . and
they were soldiers . . . and they were, by all the gods,
being *led*.

. The tower was a sullen candle with a pillar of flame
above the streakes of blazing fluid crawling through the
stonework and arrow-slits of the upper stories. The
lowest twenty feet of the wall had been built without
openings, and even above that level many of the embrasures had been bricked up against side effects of the
defenders' own flame weapons. With the top of the
tower a dripping inferno, the ground near the base of
the structure was a dead zone which none of the weapons in the fortress could reach.

The outer world swept back over Vibulenus as he
squirmed out of the gallery's dark and stinking cover.
Heat had sources again instead of being a dull ambiance. The gout that had splashed before the gallery was
now shrunken to a handful of sulphurous pools to the
right side, and the body of the archer—also shrunken—

lay for the tribune to leap as the quickest way to the wall and greater safety.

The hollow treetrunk was a slash against the sky, its muzzle-end rimmed with tiny flames. Vibulenus hoped they would not pour another jar of fluid into its breech in order to repeat the process. At the time he planned the attack, multiple spurts of flame had seemed both necessary and reasonably safe. He had not fully appreciated the way the fire clung like a solid thing wherever the fluid had ignited. The interior of the great tube must contain thousands of hot spots which would turn a fresh draft of fluid into a fireball at the breech end this time.

But that was the concern of others, while the wall was a matter for Vibulenus and the nineteen men with him.

The lower rows of that wall were blocks two feet high and three across. Their thickness was concealed until the first one was prised out, and Clodius Afer was already organizing that. The centurion wedged the thicker edge of his pick-mattock into one vertical crack while Niger and another legionary ran their crescent-bladed turf-cutters over the upper and lower surfaces of the block against which he was prying.

Vibulenus chopped the mattock blade of his own tool against the remaining edge of the block so that he and Clodius could thrust against one another. They all carried ordinary pieces of entrenching equipment, though some of the soldiers began using their swords because the blades reached deeper into the interstices of the wall. The blocks themselves were of fine-grained stone which showed no tendency to split or shatter, but the mortar in which they were laid had burned to powder.

Clodius gave a shout and leaned sideways against the head of his tool, levering that end of the block three inches from the line of the wall in a shower of gritty mortar. The tribune shouted also in unconscious imitation and thrust back, using the greater leverage of the

helve. Blood and pus from his blistered palms gleamed
on the hickory shaft, but Vibulenus did not notice it.
The stone, already loosened and held by decreasing
friction as more of it was tugged clear of its fellows,
shifted even farther than it had at the centurion's thrust.

Archers on the wings of the fortress flanking the
tower were shooting furiously. Some of the bolts struck
the rear of the abandoned gallery, but Vibulenus and
his men were protected by the wall they were assault-
ing. For all that, bits fell from higher up the tower as its
structure warped under stress of the flames. They were
not missiles as such, but a fire-wrapped scrap of battle-
ment landed close enough to the tribune to scorch his
calves, and another chunk flattened a file-closer as it
rang from his helmet.

There was too much noise for the assault to be truly
coordinated, but the veteran soldiers knew their jobs
well enough to work without direction. Clodius and
Vibulenus each levered again in quick opposition, between them prying the stone far enough for the two
legionaries to drop their turf cutters and grip the block
directly. Tendons stood out at the inside of Niger's
elbows as the tribune stepped out of his way.

"There, by Hercules!" the legionary shouted while
the block, as thick as it was high, slid out of place and
crashed to the ground. It tilted as if contemplating a
roll that would have put everyone nearby at risk, but it
settled back with a second thud.

The legionaries had broken into rough teams, not
because they were organized that way but simply because men in a tight spot look instinctively for the
support of a few fellows. Another block pitched to the
ground moments behind the one Clodius had attacked,
though it was ten feet to the side and only incremen-
tally helpful in weakening the structure. Aided by their
initial gap, the tribune and the three men with him

began to worry loose a block offset in the next layer above.

The horns and trumpets again blew the general call that would normally signal a charge. Apparently that was what Rusticanus—or the Commander?—had in mind. Legionaries protected by no more than their shields and armor began to pour over the face of the siege works fronting the tower.

Archers shot at them, but the auxilliary crossbowmen made good practice against the defenders. Without the lowering threat of the tower, archers employed by the trading guild could sweep the battlements of opponents concentrating on Roman infantry.

Vibulenus stuck his pickhead into a crevice and braced his free palm against the wall for leverage. He felt the violent shock before he heard it, fire-gnawed beams in the tower collapsing under the weight of the flagstoned top floor. Flame shot skyward in a giant version of the bellows-driven puff from the tube which had started the conflagration. Rising, wholly separated from the structure from which it sprang, a fireball expanded while its color changed from incandescent white to red as dull as that of iron quenching in blood.

"Watch it!" ordered Clodius Afer. A second stone tumbled from the wall, cracked against the first, split, and rolled to either side. Niger already had his turf cutter inserted beside the next block over and was prying so hard the thick shaft bowed.

The core of the wall was rubble, compacted between the stone facings and to an extent cemented together by time. It was not true concrete, however, and seeping rainwater had leached pockets from the material. Vibulenus chopped at it with his pick. The iron sparked but bit deep enough to crumble out a headsized chunk. Niger continued tilting his block with the help of another legionary.

Hundreds of men were joining the assault force, el-

bowing one another in their haste to attack the wall
with their weapons. Few of them had proper tools for
the job, but they did carry their sheilds. Lifted overhead by the latecomers, these provided real protection
against the increasing rain of fragments as well as psy-
chological benefit to the men concentrating on their
work of destruction.

Clodius Afer was standing on stones piled at the base
of the wall in order to hook out another with his pick
while Niger balanced him. Every time they removed a
block, the next one came easier. The crumbled mortar
would have made a ram's job more difficult, because
individual blocks had enough play to absorb shock without cracking or shaking the whole wall down.

Against the legionaries with picks, the structure had
no protection save the weight of individual blocks. Those
were no match for men with the strength and boarhound
determination of Clodius Afer and his fellow volunteers.
Including Gaius Vibulenus, who—

"Watch it!" ordered the centurion, jumping down
and back as the block he was dragging teetered on one
corner.

Vibulenus stepped clear and glanced around. To the
left of his own little group, a thirty-foot length of facing
shuddered down and outward, battering and pinning a
number of the legionaries whose individual efforts had
combined to something unexpectedly great. The gap
rose jaggedly to a peak twenty feet up the surface, a
corbelled arch sealed by the wall's rubble core.

The tremors and release from that slippage sent down
not only the block Clodius was removing but three of
those above it as well. "Come on, *back*," the tribune
shouted. He bumped into a soldier who was trying to
cover them both with a shield.

Feeling sudden panic at being trapped between moving rock and immobile bronze, Vibulenus slapped the

legionary in the middle of the breastplate and screamed, "*Back*, curse you! *Back!*"

The shadow slicing across the ruddy inferno above them snapped the tribune's eyes upward.

The teams had released the ropes which held the hollow log poised just short of the tower battlements. That effort was unnecessary now, especially since the defenders were beginning to desert the remaining walls of the fortress in despair. A collapse of the enemy's will to fight was more devastating than a breach in his walls—but it had to be exploited immediately, and a few hundred additional legionaries boosting and dragging one another up temporarily undefended fortifications could be worth a week's grueling siege work after the defenders regained their courage.

The log struck the tower just beneath the flame-wrapped battlements and clung there. Heat threw ripples in the air and made it seem that the whole tower shook. Or else—

"Retreat!" the tribune said, his voice raised but his tone again that of emotionless command as his mind distanced itself from everything physically immediate.

Niger, braced by the centurion, was clambering up the pile of tumbled stone to pry loose another series of blocks. The soldier, still looking younger than the eighteen he had been when captured by the Parthians, had lost his helmet, but sweat plastered his hair to his scalp in a black cap.

Vibulenus gripped Clodius and Niger, each by an elbow. The tribune's thinking processes were too orderly and multiplex at the moment for him to be surprised that he held two strong men without strain. "The wall's about to collapse, I think," he said into the rage-distorted face of the centurion. Clodius was drunk with haste to accomplish his business, and that monomania turned to fury at anything which attempted to frustrate it.

"Get them moving," the tribune continued coolly,

unconcerned that reflex had lifted the pick in Clodius' hand for a stroke to clear his arm. "Just away from the tower—don't try to climb back up the ramp. You too, Niger. Get on with it, boys."

The tone or the look in Vibulenus' eyes penetrated Clodius' mind before he recognized the tribune as a friend. He looked up, swore, and dragged the willing Niger with him toward the troops milling to the left of the gap he himself had torn.

"Get moving, ye meal-brained fuckers!" roared the centurion. "This fucker's about t' fall on our fuckin' *heads!*" Using his pickhandle as a cross-staff and his bellowed certainty as a goad, the squat non-com set up a motion in the troops like that of a wave sucking back from the shore over which it has swept.

Bricks blew out of embrasures midway up the face of the tower. Another floor had collapsed onto a further store of flammable liquids.

Vibulenus turned toward the right flank as Niger and the centurion bullied men to safety in the other direction. He saw no one he knew by name, though soot, helmets and emotion were effective masks. "Run for it, boys!" he called in cool arrogance, gripping a pair of the nearest men by the shoulder. One of them wore a centurion's red cross-plume on his helmet. "Get 'em moving before the wall comes down!"

Fragments of adobe brick and headsized chunks of the stone battlements tumbled with as much as seventy feet in which to accumulate momentum. Legionaries raised shields if they had warning, but this was little protection against the heaviest pieces. One legionary bounced to the ground screaming, his left forearm broken in a dozen places and the thick plywood of his shield in splinters held together only by its felt backing.

For all the injuries, at least one of them fatal, the scatter of debris was probably the best thing that could have happened to the men at the base of the tower.

Nothing the tribune could have said—no command, even if all the signallers in the legion had delivered it—could have so effectively gotten the attention of those most at risk.

In the pause that followed the crashing impacts, Vibulenus shouted, "Run or you'll die, boys! Run!" He thrust the men he held in the direction he wanted the whole force to go.

That pair moved, the centurion first glancing upward and then braying, "Mithras save us, she's comin' *over!*"

A full-sized block, tumbling and as big as any in the lower part of the wall, plunged down with just enough outward momentum to keep it clear of the tower's batter. It struck a pile of stones dragged from the base of the tower with a crash like the world splitting. Neither the block which fell nor the one it hit broke up to absorb the impact.

The block sprang outward in an elastic rebound that gave it virtually the same velocity it had at the climax of its seventy foot drop. It caromed through the legs of the centurion with the energy of a builder's dray, scarcely slowing in its crazy, corner-bobbling course into the fascines of the siege ramp which caught it harmlessly.

The man turned a truncated cartwheel, his arms flung wide by the weight of shield and spear. The stubs of his legs, both amputated at midthigh, spurted arcs of arterial blood as they described their own courses around the center of motion. When the centurion crumpled in a pile, his helmet fell off as if in benediction.

The upper face of the tower swayed like a curtain in a breeze, rippling toward either edge from where the hollow log leaned against it. More bits fell from the top, tiny until their velocity swelled then into blocks as big as a man and heavier than a dozen men.

Whether by instinct or from the tribune's warning, legionaries had already abandoned the ground on which the missiles were falling. Many of the troops were trying to climb back the way they had come, up the face of the siege ramp. They were safe enough from plunging debris, but the whole artificial valley would be covered by rubble from the total collapse of the tower. The men who had sense enough to throw down their shields and equipment would probably be able to scramble clear that way, but the others were seriously at risk.

As was Gaius Vibulenus himself. His job was done and he was a human being again with no duty except his own salvation.

There was a cataclysmic tearing sound from within the tower, shaking the ground and sending up sparks in dazzling traceries rather than balls of flame as before. The inner stonework of the wall was collapsing and dragging with it the upper portion of the rubble core. The facing was still momentarily in place despite the way the legionaries had weakened the base of it, but that could not last much longer.

"Help me," moaned the legless centurion.

The mangled soldier's eyes were staring in the direction of Vibulenus, but his words seemed instinctive rather than voiced in hope of a response. The eyes did not focus. The mind behind them was as droolingly slack as the lips.

Moments before, while the tribune was an intellect dissociated from every factor save the pieces he moved on the game board, he would have seen the sprawling amputee as a factor interchangeable with fifty-nine others in the legion. Now he had returned to being Gaius Vibulenus Caper, who had been a boy of eighteen and who recognized the centurion as the grizzled man who had punched him in the Main Gallery of the vessel that brought them—here.

Vibulenus turned and ran two leggy strides in the direction Clodius and Niger had chivvied other legionaries clear. The face of the tower would buckle outward any instant like a butterfly unfolding a broad stone wing, and anyone caught in the path of that cataclysm would be pulverized beyond the magical skill of the Medic to help.

There were legionaries on top of the wall flanking the crumbling tower. The defenders' resistance had collapsed so thoroughly that the soldiers leading the scrambling assault were able to turn and help their fellows onto the battlements instead of struggling to survive on their dangerous perch. Horns and trumpets sounded in the chaos, but Vibulenus could not tell whether they were giving orders or simply reacting to the general enthusiasm.

Metal gleamed at the edge of the siegeworks, where the palisade had been thrown down by soldiers surging toward the fortress. The sun winked on polished brightwork, the mace-studs and hackamore bosals that left the jaws of the carnivorous mounts free to raven and tear. The smokey glare of the tower stained the iron plates of the bodyguard the color at the heart of a forge, the color of the blood leaking from the stumps of the centurion.

Now that it was safe, the Commander had come to view his victory.

"Fucking *bastards!*" screamed Gaius Vibulenus, and he ran back to the dying man.

Dead, the tribune thought as he slid his hands under the hooped corselet that gave rigidity like an insect's shell to a body that was flaccid within. When he shifted the armor for a grip, the mouth gave a great sigh though the eyes did not blink.

The centurion was a heavy man, even without the weight of his lower legs, and when Vibulenus had raised him waist high he found that the man's shield was still strapped to his left arm. To clear it would require dropping the centurion and starting again the awkward business of lifting a dead weight . . . or throwing the bastard down and running from Hades gaping behind him.

Fuck it all, he'd finish what he'd started. He twisted a fraction so that the dragging shield did not foul his boots and began striding forward again.

Vibulenus had not realized how done-in he was until he started to carry the dying man. The pains that had been covered by rushing adrenalin earlier in the assault were present in full fury, and the detachment of moments before no longer operated to free his mind from the needs of his body.

All that was bearable because it had to be borne, but the weakness in the tribune's muscles was catastrophic and the final catastrophe. He was too young and too healthy ever to have had doubts about his body. There were limits to his strength: he knew that Clodius Afer was stronger than he, and that others might be quicker or faster as well.

But Vibulenus had not realized in his heart of hearts that there would be a time when a task that was within his normal capacity would find him incapable because of exhaustion. He had expected—not planned, but *expected*—to run with the centurion in his arms, praying to Hercules that he would be fast enough to get clear of the tower's collapse.

Now that he was committed, he found that he was able to grip his burden only because his knuckles were locked. Vibulenus' lungs burned so that every breath flashed him an image of the flickering inferno above, and his legs were bladders of thin gelatine which were hard put to support their load—much less drive it at a run beyond the zone of destruction.

All sounds paused, as if the world were drawing in its breath.

Vibulenus did not have to look up to know what was happening, but he could no more forebear to do so than a falling man could fail to scream. The facing of the tower was coming down like a backdrop of painted fabric. The log whose weight had propped the stone

curtain was tearing through, causing the halves of the
wall to twist outward from the slow rending trajectories
which their scale made seem lazy.

How did a vole feel when the shadow of a stooping
hawk grayed the sunlight?

Human feelings had brought Vibulenus to the gates
of the Underworld. There they abandoned him to die
or be saved by the chill intellect of command which
spared no more emotion for the body it wore than for
any other.

The tribune's muscles worked to thrust him across
the gameboard. The sound of moving air and rock grinding lazily against rock seemed only a distant whisper,
but it covered all other noise completely as the wall
prepared to bury the ground at its foot.

Striding like a distance runner, the body in his arms
as disregarded as was his own, the tribune raced toward
the mobile gallery. The body of the defender who had
bounced off the roof—the only enemy whom Vibulenus
had seen within spearlength in all the months of
campaign—lay smoldering in his path. He tripped over
the corpse and plunged into the open end of the shelter, scarcely aware that he was no longer upright nor
that the first crossbar stripped the centurion from his
arms with a smashing blow.

Boiling like the surf, stone tumbled across the mobile
gallery.

The first impact was from the front, a block ricochet-
ing up from the dead archer whom it had crushed and
blended into the soil beneath. The end of the structure
lifted as if it had not been a massive burden for twenty
strong men some minutes before. As the gallery poised,
the remainder of the man-made rockslide worried it like
a shark with a gobbet of flesh too large to bolt entire.

Had the gallery been in vertical line with the collapsing wall, the sturdy shelter would have been ground to
splinters indistinguishable from the remains of anyone

who had chanced to be inside it. Because the thrust of
the hollow log kept the wall from tilting outward, the
stone fabric crumpled from the bottom when it lost
integrity and only then sprang out to cover the ground.

The upper reaches of the wall slipped downward
smoothly, even fluidly, while the layers at their base
exploded into a fury like that of a waterfall but fed with
the inertia of stone. The mobile gallery rushed back-
wards on the wave front, disintegrating as if its beams
were not of four-inch hardwood.

The roof of mud and wicker slid into the siege ramp,
compressed the fascines momentarily, then flexed a few
feet up the face of the stabilized earthwork. The stones
driving the gallery thundered above and across it. A
few of them jounced over the lip of the Roman works
and careened angrily down the corduroy surface, spreading panic among noncombatants and those legionaries
who thought they had gained a place of safety.

Though the stone was dark, the dust into which the
great blocks ground themselves rose in a pall as white
as wheat flour. It drifted instead of rising on a column
of heated air the way the smoke had done as flame
gutted the tower.

Beneath that choking, settling shroud of rock died
Gaius Vibulenus Caper, military tribune and one-time
Roman citizen.

The first thing he remembered was fire.

Not the tower, destroyed by its own defenses—though
after a moment he recalled that too, standing like a
bloody sacrifice against the pale blue sky.

But all his mind had room for at first was the way his
body burned as it was squeezed and rubbed to bits.
There had been no sound—or rather, the cosmos had
been entirely of sound and the false lights flashing in
his brain but not his eyes, so that he could not hear his
bones breaking in sequence. He had felt the fractures,

though, the momentary slippages and loosenings as one part after another gave up the struggle with inexorable forces.

There had been no pain, then: only fire in every cell.

His name was Vibulenus. He was a soldier, and he was dead.

Everything was muted gray, an ambiance rather than a light. It could have been part of the dream Vibulenus was having since there were no lines or junctions, but he could see his own limbs. Half afraid of even the attempt, he decided to wiggle his toes—and those appendages, deep scarlet like every part of his body that he could see, moved normally.

The motion did not even make the pain worse, but the pain was already fiercer than the tribune could have imagined at any time before this awakening.

There was something beneath him, a bench or a floor, but he could not tell where it joined the walls that must surround him. He tried to roll to his feet, screaming and scratching at himself in a fury of frustrated disbelief. He had been *somewhere* just before he became here, and he could remember nothing of that other place except that he wished he were back in it.

Heat spread over the surface of Vibulenus' body and, like a blanket on a fire, suffocated the pain. His skin rippled as tremors pulsed through the muscles beneath, but *that* feeling—though disconcerting—was in no way kin to the agony of moments before.

The tribune did not even realize that he had flopped back on the floor—there was no furniture in what must be the room—until he started to get up again. The tension that his muscles had released by trembling left them feeling normal, though extremely weak. The sensation of heat vanished as suddenly as it had come on, and the pain did not return. He stood cautiously.

Instead of a door opening, the wall in front of Vibulenus dissolved completely. The room had shape

and dimensions; it was a paraboloid little more than the
man's height and twice that on the longer horizontal
axis. One end was now open, like an egg topped by a
knife, and a man—well, a figure in a blue skinsuit who
was not the Commander or the Medic—lounged there
with an expression of mild interest.

"C'mon, walk," the figure said, making walking motions with two of the three fingers of either hand. "Do
they work or don't they? Let's see 'em move, cargo."

"Where am I?" Vibulenus demanded, walking toward
his questioner. He had heard the question clearly—the
words were in the flawless Latin spoken by everyone on
the vessel except the legionaries themselves. Many of
the line soldiers were of Oscan or Marsian origin and
had learned Latin as a second language. The tribune's
nurse had been a Marsian, and he still framed some
thoughts in that ancient Italian language himself. . . .

He *was* alive, and he was the man he had always
been. All he needed to know now was *where*, in the
name of all the gods, Gaius Vibulenus was standing at
the moment.

"Where *am* I?" the tribune repeated at barracks-
square volume, striding out of the egg-shaped room in
which he had awakened. The room beyond was the
yellow-orange of clean flames, a circular hall into whose
sidewall bulged eleven man-high convexities—the twelfth
was the opening through which Vibulenus stepped.

"Hey, hey there!" yelped the other, skipping back
from the tribune. "That's no way to treat the fella who's
saved your life, now. *Look* at yourself and think what ye
were before I put the new tissue on ye."

Vibulenus had not been angry, only disoriented—and
perhaps as dangerous as the figure in blue seemed to
think he was. That thought gave him pause. He wiped
his forehead with the back of his hand, grimacing away
the brief mixture of emotions he felt when he saw the

whole limb was stained a red which only time would fade.

"Look," the Roman said, feeling for the first time that he dominated a guild employee because of his greater size, "I'm not angry with you, my man, but I need to know where I am. Are you the new Medic?"

A tunic with a narrow red border flopped from the ceiling, making both parties jump and then relaxing the atmosphere.

"Naw, I'm the Pilot," said the blue figure, bending to pick up the tunic and toss it to Vibulenus. It was not an act of friendship, exactly, but at least a form of accommodation. "He gets the walk-ins, *I* drive the meatwagon and fetch home the ones like you."

He looked at the tribune and sucked in his lips to express wonderment. "Don't believe I *ever* brought in anybody like you exactly, though. Just *look* at yourself."

"You guide the blue turtle that chooses the dead?" Vibulenus asked. All his muscles were drawn tight as he pretended to concentrate on dressing. At least the linen garment would cover some of the terrible stain on his new flesh.

"Sure," said the Pilot. "The recovery vehicle, the meatwagon. This your first time back in it, fella?"

"I suppose so," Vibulenus said. That was as close as he could come at this moment to acknowledging what had just happened to him.

He shook himself and straightened, back proud and jaw thrust out. He *was* Gaius Vibulenus Caper, notwithstanding anything that might have happened to him in the immediate past. "These others, then," he said with an imperious sweep toward the convexities in the wall. The opening through which he had stepped was now a sideways dome, though there had been no sound or motion behind him. "They're more of us— soldiers—being, that is . . . cured?"

"Would be if you hadn't been the last," the Pilot

agreed. "Depends some on just what we're talkin' about, you know—clean cut or a smash, how many wounds and how long before pickup. With you—" he paused and sucked in his lips again. "Well, you know, fella, you were pretty near the bottom of the prognosis list on all counts. Took damn near a day to dig you out after the wagon located you. Bloody lucky, you are."

"Yes, I see," said Vibulenus' mouth alone, because his mind was busy filing data without looking at it. Now just now.

"All right, fella," said the Pilot. "We're gonna be in normal space till who knows when, given how you and the others got torn up. But there's some new twists in entertainment this run, so go on and get started."

A section of floor rotated a quarter turn and opened onto a helical ramp downward. The ramp's slope looked too steep for a walking man, but Vibulenus had learned long since that angles and dimensions on the vessel were not always what they seemed.

"You must be very skillful," said the tribune as his foot poised above the ramp.

The Pilot met his eyes for a moment. Then they slipped away. Without any further attempt to retrieve the facade of superiority, the blue figure said, "Skill? Are you kidding? I can juggle five balls in the air, d'ye know? *That* takes a lot more skill than watching a console to see that the hardware's doing its job."

"Which," he concluded bitterly, "it always is."

"But. . . ." Vibulenus said. The questions in his mind were too confused to articulate, but by drawing his right index finger the length of his left arm—hairless and colored Pompeian red—he communicated everything he needed to get out.

"Look, fella," the Pilot said with a sneer intended more generally than for the Roman who was its immediate target, "you couldn't whack off somebody's head with your bare hand, but you use a sword and it's no sweat, right?"

Vibulenus lifted an eyebrow in agreement, though his arm ached with the remembered effort of swinging his sword. Heads didn't just fall off, and an armored enemy was no mere log to be hacked at until he fell. "Go on," he said, waiting for understanding to come.

"Well," the Pilot continued, "live cargo like you could never handle it, but just about *any*body from a Class One planet—anybody who could feed himself—can run the medical repair station, *or* the ship. Blazes, me'n the Medic 'r crosstrained so if I croak in the middle of a Transit, that don't matter shit t' the guild except they don't worry about a pension. *We* don't get longevity treatments like you valuable *cargo* do."

"I see," said Vibulenus, who was beginning to do just that. "As you say, I'd best be getting back to my fellows."

He had been correct about the ramp. It felt like a level surface as he walked down it, though he slitted his eyes to avoid disorientation from the room he was leaving.

When Gaius Vibulenus stepped out of wall into the corridor beside the baths, there were over twenty soldiers nearby. He knew most of them at least by sight, now, and Decimus Pacuvius Semo—another tribune—almost walked into him.

"Gaius—"Semo began as both men threw their hands up a fraction of a second after they had stopped short of one another.

Semo's tunic bore the broad stripe of a senatorial family. He had been the legion's ranking tribune in Parthia, and in a way he still was—though here it only meant that he and Falco were the Romans usually in the Commander's entourage rather than roving among the line troops.

For all his heredity, Semo remained a plump, pleasant fellow who looked and acted more like a well-bred

freedman than a mover and shaker of the Empire. The
two men had always gotten along well together; it was
without hesitation that Vibulenus said, "Decimus, do
you chance to know where the centurion I was, you
know, in the gallery with—"

"I have to. . . ." the other tribune blurted. He turned
on his heel and strode away from Vibulenus with his legs
moving more crisply than they had ever managed during training.

Vibulenus blinked, looking at the man almost running from him. Then he noticed his own hands, stained,
and raised them to touch his face. The skin everywhere
he touched himself had the tenderness of having been
scraped too hard in the baths.

Everyone knew he was dead; they could not look at
him and doubt it. Men were shying from him with the
wordless distaste with which they would have stepped
around a pile of feces in the roadway.

Vibulenus swayed for a moment. Physically, he was
as weak as if he were between bouts of relapsing fever.
The mental control that kept him upright lapsed. If he
looked around him, he saw the faces of those who
refused to see him; if he closed his eyes, he would fall
as he might fall in any event.

On the corridor ceiling ambled beads of light, cool
and pure and non-judgmental as they guided Romans.
"Direct me to the centurion Gnaeus Clodius Afer," the
tribune demanded so loudly that several men glanced
at him in surprise.

"He is in the Recreation Room," said the ship in the
Commander's voice—or perhaps the Commander spoke
only through the vessel. "Please follow the—" a pause
"—yellow dot," which popped into existence so sharply
demarcated that the tribune's ears supplied an accompanying chime which did not really occur.

Head high, back straight, Gaius Vibulenus strode off
to find the man he hoped was still his friend.

* * *

The chance that brought Clodius out the portal of the Recreation Room was so unexpected that he recognized Vibulenus instead of the other way around. Of course, the tribune had been walking in open-eyed blankness in order *not* to take any details of expression on the faces of those with whom he shared the corridors.

The centurion was in animated conversation with two of the legionaries who had been in the assault force, Pompilius Niger and a file-closer named Helvius. He raised both his hands in a gesture, looked past them, and said, "W—Gaius! By Castor, you *did* fuckin' make it!"

The cry shocked Vibulenus and the two other legionaries. Helvius looked up and muttered a curse, while Niger only froze.

"I was. . . ." said Vibulenus.

Clodius caught his companions, one in either hand, and rasped in an undertone through his broad grin, "He saved your *butts*, boys." He stepped toward the tribune. When Helvius tried to resist the pull, his biceps went white at the fringes of the centurion's ferocious grip on his arm.

"Hello, sir," said Niger with the hopeful stiffness of a pupil who fears his response may have been the wrong one and thus bring him a beating.

"I was hoping I'd be able to find you—" said Vibulenus.

A large party of soldiers jostled their way down the corridor. They pushed past the tribune without remark or reaction because he was part of a group instead of a lone outsider.

"Hoped you'd catch me up on things," Vibulenus concluded.

Clodius released his companions, took a step closer, and threw his arms around Vibulenus. The centurion's ox-like strength was all, despite his good intentions, that kept him from springing away from the tribune at the instant of contact.

The younger man became light-headed as the breath was crushed out of his lungs. His knees, already quivering, gave way and he could scarcely clasp his hands behind the centurion's broad back.

He felt better than he had ever felt before. He was not just alive, he was a member of the human race.

"Man, you had me *worried*, sir," said Clodius as he stepped away but kept his palms on Vibulenus' back to steady him. "You weren't hardly breathing when we got all that rock clear and handed you up to the turtle."

He looked back over his shoulder. "That's true, ain't it, boys? He wasn't hardly breathing?"

Both of the other soldiers raised their eyebrows in cautious, silent agreement. Niger's expression became even more fixed.

Sometimes the best thing was for all parties to tell a lie and stick to it, thought the tribune—and bless a man like Clodius Afer who had enough experience to know what those times were. He slapped the older man's shoulder in camaraderie but also as a signal that he could stand unaided again.

"Yeah, Gnaeus," he agreed loudly, "it hurt like blazes when you were picking me up. I tried to swear at you but the words wouldn't come out right. Guess that's a good thing, since you were doing the best anybody could already."

"But I thought—" said Helvius. He rubbed his balding scalp with a hand whose back curled with hair.

"Say," said Vibulenus, only partly so that he could silence the puzzled legionary. "There was another fellow in the gallery with me, a centurion. I wonder if he made it?"

"*That's* how," Niger said, suddenly animated. "He was in the *gallery*, Gnaeus. That's why we were able to, you know, find him."

The centurion nodded in distracted agreement, but
his lips were pursed to form an answer to Vibulenus'
question. "Well you see, sir," he explained, "the shed
was broken up so bad I don't guess anybody thought of
it being there to begin with. So long as it lasted long
enough to give you the edge, that's fine . . . but there
wasn't anybody else down there the turtle thought we
need bother diggin' out, you know?"

"A friend of yours?" Niger asked, and he reached out
to grip Vibulenus forearm to forearm.

"Don't even know his name," the tribune said. The
corridor and his companions withdrew as his mind su-
perimposed the face of the grizzled veteran as he had
first and last seen it.

"Just a soldier doing his job," Vibulenus' lips said.
"Just like the rest of us."

"Well, you know," said the centurion, gesturing up
the corridor in the direction the three non-coms had
been headed when Vibulenus met them, "not everybody makes it, sir. *That* sure hasn't changed."

"No, I guess it hasn't. . . ," the tribune agreed while
he remembered the blue figure in his bodyguard of
living iron, prancing daintily toward victory as men
were crushed beyond locating on the ground before
him.

"Say, but in there," said Helvius with a nod to indicate the recreation room from which they were all
walking, "they've got bears and dogs fighting with spiked
gloves on. I like it a lot better than the one they had
last, the crabs and jellyfish."

"I didn't have gloves," said Niger. Both he and the
file-closer were glad to skirt the subject of which they
would be reminded until the stain faded from Vibulenus'
flesh. "I had a little short sword and a buckler. I think
it's only the bears have gloves."

"Glad you're back, sir," Clodius Afer murmured
from close to the tribune's ear. In a normal voice, he

continued, "You know, draggin' those rocks outa the wall I thought was the hardest work I *ever* did, but—"

He paused, because as he spoke the words he realized they were false. He had been so directed on the task that he hadn't been conscious of how hard the job was.

"Well, anyway," the centurion concluded lamely, "that wasn't a patch on gettin' them cursed blocks *off* you. Don't know what we'd have done if it weren't the shear legs was right there from slewing the log on target."

"All personnel will gather in the Main Gallery for an address by the Commander," said the voice of the ship. Up and down the corridor, soldiers started and missed a step or jerked their heads around in a reflexive search for the speaker. "Follow the red dot."

All the other guide beads blinked out, including the mauve one that Vibulenus assumed they were following according to a request made before he met the non-coms. The ceiling began to stream with red dots, moving at a comfortable pace in the opposite direction.

"Oh, bugger it all," snapped Clodius Afer, but he turned around in the middle of a stride because the habit of discipline was so strong.

"Couldn't we . . . ?" suggested Helvius, gesturing in the direction they had been going. He was a bigger and possibly stronger man than the centurion, but his deference was as much a matter of relative personality as rank.

"Come on," Clodius ordered, not harshly but with no sign that he was interested in a discussion. His stride swung his three companions into the broken, ground-covering pace of a route march. "We'll do their business and then we'll take care of ours. This is the army, after all."

The tribune opened his mouth to ask what "our business" was.

Before he could get the question out, Niger laughed

and said, "Well, guess the edge's off now, but yesterday the first time, it didn't take longer 'n to walk in the room and walk back. I'd figure the Commander could wait *that* long."

"Yeah," said Helvius, "but yesterday was the first time in a *long* time any of us had a woman. Today I want it to be worth waiting for."

Vibulenus tried again to speak. No sound came out. Although he continued to stride along with the others, his body had become as hot and weak as it had been in the first moments after his awakening.

The Main Gallery was familiar because the legion mustered in it before every battle. This was only the second time they had gathered for an address by the Commander, though, and recollections of that first assembly vibrated at the back of the tribune's mind. He was afraid to look at Pompilius Niger squarely in case that surfaced memories which the other, judging from his continued banter, had suppressed.

There had been losses. Vibulenus surveyed the room from where he stood at the front, just short of the stolid bodyguards and the deadline which they marked.

It was less evident during pre-battle musters when the room shook with the clash of men moving into ranks to don the equipment they had just been issued from otherwise featureless walls. You couldn't even estimate numbers under those conditions. Besides, the glitter and sway of equipment bulked out the sparseness of the troops wearing it.

Vibulenus had seen the returns. The legion had lost eighty-three men before the start of its operations against the fortress, and the fortress had not come cheap. His fingers kneaded the muscles over his ribs, whole to the touch . . . but he could not bring himself to look down and see the stain which only natural healing would leach from his flesh.

Lights glittered in the bulkhead behind the guards. The forward door, unlocked by its spinning hexagon, drifted open and the Commander minced through with steps as precise as the tailoring of his suit.

"Why," said Clodius Afer, "d'ye suppose *that* one—" he gestured, and for a moment Vibulenus misunderstood his subject as the Commander, not the door "—moves, and the rest, they just, you know, melt away and melt back in the wall?"

None of them had an answer. Before somebody decided to fill the gap with empty speech, the rear of the Main Gallery began to tilt up unannounced.

There was commotion this time, but no panic. Not only were the legionaries used to the rising floor from pre-battle musters, they also were familiar enough with the ways of the vessel in general that moving walls did not suggest to the crowd that it was about to be swallowed.

"Fellow warriors," said the Commander in his voice that everyone heard with a clarity equal to the polish of its Latin diction, "this is both a joyful and a sad occasion for me."

A door dissolved open in the left sidewall, so close to the tribune that he could have touched the pair of mace-bearing toads who clanked through it at the head of a short procession.

Helvius was startled into a blink. Niger froze and the centurion, with a curse of real fury, leaped backward and knocked down two other soldiers in his haste to put them between him and the bodyguards.

Vibulenus stepped in front of Niger and squared his shoulders against the grip of the creatures in articulated iron. He had no idea of what he thought he was accomplishing, and his muscles seemed to have the pellucid weakness of clear spring water.

The guards ignored him, save for the one who stepped fractionally to the side in order to avoid the tribune.

Behind the first two pairs of them, four other bipeds walked. Their lack of unison and crispness was disturbing to eyes that had for a long time seen only soldiers moving in the unconscious rhythm with which soldiers walk.

All four wore the blue bodysuits of guild employees, but none of them had familiar faces. That too was disturbing, at least to Vibulenus, who wondered how many others there were whose presence aboard the vessel he had not suspected.

Three of the newcomers were frail, of races similar to those of the Commander or Pilot. The fourth was a shambling, stooped figure as tall as the spearmen the legion had met in its first battle for the trading guild. He did not push a floating cart in front of him the way the others did, and his face had the same sheen that marked the Commander—but not the Medic or Pilot.

"Your skill under my direction has been noted with approval at the highest levels of my guild," continued the Commander as the procession, closed by another quartet of guards, moved toward him. One of the figures angled off to slide his cart against the corner of the side and end walls. The barrier did not react to the inanimate object, but the figure was keeping his hands carefully out of the invisible demarcator.

"In your case," said the Commander, "the guild has responded by providing you with females expensively modified to best suit your own physiology. I believe many of you have already sampled this reward."

The slight figure beamed coldly toward his audience, who cheered and howled furiously . . . though there were a few catcalls as well. Not everyone had found the lack of females to be a hardship.

The tall, stooped figure halted beside and slightly in front of the Commander, who went on, "My reward has been promotion into the merchant service much earlier than would have been the case if my record as your command⸱ had not been so exceptional. I will transfer to the trading vessel which has joined this one, and which has brought with it my successor in your command."

He gestured toward the tall figure. The *wrongness* of the Commander's hands was a shock even after it had become familiar. The new commander at least had the normal complement of fingers.

The remaining blue-clad employees—flunkies, slaves— had pushed their carts against the rear wall, in the center and at either corner. All three turned, watching the Commander. The line of guards remained as stolid as the bulkhead behind them.

The employee at the central cart spoke to the Commander. That is, his lips moved though no words could be heard.

The Commander straightened in obvious anger with his ears twitching, but he edged forward another six inches instead of blasting the underling with a response. He paused there, his eye on the employee. Only when that person gave an abrupt handsignal did the Commander continue, "Give your new commander and his successors the same skill and courage which you have displayed for me, fellow warriors. Then you will know that my guild will continue to make every effort for your comfort and security, no matter what the expense."

There was a hum in both the ship's structure and the—voice: the mechanism, whatever it was that carried words directly to the ears of each listener at whatever distance. Both the blue-clad officers turned with settled anger behind the sheen of their faces.

Before they spoke to the nearest flunkie, the hum scaled up through bat-high frequencies into inaudibility and the barrier began to glow.

Vibulenus had been mentally alone ever since he slid between Niger and an unmeant threat. The barrier's amber radiance brought the tribune back from that internal world in which he had been staying because much of him did not believe that he was really alive. The barrier was always a presence in the memory of the legionaries, but the only previous time that it was visible was when it snarled and converted Rufus into smeared color.

This soft light was monochrome and not immediately threatening—though, like a sleeping lion, it did not seem harmless either. The flunkies and the two officers were outside the amber curtain, but the score of bodyguards with their backs against the wall appeared to have been washed with bronze.

"I will now hand you over to my successor for a few words," said the Commander, returning to his audience with the false pleasantry—not so much oily as adamantine, unscarred by any vestige of real emotion—that always marked his contacts with the Romans he commanded. Had commanded.

The tall officer's head hung forward on his neck like that of a horse. He was not an ugly man. He was not a man at all, any more than the bodyguards were men, but it was in the voice of the Commander that he said, "Fellow warriors, I was pleased to be appointed to the direction of as exceptional a group as you. I will continue to follow the example of my able predecesor."

He nodded sideward at the smaller officer. The gesture was unexpectedly quick for a skull so large; it increased his resemblance to a horse.

But he was now the Commander.

The color of the barrier had shifted imperceptibly to a soft green, an ugly color that reminded Vibulenus of scum on the pond that caught the runoff from the sheep byres at home . . . at *home*.

"Now that the key to the barrier has been changed," the voice said as the tall officer's lips moved in a different rhythm, "we are free to depart on our next assignment. Because some of you sustained severe injuries during the course of the assignment just completed, we will remain in normal space longer than usual to ensure proper healing. This is only one more sign of the care which my guild shows for you."

There was a tiny pop in the ears of the assembly. The barrier faded the way iron loses its color as it cools—swiftly and without perceptible stages. The flunkies relaxed and began to slide their paraphernalia away from the bulkhead.

"That means," the tall officer concluded, "that you have all the more time to enjoy the comforts provided for you, including the females. You are therefore dismissed to your pleasures. I look forward to our association."

He stepped backward, through the barrier. Lights twinkled as the bulkhead door opened behind him.

To Vibulenus' surprise, the flunkies and the old commander did not exit through the barrier. Instead, they fell in behind pairs of shambling guards to return through the door that formed itself in the side of the gallery. The rear doors were already open and streaming with soldiers, more than willing to obey an order to enjoy themselves.

"They really *changed* the lock," said Clodius Afer, who had moved up to the tribune's side unnoticed at some point during the address. "He couldn't go through it himself now."

The old commander was noticeably careful to keep the armored bulk of a guard between him and even sight of the men who had been under his direction. When Vibulenus caught his eye, the slim figure ducked his head to ignore the contact. They were no more than a pace apart when the blue-clad officer skipped out of the room. The guard who had shielded him followed impassively.

"Bet *his* bosses don't need a sponge to wipe their ass so long as he's around," Clodius muttered.

"What do ye figure we do now, boss?" Helvius asked the centurion. The four of them were almost alone now at the front of the Main Gallery while the remainder of the legion shuffled out the rear.

"Now," said Vibulenus clearly, "we go see the women."

He wondered how badly the lower part of his abdomen had been injured, but nothing in the world would have caused him to lift the hem of his tunic now and see what was dyed red.

"Bad as when they first announced it," grumbled Clodius. "Line'd slimmed down by yesterday, and we'd be fine now 'cept for them making such a point in the assembly."

"Well, it moves real quick, the line does," said Niger.

That was true, for they had continued to advance at a walking pace even after they reached the end of the line of soldiers intent on using the women.

"How—" Vibulenus began. He meant to add, —'much farther are the rooms?' because the corridor curved and it was impossible to see the front of the line. But there were no landmarks on the vessel and possibly no fixed locations, so his companions could have no better idea than he as to how far they had yet to go.

Instead, the tribune said, "How many of the girls are there, then?"

The non-coms looked at one another with an unexpected furtiveness. "Sir," said the centurion with his eyes fixed on a point on the wall, "I couldn't rightly say, but it's a good number. Thing is, I like t' keep the lights down, you know, and—and anyway, it's the part of a woman that's the same that's important, not whatever little ways they may be different."

"That's so," said Helvius with a ponderous lift of his eyebrows. "By Apis and Osiris, that's *just* so."

"Look, just what—" Vibulenus said, falling into his tone of command without precisely intending to do so.

Clodius interrupted him, or at least thundered on when they began to speak together, with: "There, all right, *there's* the door."

The speed troubled Vibulenus. The line was moving as fast as men could pass two at a time through the open portal at the end of this corridor. Sure, horny soldiers . . . but not *that* horny by now, the men who had been alert for the three days he had spent in the egg-shaped room unconscious.

Unalive.

Thinking about that took the tribune's mind off immediate questions. His companions seemed happy enough to leave him in bleak silence, though Niger muttered something uncomfortably to the centurion.

The legionary directly ahead of Vibulenus stepped into a cubicle the size of those in the Sick Bay. Instead of a door closing, the opening dimmed as if curtained with silken gauze. The soldier did not move, but either the floor or the whole cubicle shifted to the left with him. Simultaneously, the identical unit in front of Clodius Afer slid to the right and the diffraction smoothed from the air. The cubicles were empty.

"Go ahead, sir," said Clodius Afer. He paused, then stepped off a half beat behind the tribune.

Vibulenus was familiar enough with the ways of the vessel that he did not expect to feel concern now, even though it was not the crib that he had expected. The cubicles' similarity to the Medic's array, and the baggage *that* memory brought with it, froze him into quiescence. Without the centurion's request, he might not have moved at all, though it was without fear that he obeyed what his mind took to be an order.

The screen that appeared behind the tribune did not affect the muted lighting he perceived within the cubicle. Instead of a feeling of motion sideways, the wall in front of him seemed to slide upward. He stepped into the room beyond, small but not the closet he had more or less expected. Military brothels were no more spacious than barracks accommodations.

The room was lighted by what was little more than a red dot in one of the upper corners, but it was enough to show that the woman reclining on her left arm was full formed and had hair long enough to spill over the edge of the couch. "Hello," she said in a throaty, feminine voice. "You must be one of the tribunes, huh? I'm Quartilla."

"I—" said Vibulenus. He glanced down at the striped hem of his garment, almost black in this light. It was a sign of social rather than military rank, but no member of the equestrian order would be serving as a common soldier. She was sharp, which made the business all the more confusing, and her Latin was far too good for anyone but a true Roman.

"You can come sit down with me if you like," Quartilla offered. She sat upright with a seemingly effortless sway that brought her knees around and lifted magnificent breasts while her dark hair swirled behind her. She patted the couch.

In a—business—like this one, serving the needs of men whose lust would turn to fury if frustrated by delay, there *couldn't* be leisure. There should have been a pimp outside the entrance of the crib, itself doorless to hasten the operation. Here of course there was no need to collect the money, a sesterce or two, in advance, but one of the toadfaced bodyguards should have hulked at the entrance to prevent jostling and to jerk out of the crib any soldier who made excessive demands on the whore or her time.

There was no jostling because there was no significant delay. And there was clearly no concern about time. . . .

"How can they do this?" Vibulenus asked as he seated himself gingerly beside the woman. His intellectual curiosity was competing with his body's requirements.

His full erection proved that he need have no concern
about that aspect of the repairs made to his body, and
the dim, colored light hid the stain on his flesh.

"Are there so many of you?" he continued, reaching
around the woman's shoulders. He was sure that if he
touched her breast as he first intended he would lose
at least his ability to hear her answer. She was wearing
a garment after all, a hard fabric that fit like a second
skin but which had enough irregularity to whisper when
the tribune stroked her hair against it.

"Time passes more quickly in these rooms," Quartilla
said, running a chubby hand over the skin of Vibulenus'
throat and the neck of his tunic. "Aging too, of course,
but that doesn't matter to you. Don't worry, we won't
be disturbed."

She kissed the tribune's mouth while her gentle hand
drew him to her. He cupped her breast—full, of course,
but not as heavy as expected—and wondered whether
he could get out of his tunic.

The breast was covered by minute hard nodules.

"W—," Vibulenus said. He fumbled for her other
hand, the one that was reaching under the hem of his
tunic. "Wait."

He took a deep breath—it had no effect on his sudden dizziness—and asked, "Quartilla. What are you
wearing?" With difficulty he raised his eyes to meet
hers.

"Nothing at all, sir," the woman said, smiling as she
moved her body again with amazing fluidity. Her knees
spread wide and she rocked back on the base of her
spine to lift her vulva. "What would you like me to
wear? Anything can be provided."

The light was faint, but it was so close to being a point
source that it threw a reticulated pattern across the
female's skin when she moved. That net of shadows was
caused by the tiny roughness the tribune had felt. Now

that his eyes were adapting, he could see that Quartilla was covered by—

Vibulenus leaped to his feet, instinctively ready to strike the female if she tried to hold him. "Light!" he shouted. "Give me *light*, curse you!"

The walls glowed white, relegating the red bead to merely a decoration in the corner. The lighting was normal and thus dazzling to the tribune at this moment, but he had no difficulty in seeing that Quartilla was covered with translucent scales.

The underlying color of her flesh was pale green. The scales gave it a metallic luster.

"You're . . . ," Vibulenus said. "You aren't. . . " He didn't really have the words to complete either attempt.

"I'm not of your race, no," said Quartilla, tucking her feet beneath her fleshy buttocks. The movement was utilitarian, not seductive, but it seduced the tribune despite himself because it was made with perfect economy and physical control.

She looked down at herself with dispassionate appraisal. "But I look a lot like I ought to, don't I? I didn't used to, you know. . . ."

"I thought you were a woman," Vibulenus whispered. The light he had demanded was a pressure squeezing him and turning each pulse into a hammer blow in his temples.

"Oh, I'm much better than that," said the female simply as she met his gaze again. Her eyes in the bright illumination were a little too large, a little too round—or were men's eyes different from women's, so that he was mistaking as racial details which were only a matter of sex? How long had it been since he had *seen* a woman?

"I can give you a good time, tribune," Quartilla went on, not boastfully but with the flat assuredness of Clodius Afer discussing his century. "You and any number of your friends, in ways that no one of your own race could manage."

She shrugged. The gestures lifted her breasts in brief arcs that damped themselves quickly. Her nipples were small and erect even now. "They aren't real," Quartilla said, touching one breast as she gave it a critical glance. "Weren't—what I was born with, you understand."

She met Vibulenus' eyes again, and added with a fierceness she had not before displayed, "A lot of this body's like that, different, and I know that they—that I don't *think* the way I remember I used to. But they started with good material, tribune, and *I* don't care— the Ssrange *eat* their prisoners, except us they sold to the trading guild. I don't care!"

"Yes, they bought us too," said Vibulenus, his mouth making conversation while in his mind memories of lust wrestled with awareness of the scaled monster before him. Neither image was a reality, but reality has no emotional weight.

"I think I'd better go now," he said, and part of him did indeed think that.

Quartilla shrugged sadly and said, "I understand," as if she possibly did. "The men," she added, stretching out one plump leg and staring at the toes as she wiggled them, "usually keep the lights down, you know?"

She looked up with as much hope as she was willing to chance having disappointed. "It could be really nice, you know? I'm here to make it really nice."

"Get me *out!*" shouted the tribune in desperation, clamping his balled fists against his eyes.

"If—" said Quartilla.

"*Out!*" Vibulenus screamed. He turned and tried to batter at the door through which he had entered. It was already open, and his fury carried him into a corridor.

He sprawled there, weeping, for some minutes. He was trying to remember home, but the closest he could come to that was yellow-gray dust blowing across the plains of Mesopotamia and within it the deadly shadows of Parthian archers.

Even that memory was better than the ones which crowded it: the tower collapsing with so loud a roar that the sound bludgeoned a man groggy before the stones ground the flesh from his bones; and a green thing with scales and a sad smile, which brought Vibulenus to full sexual arousal as he lay screaming in the corridor, avoided by the soldiers who hurried past on their own errands.

BOOK
THREE

THE
TWENTY-SEVENTH
CAMPAIGN

"Sir," said Clodius Afer, centurion pilus prior and leader of the Tenth Cohort, "I think we've got a problem. Three of the boys've deserted."

"Fuck," said Gaius Vibulenus. He ducked his head and shoulders into the water. The chill shrank his steaming flesh away from his body armor, and the current sent thrilling tendrils of water down his backbone.

Either the stream or the news cooled the tribune more than he expected, because when he raised himself his torso was shivering spasmodically. The swollen yellow sun that had baked them throughout the afternoon's bloody work seemed now to glance off his breastplate with no more power to warm.

"What do you mean?" Vibulenus demanded as his palms scrubbed fiercely at his unlined, boyish cheeks and forehead. "There isn't any place to desert to that the crew won't find them."

The stream was so clear that the soldiers' boots could be seen against the gravel bottom. The spillage dripping from the tribune's face left whorls on the current, grime and sweat, red blood and most especially blood the color of drawn copper. The corpse against the bank, its arm tangled with a root, had bled out so completely that the water tumbling past was as pure as that upstream.

"Well, you know Helvius, sir," said the centurion. "He gets an idea and you can't shake him out of it." He looked around instinctively to see who might be within earshot. No one was. Vibulenus was almost alone in using the stream to wash instead of struggling for position at one of the water carts. Habit. . . . The carts were always there after a battle, so there was no need to search for local water—or even to remember the creek you battled your way across an hour before.

"Pollux and Castor," the tribune muttered. He was too exhausted to control his bouts of shuddering, and he felt that his body was on the verge of wracking itself to pieces. "Let's get, get out of here," he said and began to walk carefully out of the stream, feeling flat stones slide beneath his hobnails.

Clodius offered the younger man an arm in something more than comradeship; though the gods knew, the centurion had been in the hottest part of the fighting. Even if unwounded, he should have been weary to death.

Perhaps he was, but his job wasn't over after all—and neither was the tribune's.

Together the soldiers slogged to the bank. Pompilius Niger, who had taken Sixth Century when Clodius got the cohort, was waiting there trying to look as though he were not a conspirator. His hand helped Vibulenus up the knee-high step that had momentarily looked insuperable.

He *hadn't* been this wrung out when he stumbled into the creek to cool off. He'd have said that he was getting old if his reflection in the water did not give the lie to that thought.

But he was getting old. His mind knew that, even if his body didn't.

"All right, what happened?" the tribune said, slapping the front of his armor to shake out dribbles of water trapped between the bronze and his chest. His studded leather apron had a clammy feel as it brushed his thighs. Whatever had possessed him to splash back into the creek?

Most of the enemy who had fallen in the water had been washed away by the current. There was a straggling rank of them just up the bank and beyond it, those who had stumbled at the edge of safety or paused when they thought they had gained it.

There was no safety for those in flight from the legion. Bare backs drew swords the way iron filings slid toward a lodestone.

"The sinkhole where we hid last night?" Clodius said while Niger pursed and unpursed his lips.

"Go on," prompted the tribune.

The Commander, who had six limbs—arms or legs as he chose to use them at the moment—had sent the Tenth Cohort on a roundabout course to what he had chosen for the battlefield. It had been a nervous journey, with no local guides and only the Commander's word that the hostile force would not ambush them.

The Commander would lie in an instant, for any reason or for none at all. Vibulenus knew that; but he also knew that the guild would not throw away a tenth of a legion's strength. The vessel itself and the floating, sentient paraphernalia it sent out in the aftermath of each victory proved that the Commander could have the absolute knowledge of the enemy which he claimed.

That put him one up on Crassus; and they, the survivors of the legion, weren't the men Crassus had led to disaster either—not any more, not for a long time.

"There was that cave off the back of it," the centurion was saying. "Some locals tried to hide there with their herd when we come up."

"And I told you to keep to blazes out of it," the tribune agreed. "Some of those places go down forever."

The peasants herded leggy beasts that looked more like donkeys than sheep. Their terror when the cohort blocked passage from the sinkhole was evident in the way they grunted and flicked their ears at one another, but they had nothing to fear.

The soldiers of the enemy were squat figures, somewhat shorter than the Commander's bodyguards but built along the same lines. The peasantry was nowhere near as bulky, either from race or from diet, and some of the females might even have been attractive if you got used to ears the length of a man's hand.

"He's been wanting to get away for a long time," Niger interjected. "He even said it to you, sir. He didn't think it was leading anywhere."

"Did he figure he was going to be consul if we got back home, then?" Vibulenus snapped.

His anger was always close to the surface now. Here it had the advantage of sending a surge of warmth through his shaking limbs. The willowy shrubs fringing the creek had been trampled flat or leafless during the fighting. Their bare silhouettes marked but did not block the huge sun which was bloating into a red oval on the horizon.

"If we were home," the tribune said, arguing with himself rather than his listeners or even his memory of Decimus Helvius, "he'd have died on campaign, or on a farm. Now, well, there's fewer choices but the payoff doesn't have to be anytime soon." He looked up from the hands he had clenched in front of him.

"He could have raised sons," said Clodius simply.

"Well, he can't fucking do that here either, can he?" the tribune blazed. "If we ever get back somewhere I *recognize* or *some*body recognizes, then we'll talk about ransom or maybe even running. But not *here*."

The stars above them as they bivouacked in the sinkhole the night before had proved to anyone who cared to understand that they were very far from home indeed.

The battle had gone according to the Commander's desires and perhaps even his plan—though probably

not. The hostile force had marched straight toward the
sinkhole, apparently intending to laager a camp there,
instead of arraying themselves against the nine cohorts
which were counterfeiting the entire legion.

That wasn't by plan either: the enemy was moving in
utter ignorance. Their scouting was quite as abysmal as
that which led Crassus' army, and so many Roman
armies before his, into disaster. Though Vibulenus had
lived through a major intelligence failure, it was not
until he became used to working for the guild that he
realized how valuable knowledge of hostile dispositions
could be.

That didn't help when you were in command of four
hundred men, and almost ten thousand heavily-armed
opponents were headed for you.

"I thought I saw Helvius during the fighting, though,"
the tribune said in puzzlement. He fingered his dripping scalp and remembered that he needed to pick up
his helmet, tossed to the stream edge when he decided
to duck himself. No need to look for his shield: it had
been literally hacked to splinters by the swords and
axes of the enemy.

"Oh, he wouldn't desert *us*," said Niger in real surprise. "Nor Grumio and Augens neither. But afterwards, I saw them jogging back toward the sinkhole and
I knew what that meant." He paused, then added, "I
was looking for bees, you know."

"That's who the others are, then?" Vibulenus asked
struggling with the pin under his right shoulder that
would unlatch his body armor. It caught with an inch or
more still within the interlocked tubes of the breast and
back plates. "Grumio and Augens? And you think they'll
try to hide in the cave in the end of the sinkhole."

"Yeah, that's right," said Clodius.

"Here, I'll get it," said Niger, reaching for the recal-
citrant pin with short, strong fingers. His hands and

forearms were drenched with alien blood that fell deeper
into orange and red as it dried and scaled away.

"Leave it," said Vibulenus, batting away his friend's
hand when he had meant only to block it with his own.
"Let's go find the cursed fools before the crew decides
it has to."

The little Summoners with blue beacons atop were
beginning to drift over the field, calling men back to
the ship. There would be no immediate alarm, but the
sight was enough to spur the trio back in the direction
from which they had marched that morning in battle
order. Vibulenus' legs were weary, but his arms were
so weak that they flopped like wooden carvings unless
he made a conscious effort to control them.

The enemy's course had eliminated any chance of
striking their army from the rear while they were heavily engaged with the rest of the legion. To cower in the
sinkhole would have meant massacre by missiles hurled
down unanswerably from the rim.

Vibulenus had marched the cohort out to a hillock
with enough wood to shade them. They stood there,
bristling like a bronze-flanked hedgehog, while the hostile force broke against them in furious waves. The
legion, double-timing to the clash of weapons regardless of the heat, smashed into the attackers' rear with
nine times the force and a hundred times the effect that
the Commander had planned.

The tortoise which chose the badly wounded and the
repairable slain was still hovering over the hill the Tenth
Cohort had defended.

"They wanted us to come along, too," Niger blurted
suddenly.

The older centurion struck him a fierce blow in the
ribs with the heel of his hand, driving the breath out
despite the leather-backed mail shirt. "Shut *up* and
move," he growled.

"Why didn't you?" the tribune asked, pretending

that he had not felt an impulse to slap both the centurions for hiding the plan from him. *They* of all the men in the legion should have known better!

"Sir," said Clodius Afer in the embarrassment the tribune had hoped to spare him by ignoring the dereliction, "we thought we'd talked 'em out of it. And you had a lot on your mind just then. We all did."

"Don't know what I could've done to change their minds if you couldn't," Vibulenus said. Nor did he, now that he thought about it, which made his initial fury all the sillier. He grew angry too easily, now. He hadn't always been like that.

The skirted another straggling pile of bodies, all of them hostiles when alive. The victims wore helmets and most had, besides their ironbraced shields, body armor: scales sewn to leather, or a plate (often cast in a fanciful shape, bestial or geometric) strapped to their broad chests. The few who fought naked did so as a statement of courage like the Celts, charging at the front of the army and gnashing their teeth as if they intended to gnaw through the Roman line.

The enemy had been ill informed and ill commanded— all the chiefs, bright with gold armor and capes of brilliant scarlet, had been in the front rank, facing the lone cohort, when the remainder of the legion began butchering the force from behind. But the enemy had never been negligible, soldier by soldier, and there was Death's own plenty of them.

Without the volleys of javelins which fouled their shields and dismayed troops unfamiliar with missiles of such weight and accuracy, the native army might even have been able to reform after the first shock had worn off. It would have been a tough fight for the legion; and just possibly a losing fight.

Sometimes Vibulenus speculated in the darkness about what would happen if they were ever defeated.

The enemy's baggage train stood where the troops

had abandoned it to attack the Tenth Cohort. A few legionaries were poking through it, from curiosity or even a desire for loot. Some habits were too deeply ingrained to be eradicated by repeated proofs of their pointlessness.

The teamsters and other noncombatants among the baggage were of a physical type with the peasantry. They had so little initiative that they had simply waited, with no attempt to laager their wagons, when the soldiers boiled out of the train to attack the waiting Romans. They seemed scarcely less apathetic than the gangs of neck-chained slaves attached to the back of some of the wagons.

The sinkhole was half a mile from the battle site. Vibulenus had not noticed the distance when he marched the cohort out in close order after a chilling discussion with the pickets who had rushed in breathless with news of the enemy. Everyone had been too frightened— *he* had been too frightened—to feel fatigue.

It was a staggeringly long way back; he regretted not taking Niger's bloody-handed help in stripping off his body armor. "Publius," he said as thinking about the hands cast his mind much farther back along the path of his history with the junior centurion, "if you just possibly *did* find some bees and some honey, how in the name of Faunus do you suppose you'd get it back in the ship? Or them back?"

There was a commotion behind them in the baggage train, cause for a glance over the shoulder but not concern. Several vehicles from the merchant vessel, looking like slightly larger versions of the water carts, were gliding among the wagons. They carried half a dozen passengers apiece, men or not-men of a variety even wider than that of the legion's successive commanders. Each individual was clad in monochrome, but the selection of single colors ran the gamut from violet to a red so dark it was nearly black.

"Oh, it wouldn't be hard, Gaius," said Niger as rolling ground dropped them out of sight of the train and the field. They were not tribune and centurions at the moment; and Niger, too, was happy to return to the terms of boyhood.

"You see," he explained, so intent on his subject that he would have stepped into a flat-stemmed, spikey bush had not Clodius steered him aside, "the guards at the Medic's check, *they* don't care about anything 'cept fighting or pushing in line."

"Or," Vibulenus said tartly, "if somebody tried to slip contraband into the ship proper after they've gone through the Sick Bay. I've seen them collar people doing that, and sometimes it meant another trip through the booth to get fixed up."

"Niger, if you *don't* watch where you're going," the pilus prior interjected sharply, "you'll fall down the fuckin' side. And by Apis' dick, I'll let you lie there. If you can't talk and walk at the same time, shut the fuck *up*."

"Sorry, sir," the junior centurion answered, abashed. They had reached the sinkhole. While the trail winding down its side was occasionally wide enough for three or four men abreast, it was never regular enough to be safe for someone talking over his shoulder instead of keeping his eyes to the front.

"Here, I'll lead," said Vibulenus as he stepped ahead of his companions. He was feeling human again, tired but human. The leather backing of his body armor was clammy and beginning to chafe. As he walked down the steep incline, he tried again to pull the locking pin. It came without effort, and he flopped the breastplate wide against its left-side hinges.

"Yessir," said Niger and cleared his throat. "I mean, sure, Gaius, that's right—they grab guys with contraband. But not because *they* see it but because they're told about it."

"The Medic?" Clodius put in from the end of the line where he was apparently able to hear well enough.

"Naw, he doesn't care," the younger centurion replied. "No, I figure it's the whole ship, you know? *It* watches. But all it sees is metal, so you try to get in with gold, you get grabbed. *Lots* of guys bring in jewels, though, sometimes stuck up their ass but even open in their hands."

Vibulenus hadn't known that. He paused at the bottom of the trail to strip off his armor and prop it against a rock, watching Niger with interest. It seemed to be his day to learn unexpected things about the men he helped to lead but did not command.

"Sure," said Clodius, sealing the statement without room for doubt as he followed the others into the lumpily-flat bottom of the sinkhole. "But all that crap disappears when we march out after the next muster. They must, I dunno, give everything aboard a real goin' over whenever we're out. So it's really just there till we go into Transit. Whatever the fuck *that* is."

"But sometimes we got a couple months aboard before that, right?" said Niger. "That's time for mead to get enough of a bite to be worth doing, you know? I don't mean it'll be the vintage you bring out when your son gets married, sure . . . but it'll be mead, and that's all I'm after. Just something, you know. To remind me of home and all."

Vibulenus was picking his way along the track to the cave at the best pace possible under the circumstances. They had lost direct sunlight even before they stepped within the sinkhole, and now the sky above, though clear, was beginning to take on a rich maroon tinge that scattered very little sun into the natural pockmark.

Ground water had dissolved a pocket in limestone. When that bubble in the rock had reached the surface, or an earthquake had shaken the area, the roof had collapsed to leave a sheer-sided valley a quarter mile in

diameter and a hundred feet deep. The channel cut by
the water at one end still ran down into the earth,
probably as deep as the stratum of limestone itself.

The floor of the sinkhole was covered with debris
from the roof and windblown loess trapped by the
sides. Rock fragments, gorse-like vegetation, and quan-
tities of droppings from the animals corraled here made
the footing difficult even before the trio of Romans
reached the cave.

A hundred yards down its sloping throat, the cave
would be pitch dark even at noon on Midsummer's
Day.

"*Helvius!*" the tribune shouted. The trio could be
anywhere, not even within the cave. He stumbled forward. Breaking your neck here in the darkness might
be as effectively fatal as having your spine hacked through
by a slope-browed swordsman. "Helvius! Will you at
least come out and talk to somebody with *sense* before
you do this!"

"Careful here, sir," said Niger, whose night vision
seemed to be better than that of Vibulenus. The throat
of the cave dropped away slickly, but broad steps had
been roughed into one side. The other side. The sky
still looked bright if you looked at it directly, but that
was by contrast with the lumpy blackness of everything
on solid earth.

There didn't seem to be any peasants around—the
sound and smell of their herds was unmistakable—but
that made little difference. When the legion was to
work with local auxilliaries, the men mustered out with
the ability to speak the necessary languages as long as
they kept their helmets on. Here they had been operat-
ing alone.

So, for that matter, had the enemy: a force of heavy
infantry moving across the face of the land more as
conqueror than defender. The politics of what they did
at the guild's behest sometimes bothered Vibulenus,

but he never had—the legion never had—enough information to decide whether or not they really agreed with the choices the guild had made.

For that matter, he had never been sure why they were invading Parthia. It had something to do with the Kingdom of Armenia, he'd been told, a Roman ally . . . or with rivalry between Crassus and the partners in his political machine, Caesar and Pompey, if you listened to other opinions. He'd been scared green himself— gods! but that had been a long time ago—but he'd have been just as scared if he were being called up because Hannibal was at the gates of Rome again. Nothing political in fear.

His father might have had doubts about the expedition, but the Vibuleni had made a very good thing out of farming taxes in the Province of Asia and weren't the people to decry military adventurism in the East. Besides, a family of their stature had a duty to the Republic, to act as exemplars for lesser folk in taking arms to Rome's glory.

The tribune's fingers caressed the bone hilt of the sword which he had learned to use so much better after he left Rome's service than he ever had before.

As for the "lesser folk," the common legionaries and the non-coms who had fought their way up from that status—so far as Vibulenus could recall, their major concern had been whether the King of Parthia drank from gold cups or hollowed jewels, and which would bring more from the merchants who trailed the army to buy its loot. After a time, they all had more pressing concerns—heat and thirst and the arrows that fell like rain—but those were not political either.

And besides, by then it was too late to matter.

"Decimus!" called the pilus prior, a hand on both Niger and Vibulenus to keep them from trying to descend dangerously farther. The cave had only a slight average slope, but descents when they came tended to be abrupt. "Marcus, Gaius. C'mon and talk for a minute so we don't fall and kill ourselves, all right? It's just me, Niger, and Gaius Vibulenus—you know *he's* all right. No tricks, just a little talk that can't hurt nothing."

There was a clink from the darkness, metal on metal, and a murmur of voices made ghostly and unintelligible by the acoustics of the cave. The tribune opened his mouth to call further demands, but Clodius forestalled him by touching his cheek with the hand already resting on his shoulder.

The next sound was the one they had come to hear, the scrape of hobnails on slippery rock and the muttered curses of the men climbing back up the slope.

"A bull to Hercules for this," said the tribune under his breath. Though the problem hadn't exactly been solved yet. "I don't like to think how the Commander'd react if he heard about a desertion."

They thought the first silent flash was heat lightning, but then the little Summoner floated beneath the rim of the sinkhole and the light spinning on its top threw patches of blue against the walls instead of the empty sky.

"Return at once to the ship," it called, its voice faint but recognizably speaking in the tones of the Commander. The illuminated swatches of rock grew fainter and broader as the beam's rotation slid it along more distant curves of the wall, then snapped back to brighter immediacy.

"Return at once to the ship," the Summoner ordered as it continued to descend toward the mouth of the cave.

"Helvius, *wait!*" the tribune cried as the faint blue reflection let him run forward down the slope. The figures he glimpsed thirty feet in front of him disappeared around a bend of the water-gouged corkscrew into the limestone. The forearm of one of the men was bandaged; the white fabric flashed like a flag charged with the dark smear of seeping blood.

"Return at once to the *bzzrk*!" said the Summoner as Clodius Afer drew and cut at it with a single motion and perfect timing. He was a good man with a javelin, thrust or thrown, but with a sword the pilus prior showed nothing less than artistry.

The little egg looked metallic, but it crushed like a pastry confection when Clodius caught it with his swordedge. The blue light rotating on top blinked off, but there was a bright flash of red that seemed to come through, not from, the casing of the Summoner. It crumpled to the ground, leaving behind it a glowing nimbus and a smell that combined sharpness with something that made the soldiers gag.

"It's all *right*, boys!" the tribune shouted, plunged into darkness with the memory of a shadowed drop-off to halt him. Ahead of him faded the clattering boots of the deserters, more familiar with the footing or more reckless. "We've shut it—"

Not sound but a light froze Vibulenus' tongue. Something drifted over the edge of the sinkhole the way the Summoner had, but this was huge and all ablaze with light as pitiless as the spear which had reached for Vibulenus' eyes when he was a frog.

"Stand where you are!" ordered Rectinus Falco in a voice amplified into thunder.

As an afterthought or a false echo from the screen of light, the Commander added, "Gaius Vibulenus Caper, Gnaeus Clodius Afer, Publius Pompilius Niger: remain where you are or you will be counted among the number of deserters and treated accordingly."

The harsh light glinted from sweat and bright metal on Vibulenus and his companions. They looked at one another because at first the lighted object was blinding. The notched edge of Clodius' sword winked. There were steaming black smears across the blade where

something like tar had been carved from the belly of
the Summoner.

Moving slowly, though he could not be surreptitious
in the glare that bathed him, the pilus prior shifted the
weapon behind him and began to wipe the steel firmly
against his mail shirt to clean it. That probably wouldn't
do much good, since the remains of the little device lay
smoldering at his feet. Still, Clodius Afer had spent
long enough in the army—and in life—to know that the
best way out of an awkward situation was to deny that it
had happened—even if you'd been caught with your
cock rammed all the way home.

The object descended as regularly as if it were connected to a gear train instead of moving with a drifting,
wind-shaken look as had the Summoners and even the
water carts. The light blazed from its whole outer surface, twenty feet at least in length and broad though not
particularly high sided. Because the light was so extensive, it smothered the shadows that it would have thrown
if it were a point source of the same intensity. The
shadings that gave life and individuality to a face, even
in the bright sun, were erased. The three men looked
like a flat painting of soldiers caught in the uncertainty
that precedes death.

The object touched the ground, or came within a
finger's breadth of touching, just outside the cave mouth.
Vibulenus climbed up the path to rejoin his companions. Flow rock, limestone dissolved and redeposited
by water, gleamed in opalescent beauty on the upper
surfaces of the cave, but the stone had been rubbed
dull generations ago wherever it was within reach of a
hand.

Helvius and his companions were gone, but the red
transverse crest from a centurion's helmet lay on the
cave floor near the twist that carried the cavity out of
sight.

Their eyes adapting (and reflections from neighboring

stone surfaces) gave the Romans a view of the object,
the vehicle, that had caught them. It was open-topped
and held half a dozen figures—two of them from the
Commander's bodyguard, unmistakable in their hulking, iron-clad bulk.

Vibulenus passed the non-coms with two further crisp
steps toward the vehicle. He braced as if reporting to a
consul on parade and said, "Sir! We believe that three
of our fellows were cut off by the enemy and took
shelter in this cave. I beg a delay of the recall order for
myself and the subordinates who are here under my
orders so that we can rescue men who were wounded
and confused. Until the third watch, sir, if you please."

Midnight would be time enough. Ten minutes more,
by Hercules, would have been enough without the
Summoner's interruption.

The light dimmed abruptly. The vehicle's rounded
sides still glowed brightly enough to illuminate the
ground nearby with the intensity of a full moon, but the
light was no longer a barrier intended to blind a marks-
man taking aim. Rectinus Falco got out by swinging his
legs over the side.

The tribune with the Commander was dressed for
parade: helmet and breastplate polished, the straps of
his leather apron freshly rubbed with vermilion, and his
crest combed to perfect order. He didn't look as though
he had just survived a battle, and in a way he had not.
Falco had accompanied the Commander during this
engagement as with all those in the past.

The last of the horses had disappeared—not died, at
least not on the ground—ages ago, so many operations
in the past that Vibulenus could not remember which
one. There were always enough snarling carnivores to
mount the Commander's entourage, so Falco rode one
of those and rode it with the same panache that he had
shown from early childhood with horses.

And now he rode with the Commander in one of

the guild's incomprehensible vehicles. Not very different from riding in the ship itself, perhaps, but it was different in Vibulenus' mind—and in Falco's, he was sure.

"Throw down your weapons," the shorter tribune ordered. "They'll be gathered up later."

Falco either read something or thought he did in the motionless figure of Clodius Afer, because he then added at a higher pitch, "None of you act like *fools*, now. Remember that there aren't any restrictions on the guild's weapons now that the battle's been won."

"Yeah, now that we won the fucking battle," said the pilus prior in a voice as emotionless as the one he would have used to describe a brick wall.

Vibulenus had thought the non-com might set his sword down carefully in what amounted to an act of dumb insolence. Instead, Clodius tossed the weapon some distance behind him in the cave where its smeared, tell-tale blade clanging out of sight. He was not a man who stopped thinking in a tight place.

The tribune unbuckled both his crossed waist belts, the heavy one that carried the sheathed sword and the slimmer belt with the dagger which he could not, at this moment when it was inconsequential, remember even having drawn in battle. He would hate to lose the sword, though, sharpened often enough to change its balance and as uniquely natural in his hand now as the feel of his hair when he ran his fingers through it.

He wrapped the belts around the sheathed weapons as he heard the harness of the two centurions thud to the ground behind him. "Here," he said, offering the bundle hilts-first to the other tribune. "You take it."

"Not *me*," Falco said, kicking the side of the vehicle as he started backward. "Just *drop* it."

The lighting changed again. This time the vehicle's sidewalls became blankly metallic while its interior was suffused with light that seemed to cling instead of emanating from a discernible source. Besides the blue-suited Commander and his pair of guards in the stern, there were two—persons. One looked to be a man; the other had six limbs like the Commander himself. They wore one-piece garments of bright yellow which matched the color of the vehicle now that it was no longer a source of white light.

"I think you can keep your sword, Gaius Vibulenus Caper," the Commander said with the air of unctuous paternalism that was always a part of him—whether he had four limbs or six, and whatever the features of the face behind his mask of air. "You won't do anything foolish. Get in the wagon, now—all four of you."

Falco winced to hear himself lumped in with his rival and the two non-coms, but he obeyed as sharply as if he had been spurred. The motion he made to board, scissoring one leg over the side, then the other, provided a model that Vibulenus could follow more easily for the greater length of his legs.

Vibulenus boarded without the least outward hesitation, because he did not want his companions to make any mistaken moves. The two guild employees in yellow held lasers like the one that had fried a shield in an instant's discharge.

There was no problem. Clodius grunted as he came over the side, and Niger was too close behind him to take the hand his senior then turned to offer.

Vibulenus sat down because Falco did. The seats were three abreast, backless, and to the tribune's first thought so uncomfortable that they must have been designed for bodies not of men.

He seated himself facing the Commander, but even as he opened his mouth to continue his argument the seat began to shift beneath him. The hard surfaces flowed, shaping themselves to his buttocks, and a support extended itself to midback with an animate smoothness that almost caused him to leap to his feet screaming.

What saved Vibulenus from that and the possible overreaction of guild employees with lasers was his awareness that the same thing was about to happen to the centurions—*his* men. "Clodius," he snapped, "Niger—the seats will move when you sit down. Don't be alarmed." By speaking the words as a duty and as a tribune, he was able to restrain his body's instinctual terror before his intellect could overcome it.

Vibulenus looked back over his shoulder at the non-coms, and by that chance caught a glimpse of his rival in unguarded rage and frustration. Falco knew about the seats—of course; and of course was waiting for them to humiliate Vibulenus in front of friends, enemy, and the Commander.

Vibulenus did not smile, but it was with the air of boxer coming off a victory that he faced the Commander again and said, "Sir, these are valuable men, a centurion and two front-rankers. If you'll let us go after them with a torch—a, ah, your lights would frighten them more, I'm afraid—then I'm sure we can have them back aboard the ship in only a few hours."

"They're deserters, Gaius Vibulenus," said Falco. "The Commander knows that, of course. And if he didn't, I would have told him because it's my duty to the guild to inform him of what's going on in the legion."

The vehicle they sat in began to rise with such rock-like steadiness that it seemed the wall of the sinkhole was dropping away while they remained fixed to the ground. The lighted interior made it easier to forget what the vehicle was doing and concentrate on the Commander, whose six limbs were curled before him like the petals of an unopened rose. The face behind the shimmer could almost be that of a caterpillar. . . .

"Sir," Vibulenus said, "it was a hard fight, a *cursed* hard fight, and that's sent more people than these three off their heads before. If—"

The Commander waved the tribune's earnestness to

silence with the rosette of six fingers terminating one of his middle limbs. "My guild expects losses, military tribune," the alien figure said in perfectly-modulated Latin. "They expect me to minimize them, that's all."

The vehicle lifted vertically over the rim of the sink-hole and continued to climb at a 45° angle while the keel remained parallel to the ground. The wind past the tribune's face told him what must be happening, but he kept his eyes resolutely fixed on the Commander. Tight places did not especially concern Vibulenus, but heights were another matter.

"I'm rather glad this happened, in fact," the Commander went on calmly. "We were bound to have trouble at some point, when it sank in that you really wouldn't be going home. This incident is about the right scale—if there were a hundred of them, I suppose we'd have to do something different. And they have a better hiding place than any of the rest of you can imagine finding."

Vibulenus was dizzy. His mind was screaming, *never see home!* and trying to force its way out of the body that held it and smothered it like honey trapping a fly. *Never* see *home*.

"I suppose they thought they couldn't be seen through the rock?" said the Commander, speaking past Vibulenus toward the centurions behind him.

"We don't think they were planning anything," said Vibulenus sharply, saved again from his own terrors by the need to keep his subordinates from damning themselves by a thoughtless word. "Probably it was spur of the moment—head blows during the battle, dizziness from heat."

He was shivering and clammy as he spoke, babbling to roll through the multiplex punishments that his mind imagined the guild using on the deserters. "But of course, we wouldn't know or we would have prevented this trouble."

Falco snickered.

"No trouble, military tribune," said the Commander as the vehicle halted in the air.

They were within twenty feet of a similar craft, dark except for orange lights bow and stern like the lanterns of ships sailing well-traveled routes. In the glow from the vessel in which he rode, Vibulenus could see that there were half a dozen yellow-clad forms in the other vehicle.

The interior lighting faded or was replaced by an image like those of the mythic battles in the Recreation Room. There was no fantasy in this, however: Decimus Helvius crouched within walls of stone which were hinted rather than being fully limned. He held a naked sword in his hand, and the expression on his face was the stony determination the tribune had glimpsed that afternoon when the enemy, shouting in anticipated triumph, charged up the hill at the Tenth Cohort.

Behind Helvius squatted Grumio and Augens. The former's left biceps was bandaged—his shield must have been hacked off his arm during the fighting. Augens had no obvious injuries, but he had set his helmet between his knees and was squeezing the bronze with a fixed intensity that suggested he was in pain.

Neither of the common legionaries was looking toward Helvius or the open end of the passage. After a moment's surprise, Vibulenus remembered that none of the deserters could see anything in the lightless cave.

It could have been a trick; but it was easier to believe the trading guild could see through stone than that it would bother with trickery so pointlessly elaborate.

"No trouble," repeated the Commander in oily satisfaction. "The rest of your fellows are gathered in the Main Gallery to watch the demonstration, but I thought you might as well see it with us."

The image of Helvius turned and said something unheard to his companions.

"You should realize, Gaius Vibulenus Caper," continued the Commander's voice, "that if you had not proved yourself to be an unusually valuable asset of my guild, you would be viewing the demonstration from the ground where we picked you up. But *no* asset is so valuable that it will be permitted a second lapse in judgment as great as the one you made tonight."

The voice laughed. Technically, the laugher was "correct," as the Commander's diction always was; but instead of humor, the sound had the mechanical hollowness of blood dripping from the neck of a slaughtered hog.

"Since we're here," the Commander added, "you can watch over the side as well."

The tribune thought *no, I'm afraid of heights*, but his tongue could no more have articulated the words in this company than he could have flown home by waving his arms. Without speaking, he stood and leaned over the side. The vehicle remained as steady as an unsprung farm cart.

The vision of the three deserters continued to hang before the tribune. That calmed him more than did his grip on the coaming, though he was clinging fiercely enough to dent copper. The sky retained enough ambient light to limn the grosser features of the landscape, but it took some moments before Vibulenus recognized the circle glimpsed through the ghostly torso of Helvius as the sinkhole. The hole seemed to be the size of a medicine ball.

His arms began to shake although the backs of his hands ached with the violence of his grip.

"What are we—" started Niger, less cowed or less controlled than his fellow centurion.

Magenta fire pulsed in stroboscopic succession from the underside of the other hovering vehicle.

The air slapped after each bright surge, but the pulses followed one another a dozen times a second, faster than ears or eyes could detect the separation. Vibulenus' bowels started to loosen at the low-pitched hum, while the green complement of the laser flux rippled across the back of his eyes when he blinked.

The pulses slanted, not toward the cave mouth as the tribune expected but rather into the rock wall nearby. The limestone split apart in gouts of white, glowing chunks—not molten, but burned to raw quicklime that gnawed everything it touched with a caustic vehemence.

Over the flux ravening against the surface lay the image of the deserters, looking up in puzzlement as the cave trembled with the twelve-a-second pulses.

"*Stop* it!" Vibulenus screamed. Though he turned to the Commander, he could not escape the vision of Helvius, frowning not in fear but curiosity at the sound filling his strait universe.

The tribune must have reached out, but he was not aware of the movement until one of the toadfaced guards thrust him back with the head of his mace. The dull spikes pressed hard enough to break the skin over Vibulenus' breastbone before the Roman's body returned to immediate reality.

The ground exploded as the laser's slow gouging into refractory limestone brought it at last to a stratum through which ground water percolated. The liquid flashed to steam in an instant that shattered the whole face of the sinkhole. Pieces of rock the size of a house lifted from foundations that had held them for fifty million years, then toppled toward the center of the sinkhole.

It must have felt like an earthquake deep within the cave, because Grumio looked up, shouted something, and tried to rise but hit his head on the stone ceiling. Did they think the guild was blocking the entrance to their cave? Helvius dropped his sword and shuffled two steps forward in a crouch, his hands lifted to protect him from the rock he could not see.

The cave roof split, letting the magenta flux play on the interior. Vibulenus screamed, but his mind transferred the sound to the open mouths of the victims dying below.

Grumio was in the beam's direct path. The first pulse gnawed his body to the waist. His legs vaporized microseconds later, before they had time to fall. The legionary's iron hobnails burned with such white sparkling intensity that they looked dazzling even through the coherent pulses of the laser flux. The steel of his sword retained its shape for the instant it took to fall through the beam—belt gone, scabbard gone, and expensive ivory hilt in gaseous mixture with the hand that once wielded it.

The left arm flopped free, shriveling but not in the flux. Its bandage flashed a brilliant reflection of the beam which had vaporized Grumio.

Augens had started to rise and was not in the angled beam, but his helmet was. Bronze, gaseous or molten depending on how close it was to the center of the flux, spewed in a green flood from the impact of the light.

Reflection from the cave floor, burned white and heated to thousands of degrees by the pulses it absorbed, vaporized the legionary's feet and crisped his legs and lower body to glowing cinders. The rest of him toppled into the flux which devoured him so completely that only splinters of calcined bones reached the floor.

Unlike his companions, Decimus Helvius had time to understand what was happening to him.

The blaze behind the centurion threw his shadow in troll-like distortion down the path of his attempted flight. The beam was angled away from him, deeper into the cave, and it seemed for a moment that he might escape.

Helvius lunged forward, aided by the light though his calves burned black and the bronze studs dropped from the holes they had charred in the leather that protected his thighs. Then the cave roof collapsed onto him.

The laser continued to play on the rockface for some further seconds. Even with his eyes closed, Vibulenus could see his comrade's right foot charring in the dazzle reflected as the flux ate its way far beneath the cave.

The sky-shaking hum ended as the crew of the other vehicle shut off their weapon. A moment later, the echo from the ground ceased also. A violet nimbus around the gunvessel dissipated more slowly, as did the white glow and sound of crackling rock at the point of impact.

Vibulenus sat down. He was crying, though the fact humiliated him. When his eyes were shut, his memory reviewed the instant of destruction, but his overloaded retinas continued to pulse bright green, shrouding the horror somewhat.

"All of your fellows have watched the display," said the Commander in satisfaction, "but I'm glad you three were present at the scene, so to speak."

The rush of wind past Vibulenus indicated the vehicle was moving again. He thought of taking his hands away from his face and turning into the airstream to dry his eyes . . . but that would have meant turning toward Falco, which was unthinkable.

"There will be those who believe the scene was generated by a machine and didn't really happen," the Commander went on. "You'll be able to convince them that it was real. After all, we don't want to have to repeat the demonstration.

"This has been too expensive already."

Neither of the centurions had made a sound that Vibulenus could hear, so he had no idea of what they were thinking. For his own part, he thought he needed a woman.

And for the first time, he was willing to accept one of the creatures which the guild offered in place of women.

"I want Quartilla," the tribune said to the ship.

His companion at the head of the line, a file-closer,

looked at him curiously but stepped into the doorless alcove without saying anything.

Vibulenus followed, feeling a cool touch across his body as the blank wall appeared to open before him.

He had no idea of whether the vessel would or could deliver him to the female he requested. He had nothing to lose by the attempt. What he had to gain was tenuous, but sex is a game of the mind even if the mind sometimes plays to the body's prompting. The tribune had had personal contact with Quartilla. That made her a person, even if it could not shape her into a human being.

"Oh," said the figure on the couch. Then, "Ah, tribune . . . would you like the lights higher?"

"Quartilla?" Vibulenus said hesitantly. "You remember me?"

"You're Gaius Vibulenus Caper," the female said. "The ship told me after the other time you were here."

She paused. The lights had not gone up—Vibulenus did not know whether or not he wanted them to—but his eyes had adapted enough to see that her lips wore a smile of sort.

"I remember everyone, tribune," Quartilla concluded. "Not always their names, is all."

She was sitting on her feet with her back straight and her knees flexed together to her right side as before. Vibulenus seated himself so that his left thigh was almost but not quite in contact with those plump knees and said, with a bitterness that shocked him as the words came out, "Everyone? I find that hard to believe."

Quartilla winced, but she replied without any sharpness of her own, "Everyone is different, Gaius Caper. Every soldier, every centurion, every tribune—every crewman. I can understand how the situation would bother you. It's—part of my job to understand the things that bother men."

"Look, this is—" the tribune said. He bit his lips

and, steeling himself, laid his hand on the female's knee.

"I didn't come to fight," he went on, momentarily so focused in his own mind that he was oblivious to the texture of the skin he was touching. It was warm, perhaps marginally too warm; soft as only a woman's could be; and as smooth as thick cream. His expression changed and the words he had intended did not follow through his open mouth.

Quartilla smiled without the sadness, an impish expression that transfigured her by accenting her rather small mouth when the muscles of her cheeks curved up. She did not speak an order, but the walls glowed an off-white just bright enough to fade the red dot into a tint in its corner.

Not only was the female's skin smooth, it was a white in which only a painter could have detected a touch of green.

"I asked for further changes," Quartilla said with quiet pride. She cupped her full right breast and lifted it as if she were a farm wife displaying a prize melon. A tracery of blue veins marked the surface that was otherwise as pure as polished marble. "So that I could better perform my duties. I hoped you would come back."

Nothing better concentrates the mind than lust. It was in that knowledge that Vibulenus had driven himself to this attempt, certain that darkness and his tunic would shield his mind from certainty and that lust would overcome memories of revulsion.

There were no longer any physical cues to *wrongness*; and for the rest, Quartilla had been a person already.

The Roman threw off his tunic with a violence that was willing to shred it if the garment tried to resist his convulsive efforts. By Styx on whom the gods swear, she was a woman!

On her and in her, Vibulenus was able to forget the other men and the hint of crewmen who were not men.

And he was able to forget even Helvius and his two companions for a brief time, perhaps as long as it had taken the trio to die.

BOOK
FOUR

THE LAST CAMPAIGN

"This operation," said the Commander, a squat figure who could have passed for Clodius Afer at a distance if they exchanged garb, "is beneath me in its simplicity. I protested, but my superiors informed me that I have been tasked for the operation because of their desire for haste. I—I and yourselves—were best positioned of the units at a proper level of technology. Further, the job of ground preparation has been botched—"

"*Oh*-oh," Vibulenus muttered, resting his hand on the mail-clad shoulder of Clodius Afer. The pilus prior's angry sneer showed that Clodius knew as well as the tribune who was going to pay for the fuck-up. Not the folks in colored skin-suits who were responsible, oh no.

"—and though the personnel responsible have received reprimands," the Commander continued, audible throughout the Main Gallery despite the clash of weapons and equipment still being donned by many of the legionaries, "it was deemed necessary to task a unit disciplined enough to accomplish the task unaided. Thus I was assigned."

"Fine with me," Clodius Afer whispered, "if the smug bastard decides to handle the whole thing himself. Pollux! He's the worst we've been handed yet."

"Young, I'd guess," said Vibulenus, who still looked eighteen years old—unless you met his eyes, which were as old as the eyes of the Sphinx. "And 'worst' . . . worst covers a lot of things besides this."

He always mustered with the Tenth Cohort, standing in the front rank to the left of Clodius Afer—and by extension, to the left of the entire legion. The right was the place of honor, the sword flank; the place where the first centurion and the eagle standard marched.

But a soldier didn't fight long without a good shield, and the Tenth had been the legion's shield through every battle it fought. They'd struck some shrewd blows of their own, besides.

It was not mere chance that the Tenth Cohort was down to two hundred and ninety-seven effectives, well below the average of the nine others.

"Individual members of the hostile force," continued the Commander, "are of intermediate size and strength."

"What're *we?*" grumbled Clodius, rubbing his face under the hinged left cheek protector. There was no visible scar there, but tissue beneath the skin was knotted from the time an axe had glanced off his shield rim.

When had that been? Battles merged with one another and with the fantasies the tribune played in the Recreation Room. He wondered if Quartilla could still remember every man she had known. He had no idea of how many times he had killed. . . .

"Their armor is rudimentary," said the voice in the Romans' ears, "and their weapons, though iron, are so crude that their main effect is to permit my guild to deploy *you* against them rather than tasking a unit at a lower level."

Vibulenus caressed his left forearm where he, too, had knobs of hidden keloid that the Medic had never been able to remove. "Wonder how he'd like a stone point rammed up his bum?" he muttered, angry despite himself to be lectured by someone who knew only at second-hand about matters that were bloody memories to most of those who listened.

"The terrain is rolling," said the Commander, "and the soil coarse with no vegetation of military significance."

He paused for thought, then added, "the average temperature is lower than that of the planet where you were purchased, but the conditions for the immediate future are well within the region which you find comfortable."

"What the . . . ?" said the pilus prior. Vibulenus squeezed the armored shoulder again, for the benefit of one or both of them.

"Do your duty to my guild," concluded the Commander, "and we will treat you well. You are dismissed."

The doors in the rear of the Main Gallery never opened when the legion mustered for battle. Instead, the entire wall slid downward. The broad corridor by which the men had entered was gone, and the Main Gallery gaped through a hole in the vessel's outer bulkhead.

"Cohort—" roared Clodius Afer as he turned with a squeal of hobnails on flooring that was harder than iron.

"Century—" echoed the remaining centurions in the cohort, while their fellows in the rest of the legion did the same. In mustering for battle, the First Cohort formed up in the rear of the gallery so that it could lead the way out.

The breath of air sucked into the Main Gallery when the walls slid open was cool and dry, a good temperature in which to march in armor. You were always too hot during actual combat, but in cold weather a man could die of the shock to his system when victory or a wound let him cool off suddenly.

"About *face!*" shouted the sixty centurions in a unison gained through long practice.

In the big room, even that clashing movement was unnaturally muted, but the air itself stirred. Crests fluttered and the lighting picked out glints from steel and polished bronze. Trumpets, followed by horns, blew; and the First Cohort stepped off on its left foot.

Except for a sky as pale as goat's milk, Vibulenus could see nothing of the place they were expected to conquer. The ranks of men striding forward fell into silhouette as each left the gallery and the ship besides. It occurred to the tribune that the legion began each battle with an uphill march, since the Main Gallery was sloped for them to hear the final address by the Commander.

They might profitably dispense with the address to avoid the climb. Sometimes—and this was such an occasion—it seemed they would have been better without the address even if they had to climb a steeper slope to miss it. Why did they put young fools in command of veterans?

And again . . . Gaius Vibulenus Caper at eighteen had been a joke as a military tribune. He'd known it then and gods! when he now remembered that past, he cringed with knowledge of his callowness. But he'd seasoned into something in time. He'd seasoned into a leader.

Third Cohort was moving in its blare of signals. Why couldn't all the ranks step off together, keeping the separation they had while standing at ease? But experience proved that the legion would bunch and tangle unless the deployment were sequential, though the gods alone knew the reason.

Vibulenus wondered if he were going to die this day. Better to watch horsehair crests wave against a pale sky and to think of the legion as a machine that maneuvered on many legs.

Clodius Afer had walked up to what was now the cohort's front rank, shouting crisp, vicious orders about the alignment of his men. There were still legionaries within arms' length at the tribune, but he felt very much alone at moments like this when anything he did would put him in the way of the non-coms who had real jobs to perform.

The Commander and the guards who always flanked him—no matter who the Commander was—marched off through a sidewall of the gallery. Their mounts were stabled somewhere in the ship that Vibulenus had never seen, though it was not in the forward section behind the protective barrier. Falco and the third surviving tribune, Marcus Marcellus Rostratus, were part of the entourage.

Those who led in battle were punished for it. Safer far to ring yourself with guards like mobile fortresses and let others do the fighting. Vibulenus fingered his sword hilt and fingered the scar on his left arm . . . and he tried to concentrate on the rhythm of marching feet instead of the ragged point of a spear swelling until it was too close to be focused by his eyes.

"Cohort—" ordered the pilus prior. The Main Gallery had thinned so that the troops ahead of the Tenth Cohort, all in motion, were spaced like stakes set out in a vineyard for the grapes to climb.

"March!"

Would he die . . . and if he died, would he awaken in the belly of the ship weak and red-dyed and living again. . . . Yet again?

"Vesta, bring me home," whispered the tribune as he started to follow the legion to its latest exercise in blood and death.

The door, invisible until it opened on the wall beside Vibulenus, passed Quartilla.

None of the marching legionaries looked back, but the tribune stumbled and almost fell to the floor when he forgot that he was in the process of taking his first stride. "Quartilla!" he gasped. "What are *you* doing here?"

The woman started and would have jumped back, but the door had already solidified behind her. She bumped it, then recognized Vibulenus and relaxed enough to lower the hands she had raised clenched to her lips.

"Oh, Gaius," she said. "I'm sorry—I should have waited a little longer, shouldn't I?"

Her nod past him caused the tribune to look over his shoulder at the rest of the legion, disappearing up the sloping floor at the rate of two steps a second. Emptying, the Main Gallery was beginning to take on an air of sinister preparation. "What are you *doing* here?" he repeated with changed emphasis and a note of urgency rather than surprise.

Quartilla wore a suit patterned with irregular polygons of solid color. Instead of following the curves of her body as did the monochrome suits of guild employees, her garment seemed to have been constructed of flat panels as oddly shaped as the swatches of color—which they did not recapitulate. The form beneath seemed tightly confined as well as distorted: save for her face, the woman looked twenty pounds lighter than she did when Vibulenus visited her room.

It was the first time that he had seen her clothed.

"Well, the Pilot . . . ," she said. The tribune could not tell whether she was nervous because of the way he might react to the news or if she feared one of the manifestations of the guild would punish her for talking. "He . . . I can't enter the crew space, you know—" she waved a hand, each of whose fingers were a different color, toward the forward bulkhead "—and he doesn't like to come any distance into the cargo section. So he has me meet him here, when the. . . . When it's going to be empty."

The tall Roman said nothing. He was not even sure what he thought, except that there was a block of stone in his stomach as large as Etna and as cold as February dawn.

"It's mostly just the humanoid ones, you know," said Quartilla in a nervous attempt at reassurance.

"I've got to go," said Vibulenus with the clarity that resulted from his mind forcing words through lips from which it had become disassociated.

"Yes," she said, though he was not hearing her because now his entire body was stone. "And be careful, Gaius."

The tribune's intellectual part marveled that his body began to run toward the opening in the hall without him needing to direct the tensing and stretching of each separate muscle. Bodies were wonderous things. Minds were what got men into trouble.

He caught up with the rear rank of the Tenth Cohort just as they strode into the chill sunlight.

The sun was a green dot, low enough in the sky to cast the shadows of the enemy array halfway across the stony field to the Roman lines. Vibulenus shivered.

"Funny how it looks different depending on where you are when you see it," Clodius Afer muttered, to himself but with a sideglance at the tribune. "The sun, you know. Stars too, it seems sometimes."

"Yeah, I'd noticed that," said Vibulenus, wondering how far the Commander was going to march them across the front of a hostile army. For that matter, who in Hades was going to close their flanks? Even in extended order, the legion formed too narrow a front to match that of the mass slowly accreting toward the east.

Hercules! there were a lot of the bastards.

"Really wouldn't mind bein' back home," said the pilus prior in what was almost a whisper.

"Yeah," said Gaius Vibulenus, who did not trust himself to say more.

The ground was of gravel averaging about the size of walnuts: unattractive, but solid footing. Hobnails sparked on it as the legion tramped along in a column only six

ranks wide. The normal front rank was at the moment
the left flank of the column, while the file on the right
side would form the rear rank when the legion halted
and faced left—toward the east and the enemy a half
mile distant.

Unless the enemy attacked while the legion was still
moving sideways. That wouldn't be a disaster—they
were *veterans*, after all. But it would be one more
cursed thing along with being outnumbered ten to one
and being commanded by a kid who didn't know his
mouth from his asshole.

A horn blew.

"Cohort—" roared the pilus prior.

"Century—"

One trumpet, that carried in the command group,
sounded and all the other trumpets in the legion joined
the piercing note.

"*Halt!*" bellowed the centurions, and the legion
crashed motionless. Sparks shot from beneath boots and
from the pointed iron ferule of the javelin each soldier
carried in his right hand.

The ground looked flatter than the Commander's description of it ("rolling") but the tribune could not see
the left flank of the enemy when the halt gave him
leisure to observe them. In fact, the Commander had
marched them so far across the front that the entire
eastern horizon was filled with a line of shields whose
garish colors were muted by the light behind them.

All the vegetation the tribune could see was the same
variety, a gray-skinned plant whose center was a squat
trunk the size and shape of a large wine jar. A dozen
leaves two handbreadths wide and as much as twenty feet
long trailed across the shingle from each trunk, covering
much of the ground despite the sparseness of individual
plants. The legionaries did surprisingly little damage
when they trampled the leaves with their heavy boots,
but the cool air filled with an odor like that of bergamot.

There did not seem to be any animal life except the other army. The region raised a right plenty of warriors, if it did nothing else.

"Cohort—"

"Century—"

"Left . . . *face!*"

Scrunch—*crash!* as slightly over four thousand men turned on their left heels, then slammed their right boots down in unison. Their capes and the crests above their helmets waved like the lovely, languid fins of a reef fish swinging into position to strike. Vibulenus looked at them, turning his back on the enemy, and his heart thrilled within him. He was no longer afraid.

"Dress right—" shouted Clodius Afer, his voice as strong and no huskier than it had been when he started bellowing commands. A pause while the junior centurions echoed him, then: *"Dress!"*

The Tenth Cohort glittered as every man stretched out his right arm to the side, gripping the javelin against his palm with his thumb.

The ranks began to shift to their right as each man edged away from the extended fingers of the man to his left. The motion became increasingly pronounced as the men on the cohort's right compensated for the few inches that every one of the fifty men to their left had closed up improperly during the march.

Cursing, the pilus prior of Cohort Nine continued the process. The legion wriggled to its right with a peristaltic spasm like that of a slug advancing.

Or a snail; a bronze-armored, steel-fanged snail.

Clodius Afer began striding between the files of his cohort, shouting in what was only partly-feigned nervousness. "Come *on* you fuckers, what d'ye think this *is*, a fuckin' *defaulters'* parade? They'll *kill* yer fuckin' asses if you don't dress those *lines!* Second rank, shift *right*, yer not *bum*-fucking the first rank, you're ready t' lock *shields* with 'em!"

Each legionary stood with three feet of empty space on all sides of him: room to cock back his javelin or to swing his sword without fouling a comrade; room enough to stride forward and lock a shield wall with the rank ahead if the enemy advanced in a phalanx of its own.

It was not quite a parade formation, because irregularities in the ground skewed the array the way dense forest curves over the surface of a hill. But a parade is a purpose unto itself, sterile and emotionless. Here the legion breathed and its spearheads, sharpened as well as polished, quivered with restless animation.

There was still no one—no cavalry, no light infantry, *nothing* to close the legion's left flank. The hordes of the enemy would be all over the Tenth Cohort as soon as battle was joined, as sure as dead men stink.

There was a noise from the enemy lines greater than the whisper of equipment. Voices drifted toward the Romans on the light breeze. Warriors holding short staves upright were walking forward from the hostile mass.

Standard bearers, Vibulenus thought, or heralds . . . but it was not until he realized that the warriors were swinging their staves that he understood what the sound was.

There was a rope at the upper end of each staff and, spinning at the end of the rope's arc, a bull-roarer visible only as a shimmer in the air at this distance. The noisemakers had an angry drone, peevish in the upper registers and distinctly threatening in the lowest bass.

There were at least a dozen of the signallers being advanced from the enemy's front. They were not—could not be—tuned to identical frequencies, and the disharmonies and near harmonies that resulted raised hairs on the back of the Romans' necks the way the growl of a big cat could do.

The storm of battle was about to break over this arid plain; and unless there were immediate changes, the legion would be swept away in torrents of its own blood.

"Sir," said the pilus prior from unexpectedly beside the tribune, "who's supporting our left flank?"

Vibulenus' heart jumped when someone else broke into the mental structure he was building and all the delicately-balanced probabilities crashed down into the one gut-certainty of disaster.

"Nobody," he snapped, wholly an officer and not a man for the moment; a tribune of this legion and by all the gods its *leader*, whoever the trading guild might appoint to its command. "They've gotten greedy, and we're not going to let 'em get away with it. Order the men to ground their shields and kneel while I straighten it out."

He strode through the six ranks, oblivious to the looks of nervousness or curiosity which the nearest soldiers flashed him. Just now they existed only as statues, thoughtfully offset to provide Vibulenus a slanted path between them.

"Prepare to kneel!" bellowed Clodius Afer. It was not a standard command, but if he ordered "Prepare to receive cavalry" from the drill manual, the ranks would close up before kneeling with javelins slanted over shields.

The legion's depth was almost no distance at all to the strides of an angry man. *That* fact penetrated, and it formed a blazing backdrop to the tribune's icy resolve.

A trumpet from the command group gave the preliminary advance signal with a long clear note.

"Kneel!" ordered the centurions of the Tenth Cohort. The rank and file legionaries dropped as though the trumpet had made the ground settle beneath them.

That would make the Commander sit up and take notice, thought the tribune with satisfaction as he stepped through the sixth rank and into sight of the command group—to the rear, as always.

Behind him, the enemy was beginning to chant in unison with the pulses of the bull-roarers.

Vibulenus started to jog toward the command group, almost as far away from him as the enemy lines had been. The bodyguards oiled their armor but did not polish it, so they sat on their powerful mounts like dark lumps which turned to watch the tribune with the inanimate fascination of toads.

About and beyond them glittered the legion's silver eagle standard and the silvered bronze trumpet and horn, all carried by Romans on foot. The signallers were lowering their instruments and looking toward Vibulenus—more accurately, looking at the cohort kneeling on the flank which had caused the Commander to delay the concentus of all horns and trumpets to order the attack.

There was one figure more, a Roman in gilded helmet and breastplate who spurred his mount so savagely toward Vibulenus that pebbles spurned by the beast's pads rattled on the armor of the guards and their own mounts. The Commander had sent Lucius Rectinus Falco to learn what was wrong with the left flank.

And by Hercules, he would learn.

The carnivore that Falco rode had a pace something like that of a horse cantering, but when the clawed forepaws reached out, the creature bowed its chest so that it nearly scraped the ground. The motion by which the beast recovered, arching its back, would have pitched off any but the most expert of riders—and Falco was that, give the little swine his due.

The Commander and the toad-things of his bodyguard supported their feet in steel loops slung from their saddles—stirrups—which made an amazing difference in ease of riding at anything above a fast walk. Falco disdained them, continuing to ride Roman fashion with only the pressure of his bent legs on the beast's heaving flanks to keep him astride. Thus mounted, he rode with a verve that the guards were too heavy to equal and the Commander—all the commanders—had too much caution to attempt.

Vibulenus halted. If a messenger were coming, he had no reason to run himself into heatstroke while his equipment pummeled him. Some of the rear-rank legionaries turned to check furtively on what was happening behind them.

The carnivore closed the gap with astonishing speed. It was ridden on a hackamore that left its jaws free to rend from eye-teeth to shearing molars, and the lips were already slavering. Though of rangy build, the beast must have weighed over two thousand pounds even without the added mass of its draperies of scale armor. The tribune was not conscious of being afraid, but by instinct his left arm swung the shield so that the blazon of triple thunderbolts on its face was squarely toward Falco.

The hind claws of that cursed brute flung gravel as much as twenty feet in the air when they scrabbled for purchase.

Falco realized at the last moment that he was going too fast to skid to a halt directly in front of his rival. He tugged the reins and his mount's head to the left at the same time he pulled back with enough strength to mottle his knuckles with the effort. The pebbles that he had intended to spray across Vibulenus rattled instead on the backs and helmets of the soldiers of the rear rank as the messenger skidded to a halt.

One of the men, a centurion by the transverse crest, leaped to his feet while the mounted tribune was still trying to bring his carnivore under proper control. The non-com—Pompililius Niger, by Pollux! Of course, Niger had the Fourth Century now—thrust at the beast's snarling jaws with his shield boss, making the creature start and very nearly upsetting the rider for all his skill.

What?" Falco bleated as his mount pawed half-heartedly at the shield and Niger cocked a javelin to stab for an eye if things went further.

"Falco!" Vibulenus shouted, stepping forward to seize the other tribune's right knee and deflect his attention back to where it should be. Niger ought to have had enough discipline to ignore being pelted with rocks . . . but they were, all of them, keyed up, waiting for slaughter and wondering whose it would be. "Centurion, back to your duties!"

"Vibulenus," said Falco as he slapped the hand away from his knee, "the Commander will burn you to death by *inches*. Why have these fools squatted down in the very *face* of the enemy?"

His voice was husky with emotion and the effort of controlling his mount.

"Lucius Falco," said the tribune standing, "tell our commander that if we engage like this, they'll be all around us. We can't win if we're being pressed from three sides."

The effluvium of warm dead meat bathed the carnivore, rolling from under the blankets of armor covering the beast. Its breathing slowed from the quick gasping of the first moments after its run. During each of the intakes that filled the creature's great lungs, the whirr of the slotted disk on its chest picked up to a racing whine.

"You don't decide tactics, tribune," sneered the tribune in gilded armor, his leg moving up and down with the rise and fall of his mount's chest. "And you don't give orders."

"Falco, *listen* to me," said Vibulenus in the high carrying voice that compelled attention. "Tell our commander that we'll fight for him, but we won't let him throw us away. We went that route once, with Crassus."

He paused as arrows in his mind shot toward him from all sides, but memories of Parthia no longer froze the tall tribune. He continued, "If he doesn't get us cavalry to close our flank, or at least some auxilliary infantry—" he realized now what the Commander had been hinting about the failure of preparations "—then we form a square and march back to the ship. Otherwise we'll be killed for nothing."

Clodius and the Tenth Cohort would follow him, even in the likelihood that they would find sealed hatches and perhaps lasers when they reached the ship. Would the rest of the legion march with him also? Possibly; very possibly. He had led them before, taking the only position from which men could really be led—one step in front of them.

"I thought you were a hero, little Gaius," said Falco, and the bitterness of truth was so clear in his voice that it overwhelmed the sarcasm he had intended. "Are you afraid to die after all?"

Nothing could disturb the calm of leadership that enveloped Gaius Vibulenus at this moment. There was no room for anger, no room for personalities; no room for anything but what conduced to the result of getting support for their flank.

"Afraid to get my skull split, you mean, Lucius?" Vibulenus asked as his right hand moved. "I don't know. Are you?"

Falco looked at where his rival's hand now rested, and looked at the millennia-old eyes in Vibulenus' eighteen-year-old face. "You'll pay for this, you arrogant bastard," the rider whispered with all the venom that his fear let pass.

"Tell him, Falco," said Vibulenus steadily. "Tell him we need something to keep them off our flank and rear while we grind through their front."

Falco jerked his mount's head left and kicked the beast's haunch to tighten the turn. Its iron-scaled hindquarters brushed Vibulenus' shield as the creature broke

into a racking trot, then its canter, as the rider goaded
it back toward the command group.

"Thank you, sir," said somebody.

Vibulenus shuddered and took his hand away from
his sword. He had been gripping the bone hilt so
fiercely that the muscles ached all the way up his forearm. Not in anger. If he had chopped Falco down,
hacked through the helmet and skull until the Spanish
steel of his blade was nicked by his rival's sneering
teeth, then it would have been done coolly to demon-
strate to the Commander how serious was the demand
for support.

The trading guild understood that sort of demonstration.

Vesta, hearth and hope; bring us home again!

Vibulenus strode again through the kneeling ranks.
He paused only for a moment to grip Niger's hand,
though neither of the childhood friends spoke. The
fragrance of the sprawling local vegetation accompanied
the tribune and calmed him somewhat. Now that he
was thinking again as an individual, he was terrified by
what he had done . . . but there was no going back.

And anyway, he had been right. Execution by the
Commander could leave him no more dead than disaster in battle would. He had seen enough of the guild's
philosophy by now to realize that it would make no
attempt to recover and revivify those who had failed it,
whatever excuses the dead might have been able to
claim.

"Awaiting further orders, sir," said Clodius Afer in a
voice so neutral that it was disquieting.

Gaius Vibulenus had to remember that the actions he
took affected hundreds, *thousands,* of other men; even
after he was thinking again as a fearful individual and
not the tribune—more than tribune—who had given
the orders. "Either," he said in a voice that steadied

after the first syllables, "we'll have some help over here soonest, or we march back to the ship and discuss matters at leisure."

Or you watch me burned to charcoal and a puddle of bronze, his fear added silently.

The tribune looked toward the enemy whom he had ignored through the minutes since they ceased to be the primary threat. The Romans' actions and lack thereof appeared to have confused the hostile chieftains as well. The signallers had drifted to a halt, midway across the gap that had separated the two armies. All but one of the bull-roarers were silent, the wielders leaning on their staves, panting with the exertion they had undergone. Individually, the figures seemed to be tall and gangling, with skins whose color approached bright orange.

And gods! there were hordes of them.

"Maybe," Vibulenus said to himself aloud, "he can shift a cohort from the right to give us some depth. Six ranks isn't enough, not on this flank."

"They want us to come out," said the pilus prior with a nod toward the hesitating foe. "They aren't used to this."

"That was what happened the first time," said the tribune, voicing a train of thought wholly inappropriate at the present time. "The, you know, the first battle we fought for this guild? Those big fellas with the carts, they expected to fight a civilized little battle. Then the loser'd withdraw behind the screen of light troops and everybody'd go home."

"I'm not looking forward to this neither," said the centurion; and when Vibulenus processed the words, he too understood why he had been babbling about the distant past. He had *survived* that past.

There was a stir around the command group. Eight or ten—ten, half the contingent—of the Commander's bodyguards suddenly rode toward the left flank at a

shambling trot. They sat their mounts ably enough with
no squirming or slipping in their saddles, but because
of their size and featureless armor they looked more
like howdahs than riders.

They carried their maces upright, waving ten feet
above the saddles like papyrus stalks when wind sweeps
up the Nile.

All the warmth and strength drained out of the tribune's
body. His clammy fingers touched the hilt of his sword,
wondering whether to defend himself with the weapon or
fall on it . . . and whether the guild would revivify him
for punishment if he tried to forestall them by suicide.

Clodius Afer had remained standing when he ordered his troops to kneel. Now, looking over their
heads toward the armored riders, he said in a raspy,
carrying voice, "Boys, it may be there'll be a little
trouble in a moment. If we put our spears up the belly
of those overgrown dogs from below, then we can take
care of the prettyboys ridin' 'em in our own good time."

"I don't want—" Vibulenus started to say before it
struck him that he *couldn't* keep these men from trying
to defend him—and that he didn't want to call them off
anyway. They'd been together for a long tme, he and
the legion. Maybe this wouldn't be the worst way for it
to end.

The toad-faced guards rode past the flank of the
cohort. Instead of reining their beasts across the face of
the kneeling unit to arrest the tribune as he expected,
they fanned out to extend the line of the legion by over
three hundred feet. As the nearest of the riders halted
his mount, facing and snarling at the enemy, he turned
stiffly in the saddle. His mace head dipped in the
direction of Vibulenus, then rose again in what could
only be a salute.

"Get them on their feet again," said the tribune in a
rush of triumph and relief that elevated him beyond
human concerns. "We've got a battle to fight."

"Cohort!" shouted Clodius Afer. "Fall—*in!*"

Hidden by the scrunch of gravel under hobnails, the pilus prior muttered, "And just what're *they* doing, you think—sir?"

"They're the unit guarding our left flank," Vibulenus said, watching armored ,en rise from the stony soil like the crop Jason sowed with dragon's teeth. Shifting their grip on javelins, adjusting shields and raising reflections on the bronze bosses and edge reinforcements from the light of the greenish sun.

There was nothing in particular in the eyes that met the tribune's as he scanned the ranks: neither hope nor resignation, not curiosity or fear. They were experts who knew what the present job entailed, and knew that they could handle it.

"Not exactly a regiment of cavalry," grumbled Clodius in a husky whisper. "*Ten* of 'em. How's that going to help?"

"He gave us half of what he had," the tribune remarked with a detached shrug. "We'll call that a win. Anyway, they'll keep the natives off our backs—they look so mean."

The bull-roarers were beginning to spin again across the field.

"Mean? We'll give 'em mean," said the pilus prior as he strode away, checking the dress of his lines again.

The bodyguards must be bitter, the tribune thought, ordered to take a place in the line where they might see real action. Maybe it'd be good for them.

At least it might get a few of the bastards killed.

The command group's trumpeter blew his long preliminary call again. Bronze ranks of legionaries, their plumes and javelin points trembling, interrupted Vibulenus' view of the figure in the blue suit who was probably watching the Tenth Cohort in nervous anticipation.

The Commander had turned out to be willing to

learn from people who knew more than he did about the situation. That put him a notch up on Crassus and more than one other Roman consul.

"Signallers!" Vibulenus called as he strode across the front of the cohort toward its right, where he would find a place between the files of the Tenth and Ninth Cohorts. "Sound the attack!"

It was not his place to give that order. But, as when Vibulenus had the cohort kneel and take itself out of the battle, it was the fastest possible way to send the Commander a message he would understand.

The part of Vibulenus' mind that considered practical things expected two or three of the signallers to be able to hear his command—and perhaps none of those to obey him. Instead, all the horns and trumpets of the Tenth and Ninth Cohorts blew the concentus. His voice carried— and it carried authority to every legionary that heard it.

By Hercules, they were men and were soldiers; and so was Gaius Vibulenus.

"Cohort—" roared Clodius Afer, picking up the tribune's intent.

"Century—" from multiple throats.

First the horn and trumpet from the command group, then the signallers throughout the legion joined the concentus.

"Forward—*march!*"

The legion crashed off toward another enemy at two steps a second, while four thousand right arms readied javelins. The left flank was a half stride ahead of the remaining cohorts; and that wasn't a bad feeling either.

Vibulenus settled his shield so that the point of his left shoulder took some of the weight. He drew his sword, the same fine Spanish blade his father had bought him so long ago. Its bone hilt and the calluses of his right hand had shaped to one another over the years, and the blade—though frequently sharpened—was poised and balanced to slash a life out.

As it had done hundreds of times already.

The enemy began to chant in high-pitched voices, so many of them that it sounded like a chorus of frogs in a swamp swollen by springtime rains. The sparkling crunch of gravel beneath hobnails was the only noise the legion made in reply, but to the ears of a trained soldiers the sound of that disciplined advance was more terrible than any amount of barbarian yammer.

The tribune's grin and the edges of his sword flashed toward the enemy.

The equipment the guild supplied was solid enough, helmets forged without weak spots and shields whose laminations did not split if they were dropped. But there was no craftsmanship in that produce, no *soul*, as there was in the Spanish sword.

Sometimes it seemed that the guild did not realize even that its soldiers had souls.

The natives came on with mass but no discipline, the way surf bubbles across a strand.

"Heads up!" warned a front-rank centurion as a score of light javelins snapped from the hostile lines in high arcs. They must have been using spear throwers, because no flesh-and-blood arm could have cast a missile so far unaided.

"Company comin', boys," said Clodius Afer. "Don't lose your dress." The coolness of his voice and the unconcern for anything but his cohort's orderliness were more calming than any blustering encouragement could have been.

Vibulenus felt a sudden urge to empty his bladder. That too was calming, because the feeling had become a normal part of his life.

Being on the edge of battle was almost as normal as eating, now.

One of the darts howled down, short of the tribune but so close that he swung his shield instinctively to cover it. The missile was no more than three feet long,

a shaft of something like rattan with a small iron point
that shattered on the ground. He kicked the shaft as he
stepped past it with the disgust that he would have felt
for a snake in his pathway.

"More on the way!"

The warriors had surged around their fellows with
bull-roarers. The sound continued, but Vibulenus
doubted whether the signallers could long continue to
spin their noisemakers above the heads of the armed
warriors. Their shields were painted in geometric patterns, each unique. Some of the leaders gnawed on
their shield rims as they shambled toward the legion.

It was about time to give them something else to
chew on.

Vibulenus ran two steps ahead of the front of the
legion with his sword raised. Waves of flame and melt
water undulated through the nerves in his skin, breaking in turbulence at the hidden scars which the Medic
could not remove.

The signallers would call for the first volley of javelins, but not all the legionaries would hear the bronze
tones over the crunch of their own advance. If that
initial flight were to be launched simultaneously for
greatest effect, then there had to be a visual signal as
well.

Gaius Vibulenus had just volunteered himself as visual signal, because he wasn't willing to order any of his
men to take the risk instead. *His* men.

The tall officer twisted his head and shoulders backward as he jogged toward the enemy. The shadow of his
horsehair plume waved across the boots of the soldiers
raising their left legs a little higher than usual to balance the javelins cocked back in their right hands to
throw.

The whole left side of Vibulenus' body crawled with
fear of the enemy he could no longer see.

"*Hit 'em, boys!*" he shouted as the horns blared and

the sword in his hand swung down in an arc turned green by the light of the virid sun.

A dart flew over the tribune and thudded into the shield of a file-closer, just as the front two ranks broke into a run and hurled their javelins at the enemy a hundred feet away. The shadows of three more native missiles merged with the tribune's shadow; he staggered with shock and pain.

One of the darts struck near the boss of his shield, penetrating the three plies of wood but only bulging the felt backing. A second came down in so high an arc that it missed the shield and glanced from his shoulder where the attachments of his body armor formed a double thickness of bronze. The iron gouged a bright streak into the polished cuirass but did only cosmetic harm.

The third missile hit Vibulenus in the helmet at the same point he had been struck, ages before, by a spearman in a misty valley. The dart had been hurled as hard and flat as possible for a native arm aided by the additional leverage of a spear thrower.

There was a flash of ringing deadness in the tribune's skull, and his body started to go slack.

"*Rome!*" shouted Clodius Afer as his left arm, shield and all, encircled the tribune who was his friend and comrade.

The native ranks exploded with the death of hundreds of their leading warriors.

"Sir?" said the pilus prior as legionaries rushed past them, lifting their heavy javelins from behind their shields. "You're all right?"

"I'm all right. . . ." Vibulenus mumbled, an echo rather than an answer, but use of his lips and tongue gave him volitional control over the muscles of his body as well. He straightened and finally realized that the centurion had been holding the entire weight of his armored body until then.

The multi-throated chanting from the nearest portion of the enemy lines changed to screams as heavy javelins and the lighter missiles from the center ranks of the legion hammered the natives like wheat in a hail storm.

Vibulenus felt his head, using the back of his right hand because he had not lost his grip on his sword. His helmet was gone, but the bone beneath was solid and he could feel the pressure of his probing with both hand and head.

"I'm fine," he said, slurring the words. "Let's get 'em."

Blood from the pressure cut on his scalp dripped on his sword as he lowered his hand.

"Rome!" Clodius repeated with a nod and a feral smile as he headed for his proper place at the front with long, swift strides.

The tribune followed, though every time his right heel met the ground his vision dimmed with pain. He tried to force his eyes more widely open, as if the muscles of the lids could somehow press back the waves of pain.

The native shields were long and narrow, so the first good look Vibulenus had at the enemy he was fighting came when he strode past a native body with wide-flung limbs, pinned to the shingle by a javelin through the base of the throat. The corpse was thin with almost the angular slimness of a praying mantis. The orange cast of its skin was accented on the face and arms by rouge. The only clothing worn by the goggle-eyed corpse was a string of animal teeth that might have been intended as some sort of rudimentary body armor.

The shield beside the native's body would not have been protection even if he had interposed it between him and the Roman javelin. It was leather-covered wicker, barely sufficient to stop light darts like the one which still hung unnoticed from the tribune's own shield. This was going to be as easy as any battle could be.

Which was not to say that it was going to be easy.

The advance paused as the two front ranks of legionaries locked shields, compressing the enemy with sword points. A soldier in front of Vibulenus grunted and took a half-step backward. The tribune leaned against the legionary's shoulders and pushed, giving the man the thrust he needed to counter the weight of natives literally trying to crawl over the Roman's shield.

The legionary used his impetus to stab over the upper curve of his plywood oval. Resistance collapsed, squealing, and Gaius Vibulenus stepped into the gap opened by the advance of the soldier he had aided.

A dozen Roman javelins wobbled overhead, hurled by the rear ranks when the armored backs in front of them had stopped moving. One of the missiles cleared the friendly lines by less than it should have, thudding into the native that Vibulenus was even then preparing to stab. That was a stupid blunder, inexcusable in veterans of their experience. After the battle he'd parade all the rear ranks with gravel-filled packs until they dropped unless some individual came forward to take his punishment.

The tribune's scalp, bare and bloody, tingled with emotion at a cellular level. Had the javelin wiggled a handbreadth lower in the air, its point would have split Vibulenus' skull like a pickaxed melon, ending his duties and his life beyond help of the Medic or the gods . . . if there were gods.

Hercules, shield a soldier from harm.

The natives were packed too tightly to use their weapons properly. A warrior stabbed overhand at the tribune's face with an all-iron spear very different from the darts which had fallen on the legion's advance. Instead of a shaft, this stabbing weapon was forged in one piece with two double-edged blades joined back to back by a rod no longer than a sword hilt.

The warrior's face was painted in quadrants—red,

green, blue and a yellow turned fiery by the tone of the skin beneath it. Vibulenus ducked and raised his shield in the same motion. Wood split and the spearpoint reached an inch through the felt backing: the natives might be skinny, but they were not frail.

Instead of trying to slash around the edge of his opponent's buckler, painted in the same pattern as his face, the tribune stabbed directly at the center where the four colors met. Spanish steel slid through leather and the wicker frame with little more delay than it had made of the paint. Even dazed by the blow to his head, Vibulenus' eye had correctly gauged the flimsiness of the equipment beside the sprawled corpse.

The warrior screeched as the sword grated through the bones of his hand. He would have jumped backward, but the press of his fellows was too great.

Vibulenus put all his weight behind the swordhilt. His point met ribs and drove on into the chest cavity. His opponent cleared his own weapon with a hysterical jerk and flailed behind him with it. The victims he slashed down fell too late to provide him with any space but that he died on.

Shouting, the tribune leaped into the gap, joined on the carpet of squirming bodies by a legionary who had retained a javelin for thrusting.

His head did not hurt. The memories—Pompilius Rufus . . . Helvius in coruscating death . . . a centurion with no name, no legs, and no hope but the false one of Gaius Vibulenus—they were still present, but flows of molten glass insulated the tribune from that greater pain also.

There should have been a place other than battle where he could be free of pain, fear, and all-consuming hatred for his fate—as well as for the guild which was that fate. Vibulenus had found no other release its equal, though.

When he drank, it turned memories into nightmares

until he awakened drenched with his own sweat and vomit. The fellowship of Clodius and Niger, friends as no one would have been his friend under circumstances his birth made normal, were constant reminders of other men who had died around him, beside him, even *for* him . . . and for no human purpose.

A soldier shouldn't talk of love and should never *think* of it . . . but for all that, Vibulenus found something not far from peace occasionally in Quartilla's arms. But there were memories in that, too, and knowledge of what she was as surely as he was a Roman and a soldier. The only purity he found in life was in slaughter. He knew the feeling did not come from a healthy mind; but it was no less real for that.

For now—Vibulenus chopped overarm at a warrior who had interposed his own stabbing spear. Steel bit deeply into thin iron, but the native expertly spun his weapon like a whirled baton to bring forward an undamaged blade. The tribune punched forward his shield, knocking the enemy shield aside, then swung low. His sword cut its own depth in the warrior's shield rim and stopped only because, nearer its tip, the blade had crunched into the native's femur.

Vibulenus brought the iron-bound edge of his shield down as he stepped over his fallen opponent. Bones and teeth splintered at the blow; and another warrior, with a clear look at the tribune's torso, thrust with all his strength.

Vibulenus pitched backward off the quivering body which his hobnails gouged. There was a dent in his breastplate, centered and between the fifth and sixth ribs. The iron spearpoint had doubled back for three inches. While the warrior tried to swap ends for another stroke, a legionary crushed his face with the ferule of a javelin.

The natives' blood was pale, and it had an odor like

that of raw wool which struggled with the scent of trampled vegetation.

The tribune, half supported by a soldier whom he did not bother to thank or even look at, staggered back to his feet. Every time he drew in a breath there was a sharp pain where the spear had struck him; but even if it were a cracked rib rather than a bruise, he could still function.

He could still kill.

The fighting was beginning to open out now that the nearest surviving warriors had experienced enough of the legion's onslaught to press away from rather than toward the swordblades. A knot of the enemy had been cut off on a hillock twenty feet in diameter and no more than three feet higher than its immediate surroundings.

The warriors stood in a ring, shoulder to shoulder. Perhaps because there were no others immediately behind them to foul their strokes, the circle was defending itself ably. The height advantage permitted the long-armed natives to strike down at the eyes of legionaries attacking them, and that too contributed to the hillock being bypassed instead of overrun.

The soldiers fighting here had won many battles since they marched away from Rome; and these were the men who survived.

Titius Hostilianus, the soldier who had taken out the native who speared Vibulenus, paused to consider the defended hillock. There were twenty or so warriors here, and at least half of them bore shields painted solid blue in distinction to the multihued array of their fellows. A legionary lay at their feet. He had bent the stabbing spear when he fell on it, but its black iron point still projected through the back of his neck and spine.

Titus nodded and started to edge around the hillock. Vibulenus halted him with the flat of his bloody sword.

"Kill that one," ordered the bareheaded tribune, point-

ing the weapon toward the center of a blue shield four
feet away

The native snarled like a furious cat. His spear rang
on the sword, forcing the tribune's arm down.

The shank of Titius' javelin had bent the first time he
stabbed with the point. He scowled at Vibulenus, then
eyed the native who flashed his blade through the
empty air in threat.

Grunting, the legionary hurled his javelin. The ferule's four-sided spike tore through the shield and the
warrior's throat

Gaius Vibulenus jumped into the gap, even as the
native pitched backward. The Roman's shield thrust the
warrior to his left sideways, off the gravel knob. and a
sword slash hamstrung the native to his right.

Warriors turned, crying out at the sudden threat in
their midst. A spear cut the tribune's left thigh and
another wedged its point in the crack of his clamshell
armor, breaking one hinge and gouging into his right
armpit despite the resistance of the spreading bronze.

Everything was white pain. He swung about him like
a blinded bear, striking but not harming his assailants.
Then he stumbled to his knees in the midst of orange-
skinned bodies, Niger supporting him by one shoulder
and Clódius Afer by the other.

It had taken the nearest soldiers only seconds to clear
the hillock once the ring was disrupted. Thanks to that
and to armor with which the natives had not dealt
before, Vivulenus had no wounds that were not superficial.

He hurt as if he had rolled naked in nettles.

"Are you fucking crazy?" wheezed Niger. One front
tooth was broken, and his face was cut from his upper
lip to the left cheek guard. When he spoke, he sprayed
blood as well as spittle. "What're you fucking *doing?*"

"Needed the height," the tribune mumbled back.
"Had to be able to see." And speaking the words, he

straightened his legs to use the vantage point for which he had risked his life.

It was hard to concentrate on what he had to know as an officer in the midst of battle. It would have been easier to block severe pain, a limb crushed or the shattered-glass jaggedness of breathing with an arrow through the lung. Vibulenus felt instead that ants were crawling over him, gnawing and dribbling a poison from their tails that made his flesh burn and veins throb.

Courage can overcome agony, but it has too diamond-like a focus to deal with amorphous discomfort.

Vibulenus squinted, not because of the sun—which was too high now to interfere—but so that he could direct his attention where he wanted it. His vision kept flashing nervously from the battle scene as a whole to the centurions supporting him: Niger stolid, despite the cut in his face, but Clodius Afer visibly worried about the tribune's mental and physical state.

"No, it's all right," Vibulenus muttered. "It had to be done that way."

When he had spoken the words, which were not a lie if understood in more than a strictly military sense, his mind reasserted the control it needed and cooled his body to a support which did not intrude.

The ten cavalrymen on the legion's left had held. The relief of seeing the armored riders hulking in place like so many fortresses, their visors raised to display the horror of their features, jellied the tribune's knees for an instant so that he sagged again into the grip of the two non-coms.

It did not seem that the natives had made any attempt to attack the armored riders. The fear of monsters mounted on other slavering monsters would have worn off in time, but the crushing advance of the Roman infantry had left no time. The bodyguards were walking their beasts forward to keep pace with the legion. The warriors before them were beginning to stream away from the battle, able to do so safely because they were not anchored by contact with a foe who would slaughter them from behind.

The central mass of the copper-skinned enemy, as far as Vibulenus could see, was struggling in panic. Roman shields pressed back the warriors so fiercely that those who knew how assured was their doom if they stayed were, nonetheless, unable to flee.

Rising to his full height, craning his neck—he should have had a horse, but he would not have accepted one of the carnivores available even had it been offered—Vibulenus scanned the undulating ranks of the legion.

Success had disordered the Roman lines somewhat; but because neither pursuit nor severe irregularities of terrain were involved, the rearmost pair of ranks had retained cohesion. Even more coolly reserved was the command group, its members visible more from the height of their mounts than because of the tribune's low vantage point. Falco; the Commander; and the ten remaining guards jutted up above the eagle standard, while the trumpeter and hornblower were hidden by the waving crests of the legionary infantry.

The Commander had retained the guards whom he had not sent to the left flank. What in the names of Jove and Hades was going on at the legion's right?

"Prepare to disengage the Tenth Cohort," said Gaius Vibulenus with such startling clarity that he could be heard by everyone within spear's length of him despite the sounds of battle. "We will reverse to the right flank while developing any hostile threats to the legion's rear."

"Threat?" said Niger, stepping up on his toes to see what had led to the unexpected order.

The cackling triumph of thousands of natives sweeping toward the command group from the right flank was more answer than the tribune had time to give.

"Get the trumpeters and standard bearers, Niger,"

said Clodius Afer in instant decision. "I'll see what I can do to the front and send some non-coms back."

Men promoted for courage were going to drift forward in battle, even if they would be of greater military benefit keeping control of ranks as yet uncommitted. Usually that stiffening of the front line came at very little cost. In the present circumstances, where the cohort had to execute a complex manuever from the rear, lack of centurions and file-closers in the disengaged ranks wouldn't make matters any easier.

"About face!" Vibulenus shouted as he stepped off the hillock, stumbling on one of the tumbled native bodies because his foot had not lifted as high as he intended.

Niger slapped the tribune's shoulder in friendly benediction as the two childhood friends went off on separate errands of slaughter. The non-com's round-faced boyishness contrasted with the taller officer's youthfully-delicate features; and both visages contrasted even more with the hard-souled men who lived beneath the skin.

"Form your cursed ranks, you chaff-brained loafers!" Vibulenus shouted as he continued his staggering path back through the cohort. The pilus prior had not bothered to assign the tribune a task because there was no need to do so: Vibulenus was going to lead them from the cohort's new front. "*About* face, the fun's behind us now, boys!"

The tribune sheathed his sword to free a hand, stripping off blood on the sheath's tight lip because he did not have time to wipe the blade first. It was a bad way to treat a faithful weapon, but there wasn't any slack just now for human beings either. He physically rotated the nearest legionaries as he passed them, men who were nervous about turning their back on enemies but were unwilling to cold-bloodedly ignore an order so baldly put.

A few of their fellows followed the example and shouted

orders. Then, as Vibulenus stepped through the sixth rank, two of the cohort's trumpets began blowing the four-note recall signal.

One of the rear-rank soldiers was a Capuan named Hymenaeus. His extraction was such that when he turned and saw what was happening, it was in Greek that he blurted, "Zeus bugger me fer a heifer, here they come!"

He started to walk out, hunching to loosen his mail.

Vibulenus blocked the soldier with his shield. "*Wait* for it, curse ye! We're going to do this as *I* say."

Because to meet the new threat piecemeal would mean disaster for the cohort, and for the legion whose only hope was the cohort.

The command group was no longer a study in disinterested aloofness. The Commander's bodyguard had reined its mounts to face the right flank. One or two of the guards had enough skill to bring up their beasts lurchingly onto their hind legs so that their forepaws could ramp in the air.

That had been enough to keep the natives back on the left flank . . . but the enemy that the Commander's own party faced was quite different from warriors in the chill dawn, trying to decide whether or not to attack monsters out of nightmare. The warriors who had boiled around the legion's right flank unhindered had both momentum and quick victories—legionaries cut down before they changed front—to enspirit them.

A carnivore sprang forward, goaded by its rider or the presence of blatant enemies. It caught a native and tossed him in the air, his chest and shoulder crushed and a blunt wedge cut from the wicker shield to match the pattern of the beast's jaws.

The natives gave back. Their front, twenty or thirty warriors across as they encircled the right of the legion, spread like water flowing against a brick on a smooth table. They flanked the short line of guards as they had flanked the legion itself . . . and then they attacked the

mounted creatures from three sides with sudden wild
abandon.

"On the command, Tenth Cohort will pivot on the
left file!" Vibulenus instructed as he ran the length of
the cohort's new front. Actually, only the previous sixth
rank had faced about uniformly, though more and more
of the men closer to the old front were obeying the
trumpets. Non-coms grabbed by Clodius Afer rushed
through lines of common soldiers, snarling and cajoling
in an attempt to rebuild a formation disordered by
contact with the enemy.

"Prepare to pivot," the tribune ordered in a voice
barely audible for his wheezing. He had just run three
hundred feet, the cohort's frontage, to reach the file
that formed the open right flank of the unit's new
alignment. Already exhausted by battle and emotion,
he was scarcely able to breathe, much less speak.

The men nearest to him were the ones who must
start the pivot and march a five-hundred foot arc while
the cohort's left file merely turned on its left boot. They
could hear him; and anyway, they would follow.

"Forward!" the tribune croaked and swept his sword
out in a glittering curve.

Striding like a bronze-clad automaton, his hair bloody
and windblown, Gaius Vibulenus led his men toward
the enemy. His personality was again submerged in
duty, but the body controlled by the tribune's intellect
had very little strength left to offer.

Vibulenus could only pray—pray, and trust as experienced a team of non-coms as ever graced a cohort that
there would be troops to support the single rank which
marched at his side. He could have looked back over
his shoulder, but he knew his feet would spill him if he
did not watch his path. In a way, it did not matter
whether he led a cohort or a rank: he had no choice but
to carry out the maneuver as best he could, with however many men he had available.

Ahead of them—his pivot completed, Vibulenus was now leading his men at right angles to their original alignment—the surviving bodyguards pitched like ships in a storm of coppery bodies.

Two thousand right-flank legionaries, the first five cohorts, were tightly surrounded by native warriors. The light equipage that made the natives easy prey for the legion head-on gave them the speed to sweep like cavalry through gaps in the defenses.

Rear-rank soldiers faced around and locked shields when they recognized the new threat, but here the advantage was to the natives who had momentum and room to use their weapons while the legionaries were suddenly compressed by a double threat. The legion bristled like a hedgehog, its swords and thrusting javelins drawing blood from the yelping warriors . . . but there was no weight behind the Roman jabs, only fear, and there were ten natives for every one who fell.

"D'ye call that a fuckin' *rank?*" shrieked Clodius Afer from hearteningly near the tribune. "Slow it *down*, Piscinus, you're not runnin' fer a fuckin' bar!"

The cohort's front was thickening with men who sprinted, gasping, to squeeze between legionaries already in position and lock step with them. Centurions, file-closers, watch clerks: possibly the bravest men in the unit, certainly the men to whom an appearance of courage was most important. In battle, the two were apt to amount to the same thing.

Pompilius Niger edged between the tribune and the man to his shield-side. The centurion's swarthiness had been deepened by the flush of exertion, and blood from his cut lips splattered his forearm with oval markings. "No problem disengaging, sir," he gasped cheerfully. "Bastards run like chickens soon's we backed and 'let 'em go."

The native blood that swirled and thickened on his sword, his hand, and his arm to the elbow was yellowish and anemic by contrast to the spray from his lips.

They were a hundred and fifty feet from the swarm of enemies engaging the command group, thirty double paces measured from left boot-heel to left boot-heel. A few of the warriors who had been concentrating with mad intention on the mounted force now turned to see the Tenth bearing down on them in lockstep.

It was time.

"Charge!" cried Gaius Vibulenus, and lost the hard-bought rhythm in which he had been marching when he stumbled into a run. His headache was almost a relief, because it distracted him from the fire that throbbed in the pit of his stomach every time he drew a breath.

The world in ruddy flames, and a granite fortress falling like the stage curtain of eternity. . . .

"Let's take 'em boys!" bellowed the pilus prior from the center of the front rank, and the cohort surged forward as if it had not already crashed to one victory this morning.

The eagle standard fell with the Roman carrying it.

Only two of the bodyguards were still mounted, trying with desperate mace-strokes to protect the Commander and Falco between them. Falco had his sword drawn, but the very size of his armored mount prevented him from using the short blade to any effect.

The face beneath the gilded helmet was white with a fear Vibulenus had known only once: the moment in the Recreation Room when a ceramic spearpoint plunged toward his frog eyes.

The mounts of the bodyguards leaped simultaneously, not in snarling attacks but because spears had been thrust beneath their armored skirts. One of the toads managed to keep his seat for a moment despite the arch of the carnivore's back. Then the pain-maddened beast twisted, grasped its rider's right leg in its huge jaws, and flung the bawling guard in a twenty-foot pinwheel that ended in a crash of ironmongery and spraying gravel.

Falco turned his head as if he intended to interpose himself between the Commander and the warriors who had been temporarily disarrayed by the death throes of the carnivores. Instead, he shouted something to his mount and slapped the beast's haunch ringingly with the flat of his sword. The carnivore leaped over the kicking body of one of its fellows even as the Commander's own mount went splay-legged and spilled the blue figure on the bloody shingle.

Falco was hunched forward, his weight aiding his mount's graceful arc toward the Tenth Cohort and safety. The javelin thrown by a Roman desperately trying to break up the clot of natives intersected the gold-gleaming tribune at the top of the arc.

The carnivore struck the ground at a gallop in the direction of the ship. Falco tumbled backward, turned by the momentum of the javelin which projected from his right eye. His helmet sprang away like a bit of glittering waste stained green by the ill-hued sun. The iron point poking through the back of the tribune's skull had knocked away the gilded bronze.

The natives pausing to complete the slaughter of the command group looked up to see the front of the cohort sweeping toward them as a wall of bronze and iron and vermilion. The legionaries who had not been engaged were models of ferocious precision, their crests straight and the leather facings of their shields marked only by red dye and the lightning flashes blazoned upon them in gold.

But interspersed with that orderly threat were the men who had turned the front rank into a killing machine during the initial engagement. Clodius Afer's crest had been sheared to half its length by a slashing blow, and several other soldiers, like Vibulenus at the post of honor, were helmetless. Their shields were hacked, spangled with ripped facings and the dangling weapons they had blocked. Bosses and reinforced shield

rims were rippled with the dents and stains of the
crushing blows they had delivered.

And everywhere was blood; on the swords and the
equipment, and in the eyes of the veterans who grinned
at another chance to kill.

A few warriors broke and ran, panicked by a sight
more terrible than the carnivores and toad-faced monsters they had just cut down.

The Commander stood up suddenly, his garb a synthetic blue cynosure among the shaded variance of animal dyes. He took two steps toward the cohort, bleating
a cry for help more universal than Latin.

A warrior on the verge of flight turned and offhandedly slashed the blue figure across the front of both
thighs. Either the blade was sharper than iron had a
right to stay during a long cut, or the muscles in the
blue suit were soft as milk curd. Great wounds gaped
like mouths opening to the bone before they vomited
blood over the Commander's knees. He fell backward,
still screaming, because the muscles that should have
kept him upright had been severed.

The native who had chopped the Commander down
leaped over the sprawling body, making his escape into
the mass of his fellows. One blade of his spear trailed
droplets of blood dark as garnets.

Another warrior eyed the twenty foot distance between him and the Tenth Cohort, then raised his own
weapon to stab straight down into the Commander's
wailing mouth.

Vibulenus flung his Spanish sword overhead.

The weapon was still blade-heavy after—who knew
how many?—sharpenings, and the tribune had never
been trained to throw even a knife balanced for the
purpose. It flew straight, but the fat part of the blade
instead of the point spun into the native's forehead.

That was good enough. The warrior's hands shot up.
His shield flew in one direction, his spear in another, as

if they were pins struck down by the sword which
caromed away from the impact in a splatter of blood.

Clodius Afer, straining a half-step ahead of the legionaries to either side, decapitated the native with a
sweep of his own blade. The man was an artist, thought
Gaius Vibulenus as he sprawled face down on the gravel,
played out from exertions rather than the score of wounds
which for now he had forgotten.

For a moment the tribune could not move. His torso
crackled with dry yellow fire, and he could not tell
whether or not he was breathing.

The patter of stones and startled oaths brought
Vibulenus around to present awareness. He remembered where he was a moment before his shield slapped
him, lifted by a foot that trampled its inner rim. Men
were striding past, on their way to finish a battle and
another native enemy. The tribune was debris in their
way, to be avoided if possible because he had been a
comrade—but an obstacle nonetheless to men who would
prefer to save their remaining energies for the foe.

"Sir, y'all right?" demanded a soldier who took
Vibulenus' feeble attempts to shrug off his shield as a
request to be lifted. Because the man—he was Titius
Hostilianus; the whole cohort must have shifted to its
new front after all—had only one free hand and *that*
after dropping his sword, he jerked the tribune brutally
into a sitting posture. "You all *right?*" he repeated
anxiously.

Vibulenus let his shield slide off his left arm and
quiver against the soil on its concave face. "I'm—
Pollux. . . ." He had a bruise beneath his ribs where his
diaphragm had thrust against his bronze armor in desperate attempts to draw air into his lungs.

"I'm fine," he said, straightening to keep the cuirass
from pressing flesh already abused. "Gimme . . . you
know, help me up."

Suddenly the two men were in the wake of the battle

again. They were alone on trampled gravel with dis-
carded equipment, bodies crumpled like waste rags,
and a few legionaries hobbling but determined to catch
up with the action despite their wounds.

It felt amazingly good to stand up again. He could
breathe without his equipment pressing in ways that
made his lungs scream . . . but without the legionary's
steadying arm, Vibulenus could not have stayed upright.

The sky was thunderous with the trading vessel's
descending bulk, and the body-recovering tortoise already loomed over a shingle ridge in the direction of
the legion's own ship.

Vibulenus nodded his companion forward; it would
be pointless to try to talk until the trading vessel was
grounded and silent. Did their own ship sound like that
when it landed and took off . . .?

The tribune's spur-of-the-moment response to the
encircling native army had been successful beyond his
conception. All Vibulenus had intended to do was to
block the enemy's flanking motion and take the pressure
off the portion of the legion which already had screaming warriors on three sides.

But the soldiers in the rear ranks, though leaderless,
were no cowards. They had turned defensively to meet
a threat from what should have been the direction of
safety. When the cohort swept past them in formation,
they fell in behind the attack and multiplied its weight.
Warriors, checked by the resistance of the command
group, fled the rush to heavy infantry as abruptly as
they had attacked. Most threw away their meager equipment. Those who did not were hacked down atop it as
legionaries caught any who were in the least burdened.

And all the time, the legion's original front continued
to butcher the natives before it, though swords grew
dull and arms ached with the motions of slaughter.

Falco lay on his back, but his head was turned to the
side by the weight of the javelin's shaft. His remaining

eye had rolled up in the socket as blank and white as that of an unpainted statue, and his face was frozen into an expression of terrified disbelief.

"Wonder if he saw it coming," said the surviving tribune in a normal voice that not even he could hear over the roar of the descending trader.

Probably Falco hadn't. You don't really see anything in a panic like that, only the image of fear your mind creates for you. The image could have been anything, a warrior or the gravel as his mount fell or even the enveloping fury of a laser putting paid to a deserter's account.

Death was a point of blue steel, its edges polished smooth by a Roman hand that morning.

Rest, Publius Rectinus Falco, in whatever torments the gods adjudge you to deserve.

Several of the carnivores were still twitching in their iron blankets, dead to all but reflex that made their jaws clop and clawed feet slash at emptiness.

Their riders were utterly still. Vibulenus had wondered if the bodyguards had the tenacity of life that marked real toads, the ability to thrash for hours after being mangled. Not these. Their bodies were feathered with scores of native spears, thrust into the joints between the hoops of their armor.

The Commander was still alive.

At one time, he must have attempted to clamp shut the gouges in his legs, because both his gloved hands were slimy with his thick, dark blood. Now he only babbled sounds unintelligible even in the hush that followed the trading vessel's landing.

Vibulenus knelt—caught himself with his hands so that he did not topple flat himself. Moving was tricky; every time he did something different, he chanced total collapse.

The Commander's lips began to move slowly, as if he were still speaking, but no sounds came out. His eyes pleaded beneath a surface glitter that no longer seemed protective. Now it aped the glaze of death.

Which would shortly follow from shock and the blood loss that were natural results of the guild employee's wounds. The extensor muscles of both thighs had been slashed across, disabling him as effectively as hamstringing and with a far greater mess. The blood vessels that fed the powerful muscles were severed also, leaking out the Commander's life.

The tribune started to unknot the sash at his waist. His fingers did not work properly, and there was neither time or need to be delicate. The fallen weapon he picked up to cut the silk into a pair of tourniquets was his own sword.

"Just hold on." Vibuleenus said to the man—putatively—he was working to save. "You'll be fine. Death just gives you a different outlook on life."

"The turtle's coming, sir," said Titius. "S'pose they can load him in like they does us?"

"Why not?" said the tribune offhandedly as he tied off the right thigh. The Commander went limp, his head rolling back on the gravel from which he must have been lifting it so long as consciousness allowed. "It all comes down to the same thing, doesn't it? Whether we wear blue suits or bronze armor."

It did not occur to him to phrase the last sentence as a question.

"*Lookit* this sucker," Clodius Afer bragged. "Tell me you *ever* saw somethin' this ugly!"

"It'll do," Vibulenus said, more or less in agreement, as he surveyed the bull-roarer that the pilus prior had captured.

The sounding piece was about the size of a man's forearm and carved intricately from a single bone. Each of the holes through which air swirled to make the sound was fashioned into the likeness of a fanciful mouth.

The disquieting thing was that the result looked somehow as if it might be a miniature of a living creature
. . . and that thought was unpleasant even to men who
had become used to the toad-faced bodyguards.

"You oughta pick things up yourself, sir," said
Pompilius Niger with what the tribune supposed was
meant for a cheerful intonation. The junior centurion's
lips were so badly swollen around the cut that the
words he lisped would have been indistinguishable from
moaning by anyone less familiar with Niger than his
companions were. "Adds a little, you know, interest to
things."

"Found my sword," Vibulenus said, drawing the
weapon an inch or two from the sheath to indicate it.
He had cleaned the blade as soon as he had leisure and
the opportunity . . . using Falco's sash as a wiping rag.
He did not have a stone to resharpen the steel. That
would be done within the ship—*by* the ship, perhaps—
after the tribune stacked the weapon with the rest of his
equipment in the hall to the Sick Bay. "What have you
got? Teeth for a necklace?"

Some of the men had been doing that lately. The
ship stayed ripe with the miasma of putrefying alien
flesh for a week or two after each of the past several
battles.

"Better, sir," said Niger with a grin. He patted his
bulging leather knapsack. "I found honey. Near enough!"

A bright yellow car howled past a hundred feet in the
air. Crackling discharges played in its wake. Vibulenus'
mouth opened and his body trembled between the
choice of fight or flight . . . but the sizzling corona was
not a weapon, only a sign of someone from the trading
vessel headed in a great hurry toward the soldiers'
destination—their ship.

The legion's transport always looked mountainously
huge when the Romans straggled back to it; but even
after so many battles, Vibulenus had no clear picture of

what the vessel looked like when they disembarked. It was usually dark then, near dawn; and the ship was behind them—but it would require only a glimpse over a shoulder as he marched out. . . .

Battle was still a matter of anticipation. Every time, even though there had been so many, even though the fantasy fights in the Recreation Room had multiplied reality by a score of visions that seemed real while they were being dreamed. Neither battle nor sex brooked any rival when they had engaged a man's emotional attention.

"Now *where* in this place d'ye figure to find honey?" Clodius Afer was asking with a sweep of his arm. "I've seen *drill* fields as looked like a garden compared to this."

"Found," said the other centurion. He paused beside the barrel stem of a plant whose spreading leaves had been trampled to rags by hundreds of sets of hobnails. Kneeling instead of bending, so that the buckled lid of his knapsack remained level—it was not fluid tight—he stabbed the stem with his dagger and made a quick circular motion as if he were boning a ham.

The blade withdrew along with a plug of the stem. Behind it oozed a thick green fluid in such quantity that it must have come from a reservoir instead of being intracellular sap.

"See?" said Niger with muzzy brightness. He wiped his blade with an index finger and stuck his tongue between blackened, swollen lips to lick the green sap. "Just like honey."

"I'll take—" said Vibulenus, planning to continue, "—your word for it." But why not?

"I'll take a taste," the tribune said, dipping his own fingertip into the cavity rather than licking the digit which Niger offered him. The sap tasted sweet . . . and perhaps it even tasted like honey. The last time Vibulenus had tasted honey was too distant in time and incident for him to remember.

The sticky fluid had a smell like old bones, however, which he doubted had been true of honey.

"Well," said Vibulenus. He avoided the grimace which would have been insulting, but he wiped his finger carefully on the pebbles to cleanse it of the vile goop. "I wish you luck with your mead. It'll be . . . interesting, you bet."

"Wonder if that was the Commander bein' brought back?" suggested Clodius Afer as he shifted his loot. "Wasn't the tortoise picked him up, I hear, it was some little yellow bug from the trader. Like that one went past."

The expression on the pilus prior's face hinted that he wished he'd taken something less bulky, perhaps the spinner alone without the heavy shaft and line of the bull-roarer. It had been an exhausting battle for all of them; and under the guild, the legionaries did not have the lines of slaves that would have carried the loot they did not comprise.

Vibulenus looked at his friend, trying to remember how he had thought of Clodius when he first knew him. The pilus prior looked to be the same veteran at the height of his powers as was the file-closer who had cowed and angered a boyish tribune named Vibulenus. Clodius *was* that man physically . . . and perhaps in mind as well, more or less.

Certainly more nearly the same man than the tribune was; but the tribune *hadn't* been a man, only a boy, and he had aged a very long time since he first fought in the line at Clodius Afer's side.

Gaius Vibulenus, eighteen years old, drew his sword and almost lost it as he jumped down. A warrior thrust at him, and only Clodius' quick sideways chop kept the spear from taking Vibulenus through the chest. . . .

It was also hard to remember that men who had been side by side so many times, and through so much of the battle just completed, had not been together in the immediate aftermath. The pilus prior had led the sweep mopping up the right flank, while Vibulenus had knelt at the Commander's side when—

"Yes, it was a flying wagon from the trading ship that picked the Commander up," said the tribune as the three of them resumed their ambling pace toward their own vessel. The great doors already swarmed like the entrance of an anthill, shimmering with the forms of legionaries happy in their victory. "The tortoise came by, but it ignored him. They—I guess they don't expect commanders t' be hurt."

Killed, Vibulenus guessed with a great deal of experience on the subject, by the time the vehicle with six panicky figures in yellow suits had arrived. The tourniquets could not prevent shock, and blood loss from the wounds had probably proceeded beyond hope of recovery by the time the tribune had bound the limbs off.

"You know," said Niger, who had been sucking at his finger off and on with a contemplative expression, "they didn't pick up the bodyguards a'tall. I'd have thought they might be alive, some of 'em. Fixable, anyway," he added with a nod toward the tribune.

The three of them did not discuss the aftermath of the tower's collapse, so many . . . battles; what was a year?—battles ago. They had all received wounds since then, but none so serious that they could not stagger to the Sick Bay with the aid of friends.

"They can replace people to stand around and look ugly," Clodius said. "Wouldn't be surprised they could replace people to wear blue suits and stick their thumbs up their ass . . . though I dunno, prob'ly they've got a different kinda medic on the big ship, a veterinarian I shouldn't wonder.

"But anyhow, they *can't* replace us. Because nobody's ever been as good as we are."

Instead of clapping the senior centurion on the shoulder with a boastful echo of his own, Niger smiled oddly—

the distortion was not solely a result of swollen tissues—
and said, "Falco was there too. I guess they don't pick
up the ones they can't, you know, help."

His voice paused for a moment. The scrunch of the
trio's boots, in unison by habit, was the only sound the
men made for several seconds. Then Niger resumed,
"Mostly it'd bother me, you know, anybody I'd been
together with so long. Even ones I don't rightly know.
It'd be like it was—"

"Could've been you or me," said Clodius Afer, who
kept his eyes straight ahead.

"Like that, yeah," the junior centurion agreed. "Only
it isn't, you know? Nothing about that bastard has anything to do with me or anybody I care about. Alive or
dead. The vultures around here—" there had been
nothing in the local skies save the wagons after the
traders landed "—can have what they want of him."

Vibulenus laughed harsly and said, "As much epitaph
as he deserves." But in his heart he knew that he and
Rectinus Falco had been shoots from the same vine,
and the way they had twisted was the choice of the gods
alone.

From habit, the soldiers began to strip away their gear
as soon as they reentered the vessel. The hatch was the
same one by which they had disembarked, but now the
hall to the Sick Bay lay beyond it instead of the Main
Gallery. Like the fact that the sun rose and set—used
to rise and set—the internal workings of the ship had
ceased to be matters for comment. None of the soldiers—
none of the surviving soldiers—had enough philosophical
bent to waste energy trying to explain the inexplicable.

The line was moving faster than Vibulenus expected.
The aisle was scarcely half full even though the trio of
friends had been among the last Romans to drift back to
the vessel. Men were piling up their equipment for the
ship to process at leisure, then walking on without the
usual delay.

The Medic's voice could be heard. Though his words were unclear, they did not appear to be his usual sing-song about clearing and entering the cubicles. Over that and the shuffling murmur of men moving came repeated clangs from the device that warned someone was trying to carry metal into the vessel proper.

That happened after every battle, but the present frequency was many times greater than the usual number of accidents. Even the stupidest legionaries had long since learned that they could not sneak aboard with a knife or gold coins.

"What the fuck's going on?" Clodius Afer asked with his eyes narrowed by a frown. He leaned his shield—battered beyond conceivable salvage, but brought back because that was part of duty in the veteran's mind—against the wall and began stacking the rest of his equipment beside it. The amount of gear already deposited proved that, as the three expected, most of their fellows had already processed through.

"Maybe they've got a faster Medic," Niger suggested without particular interest. "Or maybe, you know, more booths." He touched his lips with a finger, this time as a delicate probe of his own injury.

"Maybe," said Vibulenus as he led the way down the aisle. His body was mottled with blood and bruises now that his clothes and armor no longer hid the price he had paid for the knob of high ground. "And maybe things have come a little unravelled, what with the Commander down. He was brand new, so I don't guess the guild has a replacement ready."

There were three bodyguards at the head of the moving column. Their armor was stained with gray dust pounded from the gravelly soil, and the calf and knee of one suit had bright scars showing that warriors had hacked at it.

The iron-clad toads were no less stolid than before . . . but the tribune could not look at them without remembering their fellows crumpled with feather-pointed native spears catching sun at each interstice of the armor. He smiled, though part of him objected that the toads were only dumb animals, not humans whose self-satisfied arrogance would have been worthy of his anger.

'Didn't really mind seein' 'em croak," said Clodius Afer, echoing the thought from a half step behind Vibulenus. "That's what frogs 're supposed to do, right?"

Both centurions laughed, and Vibulenus joined them.

"Move on through," said the Medic. "No, *not* the booth, cargo—" a legionary had started to tramp from habit into a cubicle "—straight on to the gal—"

The alarm chimed.

One of the toad-things blocked the side passage with his mace. The studded head of the weapon had been used in earnest recently enough that not all the residues had dried.

"Pollux!" shouted a soldier with no tunic but a cloth-wrapped bundle in his arms. "This isn't—"

One of his companions pulled him back and pointed to his feet. In the legionary's haste and disorientation, he had forgotten to take off his boots with their S-pattern of iron hobnails. That—and that sort of confused error—explained why the alarm kept ringing.

"There's a special address by the Commander," said the Medic by rote. His face, his tone did not seem bored. Rather, the blue-suited guild employee was abstracted and very possibly frightened. "Move on through, straight into the gallery."

"Well, if *that* isn't. . . ." Niger muttered angrily. "Don't mind tellin' you, I was lookin' forward t' something being done for this lip."

The three men stepped around the legionary stripping off his boots while his friend held the bundled loot. Vibulenus and his companions had left all their garments at the other end of the hall, but Clodius held his bull-roarer and his fellow carried the knapsack of—be generous: honey—by its straps.

The centurions intended to leave the objects near the cubicles and carry them into the ship when they were through with the Sick Bay. Now, brazenly, they carried their gleanings past the bodyguards who did not know to care, and the Medic who knew not to speak.

"I wouldn't have thought they could fix him up so quickly," Vibulenus muttered to himself, "the Commander. Not that the wounds were so extensive. . . ."

But it took a long time to come to terms with the fact you've been killed. Maybe it took more time than even the gods had.

The scene in the Main Gallery was chaotic but chaotically cheerful. Legionaries, a number of them still wearing tunics among their naked fellows, milled and boasted and compared their loot. Almost all the men had at least superficial wounds, but slashes and bruised muscles were too much a part of normal affairs to dampen spirits significantly.

The change in routine put life in the air the way fair day made a country hamlet sparkle. The legion had just turned near disaster into a victory as stunning and sudden as defeat had promised to be. With that behind them, nobody seemed to think that this "special assembly" could be any form of bad news.

Nobody except Gaius Vibulenus, who had been studying the guild with the mind of a man whose family owed much of its wealth to land bought from neighbors whom Sulla had executed. . . .

Soldiers have nothing to teach a good businessman about ruthlessness.

"*Sir,*" said a heavily-cheerful voice. "You'll know, won't you? What've they got going on?"

Vibulenus turned to see that it was the first centurion, Julius Rusticanus, who was hailing him.

It was surprising that Rusticanus was no worse mauled

than seemed to be the case—scores of cuts on his limbs
and several on his face, but able to talk and move with
only the half-hidden twinges that might result from
wounds received before the guild bought the legionaries from their Parthian captors. The point of the right
flank, where the first centurion stood in battle, would
have been enveloped instantly by the native army and
cleared last of all by the Tenth Cohort's counterthrust.

A tough man, Julius Rusticanus. But then, they all
were by now. Even the tribune who looked like a youth
with more lineage than strength of character.

"You're looking all right for somebody at the sharp
end, First," Vibulenus said in real approval. Nobody
was indispensable, but the first centurion's combination
of education and battle-bred experience could not have
been equalled in the legion. "But Hades, no—I don't
know, I'm not sure anybody does, in a blue suit or not.
They're stirred up over losing the Commander, that's
sure enough."

"He got chopped?" said Rusticanus. His face went
neutral; then, as he judged his audience, broadened
into a smile. "Well, that's a terrible thing to happen,
isn't it?"

He saluted and stepped back into the crowd, bending
some of his particular cronies close to hear the news.
Men on the right flank would have had no way to learn
of the command group's massacre. For that matter,
only a few hundred of the nearest legionaries would
have been close enough to see the incident or its
aftermath.

"You forget," Vibulenus said as he and his two companions drifted by habit toward the front of the gallery,
"that other people don't know things just because you
do."

"What do I know?" asked Niger, misunderstanding
the tribune's mumbled statement.

"You know," said Vibulenus instead of correcting the

error, "how to make mead." He patted the knapsack, finding the leather surface squishy but not, thank Fortune, stickily permeated with that awful juice. "Among other things."

There was a sudden commotion from the rear of the big room, catcalls. The tribune turned and caught the flash of a yellow bodysuit beyond a sudden motion of Romans toward them.

"Hey, what ye got there?" somebody cried distinctly. The edge of hectoring command in the voice would have been familiar enough to civilians in barracks town, meeting a squad of legionaries recently spilled from a bar.

"Come on," the tribune ordered curtly, shouldering his way toward the trouble. This could get out of hand real fast—maybe already had. Why had the cursed fool decided to walk a gauntlet of killers loosened by fatigue and victory? And where were the guards who *always* accompanied guild employees in the presence of soldiers.

That was easy to answer: dead on the field, enough of them, and this fellow with his yellow suit and apparatus floating before him ignorant of what a bad pair of mistakes he had just made at his life's risk.

"Get the *fuck* outa the way!" snarled Clodius Afer, clubbing soldiers to either side with the staff of his bull-roarer. Niger used the side of his fist to equal effect—neither centurion needed to be told what happened to legionaries who angered the trading guild.

The tribune and his companions were not alone. Non-coms including Julius Rusticanus converged from all sides on the guild employee, forming a shoulder-to-shoulder wall facing out against the gibes and half-meant threats. It wasn't that the centurions and file-closers were less ragged than the legionaries they backed off, or that the jostling, cat-calling mob did not understand that they were playing a dangerous game.

But the legion was a hierarchy, and the common

soldiers had the right to be irresponsible in every activity which that hierarchy did not deem to be their duty. The problem with externally-applied discipline is that it can only be specific; and it tends to eliminate self-discipline throughout the general behavior of the men it governs.

No matter here. The troops were only rowdy, not in a state of suicidal mutiny.

"What're you trying to do, citizen?" Vibulenus snapped to the guild employee, sure that the situation was under control. "Trying to get up front?"

Conceivably the fellow hadn't meant to enter the Main Gallery at all. He had the slightly purple complexion and stocky build of the current commander, a racial type as different from that of the first officer the legion had been given as either was from the Romans themselves.

But he didn't know Latin. To speak, Vibulenus leaned over the dull-finished cart the technician pushed in front of him. Instead of replying, the fellow cringed away, colliding with the back of a centurion too solid to notice the impact. He was utterly terrified and obviously understood the tribune's curt questions as a bloodthirsty threat.

Pollux! Maybe one of the guards down in front would be able to translate.

Somebody shouted, "Hey, prettiest, how'd you know I was lookin' for you?"

Quartilla touched the tribune on the arm to get his attention, then gabbled at the technician in some barbarous language or other.

The fellow looked as if he had been offered water in a wilderness. He gabbled back, making gestures toward the ceiling with his three-digit hands.

"He says," Quartilla relayed, "that he's supposed to disconnect the barrier so the Commander can come aboard." She smiled. "He says a lot of things besides, but you can probably guess them."

"All right." Vibulenus ordered. "We'll walk him down to the front, now."

There was a hushed area in his immediate presence, a result of the abrupt way the tribune and non-coms had asserted authority. Quartilla had appeared in that rebound from raucousness to embarrassment; fortunate timing, though the tribune felt sure that she could have handled without ugliness whatever situation developed. For that matter, now that he looked around, he could see that other females as well had joined the legionaries. What in Hades' halls was going on?

"Move out, boys, keep it moving," said Julius Rusticanus. When the protective screen of Romans began to move and the technician did not, the first centurion reached around the fellow and began pushing the floating cart himself. The technician gave the choked equivalent of a yelp and scuttled along after his gear.

"What are you doing here?" the tribune asked Quartilla in as much of an aside as the ambient noise and his greater height permitted. Men made room for the unusual procession, watching avidly, treating it—like everything else since they reboarded the ship—as a form of entertainment.

"We can wander when you're outside the ship," the woman replied. The smiles and armpats with which she greeted soldiers were as effective in clearing onlookers from the path as the tribune's own lowering sternness. "This time there wasn't an order to return, and we just . . . came along with everybody else."

Vibulenus had not known that the women could even leave their cubicles until he saw Quartilla before battle this morning—a lifetime ago. He thought of that meeting and missed a step because his muscles forgot to move.

"There," he said loudly, using volume of sound to dim memories with which he was not ready to deal. He made a sweeping gesture to inform the guild technician

if words could not do so. They were through the clumps
of legionaries—who had nudged closer to the barrier
than was normally the case. Four bodyguards, stolid
despite the froth and scratches on their armor, were
spaced across the front wall, but Roman soldiers were
willing to stand within the circuit that could be swept
by the long maces.

The technician jumped backward when he raised his
eyes to the bulge-eyed, broad-mouthed visage of the
nearest guard, even though the creature glanced at him
with no more interest than he showed in anything else
around him. Quartilla clucked out a direction and the
guild employee lunged forward after a moment's further hesitation.

"What's wrong with him?" Clodius Afer asked, freed
of his self-imposed duty now that the yellow-suited
figure was under the protection of the bodyguards.

"He's not familiar with any of this," the woman replied with a smile warm enough to make the tribune's
fists clench despite him. "Usually he'd never get off his
own ship except on home leave."

"Used to scare me too, didn't they?" said Vibulenus,
relaxing as he tried to recall a part of the past which he
had surmounted.

"Well, why's he here now?" said Niger bluntly from
the tribune's other side. The technician had slid his cart
against the bulkhead and was making cryptic gestures at
the end that extended back of the barrier. "Thought
they never let that down, the . . . you know."

There were subjects that would never be safe, even
for someone whose mind had compartments as rigid as
those of Niger's. Vibulenus squeezed and released his
friend's shoulder.

"They've had to replace the Commander on an emergency basis," the woman explained. She was speaking
with a familiarity regarding the crews' routines which
Vibulenus could understand easily enough, if he let his

mind consider it. "They don't have a barrier key available, so they'll clear the lock instead of replacing it."

The leavening of women in the big room was too slight for Vibulenus to get a good view of any of the others. Like the sand grain in the heart of a pearl, they attracted their own covering—in this case, soldiers in expectant circles. No harm done, even in those groupings where the women were practicing their trade under field conditions.

Like Quartilla, all the females the tribune glimpsed in the Main Gallery would have passed unremarked on a Capuan street. It was possible to forget what they must have looked like once, the way you forgot that an adult acquaintance had been an infant in past years.

The barrier lit itself in bands of light that started as a transfigured lime green and expanded toward the violet end of the spectrum in stages as distinct as those of a rainbow. There was a high-pitched crackling like pork fat being fried.

Niger turned his face away and swore.

For a moment, the plane of the barrier disappeared but the armor of each of the guards was surrounded by a ghostly nimbus. The pair nearest the center of the bulkhead were closely wrapped in sheaths of blue and indigo. The guards toward the opposite sidewalls were trebled in bulk by billowing softness of red light, causing some of the nearer legionaries to push away abruptly.

The guards themselves did not at first react, but the one nearest Vibulenus turned his bulging eyes to stare past the glow of his mace head.

The room popped, a sound that perhaps came from the ship's communications system instead of a physical part of the Main Gallery. The auras snuffed themselves. The guards snapped their heads straight again before a flicker of lights in the hexagon pattern announced the bulkhead door was opening.

The Commander, flanked by two more bodyguards,

strode through the dissolving sidewall next to the tribune's party instead of coming from the ship's forward section.

He wore a yellow bodysuit which covered his fingers instead of leaving his hands bare, a quicker clue to status among guild employees than the shimmer before their faces which Quartilla said was a barrier against bad air. Vibulenus recognized him: he had been their first commander, the one who purchased them in Mesopotamia.

Quartilla wore a tunic of many layers, each diaphanous by itself. The tribune did not realize that he was gripping her shoulders until the layers of fabric began to shift greasily beneath his pressure.

The pilot stood in the bulkhead doorway, holding a laser. The tech who had just released the barrier pushed his cart through the opening and almost collided with the crewman because both were more intent on the legionaries than they were on matters closer to hand.

The Commander had all his former nonchalance. "Brave warriors," he said in the voice which was that of every commander, "you have won a victory with the skill and courage which I learned to expect when you were under my command previously. My guild thanks you for your continued progress beneath its tutelage."

The door in the other sidewall opened as if it were composed of rime ice melting in the sun. Motion drew the usual attention, half a dozen yellow-clad techs, one of them floating a cart before him. Then there was a surge of panic from that corner of the gallery—not at the remaining survivor of the bodyguard, but because the armored toad was leading one of the carnivores he and his fellows rode in battle.

The creature did not wear its blanket of iron scales, though there were patches in the bristling fur over its withers and shoulders where that armor must have rubbed. The slotted disk was on its chest, whining eagerly and so firmly implanted that no straps or chains were necessary to hold it in place. Instead of a saddle or other riding tack, the beast wore a broad metal collar with a shackle through which was rived the cable by which the guard led the creature along.

"Castor and *Pollux*," muttered Clodius Afer. "That's bigger'n the ones they ride, right?"

Vibulenus shrugged, but he suspected the pilus prior was wrong. The great brindled carnivore was rangier than it appeared when its armor bulked the smooth tuck of its belly; but seeing the beast in a structure of human scale, even one as large as the Main Gallery, gave it an impact that it did not have when surrounded by open sky.

"A hyena," said Niger, searching back through memories of beast fights in the arena.

"Haunches're too high," the tribune objected; but for the rest, the centurion's description was a good one.

The creature, as unaccustomed to the circumstances as the Romans were, jerked at the cable and clopped its long jaws shut in a spray of saliva. Despite the size of the bodyguard and his metal-cased grip on the lead line, the carnivore threw him off balance. Men scrambled even farther back in an effect like that of a pond rippling.

The Commander's ears quivered in a gesture of irritation as he noted the beast's restiveness. Then, as his eyes swept the assembly again before resuming the thread of his discourse, he saw Quartilla in the front row.

For a moment, the face of the guild officer contorted. He turned and shot an unheard order to the Pilot which brought that subordinate erect in a terrified brace, the ready laser slapping down alongside his thigh. Even after the Commander turned back in apparent calm to the waiting Romans, the Pilot held himself stiffly and continued to swallow hard.

"Because of matters which cannot properly be blamed on you," the Commander said to the assembly, "there has been some temporary disorganization in the operations of this vessel. Let me reassure you that this will not affect you warriors in the least. Because of my experience and the success with which I moulded you into one of my guild's most valued assets, I have been requested to take over again as an interim measure."

His ears twitched. "Even though my rank would normally put me well beyond such duties."

"We were supposed to be recalled to our own quarters as usual," whispered Quartilla from the tribune's left side. "Somebody forgot."

Simultaneously, Clodius snickered on the other side, and said, "Bastard was handy and got stuck into the slot with no more ado than I'd make on latrine detail. And he ain't half pissed, is 'e?"

The squad of technicians from the trading vessel had stepped between the Commander and the door behind him. Two of them were lifting from the cart a U-shaped staple that seemed to be a fair weight for them. The bodyguard with the tethered carnivore waited nearby. The beast seemed willing to squat on its haunches, but it was making rumbling complaints in the back of its throat.

"I have called you to this extraordinary address," the Commander said, "to assure you that nothing else about the circumstances is extraordinary. Your privileges and duties as assets of my guild remain the same, and the discipline which I will enforce will be as harsh as is required for your own long-term good."

The technicians had set the staple legs-down on the floor. After fussing with it for a moment, they stepped back. The Commander glanced aside with an ear-twitch that showed he resented the way his subordinates drew attention away from his rhetorical periods.

The staple ejected angry green sparks and a hiss that

could have come from a snake big enough to swallow the Main Gallery whole. The technicians winced, but only in reflex. The Commander leaped forward with a startled cry, and when the carnivore leaped upright it pulled its handler flat on the floor with a crash.

"Well. . . ." said Clodius Afer, who—like most of the Romans near the front of the assembly—had jumped slightly at the fireworks. They had been close enough to other things to which the crew had subjected the legionaries that they did not panic, just start reflexively the way the techs did.

The Commander, who did not expect to be surprised, had just shown as little control as the animal, slavering with its hackles up as two more guards grabbed its lead line.

The staple was cool and silent, now that it had tacked itself to the floor. The techs were packing up their tools in seeming innocence, oblivious to the glare the Commander threw them as soon as he recovered his balance. It was just possible that the team of workmen did not realize how startling the flash and hiss had been to their superior.

Vibulenus began to laugh. Quartilla pressed a palm firmly over his lips.

The Commander spoke to the guards, the ship directing his words so that only echoes of angry grunting reached the tribune. The group on the tether led—even three of them together lacked the strength and weight to drag—the carnivore close enough to the staple to loop the line through.

One of the yellow-clad technicians clamped the end of the line back against itself. The fellow was being very careful to keep the guards between him and the carnivore.

"There will be another brief display," said the Commander, facing the assembly as if he had not lost his composure after all. The communications system accurately reproduced the breathiness that accompanied the way the guild officer's chest heaved. "Do not be alarmed."

The pop and sparkling as the line welded itself was so minor that only the comment made it remarkable. The technicians quickstepped out through the bulkhead door, trying to ignore the laser in the hands of the Pilot as they moved past him.

"Some of your comrades are undergoing emergency medical treatment," said the Commander in a return to his planned speech. "It is up to you to convince them that the rules which have always applied continue in force during my interim appointment. While the ship remains in normal space, the forward portion of the Main Gallery will be kept off limits by our friend here."

The Commander's arm made a coy gesture that filled Vibulenus with revulsion. Did he think they were children? Or mincing aristocrats maundering to one another while slaves pampered their bodies? He should spit out his instructions, treating them as soldiers and pretending himself to be a man!

The trio of guards still held the tether. Their armored bodies were interposed between the beast and the Commander, though the guild officer could scarcely be at risk from an animal whose like he had ridden to battle many times in the past.

"Our friend," continued the Commander in the oily manner that was as much a part of his position as the shimmer that filtered the air he breathed, "has been treated to react in a certain way to any assets of your race who come within his reach. Lest you—"

The Pilot stepped from the doorway with a set expression, gripping his weapon so fiercely that tendons stood out on the backs of his hands.

"Your Worship!" shouted Gaius Vibulenus as his soul froze and his body stepped forward into the cleared area where he had no friends or fellows. The acoustics of the big room drank his voice, but not so fully that the dainty figure in yellow could not hear him.

The tribune's hands were raised and open, a sign of supplication and in any culture proof of peaceful intent. A guard lurched forward, holding his mace out in bar.

"You have wisely chosen a creature whose savagery and power were demonstrated to us all today," Vibulenus said, still shouting. His mind considered the risk that other Romans who could not hear him would take this as some suicidal call to mutiny—and obey it.

That risk was the lesser one.

"Who could not have been amazed," the tribune continued, gesturing rhetorically as his chest halted at the mace shaft, "at the way these terrible creatures wreaked havoc among heavily armed opponents whose skill and courage threatened to overwhelm us? Not even the bravest of us would dare approach such a creature as this."

The carnivore snarled and gave a tentative pull on its line as it peered past its handlers toward the Roman. Vibulenus wondered whether he had halted inside or outside the arc the beast could lunge on its tether.

That risk, too, had to be disregarded.

For a moment, the Pilot leveled his weapon at the tribune. Then he pointed the laser at the deck and hopped backward, into the doorway again. The crewman had been drafted into duties beyond his normal competence. Now that the script had gone awry, the Pilot had either to improvise or to withdraw.

The Commander's duties did not permit him the option of withdrawing. He glanced behind him, nervously aware that if the carnivore lunged toward this nearest Roman, the cable would slice across those standing in the way.

"This assembly is dismissed," the Commander said sharply, driven to decision by the personal risk which grew if he should vacillate. "Leave at once and report to the Sick Bay for normal processing."

There was immediate movement toward the rear of the gallery. The sudden dismissal was just one more circumstance in a disorganized day.

The Commander's lips moved, and the voice in Vibulenus's ears said, "Not you, Gaius Vibulenus Caper."

Two guards advanced in response to orders grunted to them alone. They forced Vibulenus back a step as if he were a spiderlet ballooning before the wind. Rather than resist their effortless advance, he skipped ahead of them, keeping one outstretched hand on the mace helve to show that he was not trying to escape.

"Slow *down*, fish-face," snarled Clodius Afer as he and Niger—Niger blanching yellow beneath the wind-burn on his skin—stepped toward the guards on the balls of their feet.

"It's all right!" the tribune cried, sliding between the creatures in armor and the friends who would rescue him. "We're just getting away from the, the hyena!"

Maybe. Existing on the ship like fighting a war. Unless you intended to plunge in and slog forward, come what may, you needed to anticipate what everyone else would be doing long before *they* decided. And you could assume that not only would communications break down, but that everyone would put the worst possible face on whatever anyone else did.

Vibulenus didn't think his anticipation was very good. But he'd have bet his hopes of homecoming that he was the only one aboard who tried.

Quartilla touched an arm of each centurion though she did not try to hold them. "They're getting him away from the beast," the woman was saying throatily. "Careful or you'll put him in danger."

Maybe the tribune *wasn't* the only one on board who tried to think things through.

The Commander strode beyond the arc of his—

watchdog's—tether, permitting the bodyguards to release it. When they exerted themselves, the toad-things
exuded a sweetish odor with a tinge of ammonia behind
it.

Freed, the carnivore immediately relaxed. It strolled
across the front bulkhead at the limit of its cable,
sniffing at the deck which clicked beneath its claws.

"I want to—" the guild officer began. He glanced at
the centurions and Quartilla, then beyond at other soldiers staying to watch the show in the knowledge that
the mob ahead of them would not clear for some time.
The Commander's ears twitched; he turned toward his
expectant bodyguards.

Quartilla opened her mouth, but neither Clodius nor
Niger would be ruled by a woman in this.

"I would appreciate it," called Vibulenus in a tone of
icy command, "if you men would go about your business while I confer with my superior."

The face of the pilus prior went professionally blank.
Niger, more boyish in spirit as well as appearance,
blinked like a dog who has been kicked for jumping up
to greet its master. Then both minds reasserted themselves and the men stepped away, still held by Quartilla.
Clodius Afer was wearing a grim smile.

"As you were saying, Your Worship?" Vibulenus
prompted with an expression as supercilious as that of
one campaigning politician meeting another.

Close up, the Commander's face seemed to be tinged
with jaundice. Whether that was true, or an accident of
reflection from the yellow bodysuit—or possibly just
something within the tribune's mind—was beyond
Vibulenus' reckoning. His lips, which were more nearly
circular at rest than a human's should have been, pursed
and paused. At last the guild officer decided to say,
"We have noted with approval your actions on the field
today, military tribune. My guild was very pleased with

the loyalty and dedication you showed, as well as a level of initiative unexpected in an asset."

Even without the hinted motion of the Commander's ears, Vibulenus would have known that "initiative" was an attribute with risk when it appeared this far down the chain of command.

"My guild seeks to reward proper behavior," the Commander continued. He was absurdly slight when viewed from so nearby. The strength and technique which Vibulenus had gained from untold battles and drills would permit him to snap the childsized neck before either of the guards, slowed by their armor, could intervene.

"Is there some particular reward you would like to receive?" said the voice that did not come directly from the Commander's lips.

"Your Worship," said Vibulenus as his mind took over before his body began to tremble at the risk he was accepting; "I would like to lead my fellows home and arrange the recruitment of new legions of full strength for you."

That was ridiculous—Romans enlisting as mercenaries for foreign traders! But if the guild let them march home, then the aftermath could be dealt with somehow, some way. . . .

"That's ridiculous," snapped the Commander. "If you can't—" He started to step back between the body-guards who flanked him.

"Then, sir," the tribune continued without hesitation or evidence that he understood his rebuke, "perhaps you could arrange that one of the females be withdrawn from—" he licked the lips that had just gone dry "—general duties and place her at my service. The woman Quartilla."

He did not dare to look behind him to see whether she was in the room or even within possible earshot.

"You want one of your own?" the guild officer said

with amusement, shifting his weight back onto his leading foot. "Very interesting."

His dainty fingers made an uncertain gesture at the tight legs of his garment. "If I were to be abandoned to this wretched duty for any length of time, I'd make a study of your behavioral patterns for my own amusement."

Vibulenus' tight smile was a mask that waited for an answer that he dared not anticipate.

"Yes, of course," said the Commander. "We grant your petition. Now, go on and carry out your duties, remembering that the eyes of my guild are on even the least of its assets."

The slim figure turned and strode through the bulkhead door, giving a wary glance at the carnivore who paced before it in guard. The toad-things followed their master by pairs, without audible summons.

Only after the last of the armored monsters disappeared into the forward section of the vessel did the Pilot leave the doorway. The portal closed, sparkling like lightstruck dew.

Gaius Vibulenus Caper turned, feeling disoriented by the complex of emotions which eddied through him.

It takes time to clear a structure of four thousand men, even when the entire back wall gapes open. Quartilla and the two centurions had obeyed Vibulenus' order, but they were still within fifty feet of the tribune when he turned around.

The three smiled when Vibulenus' head-to-head discussion ended without sudden violence. Niger waved at his old friend and Clodius Afer called a comment which could be heard only in its cheerfulness.

The woman stiffened while her ears received a message which others did not. She looked at Vibulenus, returning to them at the slow pace which his stiffening wounds required. Then, unexpectedly, Quartilla began to run across the front of the Main Gallery, away from the tribune.

"Quartilla!" Vibulenus called. Niger put out a hand, but neither of her immediate companions made a real attempt to stop her. The woman was even fleshier than his Roman ideal of feminine beauty, but her bulk was more muscle than fat—and unlike the men, she had not just fought a grueling hand-to-hand battle. "*Quartilla!*"

What would have been a wall in the far corner, if a soldier ran against it, dissolved into a doorway in time to pass Quartilla. An instant later it was again gray metal, or at least what passed for metal on the ship.

The tribune carefully joined his companions.

"What got into her, Gaius?" asked Pompilius Niger as he gripped hands with his childhood friend.

"Better question'd be why all the good-time girls were loose t' begin with," said the pilus prior. "Not that I care." He patted the tribune's shoulder gently with an iron-hard palm. "Sir, you . . . Aw, fukkit, I'm glad to serve with you, that's the size of it."

Vibulenus' height made it easy for him to drape his arms over the shoulders of both other men. "Good to serve with you guys, too. Hercules, with *all* of us." He nodded toward the back of the gallery, still crowded with legionaries, and started his own companions moving in that direction toward the Medic and the baths.

"But you know?" the tribune added in a voice whose mildness deceived neither of his hearers, "Sometimes I don't think a great deal of the folks we're serving *for*."

They were nearing the head of the line to the Medic's booths when they heard the shout from down the hall, "Does anybody see the tribune? Gaius Caper?"

"Oh, fuck off," mumbled Clodius Afer, but he was grumbling at the situation more than he was the searching legionary. A blow turned by the mail covering his right biceps had gone unnoticed during the battle, but the muscle had begun to swell into purple agony as soon as the pilus prior sheathed his sword.

"It can wait," Vibulenus muttered; but maybe it couldn't, and he stepped aside to look in the direction of the summons.

There was less of a crush awaiting the Medic than the Tribune had expected. Given the option of obeying the Commander's injunction or not, many of the men with lesser injuries had gone to the baths, the bars, or the women instead.

Even Clodius Afer and his companions had detoured to a hall of sleeping rooms which the pilus prior designated the Tenth Cohort's barracks area. The Tenth had been doing that after the past dozen or so battles, and the rest of the legion had followed suit immediately.

There was no lack of space within the vessel, and the trading guild obviously did not care whether or not accommodations were organized; but it was good for the men to have something they could treat as home, and it was good for a unit that fought together to keep its cohesion out of battle as well.

Among other things, it gave the troops a place to stash their loot under guard for the days or weeks until the vessel "entered Transit space"—and all the soldiers awakened together to be marched against a new enemy.

"Has anybody seen—sir, *there* you are! We need to talk to you, I'm sorry."

"Of course, Marcus Rusticanus," said the tribune. It wasn't one man searching him out, it was the first centurion with an entourage of at least twenty other soldiers. The latter began babbling excitedly to friends and acquaintances waiting in line while Julius Rusticanus approached the tribune—with a salute.

The Medic called something nervous but unclear in the clutter of other sound. The two bodyguards became restive also, if not actively hostile. They stepped toward the gathering which completely blocked the aisle, brushing Romans aside with their iron shoulders. Swearing softly, Clodius Afer turned to face the new threat.

"Outside," Vibulenus ordered in instant decision. He wished he felt better—and his physical condition was less a burden than the way his stomach dropped in black spirals whenever he thought of Quartilla.

"You heard the tribune!" roared the first centurion to the mob of men who had done no such thing. "Turn around and move *out!*"

Obedience was so quick and so complete that Rusticanus could begin marching immediately toward what had been a solid clot of men at the moment his leg swung forward. Vibulenus fell in step beside the senior non-com, marveling at the way discipline made of soldiers something greater—or at least different—than their numbers alone.

The Medic gave another startled squawk. The tribune glanced behind him and saw not only Clodius and Niger, but the soldiers who had been even nearer the booth as well—following because Rusticanus had said the tribune had ordered them to do so. The guards halted, no longer concerned, but the Medic had enough initiative to wonder what was happening.

The sudden, accidental display of his authority made Vibulenus tingle with pleasure, but there was a frightening core of responsibility within it also.

"Sir," said Julius Rusticanus even as the tribune's mouth opened to prod him, "I think. . . ." He rubbed his bald scalp fiercely. "Sir, if you come to the Rec Room, you can see it for yourself. That's better than me trying to tell you."

Presumably they were marching in that direction already as they followed an orange bead out of the Sick Bay and into a cross corridor. The floorplan of the ship normally did not change between embarkation and landing; but even when fixed, the maze of corridors was so complex that it was easier to ask for a guide bead to your destination than it was to grope along without one.

"These men came from Recreation?" asked Vibulenus,

gesturing with spread fingers toward their entourage instead of giving a nod. The motion of walking was more than he could comfortably accept, and a good brisk shake of his head was likely to drop him to the floor in blinding pain.

He didn't imagine that anything so badly required his presence that it couldn't have waited for him to be refashioned into comfort by the Medic's cubicles. The first centurion—whose freshness and clean tunic proved he had at least been to the baths—thought it was that level of emergency, though. Rusticanus was a solid man and had the information, so the tribune would be a fool to second-guess him.

"Yessir," Rusticanus answered. "A lot stayed back though, and I just hope they kept the lid on." He paused, rubbing his scalp, before he added, "Figured I'd better come fetch you myself, sir, so's you'd know there was a rush."

"Good judgment, First," Vibulenus said, grinning wryly in his mind. He should have been pleased at his own accurate and self-sacrificing response to the situation. Instead, he was thinking that if he were a little less dutiful, he wouldn't feel like a gladiator being dragged out of the arena on a hook—and he'd be better able to deal with whatever the problem was.

The soldiers ahead of them turned into the Recreation Room, slowed by the number of men already standing inside. The circular, domed room expanded when all its couches were full, so the tribune had never seen it overcrowded. Now, though there must have been at least a thousand men packing the aisles and open areas, only a handful were actually lying back to enter the room's fantasy world.

"Move aside!" bellowed the first centurion. "Move aside for the tribune!" Soldiers obeyed by leaping onto the couches, the only space available. Many of them shouted, some cheering Vibulenus but others calling messages of anger uncertain in the confusion.

What in *Hades* was going on?

The tribune sat down on a couch, started to swing his legs up, and quickly decided to lay his torso down first. The strain of balancing his upper body while trying to lift his legs with his belly muscles had sent sheets of white fire across the back of his eyeballs.

"Easy does it, Gaius," said Pompilius Niger from the next couch with a grin that opened the cut in his lips. He reached across with one broad hand and lifted the tribune's feet onto the couch. The two of them, and Clodius on the tribune's other side, lay back together.

Vibulenus found the battling animals of the Recreation Room—a different set every voyage—to be a splendid way to sharpen his skills as well as a matter of amusement. No doubt that was what the trading guild had in mind when it provided this "game" at what was as surely great expense as the gladiatorial shows with which politicians paid for votes throughout Rome's Latin-speaking domains.

Real drill with weighted swords was the only way to develop muscles for battle, but timing and judgment could be taught better on the mental fields of the Recreation Room. Pain was the penalty for misjudging an opponent's strength or speed: instant, agonizing pain that was wholly real until another dream figure finished you off. Learning that sort of lesson on a physical battlefield was likely to cost your life—permanently, despite the magic of the trading guild. Certainly it took you out of action when your friends might need you.

But lessons in tactical maneuver were more important, at least for the tribune, than training in the physical aspects of battle. Though the contending armies were marshalled from animals and were often equipped in equally silly fashions, their tactics were those that could be applied to bodies of men.

Vibulenus could not *change* the movements and dispositions of the armies: those proceeded according to some higher law, just as the legion in the field was commanded—if not led—by a figure in a blue bodysuit. But the game aspect of the situation, the certainty that no permanent harm would occur to his real flesh, let the tribune study the fantasy battles with a detachment that carried over.

That morning he had pulled a cohort out of line, changed its front, and smashed a new threat without panic—because he had so often in his mind been a participant when the wheels came off a maneuver in the face of the enemy.

The first feeling Gaius Vibulenus had when his consciousness entered the fantasy scene was physical relief. The Recreation Room did nothing to alleviate his injuries the way the Sick Bay or even a bath would have; but by isolating the tribune from his body, it deleted the body's pain for the time being.

The next feeling was incredulity. Almost at once it became anger that hissed like a red-glowing sword being tempered in an oil bath . . . but he directed his mind downward, into the action, because he had come here to get information.

The animals on one side were spearmen who carried huge shields and rode to battle in wagons. They were more manlike than not, but their skins were purple and they had long feathery appendages in place of ears.

The animals on the other side were Roman legionaries. This battle was the first one the legion had fought on behalf of the trading guild.

Vibulenus directed his consciousness into one of the giant aliens. Vagrantly he considered entering the mind of a Roman, of poking and sampling the memories of a fellow who might lie on the couch beside him. The thought squeezed the tribune with nausea even though he did not at present have a stomach to turn. As suddenly—

he was a warrior with a harness of bronze bangles, more ornamental than protective. He gripped the rope frame of his jouncing chariot with his left hand; in his right was an iron-headed spear half again as tall as he was. The cartwheels and the hooves of the team threw up reeds and mud and water as the vehicle lurched out of the swampy depression at the valley's center.

The slope above them held the hostile army which was advancing like a single monstrous creature.

The driver hauled back and left on his reins, swinging the chariot to a broadside halt in front of the enemy. Two of the other warriors vaulted from the vehicle while it was still slowing, slamming Vibulenus off balance in their haste to plant themselves on the ground.

Fools. That's exactly where they would wind up—at the leisure of a burial party.

The part of the tribune's mind that came with the body he now inhabited did not understand the army that was tramping down at him. It glittered with metal, each warrior dressed in the trappings of a great chief. But those same warriors moved as a single serried mass, each front-rank champion advanced only a long stride in front of the followers arrayed behind to his right and left.

It was not a wedge formation. It was the edge of a saw sweeping toward Vibulenus.

He strode off his vehicle, heartened by the rumble of the bronze gongs in each of the cars lurching toward the enemy. Now free of the need to stabilize him, his left hand gripped the shield and swung it in front of him. The strap's friction irritated his neck despite the leather throatlet he wore against that problem, but his muscles made nothing of the shield's weight. The consciousness that was a Roman tribune remembered that the shields of hide on heavy wooden frames weighed around a hundred pounds apiece.

That same mind also knew the way to break the Roman advance, to smash the legion's integrity so that the mass of light-armed thralls on the hill behind Vibulenus and the other champions could nibble clots of Romans like nodes of sand in the surf. He opened his mouth to shout orders to his immediate companions, and the rain of javelins washed the words back down his throat.

Vibulenus' shield was like a section of leathern tower. Its lower rim was only a handbreadth off the ground, but it was tall enough that he could duck his head and broad shoulders to safety without lifting the shield higher. Javelins were the weapon of thralls, a part of him thought, not of warriors who dared challenge—

The javelin that struck the upper edge of his shield buried its point in the frame and did not penetrate. It slapped the shield back against Vibulenus' skull hard enough to dizzy him for an instant, and one of the three other missiles went far enough through the center of the hide to prick his left biceps.

The second flight was already arching down.

The chariot overturned with a crash behind Vibulenus, throwing sod and bits of broken wheel against his calves. He lunged forward, away from the touch and toward the real threat, the ranks running forward as they drew swords much heavier than the knife in Vibulenus' sash which he used only to silence the screaming wounded.

The weight of javelins clinging to his shield dragged its edge against the ground and made him stumble. His toes hurt where they stubbed the shield rim, and the javelin hurled by a strong man scratched both his left arm and his chest as its point slammed several inches through the thick leather.

That did not make the body's consciousness afraid: he was a warrior, a champion who met the best each enemy offered and slew them, knowing that he would be slain in turn some day. But the near escape made him respectful of missiles that were more than the stone-weighted ox-goads his own thralls hurled.

"Lock shields!" the tribune's mind ordered through the warrior's lips. Normally, champions would duel before the weight of reinforcements to both sides made the engagement a general one of armies and shield walls. But this was not a normal battle. . . .

Oxen bellowed in terror as three of them dragged the overturned chariot and the yoke-mate which was interested only in biting off the javelin that quivered in its haunch. The warrior who had stepped off with Vibulenus was still all right, though a javelin with a bent shaft dangled from his shield face also.

The pair who had jumped from the chariot a moment earlier had been off balance when the missiles struck. One was down his face, a javelin at belt height beneath him and three more fanning from his back which he had turned in staggering away from the first. The remaining warrior was upright, but only because he leaned on his grounded shield to take the weight off the right thigh from which a javelin protruded.

If they, even the four of them, had been able to lock shields and match their long spears against the swords of their immediate opponents, strength and armament would have taken them through the legion like a thorn in an ox's thick hide. Only for a time, no more than minutes—but they were champions, warriors who lived for the glory of dying on the heap of their slain. By robbing the hostile advance of its momentum and turning the ranks inward, Vibulenus' fellows and similar knots of warriors could disorganize the legion into a milling body of men.

Individually, each of the spearmen in the chariots being lashed toward the battle was more than a match for a legionary, despite the latter's armor. But the chance of fighting on those equal terms had been drowned in the rain of javelins, and in the personal code of the other warriors who did not have the mind of a Roman tribune to direct them.

All that could matter now was individual combat, death or survival. Gaius Vibulenus Caper would be alive at the game's end; but the test was real, and the pain would be very real.

What came within range of Vibulenus' spear was no longer an army moving in lockstep but rather a handful of individuals with alien faces framed by helmets forged all of metal. The one squarely fronting Vibulenus raised his shield as he judged the angle of the spearhead and let his sword drift back to take a full-armed cut as he ran into range.

Vibulenus stabbed overhand at the center of the Roman shield, knowing that the boss was reinforced with bronze—and knowing also that his strength and stout spear were enough to smash through all resistance.

The Roman lurched backward, losing his sword and his footing as the iron spearhead broke both the bones of his left forearm. Others jumped aside, thrown off balance as they tried to close up their ranks. Like all participants in Recreation Room fantasies, the wounded man had been shouting in Latin. The screams with which he now assessed his severed arm were even more universal.

Vibulenus shrugged to settle his shield strap, remembering that the equipment was awkwardly heavier than it should be because of the javelins dangling from its face. If the pentration of the Roman missiles had shocked the warrior's mind, then he had taught the nearest Roman how effective a broad-bladed spear could be when thrust by a strong arm.

He jerked his point clear, splintering plywood from the vermilioned shield face, and felt all the way up his forearm the shock of Clodius Afer's chopping blow against the spearshaft.

*Vibulenus hadn't recognized his first opponent, a
soldier who had died too long in the past for his face to
be a memory. But these features were those of the man
on the couch beside him, disconcerting because the
image Vibulenus fought did not yet wear the transverse
red crest of a centurion.*

*And this time, the military tribune had far more
combat experience than the veteran file-closer brought
to the battle.*

*Vibulenus swung his spear sideways like a cudgel.
The instinct of the warrior whose body he shared would
have been to withdraw the weapon for another stabbing blow, but the tribune's mind knew that would be
quick disaster. Clodius Afer, quicker and armed with a
cut-and-thrust sword, would be inside the warrior's
shield and disemboweling him in a fingersnap.*

*But the file-closer did not expect a spear so heavy
that, clubbed, it could slam aside a legionary shield and
dent a bronze helmet in sending the wearer splay-
limbed and unconscious.*

*Swords chopped at Vibulenus' left side, but the shield
covered him there and fellow warriors were running to
his support. A Roman, charging through the ranks at a
dead run, tried to jump the sudden sprawl of Clodius
Afer's body. His boot clipped the file-closer's flailing
arm so that his knees bent and he skidded down on his
back.*

*The Roman's round shield was flung sideways, no
protection at all, but Vibulenus knew the breastplate
had been cast from bronze heavy enough to turn his
spear at the slant with which it would receive the
thrust. He stabbed instead for the face, white with
terror. It was only as his point slid beneath the helmet's
lower rim that he realized the eyes through which his
broad blade was cutting were his own.*

Vibulenus screamed. Even after he leaped from the
couch in the Recreation Room, he could feel his hand

tingle with the bones crunching in his own image's forehead.

Pompilius Niger wrapped his strong arms around the tribune's chest and shouted through the bleats of revulsion, "Sir! Sir! You're here again!"

Vibulenus let his body sag against his friend while he mastered the terror and fury of his mind. There were staring faces all around him, but the expression of their own emotions had blended into a general concern for the tribune.

For their leader.

"So that's what the bastards've thought of us all along," said Clodius Afer in a harsh, deadly whisper. Both he and Niger must have lifted their heads back into reality as soon as they understood the incident around which the Recreation Room had woven its current game. "Like dancing bears . . . or *frogs!*"

The disgust in his voice reminded Vibulenus of how much his friend hated smooth-skinned amphibians. Certainly there was something in the current revelation about the Rec Room—and about the legion's status—to horrify and enflame every Roman aboard the vessel.

And it was the duty of Gaius Vibulenus Caper, military tribune by the whim of Crassus and leader of the men around him by the will of the *gods*, to keep that flaming anger from exploding in a suicidal fashion.

Calm again, so frigidly controlled that his mind did not notice the way his right hand—spear hand—was quivering, Vibulenus used Pompilius Niger for a not-wholly-needful brace as he stepped up onto the couch on which he had recently lain. Rusticanus said something, but the tribune ignored the words. He already had enough information to deal with the immediate situation, and this was not the time for long-term planning.

But by Jove and the Styx, the guild would pay: for this, and for everything.

"Fellow soldiers!" shouted Vibulenus, words that he
and no creature in a blue suit had a right to speak. "You
will not raise your voices, you will not attempt to damage the ship or the crewmen or your fellow soldiers
because of your distress at what you've seen here."

The snarling response from the faces lifted toward
him was unplanned, instinctive.

Vibulenus raised his arms with his fingers spread in a
gesture of forcing back the anger by sheer dint of personality. The men quieted, his men.

"You brought me here to see this," the tribune cried
into the feral silence, "and I have seen. Now, leave the
matter in my hands."

He could feel the hatred boiling in the domed room,
even without the growls and the anguished voice nearby
which called, "No! We gotta *kill* the bastards!"

Vibulenus chopped his arms sideways and back, stilling the tumult again. "I give you my word," he said in
a voice as clear as light dancing from the edge of his
Spanish sword, "as a Roman, and as the man who
fought at your head on more fields than any of us can
remember . . . this will not pass unchallenged.

"I swear it to you. *I* swear it to you."

He waited a moment, then dropped his arms. The
sounds that exploded into the room where no less bloodthirsty than those of moments before—but these were
cheers.

The tribune was shaking with reaction, but the injuries and malaise he had brought from the battlefield
were gone. He had thought slaughter was the only
thing that could take him wholly out of himself, but he
had been wrong.

He stepped down.

"What do you want us to do, sir?" demanded Rusticanus in a husky voice while Niger, wrapping the
tribune again in an arm, babbled excitedly, "What're
you going to do, Gaius?"

Vibulenus looked from one man to the other, taking in the way other soldiers were pressing toward him from all sides with hopes, advice, and congratulations on their lips.

Clodius Afer grinned sardonically, but it was his back and spread arms which provided the tribune with breathing space.

"Out," Vibulenus said, nodding toward the nearest doorway because he knew his voice might not be audible in the commotion.

"And then," he added for himself alone, "we plan how we're going to go home."

The soldier ahead of Vibulenus cycled sideways. "I still think—" the tribune heard Clodius Afer grumble as they stepped together into the paired cubicles.

"Quartilla," said Vibulenus, and he walked into the woman's room through the dissolving wall. "I need to talk to you."

Clodius had insisted the tribune should go to the head of the line on the basis of planning needs if he were unwilling to pull rank—and he *had* the rank, had earned it, so there was no reason not to claim its perquisites.

Vibulenus had refused on the grounds that they were all in this together, however you defined "this" . . . and that there was no real haste, that he'd processed through the Sick Bay, eaten, and drunk already.

And all that was true, to the seasoned veteran Gaius Vibulenus Caper at any rate. He smiled at how the boy-soldier Vibulenus Caper would have reacted to the notion of eschewing the honors due his rank—the boy who had not yet fought beside his men in a hundred fields, fought and died. But the real reason he had not cut in at the head of the line to the women was cowardice. There was solace in the thought, a psychic mudwallowing in the fact that he was afraid and that he was giving in to that fear—somewhat.

He was here in the room lighted by a bead in the back corner, and Quartilla was facing him.

Vibulenus hadn't been a gallant—Carrhae and capture had come too soon for the boy to have developed polish even if the inclination were there. There had been a woman during the season he spent in Athens attending lectures by the philosopher Aristaneus. An Argive of good family, she claimed . . . a Carian from some nameless crossroads, Vibulenus had suspected even then. Everything about her was as false as the red of her hair, and Vibulenus' passion had been false as well—a boy's nonsense modelled on the poetry of Catullus and Theognis, and it hadn't prepared him to really care.

"I would have discussed it with you first," the Roman said softly, "but the offer was spur of the moment and there wouldn't be . . . time."

He was standing with his back straight and his hands gripped firmly so that they would not wash themselves in his nervousness. He was not skirting the discussion of his plans to take the ship home to Campania: he did not even remember those plans in the crash of personal emotions which, as always in a human, managed to claim precedence.

"You . . . ," Quartilla said. She patted the couch beside her. She wore wristlets and anklets strung with tiny bells which sang at every movement. "Come, sit down, of course. You—must have been very brave for the guild to allow you. . . ."

The tribune sat very carefully and faced the woman, because he forced himself to do so. "Brave's easy," he said, meaning physical courage. He was blackly amused at how much easier it was to face spears than it was to face the fact that he had blithely destroyed a relationship that just might mean more to him than life did.

"Everybody was brave," he went on, able to make his tongue function even though it was dry and his mouth was so dry he thought it would crack. "Either they were pleased because I was smart enough to pull the pan out of the fire when they fucked around—"

Vibulenus took a deep breath. "Or else," he went on, letting the words tumble out in their own time, "they liked the way I tried to save the Commander's life. Which was a stupid mistake, and the more so if it earned me the chance to make a *worse* stupid mistake. All I can say about either choice was that I did what I did; and I—wish I hadn't."

"I'm a slave," said Quartilla.

"We all are," Vibulenus broke in savagely. "We're less than that."

She waved him silent in a silvery murmur from her wrist. Apart from the bells, she wore nothing on her body—though her hair was piled around crystalline combs which refracted the dim red light.

"I'm a slave," she repeated, "but I can forget that, usually, with the part of me that *lives*." Her hand gripped the tribune's, and her eyes demanded that he meet hers. "Do you understand?"

He gave an upward nod of assent, afraid to speak but filled with sudden hope that it wasn't over, that there was something between them still to salvage.

"I'm *good* at what I do," Quartilla said with fierce emotion that was neither anger nor very far apart from it. "I have my pride, and maybe that's because of what they did to my mind after they bought me, the guild, but it's *all* I have. You had the *right* to make me your personal slave, Gaius Caper, you earned that and I'm very pleased for you.

"But why in the name of the god you worship did you decide to exercise that right? Why did you rob me of all the little fantasies that left me free in my own mind?"

"I thought . . . ," the tribune said. He turned suddenly away and slammed the wall with his fist in a blaze of self-revulsion.

He hadn't thought. He had wished and acted on the wish, unwilling to consider anything but the way he wanted his world to be structured and arrogantly certain that his power to choose also gave him authority over the outcome of his choice.

He didn't want to die now. He wanted to have died that morning, before he had time to speak to the Commander and claim the reward which destroyed more of his life than remained.

There was a whisper of bells. Quartilla set her hands on his shoulder blades. Vibulenus let his shoulders loosen, but he would not, could not, turn around. He hid his face in the crook of his right elbow and squeezed back his tears of frustration with the muscles that enabled his sword to shear through simpler problems.

"Gaius," said the woman gently, "you could have asked that you never have to fight again. Yourself. They would have granted that, you know. There are twenty of us, the females, but they have only one of you among so many swords."

"Quartilla," the tribune said as he turned with his eyes still closed, "I will not—fail to think again." He did not offer to undo what he had done, because he *could* not change the past, change his words. He would ask the ship, the Commander, that the woman be returned to her regular duties; but that would not change the fact that he had made her a slave, of his whim or *any*one's whim.

"Truth," he said in a flat voice, "isn't as important as perception." He wasn't even close to considering whether he could live with the situation he *now* perceived. For now it would be enough that he be permitted to try— that *she* permit him to try.

Quartilla smiled as he met her eyes, but it wasn't a particularly happy smile.

He didn't, now that he was aware of externals again, remember when he had stood up. His knees were quivering and he wanted very badly to sit down again, but—

"We'll either get through this," said Quartilla gently, "or we won't. And 'won't' could be a very long time for both of us, the way things are."

She took one plump hand from Vibulenus' shoulder and gestured toward the couch. The tribune read the gesture in his peripheral vision, still afraid to break the eye contact he had regained. He sat or collapsed, and Quartilla curved gracefully down beside him, her breast wobbling momentarily against his elbow.

"I want to change the way things are, Quartilla," Vibulenus said. "I want to take my men home, and I need your help."

"Gaius," said the woman with new concern in her eyes. "You *can't* go home."

"And just now," the tribune continued, without recognition that he knew something had been said in the interval, "I want most of all to think that you'll forgive me for what I did."

Quartilla slid her left hand from Vibulenus' shoulder to the back of his neck. Her fingertips toyed with his scalp while her free hand plucked open the knotted sash of his tunic. She smiled again.

Vibulenus knew that he was not being given an answer, however much his body was willing to believe otherwise.

But he knew also that the woman was willing to try to work through it; and that was perhaps as much undeserved mercy as he could have accepted anyway.

The sweat of Tenth Cohort in sword drill overloaded the Exercise Hall's ventilation system with an effluvium made bitter by fatigue poisons. Men grunted, and the clack of practice weapons was supplemented frequently by the duller sound of a riposte getting through to human flesh.

"Up, Decimus, *up*," snarled Clodius Afer as his swagger stick—which looked like, but probably was not, vine wood—prodded the legionary who had just been knocked down by a head blow. "You're favoring your right hip, and that's why he's coming over your guard."

Decimus' duelling partner, a gray, featureless automaton like the hundreds of others in the Exercise Hall, waited with its sword crossed over the face of its shield—both pieces of equipment equally-gray extrusions from its body.

"Yessir," the legionary muttered, though his eyes were crossed, and the only movement of which he seemed capable was to clench and unclench his hand on the hilt of his practice sword, formed from the same material as the automaton. It was heavier than a real sword, and—though its edges were rounded and slightly resilient—a blow from it could send a man to the Sick Bay easily enough.

"Let's get him checked over, pilus prior," said Gaius Vibullenus, threading his way a step behind Clodius through the ranks of duelling pairs.

His own temple throbbed in sympathy with the blow Decimus had taken. The Medic had assured him that there was no organic injury—the booths would have seen to that. But something in the tribune, his mind if not his body, remembered the blow it had taken in the ancient distance.

"Cohort," roared Clodius Afer, "*at ease!*" He would not have had to raise his voice, because in this room a unit leader spoke directly to all his men as if he were the Commander. Battle practice for a pilus prior, however, was not limited to exercise in swinging personal weapons.

At the Roman's order, all the automatons froze into their upright position, waiting for another command to reactivate them. Soldiers who had kept moving on adrenalin knelt, wheezing and supporting themselves on

the shields which, like all their practice gear, were
overweight. Drill *had* to be harsher than the real thing,
because real battle could not be halted save by victory—
the victory of either side.

"Good drill, boys," the pilus prior said mildly, this
time letting the vessel's communications system do the
work. "File-closers and watch clerks're responsible for
getting whoever needs it to the Sick Bay. Rest of you,
stack arms and dismissed."

"Yessir," repeated Decimus in the hubbub. He was
still playing with his sword hilt on the floor. The file-
closer from that century clumped over, swearing softly.

"Not bad," Clodius Afer said to the tribune as men
streamed past them. "They're good. Pollux, they're the
best."

"Stacking arms" meant carrying all the practice equipment to the wall at the distant end of the Exercise Hall
where the smooth gray surface would reabsorb the helmets and body armor, swords and shields. With dismissal as a spur, the men moved as fast as their
exhaustion would permit them—and that prevented their
muscles from cramping as they would if allowed to cool
suddenly and completely after that level of exercise.

"They'd better be good," Vibulenus answered grimly.
"We've got to make our play soon, before the ship goes
into Transit. And if we try and it doesn't work . . . they
won't let things be. The Commander won't."

"Nobody in the whole fuckin' legion won't be willing
to try, sir," said Clodius Afer, flexing his swagger stick
gloweringly to the curve just short of breaking. "Nobody
said there wasn't a risk when they swore us in, did they?"

"In Capua," the tribune said, with a bitter smile
because he remembered little of the city save its name.
Would he recognize his father's face?

"In fuckin' Capua, and that's where we're goin' back,"
said the centurion in what was more a soldier's prayer
than agreement.

"Let's go take a look," Vibulenus said, shrugging. Today neither he nor the pilus prior had donned equipment themselves, but he thought he might return later for some individual exercise. His mind alone could not burn off the nervous energy with which his plans filled him. "Quartilla'll join us there."

"I swear those dummies, they hit harder every time," said Pompilius Niger, jogging drunkenly from the wall where he had dumped his gear. He was not gasping, but he drew in full breaths through his mouth in between phrases. "You guys willing t' head for the baths with a fella been doin' some work?"

Vibulenus briefly surveyed their surroundings. None of the hurrying legionaries showed any particular interest in the three of them. "We're going to the Main Gallery, going to take a look. Wouldn't mind another set of eyes if you're up to it."

"Sure, why not?" agreed the junior centurion. He put a hand on the shoulder of each of his companions and sagged there momentarily, miming total exhaustion. "Sure. You know," Niger continued, setting the trio a brisk pace through the door, "if enough of us stare at it, maybe its teeth all fall out, hey?"

"That still leaves the claws, don't it?" Clodius noted dourly.

"Guide to the Main Gallery," said Vibulenus to the ceiling, and a red dot appeared.

"Thing is," Niger went on, his breathing under control and a serious frown on his face, "we do need to. . . ." He touched his friends' shoulders again, though without looking up from the floor. "Look, guys, if we *don't* do something, there's going to be trouble. Maybe not just now. But sure as shit, when we wake up after Transit and they issue real weapons—somebody's going to put a javelin through the Commander."

"Gonna try, anyway," the pilus prior agreed.

"And then," Niger concluded morosely, "I guess we

can all figure out what's going to happen. Might be wrong on details . . . but it won't be a *detail* sort of job the guild does on us."

"We're going to do something," Gaius Vibulenus said flatly. He spoke with the absolute certainty he felt, although he could not have explained *why* he was so certain. Not quite.

"You know," said Clodius Afer, after a few moments of tramping forward during which all three men remembered laser blasts, "I didn't know the girls were still loose on the ship. I mean—" Suddenly it didn't seem to be a safe topic of conversation after all. "—you mentioned Quartilla, you know."

"Ah, that's right," said the tribune. He corrected his mumble after he got out the first few syllables, but he fixed his eyes on the guide bead. "Ah, Quartilla's status, that changed. And I was going to change it back, you understand, but she thought it was good just now that she could come and go. . . ."

"Sure, I understand," said Clodius Afer. What the pilus prior *did* understand from the emotional loading in his friend's voice was that they'd better talk about something else.

"Wonder if they close this place and steam it down like the little rooms," said Pompilius Niger, turning into the Main Gallery and supplying the perfect change of subject. Vibulenus had continued to walk past the bead at which he had appeared to be staring.

"The way they move it around," the tribune said in a subdued but reasonably normal voice, "they may be able to turn it inside out and shake it clean."

The echoless nature of the Main Gallery expanded its great real size into the ambiance of a twilit plain. The floor was level, and for a moment nothing at all moved within the black volume.

The beast rose, haunches first, and stretched in silhouette against the forward bulkhead which was the only source of light.

"Good, I was feeling lonely," said Clodius, but there was a grim tone overlaying the joke.

They walked in unconscious unison toward the waiting beast. The forward bulkhead quivered with a red glow so deep that it *felt* brighter than human eyes could perceive. The creature began to growl. Though the room's noise-deadening acoustics must have absorbed the physical volume of the sound, the hatred behind it was projected like a volley of missiles.

"Got slack in his chain, the bastard does," observed Niger. They were walking gingerly now, as if they stood on glass or eggshells. "Hopes we'll come maybe a step too close to look at him, he does."

The side entrance opened and closed soundlessly, but the motion took the men's attention as well as that of the giant hyena. The beast turned only its head and, after a moment of observing Quartilla's quick-footed figure in silence, began to growl again.

"Milady," muttered both the centurions, glancing away in at least the semblance of being embarrassed as Vibulenus and the women kissed demurely.

Quartilla wore sandals, a tunic, and over that a dark blue woolen stola. The garments were chaste and had as much the appearance of being Roman as she herself had of being human.

"That's gonna be a bitch t' deal with," said Clodius with his eyes on the pacing, growling carnivore only twenty feet in front of them now. "And I just don't see any choice."

"Unless you could, ah, lady," said Niger as his tongue and words wrapped a sudden idea clumsily. "I mean, maybe it'd let you get past it t' the door since you're not—I mean, maybe you're like the Commander or the guards to it and it'd let you be?"

"I'm not," said Quartilla with a smile that replaced a

blank expression as soon as Vibulenus' hand reached over to squeeze hers. "It wouldn't swallow down pieces of either one of us, Publius, but it wouldn't hesitate to bite those pieces out."

"Wouldn't help anyhow," muttered the pilus prior. The older veteran scowled as he watched Vibulenus step cautiously nearer to the tethered carnivore. "Only use to getting the door open's so the rest of us can get through. Which we sure don't do while *that's* still standing there, grinnin'."

Vibulenus was close enough to really hear the growls now, and the hair at the back of his neck rose in response. The whine of the slotted disk on the carnivore's chest was a waspish undercurrent to the deliberate sound, doing what it could mechanically to make the Roman even more uncomfortable.

There was a loop of slack in the cable, cunningly or even intelligently hidden behind the creature's pacing feet, but the mark of its claws in an arc of the flooring provided the tribune with an accurate deadline.

If he stepped within the jaws' length of that line, he was dead.

This close, he could feel the pressure of the carnivore's exhalations. Its breath did not stink, exactly, but its odor was of something darker than the vegetation-based smell of any animal of similar size in Vibulenus' past experience.

"You *can* fix the lock?" Clodius Afer asked from closer than the tribune had realized.

"Yes," Quartilla answered simply. Then she added, "I've—never touched the bulkhead, of course, because of the barrier. But I've seen the pattern lighting up before the door opens, and I've seen crewmen tap out the same pattern in the hexagon there when they open it from this side. It never changes."

"Well, I figure," said Niger, "that we take the practice equipment from the Exercise Hall, like we planned.

I don't care *how* mean this bastard is, there's enough of us t' put him down regardless."

The carnivore suddenly leaped to the limit of its tether, snarling rage and crashing to a halt with its hind legs on the floor and its foreclaws slashing the air above the Romans and Quartilla. The centurions broke back instinctively, one of them sweeping the woman away more swiftly than her own muscles and training could take her.

Vibulenus stood his ground, lost in observation that freed him from the panic that experience had taught him was false. He had come here many times since the day they had last reboarded the vessel.

"That won't *work*, don't you see?" snarled the pilus prior in anger that he could direct at his subordinate instead of his own fright. The tribune's three companions were picking themselves up from the floor, throwing concerned glances toward their leader. Even the carnivore had subsided, flopping down and beginning to gnaw the staple to which it was attached.

"Well, have you got a better idea?" Niger snapped back. "Piss on it and hope it shrinks and goes away, maybe?"

Clodius, offering a hand which Quartilla accepted for the sake of diplomacy, said, "Well, the trouble is, if we have a full riot out here they'll for sure be waiting if we come through the door."

He nodded toward the bulkhead and its geometric design. At this point, the senior centurion was even more embarrassed at taking his anger out on a friend than he was for the way he dodged away from claws that could not have reached him anyway. "Sure, we can take it out . . . and sure the price'll be cheap enough for what the payoff'll be. But no way I see it bein' quick enough and quiet so's it does us any good."

"Niger," said Gaius Vibulenus.

"Gnaeus," said the junior centurion to Clodius, "you

may be right and—" he raised his hands to bar angry protest "—I figure you are, that's how I read it too. But—"

"Niger," the tribune repeated as he faced around again. For a moment he seemed to glow with a transfiguring thought. His companions gaped and fell silent. Even the rasp and whine of the carnivore's frustrated attempts on its tether ceased, leaving only the keening disk on its chest to compete with the Roman's presence.

Vibulenus said, "How is your mead coming along?" His words were as distinct as they were unexpected, penetrating his hearers as clearly as if he had tapped into the vessel's communications system.

"It's . . ." said Niger, pausing to swallow and to collect his thoughts. The tribune gathered the others to him as he began to walk toward the doors in the back of the big room.

"It's shaping up fine, Gaius," Niger continued. "Added some more water this morning. Doesn't have a real bite, yet, but if we don't Transit for another week, two weeks it'll be plenty good."

"It'll be plenty good sooner than that, my friend," said Vibulenus. He put an arm around Quartilla's shoulders and pulled her close, but he did not look at her for the moment. The tribune's eyes were turned toward the nearing exit, but his mind was focused on a red future.

"Sir?" said one or the other of the centurions.

"Pilus prior," said the tribune as they stepped into the hallway, "we'll give the men the remainder of the day to rest. I want to use the Tenth Cohort."

"Of course, sir," replied Clodius Afer. He sounded more shocked that any other unit could be considered for the operation than he was at the implication that the operation was about to go on line.

Quartilla's body shuddered reflexively, but she immediately squeezed herself to a closer bond with the tribune.

"We'll proceed to the Exercise Hall as usual," Vibulenus continued. His companions were following his lead, but he was simply walking—moving his body so that his racing mind did not bounce off its physical trammels. "Pick up practice equipment and carry it to the Main Gallery. *March* here with it."

"We'll need to inform the men," said Niger, sketching his own mental picture of the operation and the duties *he* would be required to perform.

"Non-coms the night before," replied Vibulenus decisively. "Common soldiers by their centurions as we exit the sleeping room. No noise, no fuss. Especially no cheering. There'll be plenty of time for that when it's over, and I want *us* to be leading the cheers."

Though the alternative wasn't unacceptable, noted the part of the tribune's mind which was willing to consider all possibilities with an icy logic. Because if the mutiny failed, the leaders who planned it were certainly going to gain freedom of a sort.

"Open your mouths again," said Niger in a low voice to the pair of soldiers babbling as they entered the Main Gallery, "and I'll choke you with your teeth."

Vibulenus was terrified. Not of death—death would be a release. He was certain that he was about to fail in front of his men, in front of his friends.

In front of Quartilla.

They had marched to the gallery six abreast, each century forming a file. As the cohort entered the big room, several of the centurions fell out to check the order of their men before running to the front of the column again.

The beast guarding the bulkhead began to growl deep in its throat. The sound was caressing, almost welcoming.

Clodius Afer began to growl back, rubbing the smooth blade of his practice sword against his thigh as he led the cohort from the right hand corner.

The men carried swords and shields, but the helmets and body armor of the same dense gray material had been abandoned in the Exercise Hall. The centurions, Clodius Afer strongly with the majority, had decided that the additional burden would be more of a hindrance than any benefit the dummy armor would confer. Nobody thought there was a chance for a soldier who got squarely in the path of a bodyguard's mace or the jaws of the carnivore here.

As for a laser—it should be quick, which was as much as anyone needed to think about *that* possibility.

"The quicker, the better," muttered Vibulenus, who had also paused beside the entrance to take stock of the situation.

Quartilla, who understood part of what the tribune meant by the comment, smiled and fell into step beside him as he paced to overtake the head of the column.

Vibulenus and the woman did not carry the practice gear that was about to get combat use. Instead, they each bore one of the leather knapsacks into which Niger had divided his "honey" upon return to the vessel.

In order for fermentation to proceed, converting sugars into alcohol, the honey had to be thinned with water. The greased leather packs were not perfectly watertight, especially along the seams, but they provided the best container available within the legion's portion of the vessel. They were sticky, and the reek of the original contents (which Niger continued to call honey) had not been improved by what was, after all, a process of decomposition.

The knapsacks were what Vibulenus needed now, and behind him every Roman on the ship.

The tribune started to laugh. It felt good to be moving, even toward the carnivore stretching with the deadly intensity of an all-in wrestler preparing for his bout.

"All right, sir?" asked Niger, jogging to the front of the column.

The Main Gallery had the aspect of a battlefield at evening. The single understrength cohort debouching into it emphasized, rather than filling, the room's emptiness.

"I was just thinking, Publius," said the tribune. "That we might win."

"Sure, sir, we're with you," the centurion replied—to what? What did Niger think he'd been told?—as he slipped back to deal with a confusion of voices at the rear of the line.

The formed cohort had inevitably swept up legionaries from other units who had been walking the halls on their own business. These confused, excited hangers-on were causing the commotion which Vibulenus had feared and which Clodius Afer's troops had themselves avoided. File-closers and another centurion besides Niger silenced the unarmed audience with whispers that ranged from warnings to threats.

The carnivore stepped delicately forward to the end of its tether and reached out with a forepaw. Then the beast turned and circled back around its staple. It had determined the zone within which it could kill, like an expert gunner ranging his ballista at the start of a siege.

Well, Gaius Vibulenus knew what that zone was also. He paused just beyond it and undid the thongs closing the knapsack's flap.

The beast remained huddled between the staple and the bulkhead whose door was invisible save for the pattern forming its lock. An optimist might have said the carnivore had retreated in fear of the armed cohort being halted by handsignals behind the tribune.

Vibulenus knew better than that. He understood the growls that the creature could not suppress for all its wish to entice its prey closer; understood the appraising glint in its eyes when it turned them toward the Romans. The beast was not sure that it could kill all the men about to attack it; but it was looking forward to an opportunity to try.

Oh, yes. . . . Gaius Vibulenus Caper knew *just* how the creature felt.

Quartilla stepped to the tribune's side, and he snarled, "*Back*, by Pollux! Don't be in the way now."

There was a rasp of orders muted by the gallery's acoustics: Clodius opening his unit into a twelve man front by bringing the half-files forward. That was an ample frontage to deal with the carnivore, and it retained some semblance of order for the moment at which the woman, Fortune granting, opened the bulkhead door which would pass no more than two men abreast.

The tribune placed every element of his surroundings in its proper niche on the gameboard of his mind—himself as well, because his body was a primary piece in the exchange that was about to begin. Then he stepped forward, into the carnivore's range, swinging the knapsack of half-worked mead.

The beast was faster than Vibulenus dreamed. All of his planning had been based on subconscious recollections of the way the carnivores moved on the battlefield—carrying heavy, iron-clad riders and wrapped in several hundredweight of armored blanket. The creature had been bred in a place where things were heavier; and under conditions like these which men thought were normal, its speed was almost reflex quick.

Vibulenus had no time to use the knapsack for a weapon as he intended, but it saved his life anyway by providing a target for the claws which could easily have crushed into his chest from both sides or slapped his head against the sidewall while blood spouted from the stump of his neck.

The knapsack exploded in a sticky geyser—honey dissolved in water already slightly alcoholic with decay products from the bacteria which the mixture supported.

It splashed the ceiling thirty feet above and bathed the jaws and shearing teeth which the beast slammed down on what it thought was a victim.

Vibulenus had intended to retreat as soon as his presence brought the carnivore out in a lunge. The knapsack, heavy with its fluid contents, would propel him backward while it sped to its target.

Now he sprawled on his face, legs tangled beneath the forepaws shredding the knapsack. The strap had fouled his wrist as the beast snatched it away; that slight contact had been sudden and forceful enough to spin the Roman and drag him toward the slayer.

Quartilla swung the pack she carried.

The side-arm motion had an authority which belied the sausage-like plumpness of the woman's limbs; her delicacy of touch might have been expected by any of the men who had shared her couch. The knapsack struck and gushed its contents over the slotted medallion whining on the creature's chest.

The flashing power of the mounts with which the guild provided its command group came at a price in food and the oxygen needed to convert that food into energy. The same homeworld gravity which built the creature's muscles held an atmosphere dense enough to support their physiologies. They could no more breathe unaided the ship's air or that of any of the worlds on which the legion fought than a human could survive in the atmosphere of Mars.

The supercharger, which rammed air into the creature's lungs at the density which they required to function, filled with mead. It stalled out, shrieking.

Clodius Afer dropped his shield. His left hand jerked the tribune clear while his right swung the heavy practice sword fast enough that it managed to whistle on its way to the joint in the carnivore's forelimb.

Pure honey—sap—would have been too thick to flow into the compressor with the necessary abruptness; a fluid thin enough to drink would have been spewed out the side-vents of a unit intended to operate in heavy rain without discomfort to its wearer. The half-worked mead, gummy with undissolved sugars in an alcohol mixture, smothered all chance of oxygen reaching the creature's lungs as surely as immersion in a lake could have done.

The beast spun, slashing for the non-existent opponent who covered its nostrils. The pilus prior's blow struck with all the veteran's strength and the mass of his dense club behind it, but the carnivore did not notice the bone-crushing impact in the midst of greater pain. A paw flung Clodius aside with long cuts on his shoulder, because that happened to be in the path of the creature's panicked thrashing.

Bare feet and gray, fifty-pound shields battered past the tribune as the cohort charged unordered. It was a bad idea, but a soldier too disciplined ever to fight on his own initiative is as useless as a warrior too rigidly honor-bound ever to avoid combat. Practice swords arced in curves, smooth-edged clubs that shone greasily in the bulkhead's deep glow.

Vibulenus' perception had become a packet of still pictures without a clear timeline to connect them. The images were not jumbled—each was crystalline in its sharpness. Claws meeting in his knapsack, breaking a line in the skin of his hand but not tearing off that hand; Clodius rolling clear, his hand scrabbling for the sword he had dropped and a smear of blood on the floor beneath him; Pompilius Niger, six feet in the air, with a surprised look on his face and the clumsy shield flat against his chest where it transmitted the thrust of the carnivore's kick.

And Quartilla, palming the doorlock as light glinted in response and men with demonic expressions battled a monster behind her.

There was a sword beside Vibulenus, visible in flickers as shadows and feet scissored across it. The tribune hunched his shoulders against the knees and shield rims that struck him as his men surged toward the fight. He gripped the swordhilt and tried to lift the weapon. A legionary was standing on the blade.

Vibulenus' frustration transmuted itself into strength so abrupt that the legionary was levered against the backs of his fellows with a bleat of surprise. The tribune dodged—and wedged, by brute strength—through men concentrating on the dying guardbeast instead of the real goal.

The lockplate flashed, silhouetting Quartilla's palm momentarily. The door began to float inward.

"Tenth to me!" screamed the tribune as he slammed past Quartilla with a lack of ceremony which he suspected was the only thing that could save the woman's life.

He was correct.

The light within the corridor beyond was lemon yellow and bright only to eyes adapted to the red/infrared of the Main Gallery. The bodyguard reaching for Quartilla's throat was naked, but his fingertips were armed with unexpected claws.

The bodyguard's reach was almost as long as Vibulenus' arm and the sword extending it, but "almost" was the margin of survival. The tip of the practice sword ended its overhand chop between the bulging toad eyes. Clodius Afer himself might have been proud of the accuracy of the blow and the muscle behind it.

The bodyguard was seven feet tall and, without his armor, as ropily powerful as the carnivore on watch. The edge of the practice sword was too rounded to cut, but it was an edge nonetheless. It focused the inertia of the blow in a line which caved through the bones of the victim's flat forehead.

Vibulenus' weapon rebounded. The bodyguard stag-

gered backward, bleeding from its ear flaps and with
both eyes jouncing at the end of their optic nerves.

"*Rome!*" shouted the tribune as he darted forward.
Shouts merged behind him into a single wordless snarl.

Naked, the bodyguards looked less like toads than
they did in their armor. Their legs were shorter than a
man's, much less a toad's, in comparison to the length
of the torso; the bodies were rangy without iron hoops to
bulk them out; their skins were smooth and the color of
polished bronze except for the hands, feet and faces of
richly-marked mahogany.

The bodyguards came from both sides of the corridor, through what appeared to be partitions but were
only screens of coherent light. Their duties were too
deeply ingrained for the creatures not to fling themselves into battle without hesitation; but they were
unprepared, and the soldiers who spilled forward after
Vibulenus had dreamed of this moment for weeks.

The tribune's headlong rush took him past the rooms
nearest the door where the guards were billeted. There
was fighting behind him, but there was no lack of men
to handle it. He was running for the main chance in the
desperate hope that he would recognize it if he stumbled into it.

The mutineers were completely out of their depth
now. Quartilla knew no more of life in the forward
section than the Romans did. She could pass through
the transport system the crew used within the main
body of the ship, but forward was entered only through
the bulkhead door which they had just forced.

A blue-suited crewman leaped into the hallway—the
Pilot, not the stocky, mauve-faced fellow who was now
the Medic. Behind him was a room of floating dodeca-
hedrons, some as thick as a man was tall. Each facet
was a different picture, most of them mere swirls of
color. Together their light shadowed the crewman's

face without hiding the scowl of manic rage or the laser he was raising to aim.

The practice sword did not spin with the glittering beauty of Vibulenus' own weapon, saving the Commander on the gravel field where last they fought beneath a sun. It flew true, though, smashing the guild employee backward into the drifting shapes that eddied to avoid his touch.

The Pilot's face was bloodied and his shoulder possibly broken, but his life had not been risked by a sharp edge—a result as important to the tribune as the fact the laser had spun away from the impact.

"*Got 'im!*" bellowed Clodius Afer as he raised a dagger—a real one with a hilt fit for two Roman hands, part of some bodyguard's equipage—to finish the job in a fury as red as the blood from the scratches torn across his chest and arm.

"*No* by Hercules!" the tribune screamed, tackling his berserk subordinate because he knew no words could now restrain a man whose rage had overwhelmed weeks of careful, mutual planning. His hands locked on Clodius' right wrist, and the pause in which the centurion threw off the hindrance was time enough to reinstate training and sanity.

The walls here were real enough to slam Vibulenus back toward Clodius when the pilus prior shook free. The tribune had been pounded worse—even in his men's scramble to attack the guardbeast—and the amount of adrenalin singing in his blood at the moment would have permitted him to ignore amputation, much less a few more bruises.

"*We need him*—" the tribune cried, as much to the dagger as the man who held it.

"*Pollux* sir!" Clodius Afer was shouting, bloodlust melted on his face into a mask of horror. "I swear I didn't—"

The wall behind the tribune dissolved. The Medic

stood in the broad opening. Behind him was a room
whose air seemed filled with bright fracture lines, as
different from that in which the Pilot sprawled as either
was from any room Vibulenus had seen before.

In the Medic's hands was a laser.

The crewman could have burned the two Romans in
halves before they reached him, but Vibulenus and his
centurion were the killers in this tableau of mutual
surprise: the Medic was paralyzed by the face of death
while the soldiers were unaffected by the black reality
waiting at the laser's muzzle.

The tribune threw himself at the crewman's knees.
He was off balance and facing the wrong direction, so
his target was just an estimate of what he thought his
hands could reach. Either the laser would carve him with
the deck for a cutting board, or he would jerk the
Medic flat after the weapon had disemboweled Clodius
Afer in a gush of sparks and blood.

There was always a cost but it didn't help to consider
what, while you were paying.

The Medic displayed lightning-quick reflexes despite
his sedentary background. He tossed the laser down as
if it were hot, bouncing it off the lunging Clodius Afer
by chance rather than by intent, and dived squealing
away from the Romans.

There was chaos near the entrance to the forward
section. The screen of light to one side of the aisle had
vanished. Instead of furniture—or the marsh the tribune
had half expected from the wizardry of the vessel—
the bodyguards had been living amidst a rocky environment similar to a windswept knoll in northern Mesopotamia.

The barracks area was littered now with equipment
and bodies. Some legionaries screamed or moaned, struggling to cover their wounds or pawing feebly at the
hands of friends trying to help; but the quintet of guards
visible were dead, pulped by Roman clubs and hacked

with edged weapons the guards themselves had no time to use.

Death did not save the toad creatures from further attack. Legionaries were still pounding at bodies which were beginning to flow over the landscape on which they sprawled.

Fighting might be going on in the other half of the billet—men ducked in and out, ignoring walls which they had learned were only cosmetic—but if there were still guards resisting there, they could not be a threat to the mutiny any more. The legionaries who were struggling through the bulkhead door, now in total disorder, ran toward Clodius and their leaders for want of battle nearer.

Vibulenus scrambled on his hands and knees to catch the wailing Medic, also on all fours.

"ClodiussavethePilot!" the tribune screamed behind him in a single breath, knowing that only the pilus prior was likely to have enough presence of mind not to treat the dazed crewman the way the guards were being handled. He had given orders and explanations, clear and convincing in the moments before the attack. Men balked of a chance at the real fighting were going to pound away their prebattle fears—together with their only hope of seeing home—if there were no one with discipline in place to stop them.

The Medic buried his face in his crossed arms. Vibulenus sprang on him like a dog on a rat.

"Don't!" the crewman wailed in Latin. *"Don't! Don't!"* He was stockier than Vibulenus and possibly as strong, but the fight had been stunned out of him by the homicidal intent he saw on the faces of the Romans rushing toward him.

"Where's the Commander?" the tribune demanded, shouting to be heard over the uproar. He rose awkwardly to his feet, dragging the Medic with him as an unresisting dead weight. Vibulenus' back now ached with memory of the trampling haste of his men determined to join in slaughtering the carnivore.

"I've got this one, Gaius!" cried the pilus prior, who clutched the Pilot to his chest as if they were lovers. The crewman was either struggling or writhing in pain as fractured bones grated under the centurion's grip; but without the hand which Clodius held out to stop his subordinates, pain and life would have ended abruptly for the Pilot.

"The Commander!" Vibulenus shouted. "The Commander!" He began shaking his captive.

Men, clumsy with the shields they still bore, clustered around their leader. The lines in the air felt like cobwebs, but they formed again like designs in smoke when a soldier passed through them. Some of the legionaries swatted at the figures, then drove their way back out of the Medic's room when they had time to appreciate its uncanniness.

The stocky crewman was whining syllables that were not Latin if they were a language at all.

"The Commander!" Vibulenus shrieked, jerking the blue figure back and forth in fury and frustration.

Quartilla, with a bruise on her cheekbone which became a pressure cut as it mounted toward her hair, squeezed between legionaries to touch the tribune with one hand and the Medic with the other. "Let me," she whispered to Vibulenus; and, in a fluting trill which seemed to be a language after all, began to speak to the captive.

The Medic pawed Quartilla gratefully with his three-fingered right hand, but his eyes were unfocused and his left hand stroked the tribune with the same limp thankfulness. In Latin, though he seemed unaware of both his language and his audience, the crewman said, "He's at the end, of course. Me here, the Pilot across, him at the end."

A dozen legionaries at once began battering with

practice swords on the wall which closed the corridor leading from the bulkhead door. Two men shouted for space as they stamped forward, carrying the ten-foot, iron-headed mace which had belonged to a bodyguard. They crashed their makeshift battering ram into the wall. It rebounded out of their hands, sending the nearest legionaries hopping. The wall was unscarred.

"Get us in," said Clodius Afer to his own prisoner, his voice a low growl more threatening than the dagger which he now recalled and waved before the Pilot's face. The fingers of the centurion's left hand were wrapped in the fabric covering his captive's chest. The bodysuit did not tear, but where the material was most strained, its color became a glistening, silky green.

"Un*lock* it, bastard," Clodius ordered in a voice like stones sliding, while he turned the Pilot deliberately to face the blank wall.

"I can't," the Pilot said in what started as a choked whisper but quickly built into a terrified babble, "because it's only him from in*side* as controls it!"

"Clodius!" shouted the tribune who saw death in the pilus prior's rigid face an instant before the dagger lifted.

The weapon poised in midair. It was forged in one piece—blade, hilt and crossguards—massive and dingy gray except for the edges and the scratches on the hilt left by the iron gloves with which its normal user gripped it.

"Sir?" said Clodius Afer pleadingly; but the fact that he had bothered to respond at all meant that he understood the order and would obey.

The Medic had recovered himself enough to be sure of his surroundings and to talk to Quartilla in his melodic birth tongue. His face quivered with terrified animation as he made frequent one-finger gestures which were not attempts to point at anything in the immediate environment.

"He's telling the truth," said the woman when Vibulenus dared glance away from his pilus prior. A single legionary continued to hammer vainly at the corridor, but all the others hung in restless anticipation, waiting for the information or the event which would give them a goal again.

"There's no way into the Commander's quarters except through that door," Quartilla continued, "and it's controlled by the Commander's voice. There's no way out either."

"He says," said Clodius Afer, pushing toward the invisible door through men who scurried from his authority and from the anger in his eyes. The wrinkling grip across the front of the bodysuit made the Pilot seem shrunken in on himself as the centurion dragged him along.

"He *says!*" the pilus prior shouted as he stabbed the dagger into the center of the blank wall.

Blood scabbing across Clodius' right shoulder was jeweled with bright, fresh droplets as the muscles bunched beneath the skin. There was a thunk and a musical *twang* that would have been loud even in a room not hushed like this one.

Clodius' arm was numb to the elbow. He fell back a step, eyes widened in surprise. The dagger hilt was still in his hand, but the blade had snapped off at the crossguards and lay, still quivering out nervous tones, on the floor of what had been the Pilot's quarters. He dropped the iron hilt.

"No," said Pompilius Niger in a voice of unexpected certainty. "We'll use this."

The junior centurion had a bruise across the forehead where his shield had caught him while it blocked the carnivore's kick. He had lost or abandoned the practice weapons. What he now carried in his rough, capable hands was one of the lasers with which the crewmen had tried to face the mutiny.

The Medic trilled something that was an oath in any language. In desperate Latin directed more toward Vibulenus than it was the woman—authority taking precedence over mercy at this moment, though the reality of the situation was not what the crewman perceived—he said, "Please don't let him—if he touches the wrong thing, all of us, the *ship* even."

Men made way for Niger the way they had for Clodius, but this time the threat was in his hands instead of his face. In hot blood, most of the legionaries would have charged the beam weapon with the same reckless abandon the tribune and pilus prior had shown. Now, though . . . nobody wants to die *after* a battle, and memories of the laser demonstrations were still bright and terrible.

"Everybody move back," said Vibulenus, raising his voice to quiet the babble. Another problem occurred to him—his duties did not end with mutiny, unless the mutiny itself were ended—so he went on, "Fifth and Sixth Centuries, return to the Main Gallery. Keep people out, and tell them I'll make a full report as soon as we've mopped things up in here."

And might the wish father the result.

There was a stir and more obedience than the tribune had really expected. The ship was uncanny in many fashions. Familiarity did not help legionaries understand how the walls moved or carts floated through the air.

But these *were* familiar occurrences now, whereas the laser still commanded the awe which a nearby thunderbolt would receive in the legion's Campanian homes. The order provided an excuse to get away from something that even brave men would prefer to shun.

Clodius Afer had no visible qualms. He strolled back to the tribune and Niger, flexing the numbness out of his empty right hand. The Pilot, who was trying to hug his injured right shoulder, had no more control of his movements than would a dufflebag in the centurion's grip.

"Now," said Clodius to his captive in a tone of catlike menace, "why don't you tell us how to make this work?"

The two crewmen looked at one another with mirroring expressions of blank-eyed terror. The faces of the Romans around them ranged from expectant to ravening, with Niger's features the worst for their demonic calm. The junior centurion pointed the laser at the Medic's chest. His hands began to prod the bumps and knurlings on the weapon's surface.

"Don't!" shrieked the Pilot. "If you fire it here, you may strand us in normal—"

The pilus prior slapped his prisoner. His calloused palm cracked like a ballista firing, and the Pilot flopped stunned against the grip on his chest.

"I'll tell you *just* how to do it," said the Medic in a voice of manic calm. He spread both his hands, vaguely purple where they extended beyond his suit, toward the laser. It was the gesture of an adult placating a raging child—or of a suppliant before his god. "But *please*, don't touch the controls until I show you."

"Give the laser to Quartilla," Vibulenus decided aloud.

Clodius looked surprised, while Niger looked as if nothing could surprise him. With no more hesitation than if he had been asked to deliver it to the tribune or one of the other men, he handed the woman the tube with excrescences molded into it instead of being welded on. An article of plumbing, a length of foundry scrap . . . except that it burned like the heart of Phlegethon, and that made it useful.

"Please . . . ," said the Medic in a voice that was quiet though not calm, the way a cat in ambush is quiet. "If you will point the other end—yes, like that, goodlady—toward the wall, the door."

Groggy, stunned enough that immediate consequences did not terrify him, the Pilot said, "You know what happens if she hits the navigation bank. Is this where you want to spend eternity?"

Clodius slapped him into a daze again.

The Medic made a swallowing motion higher in his throat than a Roman would have, then continued, "Now, goodlady, slide the piece just above the trigger—where your index finger is—back."

"Which piece?"

"Either side—yes, that's fine, it slides, yes, goodlady. Now—"

Vibulenus was wondering why the Pilot had spoken in Latin to his fellow. Stunned, yes; but under the circumstances, probably because they had no other common language.

The guild could achieve wonders, miracles—but it had a cheeseparing attitude that reminded the tribune of wealthy men at home who served fine wine to their immediate companions at dinner, but sent lees and vinegar to the lower tables. The Commander's duties required universal fluency, but those of the crewmen did not.

Quartilla spoke all the ship's languages.

The laser's pale beam struck the door in a dazzle that could have been the tribune's sudden anger.

Startlement lifted the woman's finger from the trigger instead of clamping it there. Even so, the microsecond pulses had blasted cup-sized depressions in an ascending line across the face of what had been a blank wall. The material which had shrugged off a ram and a steel point slumped at the touch of coherent light. Bits which sprayed from the surface left sooty trails behind them as they sputtered through the air.

"Don't!" shrilled a voice. "Don't do that!"

Vibulenus spun around, keeping his grip on the Medic only by reflex. The words had come from—

The words had come from just beside the tribune's ears. The Commander had spoken, rather than someone in the immediate vicinity.

There was momentary silence except for the curses of

a few men, close enough to the door to be burned when it spattered on them. The yellow-green surface of the wall was angry pink around the cavities and dull gray at their heart. It looked like pustulant worm damage on the skin of a fresh pear.

"Again," said the tribune softly, and Quartilla steadied herself over the laser tube.

"Wait!" bleated the voice. "I'm coming out! Put that down, I'm coming *out!*"

A legionary who had been smothering sparks on his thighs grinned and straightened. He cocked his practice sword back in an unguarded fashion that would have gotten him killed on the battlefield or knocked silly by an automaton in the Exercise Hall.

"*Not* without orders, ye fool!" snarled the pilus prior. He shook the Pilot as he would have a swagger stick. The loose-limbed crew member moaned softly in response, but the abashed soldier lowered his weapon.

"Put down the laser!" demanded the Commander's voice.

"Quartilla," said the tribune in a voice that crushed other sounds with its glacial power, "on the count of three I want you to begin burning the door until I tell you to stop. One—"

"*Wait!*"

"Two—"

The wall dissolved like most other doorways in the ship. There was a line of what appeared to be smoke where the laser had cut, but it settled out of the air quickly as a handful of gray dust. The Commander, with his arms crossed in front of his face, stepped through it.

He was wearing a blue bodysuit again. Even had he wished to, Vibulenus could not have avoided remembering his first sight of the slim figure. The Commander had watched Parthian guards driving their Roman prisoners onto the vessel that was intended to be the only home the legionaries would know for the rest of their lives. The figure in blue had watched with the detached interest of a cattle buyer.

And it no longer hurt to realize that the Commander had thought of himself in just that fashion, a human who bought and managed animals.

"Glad to see you, Your Worship," said Gaius Vibulenus in a kittenish tone. "Most glad to see you like this."

The Commander lowered his hands, and gods! but it *was* good to see the terror on his face.

The Commander's personal quarters were a forest— not a glade on a Campanian hillside, but no stranger than a score of woodlands through which the legion had battled. Trees with willowy trunks rose in gold-barked splendor above the level which Vibulenus could see through the doorway. Tendrils hung down, fringed with blue-green foliage that marched along the twigs in connected rows like an eel's fins instead of being separated into leaves. The air had a sulphurous tinge, not quite unpleasant. Several of the trunks were six feet in diameter.

"Throw your traps down, you two," said Clodius Afer, nodding his clenched right hand toward a pair of legionaries. "Hold 'im by the elbows, just *hold* 'im—but no mistake."

He looked in surprise at the Pilot who dangled in his big left hand. "Here, two more of you take this one—and the Medic, too. Pretend you're good for something beside scratchin' yer butts."

As he spoke, the pilus prior let his gaze wander across the guard billets his men had cleared. Tired soldiers squatted on the deck or braced themselves against rocks designed for the comfort of inhuman forms. Where they could, they avoided the remains of the toad creatures who had lorded over them for—how to measure the time? But avoidance was not always possible, and some of the men were too weary to care that the surface beneath them was greasy.

Clodus grinned, and the men grinned back at their bloody centurion. Their mutual pride glowed like a hot furnace.

"This all can be forgotten," said the Commander. Either his control or the ship's communications system kept his voice calm, without the tremolo of fear which the tribune had hoped to hear. "For the sake of my career, you see, so you need not doubt me. The— damage—" he wriggled his short, pointed ears "—can be assessed against the recent battle, a mere entry error in the damage report. It will be all forgotten."

"No," said Pompilius Niger. "It won't be forgotten. Lots of things aren't forgotten." He reached out slowly.

Vibulenus poised to act if needs must, but the bovine, childish-looking centurion only drew the tip of his index finger down the face of the Commander. The guild officer shuddered but could not draw away against the grip of the strong men holding him.

"I'll never forget Rufus, your worship," Niger added with the gentleness of a chamois whisking over a swordblade.

"Bring him into here," said Vibulenus, walking toward the Commander's quarters as he spoke. "The Medic— both of them, bring them too."

The tribune's right hand hurt from the strain he had not noticed when he was gripping the crewman. He felt a momentary hesitation—mental, not quite transmitted to his body—before he stepped through the doorway. In this place there could be deadfalls—or the vessel's dreadful equivalent of them, invisible partitions that would sizzle away the blood and bone of an intruder.

But Quartilla was at his side, and if he paused she would be the first into . . .

A forest in which the air was unexpectedly warm and dry, and where several of the trees shot up to a height of several hundred feet unless that were an optical illusion. No snares in the doorway, no lethal barriers.

There was nothing which suggested the guiding or working of a ship either.

"What does he have to do with making the ship go places?" the tribune asked without looking over his shoulder. He was bending his right fingers back against his wrist with the other hand. "The Commander?"

"He just . . ." the Medic said. "I mean, I think he just orders him—"

"What are you doing?" demanded the guild officer in rising inflections that pierced like the voice of a senile woman. "You're safe now if you'll stop this mad—"

The voice cut off.

Vibulenus turned. No one had touched the Commander. Niger was pointing a finger at the blue-suited officer's face and smiling.

The Medic reached out toward the Pilot's head to steady and direct it. The slighter-bodied crewman was standing upright again, but his face bore mental and physical vestiges of the punishment he had received.

"Hey!" said the soldier holding the Medic's right elbow. He jerked his captive back sharply.

"*Tell* us," the Medic begged his fellow. "He doesn't set any controls, does he?"

"*Him*," mumbled the Pilot. He tried to rub his face with a hand but was prevented by the overzealous legionaries gripping him. "*He* just tells me it's my fault the other bastard got cut so *he* has to take over this zoo again. Have me demoted, *he* says."

"Your choice, Publius," the tribune said softly to Pompilius Niger. "He was your cousin."

"Yes," said the stocky junior centurion.

Niger had been staring at the guild officer. Now he reached out to the crewmen, taking each man's chin between the thumb and forefinger of a hand. The Medic froze. The Pilot struggled reflexively; but he could not move his head against the two-finger grip, and the attempt brought him back to full consciousness.

"Now . . . ," said Niger, letting his eyes travel from one crewman to the other. "We're going to give you a demonstration of why you will obey every order which Gaius gives you, without argument or hesitation.

"We call it crucifixion."

The Commander began to scream. The screaming went on for a long time.

"This was the last unit, sir," said Julius Rusticanus at the doorway of the Commander's quarters.

"Very good, First," said Gaius Vibulenus, giving the first centurion an upward nod which exhaustion kept from being as crisp as he would have liked.

Quartilla, empathetic or just lucky in her timing, began to massage the tribune's neck and shoulders. The black certainty of the laser still lay across the woman's lap.

"March them out then," Vibulenus continued, relaxing visibly, "and await further orders."

"*Century*—" Rusticanus roared.

"Century!" repeated the centurion of the particular unit, Sixth of the First, in a pale echo of the first centurion's incomparable bellow.

"March!" Rusticanus ordered, and bare feet slapped the floor as the century exited the forest scene in close order and perfect step.

Every legionary aboard had now been brought into the Commander's quarters for a view of the price men had exacted from—not men. Most of the centuries filed in and out in boisterous good humor, but Rusticanus had set his own stamp on the conduct of the First Cohort.

"Sir," he said as the men marched toward the exit into the Main Gallery where most of the legion already waited. "I—I'm very proud to serve under you. You did . . . you did what you promised us you would."

"Thank you, First," the tribune said, feeling pleasure tingle beneath his skin despite his weariness.

"But you should have had me with you—" his broad hand gestured around him, fingers spread "—when."

The first centurion made an about face as sharp as a surveyed angle and marched out after his men.

Clodius Afer assumed a full brace, looking at a knob of tree-trunk, and asked, "Further orders, sir?" in a raspy, impersonal voice. He did not want to prod his friend, his *leader;* but until the operation was complete, the pilus prior would be wound up tight as the springs of a catapult.

He knew very well that the operation was not over.

Niger's century was on duty in the forward section, half of them sprawled in the outer area while the remainder wandered in the glade which formed the Commander's quarters. Their centurion sat crosslegged with his back to a tree, smiling faintly but not speaking except to briefly answer direct questions.

He could not even be said to be watching the Commander, though he was not looking anywhere else.

"All right," said Vibulenus in a sharp voice intended to rouse his own mind as well as bring those around him to attention. He stood up and pointed his index fingers at the crewmen tied to daggers driven into one of the giant tree boles. "*You,*" the tribune demanded. "Where is the ship controlled from?"

The Pilot winced with trapped-animal panic—he might have been dopey with the pain of his ribs and shoulders. The Medic craned his neck to see the other crewman. Because of the trunk's curve they could not see one another's face without straining.

When the Pilot still said nothing, the Medic flung his gaze again on the Roman tribune and said, "It's in his quarters, the whole thing, but you can't work the controls yourselves, you know—"

"Yes, we know," said Vibulenus with a vague smile at

the fellow's desperation to prove he was indispensable.
They already knew that; the tribune himself did, at
least.

Niger stood with a mechanical rather than fluid grace,
each joint of his close-coupled frame moving by small
increments. There was certainly a way to provide the
Commander's quarters with real furniture, but it was
not worth the bother of learning—and very possibly, it
was under the Commander's control alone.

The junior centurion put an arm around Vibulenus'
shoulders and hugged him. Quartilla, standing at the
tribune's other side, laid her fingers on her lover's
biceps, and the troops of the century on guard began to
move closer to hear what was about to happen.

"We can set a course for a lovely world," the Medic
said, nervousness speeding his voice so that the words
tripped across one another. "Anything you want, whatever's lovely to *you*. And—"

"You'll set our course for home," said the tribune.
"For Capua. For—"

"*No*," said the Pilot.

They had all been ignoring the slimmer crewman in
his silence and his daze. Vibulenus moved to his side
for a better view of the fellow. Niger, a non-commissioned
officer again, made room through his crowding soldiers
with a snarled order and a shove that could have moved
oxen.

"There's no home," the Pilot went on, meeting the
tribune's eyes with a bright terror which proved he
understood well the temper of the men around him.
"We can take you—many places, almost anywhere, places
the Federation will never learn about. But if we take
you to Earth—"

"Look at him," said Clodius Afer to the captive. He
swept his arm to the side, clearing by his authority a
path as wide as what his junior had managed with
physical effort. "*Look* at him!" the pilus prior shouted.

The Commander was on a tree facing his two subordinates. The undergrowth which might have interfered with the view was gone, trampled down or hacked away. The shimmering filter of air before the guild officer's face was studded with sweat like that of a human. When he moaned, the droplets shuddered and occasionally splashed down onto his suit where they vanished in the fabric.

A number of the soldiers had gleefully helped, but no one had disputed Niger's right to drive home the daggers that pinioned the Commander to what had been part of the luxury in which the guild kept him.

His arms were outstretched, and his fingers twitched beneath their blue covering. The daggers by which he supported his upper body had been driven through his wrists, where the network of sinews and bone could accept a strain that would have torn apart the lighter structure of his palms and let his torso slump forward.

The Commander's legs were flexed sharply at the knees and turned to his right side. His feet had been drawn up to provide a cushion of sorts for his buttocks. Then the third spike had been hammered through both heelbones and deep into the wood beneath.

The slight, blue-clad figure was alive and would remain alive for a considerable time before shock or suffocation carried him off. The blood which dripped with spittle from the corner of his mouth was only from the way he bit himself while gnashing his teeth in agony.

"What's your Federation going to do with you," said Clodius Afer, his voice harsh but no longer shouting, "that's going to be worse than that?"

The Commander whimpered.

"You don't understand," said the Medic who was closing his eyes tight and then reopening them, not blinking but more an unconscious attempt to wring visible reality into a more acceptable guise. He was almost whispering, but he got somewhat better control of himself when Vibulenus looked back at him.

"You've been gone," the crewman explained, "not the time you've been awake on the ship or on the ground, but all the time the ship's in Transit, too. Do you understand? You haven't been home for *thousands* of your years. There isn't any home *left* for you."

Quartilla stroked the tribune's back, her touch sensuous, this time for its power rather than its delicacy. "Yes," she said in answer to the question her lover has not needed to ask aloud. "He's telling—"

She paused to rephrase. "He's not lying."

Existence was sand, rushing down a slope to bury the soul of Gaius Vibulenus Caper in tiny, harsh realities. Everything they had fought for, everything he had promised these men who trusted him—

He had promised them a chance to live free and live as men. Whatever else home might be was less important than that.

"We never thought it would be the same," Vibulenus said. His voice stirred echoes even from the rough boles of the synthetic trees. "It wouldn't have been the same if we'd marched back from Parthia with all the loot of Ctesiphon in our baggage—home would have changed, and we would have changed even more."

"All right," said the Pilot in a voice like twigs snapping. "Cut me loose and I'll take you to what you think your home is."

Quick hands moved, anticipating Vibuenus' nod of assent.

"I warn you, cargo," said the Pilot as his face worked against new pain as his injuries were jogged. "You don't understand what you're doing."

"Perhaps we don't, guild crewman," said Gaius Vibulenus. His right hand and those of his two centurions gripped each other in a knot as tight as that which Alexander cut at Gordion, and the soft warmth of Quartilla beside him was hope itself.

"But we understand that we are Romans."